A TASTE OF CHRISTMAS

CHRISTMAS ROMANCE COLLECTION

MELISSA HILL

CONTENTS

A TASTE OF CHRISTMAS

A HOLIDAY NOVELLA

SITTING in the back of the Uber taking her to her father's house, Kelly Bennett looked out the window as they drove from the airport through Whitedale Pines, the town that she'd grown up in and which was never far from her thoughts.

The driver, a heavy-set man with warm blue eyes glanced at her in the rearview mirror. "Lemme guess -- you're a native?"

She laughed. "What gave it away?"

"You're heading into the part of town that only people from around here go to. Everyone else just wants to head up to the ski resort."

Kelly shook her head sadly.

She'd gleaned snippets from her dad, that the five-star EdgeLake resort hotel that had opened this winter season had not quite been the godsend some of the locals had been hoping for.

Rather than attracting more tourists to the local shops and businesses, pretty much everyone now stayed in the luxury resort's expansive grounds.

"I'm definitely a native," she admitted, smiling at the snow-covered pine forest. "Born and raised."

"Where are you coming from now?"

"Geneva."

She watched his reflected eyebrows go up.

"Switzerland, huh? Lemme guess -- you work for the government or something?"

"Nothing like that. I've just been in Europe to study and work in different restaurants learning my craft."

"What are you -- a chef or something?"

"A chocolatier."

The driver nodded and gave her a thumbs up.

"Nice. That would have been my dream job when I was growing up," he told her. "If there's one thing that I can never get enough of, it's chocolate."

"I know," she agreed, smiling. "There's just something magical about it, right? You could be having the worst day of your life and when you pop a piece of chocolate into your mouth, everything else seems to go away -- at least for a little while."

"Couldn't agree more. I've always felt if there was more chocolate in the world, there'd be a lot less problems."

When the Uber pulled up in front of the snow-covered split-level house she'd grown up in, Kelly found an over-whelming sense of warmth flood through her -- and it was only amplified when she saw the large man flinging open the front door and rushing out to meet her.

Bradley Bennett looked like the kind of man who could easily go toe-to-toe with a grizzly bear and come out on top but Kelly knew her father to be one of the gentlest and kindest men she'd ever come across. There was a tender streak in him that few people ever got to see and Kelly had often wished more people knew the man the way she did.

She barely got her door open before she found herself scooped out of the back of the car and pulled into an embrace that made the years melt away and sent her back to being a little girl first wanting to know where chocolate came from.

"So great to see you, honey -- you have no idea how much I've missed you."

"I've missed you, too, Dad."

"Let's get your things and get you settled in. You and I have got a lot of catching up to do. It's been too long."

Kelly nodded, tears unexpectedly welling up. She'd told herself that she wasn't going to get all emotional when she saw her dad but that resolution had been very short-lived.

After her mother died when she was a young girl, a lot of people in town didn't believe Bradley Bennett could raise a child alone. After all, the man was a foreman in the lumber yard and there was nothing soft or gentle about him -- or so they thought.

Granted, her father could be tough when he had to be, but he could also show a tenderness and warmth to others that would totally catch them off-guard.

She allowed herself to stay in his arms for a few more moments, then pulled away and said, "I'm seriously hoping that you decided to make your pot roast stew. That's all I've been thinking about since I left for the airport."

He grinned. "What do you think?"

"I think the sooner we get inside out of this cold, the sooner I can have the best comfort food in the world."

"THAT WAS INCREDIBLE," Kelly said a little later, shaking her head in amazement at the now-empty plate that had contained an almost obscene amount of her dad's famed stew.

Bradley grinned. "As good as that fancy stuff over in Europe?"

Kelly laughed. "Dad, if I were to bring this to some of the restaurants over there, they'd be kidnapping you to work in their kitchens before you knew it. That was just what I needed. Thank you."

She was amazed at just how much she really had missed home comforts. Yes, Switzerland was wonderful, and she'd seen sights and visited places that so many others never would – but in the end, what mattered to her was how a place made her feel.

"You have no idea how much I've missed Whitedale," she said.

Her father gave her a long look, then nodded. "Yeah, I do. Back before you were born, back even before your mother and I got married, I spent some time trying to figure out who I was and where I belonged. I went to different places, looking for the place where I'd feel like I was meant to be – and after a year or two of not finding whatever it was that I was looking for, I came back to the mountains – and that's when I realized it was always where I'd belonged."

Kelly smiled. He really did get it.

"Then, once I met your mother and the two of us started to get serious, I realized Whitedale Pines and I were always going to be joined together."

"Don't get me wrong – Europe's amazing, it really is, but it's not like it is here. The minute I got back, it felt like the town had just come right up to me wrapped me in a warm blanket and took me inside on a cold winter's night. This is the only place that I've ever really felt a true connection with."

"Well, then … no time like the present." Her father reached into his shirt pocket, then, and took out what looked like a folded piece of paper. "I saw this in the paper a couple of weeks ago and I thought it was something you might be interested in."

Curious, Kelly took it from him and saw the newspaper headline, *A Taste of Christmas*. Unfolding it, she quickly read the contents of the article and when she was done, she found herself smiling.

"Hershells Chocolate is actually opening a location here in town?" she asked, stunned. "That's incredible."

"Yes, and even better, they're having a competition to find a new product for the Christmas market to roll out everywhere next year. And I'm pretty confident my little chocolate girl would have a great shot at winning."

Kelly's mind was spinning. When she'd decided to come home for the holidays, it had been for two reasons – wanting to see her father had been the first reason. She hadn't given too much thought about the second reason – at least, until now.

"What do you think, Kellybug?" her dad asked.

"I think," she told him, smiling, "that I need to get back into the kitchen and start working some chocolate magic."

THE FOLLOWING EVENING, Kelly watched as her best friend, Cindi moved through the crowd at The Black Run Inn, set two Manhattans down on the table, then slid into the booth beside her.

Cindi and Kelly had been inseparable from the moment they first met in tenth grade in Mrs. Donovan's class.

Cindi was tall, with fiery red hair and emerald green eyes, with the kind of quick wit that was a prerequisite to be friends with Kelly.

"I can't believe how good you look!" her friend gasped, raising her glass to Kelly. "Radiant even. Europe must agree with you."

Kelly touched her glass to Cindi's and smiled.

"Not as agreeable as you'd think. Don't get me wrong – it's a wonderful place to be, you know, but believe it or not, not nearly as welcoming as here."

Cindi rolled her eyes. "Sure – that's why so many people are breaking down the door to spend their vacation in Whitedale Pines."

Kelly looked around at the small crowd in the bar and said,

"Well, it looks like there are plenty of people visiting right now."

"They're just here for apres ski. Nothing more. When the hotel chain first approached the city council, everyone thought it meant we'd be seeing a ton of new money coming in but that's not what happened," her friend said bitterly.

Kelly knew the story. Yes, construction of the snazzy new EdgeLake hotel had initially brought in job opportunities for a few locals. But then investors started building up other businesses around the resort – ones that took away from the local economy.

Soon enough, the only businesses that were seeing any kind of growth from the hotel were the ones that the chain had helped set up.

"There's something that I've been meaning to talk to you about," Kelly murmured.

"What's that?"

"Well, if I'm going to be totally honest with you, there's a good chance that I might be thinking about coming back home."

Cindi's eyes widened. "Oh, my god! What happened? What's going on? The last I heard, you were loving European life and starting to get really serious with that guy."

Kelly sighed. Yes, Grant – handsome, clever and witty Grant.

"I was getting serious with him – and he was getting serious with my roommate, so things didn't quite turn out the way I'd hoped."

Cindi sipped her drink, and after a moment, she said, "Well, I can honestly tell you that I'd *love* to see you coming back home. It would be perfect."

"But to do that," Kelly said, "I need to do something to make a name for myself here if I'm to find a job – and my dad told me about that Hershells competition."

Cindi clapped her hands together. "Oh my gosh yes, that would be perfect for you! You enter the competition, you blow everyone away with one of your amazing creations, land a job with Hershells – and the next thing you know, you're living in your own snow palace in the mountains. You have to do this, Kelly! You have to!"

Cindi's enthusiasm was infectious and she found herself grinning.

"OK then. Any good ideas for a taste of Christmas?"

was perfectly good in theory. But it just didn't have the same *feeling.*

"The presentation is tomorrow," she told him, "and I still don't have it where I want it to be. It's close. So very close; just not quite there."

He kissed her on the cheek then, and said, "Well, I know from experience there's no point in trying to talk you out of anything you've set your mind to, so just make sure you try and get *some* rest tonight, OK?"

She went over to the stove and dipped the tip of a teaspoon into the melted white chocolate, then carefully lifted it out and tasted the sample.

No. It still wasn't there. She had gotten so close, but this still was not matching the memory she'd carried with her.

But maybe it was enough.

CHAPTER 5

KELLY HANDED her father a sample of the recipe she'd spent endless hours working on and watched him put it into his mouth.

For a moment, she didn't notice anything out of the ordinary – and then, he slowly smiled and nodded.

"Kelly, this is absolutely incredible. I've never tasted anything like it. It's like you've managed to get an entire mug of hot cocoa with marshmallows inside a single piece of chocolate. I – I can't believe how good it is. This is amazing."

"Thank you," she said proudly. "It's called SnowDrift. "Still not quite as good as what we used to get at the Snowflake Cafe, but close."

"I think it's perfect," her dad assured her. "This will definitely get those judges falling all over themselves to hand you the prize."

"I hope so."

"You got everything ready then?"

Kelly nodded. For the first time in a while, she felt like her life was back on track and that things were going just the way she wanted them to go.

"My presentation is at three o'clock. That'll give me more than enough time to make sure I've made a backup batch – just in case the unexpected happens. If there's one thing they made us learn in the academy it was to never leave anything to chance."

THAT AFTERNOON, Kelly took one last look at herself in the mirror, making sure she looked every bit the professional.

Her hair was pulled back into a ponytail and she had applied enough makeup to accentuate her features without being over the top.

The pink skirt and white top combo was one of the nicest outfits she had, and all in all, she was satisfied that she looked like someone whose chocolate creation should be given serious consideration by the Hershells Corporation as a new product.

Something was bothering her, though. She wasn't sure what it was, but there was an annoying little tickle in the back of her mind. Every time she thought she'd figured it out, it again moved out of reach.

Her phone rang and she reached for it, grateful for the distraction.

It was Cindi.

"Hey, there," she greeted, smiling. "what's up?"

"I just wanted to wish you luck, that's all," her friend said. "I saw your dad at the gas station and he told me that you'd finally come up with a recipe you were satisfied with."

"Knowing my father, it was probably more like telling you that I've come up with the most incredible chocolate creation in the entire world."

"Yeah, you're right. The way he's talking, you might as well just change your name to Willy Wonka and start your own factory."

CHAPTER 6

In the EdgeLake resort's grand ballroom, Kelly studied the faces of the three judges as they each tasted her Cherry Snow-Drift presentation sample.

Although she'd never met any of them personally, she knew them by reputation:

Eleanor Crum was the executive editor of Chocolate Magic Monthly, the premier online and print digest of all things chocolate. Kelly watched the woman's previously stony features melt as she let the confection dissolve in her mouth.

Adrian Tindersen was there on behalf of the Hershells' Chocolate empire. His dark eyes held Kelly's gaze as he put the sample on his tongue and closed his mouth.

A few moments later, she saw him nod imperceptibly and she found the breath she'd been holding escape.

Julian Gascard of Chocolat LTD, the worldwide distributor of every high-end chocolate ever created. Chocolat LTD was the Cartier of expensive confections, and the small elderly man with a shock of white hair kept his features impassive as he tried a piece of her offering.

After they each wrote down their opinions on the cards in

Cindi rolled her eyes. "You don't get it, do you? Sam's a guy, and like most guys, he's not someone who's going to go around and talk about his feelings and stuff. But everyone knows how he felt – it was there every time the two of you were in the same room together."

All of this was too much for Kelly to handle at the moment. She pushed thoughts of what Sam had said out of her mind and focused on something else – like why in the world her ex had been entering the Hershells competition.

"Last I heard, he was still a ski instructor. Since when is he into chocolate-making?"

"He is, but his mom's place isn't doing so well these days and I guess he thought this might help. You know that he was always great in the kitchen too."

Kelly smiled again at the memory of The Snowflake Cafe - and its comforting hot chocolate that had inspired her very own creation.

"I can't believe the cafe's having problems. I'd have thought the place would still be packed out."

Cindi shook her head. "Only the locals go there now. The shiny new restaurants up at the resort are where everyone else goes. Without tourists, Whitedale is slowly dying."

CHAPTER 8

THAT NIGHT AT SUPPER, Kelly told her father about what had happened with Sam and what she'd found out from Cindi.

Her father listened quietly, and when she was done, said, "Well, I'm not surprised."

"What do you mean? You're not surprised that I ruined Sam's presentation?"

"No, of course not. I know that was an accident, Kelly. I'm talking about his reaction."

"Dad," she protested, shaking her head, "he said that I broke his heart. How in the world is it possible to break someone's heart who hasn't even told you how they feel about you?"

Her father leaned back in his chair and gave her a steady look.

"Hmm -- so, before you left for Europe, you told Sam how you felt about him, huh?"

Kelly opened her mouth, then closed it, then shook her head and admitted in a soft voice, "No."

"Why not?"

"Because what we had was so good that I didn't want to go and ruin it by making it weird. Does that make sense? I mean, glad that you're back in town. We've got a lot of catching up to do."

And with that, he went back inside.

Kelly stood there for a moment, unsure whether or not she'd made any progress – but, at the very least, they were talking again.

She'd just have to see if it went beyond that.

WHEN KELLY GOT HOME, she found her dad up in the kitchen, sitting in front of a mug of steaming cocoa. She noticed the second cup sitting in her spot and she sat down across from him.

"Why are you up so late?" she asked.

"I could ask you the same question," he told her. "I suppose neither one of us could sleep."

Kelly sipped the cocoa, and let her tongue experience the sweet warmth as she drank it.

"I went to see Sam."

"I figured you would," her father said, grinning. "That's the way the two of you always were. Whenever you had a fight, neither one could just walk away. That's the way it was with your mother and me too."

Mentioning her mother made Kelly's heart ache once more. Although Gloria had passed away many years ago, Kelly still felt the sadness of knowing that the woman she loved more than life itself was gone forever.

"You two had a great marriage."

"Yeah, we did. We had our ups and downs, of course, but in the end, we always knew we were each other's best friends and that's all that mattered."

"You were lucky."

"No luck to it, honey. You just have to be determined not to let life screw things up. You and Sam might not wind up together. That's not for me to say. What I can tell you, though, is I've seen the way he used to look at you when you didn't know he was watching and there was nothing in his gaze but pure devotion."

"Why is everything so complicated?" she muttered, shaking her head.

Her father laughed.

"Things are only as complicated as we make them, honey. Like most great recipes, the trick is to just keep things simple."

CHAPTER 10

WHEN LAURA WEST went into her cafe the following morning and found her son with a cup of hot cocoa and her homemade marshmallows floating in it, she sat down across from him at the small corner table.

"Okay, what's going on?"

"What do you mean?"

She'd never had the heart to tell Sam that he had the worst poker face.

"The only time you put marshmallows in cocoa is when something's bothering you. What is it?"

He looked down into the cup, remembering all the times his mother would give him a cup of this stuff and just wait for him to open up.

"It's Kelly."

Laura sighed. When she'd heard that Kelly Bennett was back in town, she'd been careful not to get her own hopes up. She remembered the Sam he had been back then when they were together -- happier, freer, less guarded.

All of that had changed when Kelly left for Europe. Some-

MELISSA HILL

thing had gone out of him. It was as if his inner light had been dimmed.

Now she wondered if that light could shine once again.

"What about her?" she asked, keeping her tone neutral.

"She came to see me and we kind of got to talking about things. Part of me's glad to see her, but another part is warning me to keep my distance."

Laura gave him a small smile and shook her head.

"I don't know what's going on between you two now that she's back in town but I do know that no one wins when you hold back from your feelings. I also know you're worried about whether or not you could get hurt again and even though that's a valid concern, if you keep your distance, you just might be making sure that you never get hurt -- but at what cost? What could you be giving up to stay safe?"

"So what do you think I should do?"

"I think you should and Kelly should give each other the chance to learn what it is that you both want," Laura assured her son. "All the very best recipes are born from patience and time."

KELLY'S HEART was pounding as she found herself back at the EdgeLake hotel explaining to the Hershells people what had happened with Sam's presentation, and why she thought he should be allowed an opportunity to showcase his talent.

"Kelly, while it's very commendable for you to come here on behalf of your friend," Hershell's representative Tindersen said, "I'm afraid rules are rules and we have to abide by them."

"But he would have been able to enter the competition if I hadn't ruined his entry," she protested. "I hope you might consider giving him another chance. If you look at the video footage from the lobby, you'll see that I'm telling you the truth."

He nodded sympathetically. "Oh, I'm sure you're telling the truth but again, my hands are tied. Besides, there really wouldn't be much point for him to be competing right now, since we've already made our decision." He smiled broadly. "Congratulations. SnowDrift is as of today officially a new Hershells' holiday creation."

Kelly just stood there, stunned. This was what she'd been hoping for of course, but now that the moment had arrived – she felt even worse on Sam's behalf.

"I – I won?" she asked, her voice shaking. "Are you sure?"

He chuckled. "Please – there's no need to be modest here, Kelly. SnowDrift was outstanding and will be an incredible addition to the Hershells' holiday line for years to come. But for this year only, we're going to launch by making it entirely exclusive to this resort. Visitors will be coming from far and wide to experience the famed EdgeLake SnowDrift."

This was a disaster. She couldn't let this happen.

"I'm sorry," she said then, "but I'm going to have to withdraw my entry."

Tindersen stared at her. "What are you saying?"

She thought fast. "I'm saying that I can't possibly proceed knowing I caused another competitor to be disqualified. I hereby withdraw SnowDrift and myself from the competition."

After a moment, Tindersen cleared his throat and said, "Well, you can certainly withdraw, but I'm afraid you cannot do the same with your presentation. The rules were quite clear. All entry recipes become the intellectual property of the Hershells Chocolate Corporation, regardless of whether they are chosen as the overall winner."

Kelly's mouth dropped open. "You've got to be kidding me! How is that even legal?"

"It was all laid out in the submission information. So, you see, you can choose not to be our winner, but we still own the rights to SnowDrift."

"You've got to be kidding me!" Cindi repeated later, almost choking on her coffee. "That's horrible!"

Kelly sighed, feeling sick to her stomach. The two of them were in The Little Dripper diner, and the only thing keeping her from crying was knowing they were in public and she didn't want to make a scene.

"Believe me, I couldn't believe it, either. How could I not

have studied the rules more closely? If I had known that all entries became Hershells' IP regardless, I never would have entered."

"But you still withdrew?"

"Yes, but it doesn't matter. They still have my recipe and that kills me. They're going to wind up making money off my marshmallow chocolate creation. EdgeLake Resort too"

Cindi looked uncomfortable and Kelly looked at her, eyes narrowed. "What is it? What's wrong?"

"It's nothing. Really. It's nothing."

"Cindi, you're an even worse liar than I am – and that's saying something. You're hiding something from me."

"It's about the recipe," her friend said, softly.

"What about it?"

"Um – remember when I used to tell you how much I loved your marshmallow white cocoa and you said that I could thank Sam's mother for that. Because she gave you the recipe."

Kelly frowned. That couldn't be. She'd been making hot cocoa that way for years, ever since...

...ever since she'd gotten the recipe from Sam's mother.

Her hand flew up to her mouth and the world suddenly seemed very unsteady. All of a sudden, she was having a hard time breathing and it took a tremendous effort of will to keep from passing out.

"Oh my gosh, Cindi," she whispered, her voice shaking and tears finally beginning to come, "what have I done?"

CHAPTER 12

THIS TIME, when Sam saw Kelly outside his house, he smiled and stepped outside.

"Hey," he said. "what's up?"

"I've got something to tell you," Kelly began. "I went to see the Hershells people to ask them to give you another chance, since I ruined your presentation but they said they couldn't because of the rules."

He nodded. "Yeah, I figured as much. I also figured you'd try and make things right, Kelly, but it's okay. It's just as well, really."

This was not what she'd expected. She'd expected Sam to be upset, more angry at not being given a chance to show off his skills, but instead, he seemed...defeated.

"What do you mean, 'it's just as well?'"

"Well, I was talking with the guys up at the slopes about this whole mess and Tommy, whose brother works for the city, told me that Hershells is no longer opening a location here in town."

Kelly's eyes widened. "What? I thought it was already a done deal."

Well, that was good news at least.

"Yeah, that's what everyone thought. Then, out of left field, they announce they've done a major deal with the new hotel and they're setting up a Hershells chocolate emporium right inside the Edgelake resort. Which of course means that once again, our little town isn't going to see a dime."

"I can't be the reason that the resort winds up destroying everything, Cindi. I can't. What do I do?" Kelly kept shaking her head; she had to think of something to make things right.

It was bad enough that she'd ruined Sam's chances at the competition, but to have given away his mom's homemade hot cocoa recipe to help the resort damage the town even further …

"I know you're upset but you can't blame yourself for this. You didn't know this was going to happen. You just wanted to win the contest — and you did. You didn't know Hershell people were going to do this."

Kelly looked around the Snowflake Cafe, taking in the few customers who were there. They were all regulars — people who had grown up in the area and who had had some of their first dates in this very spot, possibly in the very booth she and Cindi were sitting in.

"It's just so hopeless."

"Let's face it, this is how it always is, isn't it? The big corporations wind up stepping all over the little guy out there and no one can stop them. They've got the money to put the politicians in place and that's all that matters. After that, it's all over for the small-time places. You either play ball with them or you get swallowed up whole. But …you know it's not over yet, right?" Cindi continued archly. "Just because things are looking bleak now doesn't mean they can't change."

"Yeah, well, it would take a miracle to change things now, and I don't think either of us has got one handy."

A thoughtful expression crossed Cindi's face then, and she slowly smiled.

"Okay, you and I might not be able to work miracles," her friend finally said, "but I know someone who just might."

CHAPTER 13

THE FOLLOWING DAY Cindi texted to say that she had some 'amazing news' that couldn't wait and she'd meet Kelly at the cafe before the lunch crowd came in — although the term didn't really apply to the five or six customers that showed up after noon.

But her friend was running late — as usual.

Kelly was about to message her when the door opened and Cindi came in. She looked as if she were out of breath and when she sat down across from her, there was a manic look in her eyes.

"What's going on?" Kelly asked. "What's this amazing news you've got to tell me?"

"First," Cindi said, "I need you to promise me that you're not going to get mad."

In the past, Cindi had taken it upon herself to do things that others might not approve of and before she told anyone anything, she *always* prefaced it with "I need you to promise me that you're not going to get mad."

"Cindi, what have you done?"

"So," her friend said, "you know how you've never had a social media account?"

"Yes..." Kelly replied slowly, a growing feeling of unease moving through her. "What have you done?"

"Well, I went ahead and set you up with TikTok."

"Why would that make me mad?"

Cindi glanced down at her hands and said, "Well, one of the first things you did was tag Hershells Chocolate HQ about SnowDrift."

Kelly stared at her. "I did what?"

"You told the world about how they rights-grabbed your recipe and then challenged them to a head-to-head chocolatier competition. They accepted — and one of my friends who works for TMZ made the whole thing go viral. SnowDrift's actually trending, Kelly."

Kelly's eyes were wide. "How could you do that? What were you thinking? Besides, I don't have anything else last minute that I could use to go up against Hershells. I'll be humiliated."

Cindi gave her a long look and shook her head.

"That's the stupidest thing I've ever heard. If anyone can compete with a world-famous chocolate corporation, it's you."

CHAPTER 14

SAM HAD BEEN DOZING on the couch when the pounding on his door woke him up. He rubbed the sleep out of his eyes and opened the door.

"Sorry," he said. "You just woke me up from a nap."

Kelly pushed past him and when he turned around to ask her what was going on, she said, "I need your help."

He ran a hand through his unkempt hair and stifled a yawn. "Sure, but what's going on, Kelly?"

"You are and I going to compete against Hershells Corporation in another contest. Head to head this time."

Sam stared at her, confused. This wasn't making sense.

"Have you been drinking?" he asked, sniffing the air to see if he could detect the smell of alcohol.

"No, I'm not drunk. Guess what Cindi did?"

Sam shook his head. "Probably something I don't want to know, if Cindi's involved."

"It's actually a good thing this time. She challenged the people at Hershells to another contest. Someone she knows at TMZ picked up on it, and it went viral — so the Hershells' chocolatier team is going to compete against us. Right here in Whitedale."

Sam stood there, still trying to process what he was hearing. "But how? You told me that Hershells has the rights to your creation."

Kelly gave him a mischievous grin and said, "But they don't have yours. I only got a glimpse of it before it was smashed to smithereens. But between you and me, I'll bet we can make something that'll knock their chocs off."

SAM TOOK a tentative taste of the latest chocolate batch and frowned. What he was experiencing in his mouth was not what he'd been expecting. He glanced over at saw Kelly watching him.

It was a day later and they were in his mother's kitchen, trialling ways to combine unique flavors for another winning recipe.

He grimaced and said, "Okay, you were right. A touch of peppermint isn't what's needed here."

She laughed. "I did try to warn you."

"It seemed like it would work when I was thinking about it though," he protested.

He looked around the cafe's kitchen and shook his head. It was a total mess. He and Kelly had been at it all day yesterday and again today but it seemed like they were no closer to finding what they were looking for.

While his entry to the original competition had been a chocolate and candy creation, there was nothing especially new or original about the recipe itself.

Kelly's unique chocolate flavour combos for SnowDrift had

been streets ahead, so if they were to have any chance of winning this, they needed something along those same lines.

But the competition was tomorrow, which meant that time was running out and a much-needed breakthrough would need to happen soon.

Kelly put some of the used pots into the sink and began to wash them.

Sam picked up a cleaning cloth and started to wipe down the stainless steel counters and put their equipment and ingredients away. The cafe would be open to the public soon and he'd promised his mother that he wouldn't leave her to clean up after them.

"I hate to admit it," he said, after a silence, "but I'm beginning to think that this isn't going to happen. I just don't see how we're going to pull this off."

Kelly looked resigned too and he hated seeing the defeat in her eyes.

"You might be right," she admitted softly. "If we don't find what we're looking for by tonight, I think we're just going to have to face reality."

"We've tried everything, Cindi," Kelly told her friend later. "Some of Sam's ideas are good, but none of it is outstanding. SnowDrift was my absolute best creation - and I just don't think that I'm going to find anything to beat it. To say nothing of the fact that it wasn't entirely mine after all."

"Well, you still have tonight, right? At least you've got a chance."

Kelly sighed, shaking her head. "Yeah, a few more hours to come up with an amazing recipe that is going to compete with the original amazing recipe. Gee, how hard could that be?"

"Come on, Kelly -- if anyone can pull this off, it's you and Sam."

Her friend regarded her for a moment, then asked, "So, how are things between the two of you?"

Kelly smiled. "Well," she said, "pretty good, actually. We haven't been able to focus too much on the whole situation with us because we're so focused on a way to win this."

"Hey, I'm sorry that I sort of took the ball and ran with it this way. I mean, if I hadn't jumped the gun with my friend at TMZ, none of this would be happening. And you certainly wouldn't be having this whole live-streamed battle either."

"What?" Kelly's heart pounded afresh. "You didn't tell me that."

"Yep. The Hershells team are so confident they'll win that they want the whole world to see it."

Oh boy, Kelly thought. Suddenly things had gotten even more hopeless.

CHAPTER 16

SAM ENTERED his mother's café after work that evening and found Kelly already in the kitchen. She had several pots of melted chocolate warming and she gave him a bright smile.

"By any chance did you come up with a really amazing idea to save the day while I was on the slopes?" he asked.

Her smile faded. "No, actually. I didn't. I've been racking my brains but I've got nothing that's even going to come close to the SnowDrift recipe."

Sam went over to the counter and looked at the various ingredients lined up – slivers of almonds, white chocolate shavings and vanilla extract, along with orange extract, dark chocolate and a dozen more different varieties of essence and oils.

"Well, we've got one last shot," he said. "Let's see what we can do."

Three hours later, he wasn't feeling so confident. "It's hopeless," he groaned, shaking his head. "Maybe it's just not going to happen."

It was almost time to start cleaning up for the night. Like it or not, they were going to have to simply go with the closest thing they had to what might stand a chance – but it was a very slim chance.

They'd concocted a milk chocolate orange-infused bar with hints of dark chocolate and white chocolate swirls. A nice combination but both of them knew it was lacking that certain 'something' that would make it magnificent.

"So, I guess we're just going to go with this," Kelly said. "The way I see it, it's our best chance."

He nodded. "Yeah."

Then seeing the dubious look on her face, Sam stood up, "I'll be right back. I've got something that'll cheer us both up."

She waited and a couple of minutes later, he emerged from out front carrying two steaming mugs of hot white chocolate cocoa.

Kelly breathed in the familiar scent and wrapped her hands around the mug. "I remember whenever I got a bad grade on a test, I'd come to the café and your mom would make me a mug of this. It would cheer me right up."

Sam sipped it too and despite everything, found himself smiling. "It's the cherry in the marshmallows," he told her.

Kelly frowned. "What?"

"Mom always made her own marshmallows for the cocoa. She hated the way prepared marshmallows tasted, so she made her own with a hint of cherry essence. That's what makes this so great."

Kelly stared at him, her mind suddenly racing.

"Sam, I think I know what to do," she gasped, trying to keep the excitement out of her voice. "I think I know how to beat Hershells."

CHAPTER 17

THE FOLLOWING AFTERNOON, Cindi and Sam stared at the huge
crowds gathered in the main ballroom of the EdgeLake Resort.
As large as the space was, it was still completely packed
with onlookers ranging from businesspeople in custom-
tailored outfits to tourists in full ski garb.

"All these people here to watch a competition?"

She laughed. "Wake up and smell the chocolate, Sam.
Nothing gets the online world worked up like a 'David versus
Goliath' piece – and Hershells is definitely the Goliath in this
story."

"Is it weird that I've got an overwhelming urge right now to
make a mad dash for freedom and never look back?"

"It's going to be fine. You guys are going to be fine. Just
relax. I'm sure the two of you have come up with something
truly amazing."

He looked away uncertainly and Cindi frowned. "Sam?"

"Yeah?" he asked, still not looking at her.

"Exactly what is it that you're not telling me? I know something's up because when I tried to call Kelly earlier, it went
straight to voicemail."

He sighed. "Okay, here's the thing – I don't actually know what's going on either. Kelly wouldn't tell me. She just said that she thought she had a way to win this, but she had to try something first."

"Uh-oh," Cindi murmured.

"We're just going to have to trust her," Sam said, hoping his voice sounded more confident than he felt.

Then a few minutes later, Kelly appeared, carrying an aluminum foil-wrapped tray and rushed over to them.

She saw the panicked look in Sam's eyes and did her best to act confident.

"Sorry I'm late!" she said, cheerfully. "I had some last-minute things I had to take care of."

Cindi looked down at her phone, "Okay, so here's how it's going to go down. There are three judges – Leonard Barstow from Chocolate-To-Go, Yolanda Cortez from Godiva, and Georgina Hoffsteder from Ghiradelli, eek!"

Complete and utter juggernauts in the chocolate industry, Kelly realised gulping.

Sam leaned across and asked her, "So what did you make?"

Kelly gave him a tight smile. "You're just going to have to wait and see."

CHAPTER 18

"LADIES AND GENTLEMEN, may I have your attention, please."

The emcee, a short individual who looked somewhat unnerved by the size of the crowd gathered, nervously tapped the handheld microphone. There was a feedback screech and a young woman fiddled with some equipment behind the elevated platform they were on.

Off to the side, was a table where the three judges sat. They were quietly talking among themselves, looking indifferent to the mass of people in front of them.

"Ladies and gentlemen, may I have your attention?" He tapped the microphone again. This time there was no feedback and the crowd's conversation faded away to a low murmur.

"Thank you," he continued. "The rules of engagement in this competition are simple -- each entry will be presented to the three judges sitting here, and each will vote for their preferred choice. Whichever entry gets two out of three votes will be deemed the winner."

Kelly stood off to the side, looking over at where the team from Hershells stood.

Adrian Tindersen was watching her and there was a dark

expression on his face. Ever since she'd tried to withdraw herself and SnowDrift from the competition to help out Sam, she had a feeling that the Hershells rep wasn't too fond of her.

And if things went according to plan, he'd likely be even less fond of her.

"An earlier coin flip has Team Hershells presenting their entry first."

One of Hershell's in-house chocolatiers had a crystal tray in hand as he approached the judge's table. He handed each judge a smaller crystal plate, upon which was a sampling of their entry.

"Thank you for this opportunity to present the newest addition to the Hershell confectionary family -- SnowDrift," Tindersen announced loudly, and Kelly gasped.

They were actually going to use her very own recipe against her?

Well, this was awkward...

She held her breath as each judge took a small taste of the chocolate, holding it in their mouths for a moment, nodding satisfactorily.

After that, they took a larger bite and made their notes on small notepads in front of them.

The emcee then turned to Kelly, who duly took the aluminium foil off her latest creation, revealing small blocks of white chocolate with pink swirls on tiny paper plates.

She approached the judges and handed each of them one. "Hello. I'm Kelly Bennett and I'm also presenting my very own SnowDrift creation."

CHAPTER 19

THE EMCEE LOOKED CONFUSED, the judges raised their eyebrows but Tindersen immediately rushed to where Kelly stood.

"What is the meaning of this?" he glared.

She gave the Hershells rep a sweet smile.

"Well, to make this a truly fair contest, shouldn't we see which version of the recipe - *my* recipe - is best? And which chocolatier can create enough flavour nuance in SnowDrift to win."

Tindersen turned to the judges. "This is ridiculous! She can't use the same recipe! Hershells own the rights to the SnowDrift recipe!"

"Actually," Kelly said, shaking her head, "you own the rights to the SnowDrift recipe I presented last week. *This* is not the same recipe."

"What do you mean?" he scoffed, unperturbed. "Regardless, this is completely unacceptable. Judges, what say you?"

The three judges duly conferred and nodded towards the emcee, who went over to them and spoke in hushed tones.

Finally, he came forward, looking somewhat perplexed.

"Well, this is unusual," he said, clearing his throat, "but the judges have indeed decided to allow both entries."

"But Hershell owns the rights to ...."

"Perhaps," the emcee agreed, nodding, "but Ms Bennett has already affirmed that her recipe is *not* the same. If the taste is identical, they've decided that Hershell's SnowDrift will be declared the official winner. If however the taste differs, they will then attempt to choose the better of the two."

Tindersen glared at Kelly but reluctantly went back to his side of the stage.

While Kelly stepped back to where Sam and Cindi were standing, watching in amazement.

CHAPTER 20

HALF AN HOUR PASSED while the judges deliberated and discussed. Kelly was going out of her mind. What was taking so long? Had this been a mistake after all?

She had thought about consulting Sam before making this Hail Mary attempt, but in the end, decided to confide in Laura. That way, if things went south, at least Sam's mother knew that Kelly had tried her best to make things right.

She was broken out of her thoughts by the tapping of the microphone, and the murmurs of the crowd around them faded away.

"May I have your attention, please? The judges have come to a decision."

Kelly and Tindersen both approached the podium and stood there.

Her heart was pounding. She risked a glance at Tindersen but she couldn't tell whether or not he was nervous.

"Well, this is it, I guess."

He looked at her with disdain, slowly shaking his head.

The emcee had a sheet of paper in his hand. He looked at it, then looked at both entrants.

"It seems as if the judges' decision is unanimous," he said, unable to keep what sounded like surprise from his voice. "The winner is ... SnowDrift by Kelly Bennett."

For a moment, she stood there, completely frozen in place. Then, she heard the sound of the applause washing over her and Cindi and Sam cheering alongside her.

She turned to stare at Tindersen's face, frozen in disbelief.

Turning back to the crowd, she waited until there was relative quiet to say what she had to say.

"First of all, this feels amazing, but I'm not the only one winning here today. If it wasn't for my family and my friends and the special people in this town, I wouldn't be in this position."

She smiled at Sam and Cindi, then turned back to the crowd.

"For those interested, you'll be pleased to know that exclusive rights to this - the official cherry choc SnowDrift recipe - belongs to Whitedale's Snowflake Cafe. If you too like the taste of our creation, a website will soon be up and running and available for worldwide orders."

CHAPTER 21

Sᴀᴍ ᴘʟᴀᴄᴇᴅ the last dozen boxes of SnowDrift into the shipping box and placed a mailing label on it. He set it by the front door and let out a long sigh.

Kelly looked up from behind the counter, "We've got two dozen more orders due tomorrow. That's fifty-three batches! Looks like we're going to have to pull another overnighter."

Sam groaned but went over to her and put his arms around her, looking at the computer screen.

Just weeks ago, his mum's café was on the verge of complete collapse and now thanks to SnowDrift, business was booming.

Right after the competition, the orders started flooding in, along with requests for interviews and public statements. Cindi handled all related social media requests for the Snowflake Cafe, and from there, several more of the local businesses hired her to update their social media presence.

The result was astonishing.

People were actually flocking to Whitedale to visit the small Mom and Pop business that went up against a mega-corporation and won.

The negative publicity generated by Hershell's original

SnowDrift rights grab made their stock prices plummet – and they abandoned the launch of the new product and pulled back on their plans to open up in the resort.

The Edgelake hotel for their part, had reached out to ask if Kelly and Laura would consider concoting a special recipe exclusively for their brand.

"So when are you going to tell me how you knew you were going to beat Hershells?" Sam had asked afterwards.

"Like I said – it wasn't the same recipe. When I made the first batch of SnowDrift for the presentation, I mixed marshmallows and hot cocoa in melted white chocolate. Directly inspired by my memory of your mom's, but not quite."

"But that's just cocoa powder, sugar, dry milk and flavour essence."

Kelly grinned. "Sure – but the second time for the competition, I also used her very own *homemade* marshmallows, like you said. All I wrote down in the first recipe was 'miniature marshmallows'. I didn't even think about them being homemade with the cherry essence until you reminded me. And *that's* why we won."

Sam stared at her. "So, in a way, you're saying that - "

Kelly nodded, grinning as she popped a piece of the winning recipe in her mouth. "Yep. It's your mom who's responsible for all this...winning the competition, filing the cafe, bringing tourist business back to Whitedale and ..."

Sam pulled her towards him, his eyes gleaming with delight.

"And us back together," he concluded, kissing her, a taste of Christmas still on her lips.

A WONDERFUL LIFE

A NOVEL

CHAPTER 1

2.55 p.m.

HERE GOES NOTHING....

Abby knew Kieran would already be at the church, probably joking with the best man.

He wouldn't be a nervous groom or worried about a no-show, though she couldn't help but wonder if he'd be a teeny bit unnerved about the idea of committing to one woman for the rest of his life?

She swallowed hard as she stared out the window of the car. Her palms were clammy and she resisted the urge to wipe them on her dress.

3.05 p.m. She felt her heart rate speed up. They were just minutes away from the church now and for a brief second, she thought about telling the driver to turn around. She could just lay low at home for a while, wait for all the fuss to blow over.

Yet Abby knew she couldn't – not now. Not when she'd come this far.

3.08 p.m. They reached the church grounds, and as the car approached she spied guests chatting in groups outside the entrance. Then a flurry of shuffling and stubbing out of cigarettes as someone noticed the wedding limo appear, and they quickly piled inside.

3.10 pm. "Here you go," the driver announced, slowing the car and despite her nerves, Abby managed a smile.

"Thanks," she mumbled, running an apprehensive hand through her freshly-styled blonde curls. Did she look OK? Was her make-up good?

Talking a deep breath, she reached for the handle but the driver was already holding the door open on her behalf.

"Thanks," she said, stepping out gingerly. But as soon as she left the security of the car, her mind began to spin and her heart raced even faster.

What the hell was she *doing*?

But there was no more time to think about it, when somewhere in the distance she heard organ music start up, and the bridal march begin.

Somehow, her jellylike feet managed to take her through the doorway and inside to where her beloved stood waiting to pledge his marriage vows. She saw guests turn and smile in the dreamy way that people did at brides and wondered how much more she'd be able to bear.

Then Abby's gaze finally rested on Kieran waiting at the top of the aisle and little black spots danced before her eyes at his expression. His easy smile and glance of pure adoration as he watched his bride approach was almost enough to shatter her heart in two.

And when his wife-to-be took her place beside him at the altar, Abby knew she was done for.

It really was all over...

3.15 p.m. Tears streaming down her face, she slipped numbly through a side door and stumbled outside to where her taxi was still waiting.

"You all right love?" the driver asked when she was back in

the car. "You weren't long." Then, noticing her tearstained cheeks, he added in a kind voice, "Ah, weddings can be very emotional sometimes, can't they?"

She could only nod.

Some time later, the taxi deposited her at the front door of her flat, the one she and Kieran used to share before ... everything.

But there was no point in thinking about that any more, Abby thought, her eyes red-rimmed as she paid the driver.

He was officially lost to her, and no matter how much she'd hoped he might change his mind or prayed there would be some last-minute hitch, she'd seen today with her own eyes that there was no going back.

No matter how much she'd loved him – how much she *still* loved him – her ex was gone forever.

All Abby could do now was get on with her life and try to forget him.

CHAPTER 2

"YOU'VE FORGOTTEN, HAVEN'T YOU?"

"Forgotten … what?" Abby replied absentmindedly. She cradled the office phone handset between her neck and shoulder and sifted frantically through the pile of papers on her desk.

"Mum's birthday dinner?"

The papers fell limply onto the desk, almost in tandem with her insides.

"I knew it," her sister Caroline groaned. "That's why I thought I'd better give you the heads-up…"

"Thanks sis," Abby replied, meaning it. She checked her watch and saw that it was after six pm. If she left soon, she'd have just enough time to scoot back home, get changed and make it to the restaurant on time.

"What are you doing at the office anyway? It's Saturday, Abby. Mum was right – you really *are* doing too much."

"Ah, just trying to keep on top of things," she replied airily, unwilling to admit that work was pretty much the only part of her life right now over which she felt some semblance of control. Notwithstanding the fact that she *liked* working hard at the accountancy practice. It gave her sense of purpose, kept her focused and helped her keep her mind off ... things.

Caroline harrumphed. "It's really not good to be slaving away in an office at the weekends; you should be out enjoying yourself."

By now a well-worn argument of her sister's, who by contrast loved nothing more than going out and enjoying herself. But it was different for Caroline, who had a lovely husband and a lovely life and not a care in the world. She'd never experienced anything close to the heartbreak Abby was suffering.

"But I'm out with you guys tonight, aren't I?" she replied easily. Although whether or not this constituted 'enjoying herself' was debatable.

"Yes, but knowing you, you'll be fidgeting during the first course and making excuses to leave by the third."

"That's not fair," she retorted, stung.

"Well, it might not be fair but it's certainly true." Then Caroline's tone softened. "Look, we're just worried about you, OK? Lately you don't seem to have time for anything but work and we've hardly seen you since ..." She paused slightly. "Well since all.... that. "

The break-up had happened ages ago, but her sister didn't know that Abby had gone to see her ex get married a couple of weeks back – no one did.

As far as her friends and family were concerned she hadn't seen or heard from him in months. She couldn't reveal that she'd actually gone to the church for Kieran's wedding, nor admit how pathetic she'd been in thinking that he might change his mind.

She recalled the look on his face as he watched his bride walk up the aisle towards him ... like there was nobody else in the room. At that moment, Abby would have been lucky if Kieran even remembered her name.

How had that happened? How could he have gone so quickly from planning a future with Abby, to actually marrying someone who, a few months before she'd never even *heard* of?

"Abby? Are you still there?" Caroline's voice broke into her thoughts.

"Yes, yes, sorry–I was just …" she paused, "looking for a file." No point in trying to talk to Caroline about this; her sister had little time for sentimentality and even less time for Kieran.

"You really are a workaholic. Well, hurry up and get finished and I'll see you at eight, OK? Oh, and be sure to pick up a card for Mum on the way–I'll add your name to our present if you like, or did you remember to get something for her?"

Abby winced, feeling like an absolute heel. "No, it completely slipped my mind–time's just flown by and –"

"Not to worry, as I said, I'll add your name to ours. It's a couple of tickets to *Les Mis* at the West End."

"Lovely, thanks."

Caroline and her wealthy husband Tom rarely did things by halves. But at least her elder sister had actually *gone* to the trouble of getting their mother a present, whereas Abby had been so caught up in her own little world, she hadn't even remembered the day itself, let alone got her mum a card. What kind of daughter was she?

"So I'll see you later then? Eight o'clock, remember?"

"Sure, thanks again for the reminder," Abby said before hanging up.

She sat forward in her chair with a deep sigh, and automatically resumed her search for the missing file. She was annoyed with herself for forgetting her Mum's birthday and somewhat deflated by the fact that Caroline had in a roundabout way, brought up the subject of Kieran.

Granted it was always there, but lately she was making a conscious effort to keep it to the back of her mind.

Why was this *so* hard to get over? He'd wounded her deeply, devastated her actually, yet still she just couldn't forget him. She couldn't forget the times they'd shared together and how much she'd loved him. Couldn't forget the way his skin always smelt slightly of coconut, the taste of his lips on hers, the dizzy warmth she felt when he smiled.

Abby didn't think it was even truly *possible* to forget the love of your life.

And it was driving her crazy.

CHAPTER 3

SHORTLY AFTER WORK, Abby arrived at the restaurant to find Caroline and Tom, her mum and her brother Dermot already seated and awaiting her arrival.

"Happy Birthday Mum!" She put her arms around Teresa and gave her kiss on the cheek. She'd felt so guilty after Caroline's call that she'd picked up a bunch of flowers on the way, but felt even worse when she realised how paltry her shop-bought bouquet looked compared to the oversized exotic arrangement already resting alongside her mother's chair.

"Hello love," Teresa stood up and returned her youngest daughter's hug. "Thanks for coming."

Thanks for coming? Taking a seat across from her, Abby felt even worse. Was she that unsociable these days that her mother had to actually *thank* her for turning up at a family gathering?

"Mum, have you heard from Claire?" Caroline asked, referring to their oldest sister who lived in New York with her husband.

Teresa smiled. "Yes, she called shortly before I came out, and she and Zach sent me the loveliest card."

"How is she?" Caroline asked, taking a sip from a glass of

champagne. Her sister had ordered a bottle of the most expensive bottle on the menu to toast their mother's birthday. It was the kind of thing that used to drive Kieran demented.

"I don't know how Tom puts up with it," he would say. Although her brother in law was a man of few words (hello and goodbye being about the extent of them) Tom was as easygoing as they came, and didn't seem to mind his wife's spending. He adored Caroline and worshipped the ground she walked on, something that Abby had always secretly envied.

"She's in good form," Teresa said, referring to Claire. "They're hoping to try and get home for a visit soon, but it's just so hard for Zach to get time off from work."

"Still no word on the ... other yet?"

Abby knew that Caroline was inferring Claire and Zach's hopes of having a baby. At thirty-eight, her elder sister, unlike some of Claire's social circle, was unwilling to go down the IVF route.

"Sadly nothing to report yet," Teresa confirmed.

Claire had called often in the aftermath of the break-up with Kieran, and Abby had been meaning to catch up with her many times since but had just never got round to it. "I must give her call soon," she said.

"Do she'd love to hear from you," Teresa smiled. "So how have you been yourself, love?" she asked then. "How's work?"

"Oh, very busy." Abby shifted with discomfort at having the conversation directed to her.

"Yes, Caroline tells me you've been working late in the office a lot," her mother ventured softly. "You shouldn't do too much, pet–work isn't everything, you know."

But it's all I have now, Abby wanted to say but didn't. None of them really understood that without work to concentrate on, she would have fallen apart a long time ago. "I know Mum," she said with a forced smile.

"Well, I might have just the thing to take your mind off

work Abs," Caroline trilled. "There's this fab new place in town called *Rapture*. It's a day spa, and they do all sorts of relaxing and de-stressing treatments. The three of us could go together for a pampering day sometime–my treat and–"

"Not my scene really," she told her sister with a weak smile.

"Oh, OK then," Caroline seemed a little taken aback by this steadfast refusal. "Well ... maybe you and I will try it sometime anyway Mum, what do you think?"

"Maybe sometime when Abby's not so busy," Teresa said gently.

"Well, just don't make work your only focus," Caroline said, topping up everyone's champagne glasses. "You know what they say about all work and no play ..."

Again, Abby was struck by the stark contrast between their lives. Her sister was so fortunate; she had a husband who adored her, a big house in Dalkey and not a care in world.

Yet she wouldn't dream of begrudging Caroline her perfect life. Circumstance just worked that way; some people had all the luck, while others - she thought glumly - very definitely did not.

CHAPTER 4

THE FOLLOWING MONDAY MORNING, the phone rang, and toast
still in hand, Abby answered.

"Hello stranger!" Erin said chirpily.

"How are you?" Abby smiled. She hadn't seen or spoken to
her best friend in an age. But while she'd love a chat, she didn't
have a whole lot of time right now ...

Erin seemed to read her mind. "I'm great, but I know you're
probably heading out to work soon, so I won't keep you." She
sounded excited. "The girls and I were out for a few drinks last
night and …. we came up with an idea for a sunshine mini-
break –just the four of us. What do you think about Dubai?"

"What do *I* think?" Abby knew little about the Middle East,
other than it was boiling hot and a long flight away.

"None of us have been there before, and it's supposed to be
great– sunshine, great shopping, and we'd have a good giggle.
We were thinking maybe next month–round Halloween?"

"Ah, I don't think so Erin," she said to her friend, the
thoughts of a trip to a exotic destination way down on her list
of priorities.

To say nothing of her fear of flying.

"Come on, you've been working every hour God sent these last few months, surely you're due some time off?"

"I really can't, things are just too busy."

"Well maybe we could put it off for a while then, find a time that suits everyone?"

"Maybe," she said non-committally.

"Abby, are you OK? Every time I talk to you lately you seem totally preoccupied with work, and this is the third time in weeks that you've turned me down." Erin sounded hurt. "I'm sure you're still finding things tough but– "

"Sorry Erin, but can I give you a call back later?" she interjected. "I really have to go. I'm running late as it is."

A brief silence. "OK."

"Look, you guys go ahead and book the trip without me anyway," she went on, trying to keep her voice light and upbeat. "We'll try and meet up soon, I promise."

"Fine." Erin sounded a little put-out.

"Talk to you soon, OK?" With that, Abby hung up and gulped down the rest of her coffee before grabbing her coat and hurrying out the door of the flat. She checked her watch. Eight thirty-five.

She was *definitely* going to be late.

She hurried down the street towards the city centre, needing to negotiate her way through a throng of people getting off at a nearby bus stop and in her haste, almost collided with a pedestrian coming in the other direction.

"Sorry," she said, ducking out of the woman's way, but in doing so, veered beneath a ladder up against a nearby building.

Good thing she wasn't superstitious...

It was Abby's final thought before there was a blinding flash and suddenly, everything went dark.

CHAPTER 5

FINN MAGUIRE WAS in a hurry and Lucy wasn't helping. The ceremony was due to start at two-thirty and there she was, still lingering over lunch, not a care in the world.

"Luce, hurry up and finish that, will you? We'll be late."

Lucy looked up and with a barely imperceptible sigh, sulkily walked away.

"Oh, come on–there's no need to be like that," he called after her. "You know what the traffic's like; it could take us an hour to get there."

Actually an hour would be good going, despite the fact that they only had to travel twelve miles. But knowing the M50 traffic, the journey to the school could take that and longer.

He grabbed a jacket and stole a quick look at his reflection in the hallway mirror on the way out, realising then that he'd forgotten to run a brush through his hair and it was now sticking up in thick, dark clumps all over his head. Blast it anyway, Finn thought, trying to smooth it down, and thinking it was a very good thing that they only had to make themselves look presentable now and again.

While Lucy looked great after a stint in the salon the day

before, he was very definitely letting the side down, what with his sticky-out hair and a five-year-old suit that was crying out to be replaced. It was in fact a blessing that he'd even remembered to shave this morning, so unaccustomed he was to formal gatherings.

Having done his best with his unruly hair, Finn locked the front door and went outside to where Lucy was waiting patiently alongside the Jeep.

His heart melted at the sight of her downcast expression, and for the first time that day he reminded himself that even though this was a celebration, it wouldn't feel like that for her.

"Hey, I'm sorry for shouting at you, OK?" he said, unlocking the car. "I was in a hurry and it's getting late, and you know how I much I hate being late, don't you?"

Refusing to meet his eye, she settled herself on the front seat. OK, so he wasn't getting away with it *that* easily today, Finn thought with a sigh.

He started the engine, deciding he was probably better off just staying quiet and letting her sulk. She'd snap out of it–eventually.

"I know these things can be hard for you Luce, hell they're hard for me too in a way, but you should be very proud. This is what–the fourth ceremony we've been to, and not one of our lot have ever failed to make the grade, have they?"

He glanced sideways at her, but she continued staring forward, her gaze fixated on the road in front.

"I know you'll miss them; I'll miss them too, but they're at the age where they need to make their own way in the world. And they'll be fine; you and I have made sure of that, haven't we?"

But it seemed there was still no consoling poor Lucy today. Fully-grown adults or not, at the moment she was still missing her babies, although Finn knew that this would change once the ceremony took place.

"You're the best – you know that don't you?" he said, reaching across and ruffling her fair hair, wishing again that instead of nagging her to hurry up, he'd had the good sense to try and understand what she might be going through.

Still there was nothing he could do or say now, he thought, pulling into the school gates. People were milling outside the main hall and the ceremony was about to begin.

"Finn–up here. I've saved a seat." As he and Lucy entered the hall, Finn looked up to see his colleague Angela waving at them from the front row.

Ignoring a deep sigh from alongside him (for some reason Lucy had never really taken to Angela), he made his way through the crowds to where she sat.

"Hey, thanks for that. Busy today, isn't it?"

"It sure is. Did you two get a chance to see the guys? Are they all really excited?"

"Nope, think better not to," he muttered out of the corner of mouth with a sideways glance at Lucy.

"Oh, of course, silly me." Evidently sensing some tension, Angela sensibly decided to change the subject. "But don't you scrub up well," she said, flashing Finn a flirtatious grin. "Great suit."

"Thanks." He self-consciously loosened his tie. "Em ... so do you."

Angela did indeed look good in a clinging black dress with a disconcertingly low neckline that Finn wasn't entirely sure was suitable for the occasion. Still, what did he know? His fashion knowledge extended to his work attire of mostly jeans and T-shirts, and as social outings were pretty much limited to occasions like this or the odd night out in the pub, he couldn't really comment on whether or not Angela had got it right. Women were a bit of an enigma as far as he was concerned.

"Thanks–and I'm so glad I remembered at the last minute to wear waterproof mascara."

"Waterproof mascara?"

She opened her handbag and took out a small packet of tissues. "I always end up bawling at these things, don't you?"

But Finn had no time to reply, as just then a voice he recognised spoke softly through the tannoy.

"Ladies and gentlemen. I'd like to welcome you to what is always a hugely important event in our calendar. Today's graduates have studied hard and are now ready to tackle any challenges the world throws their way. We're gathered here to celebrate their achievements, and to set them on the road to even greater things." He paused and looked to his right, before smiling. "I'm going to introduce them to you now, but for the benefit of those members of our audience in attendance for the first time, can I remind you not to applaud."

Finn nodded approvingly at this. He had forgotten to make this announcement last time and the applause had really unsettled the graduates.

"So without further ado, I'd like to introduce to you, in alphabetical order– " As the director began calling out names, Finn laid a gentle hand on Lucy's head, "Marie, Maisie, Martin, Michael, Michelle, Molly and Morris."

When the first appeared, there was a brief clap from someone who'd obviously forgotten Brendan's earlier warning, or who'd got so carried away that they couldn't help themselves.

And Finn realised, there was also a brief whimper from Lucy when she spied her babies, and as each walked on in turn she moved her tail every so slightly, until eventually when each had emerged, stood up on all fours and wagged effusively.

Lucy and Finn watched proudly as their three charges one-by-one turned and quietly stood to attention alongside their fellow graduates.

"Ladies and gentlemen," the director continued with a flourish. "I'm delighted to present to you this year's Leinster

Guide Dogs Trainee class. Now fully qualified, today they'll be officially presented to their new partners - for which all of us here hope will be a long and mutually fulfilling companionship."

"WELL, that wasn't so bad, was it?"

Once the graduation ceremony was over, Finn attached Lucy's leash, and went outside to where the newly inaugurated guide dogs were chasing and wrestling with one another on the grass, their ex-trainers and their proud new partners surveying them from the sidelines.

Now off duty, the younger dogs were making the most of what would probably be their last few hours together as a group, before each in turn went home with their visually impaired partners.

It was a wonderful day and a true validation of the work that Finn and his fellow trainers at the Leinster Guide Dog Centre carried out from year to year.

There was nothing more satisfying than taking a mischievous puppy and grooming it to become a worthwhile and essential aid to the visually impaired. But while Finn like most of his colleagues at the centre, had huge affection for each and every dog they trained, he also had a deeper additional attachment to the ones Lucy had given birth to.

A retired assistance dog of some years, the Lab's even temperament and keen intelligence made her an ideal candidate for the centre's breeding programme, and she'd so far produced three different litters who had gone on to become model trainees.

Her earlier sombre mood now greatly improved, Finn released Lucy from her leash and she raced off to join her offspring while he went to speak to the adults.

"Hey everyone. Enjoying the day?"

"It's fabulous," Melanie, a partially-sighted woman in her thirties who had been partnered with one of Lucy's pups smiled in the direction of the dogs. "They seem to be enjoying it too." Now Lucy was lying on her back, all fours in the air, happily letting the younger dogs climb all over her. "That's yours, isn't it? Michelle's mum?"

"Yes."

Since Lucy attended the centre only throughout the breeding programme and for a brief period after giving birth, she didn't have much contact with the dog's eventual companions, except on days like today.

Typically, she stayed at home with Finn, who as well as being a qualified guide dog trainer also acted as a puppy raiser for some of the potential trainees.

When the pups were about nine weeks old he brought them home for a while to help socialise and get them used to their environment, teaching them good behaviour and manners as well as get them used to living indoors, something they needed to do should they eventually be suitable as guide dogs.

"She's gorgeous; obviously knows how to put them in their place too." She and Finn laughed as Lucy nipped one of her charges for being too overzealous in his energy. "Someone told me she was a working dog herself once, but she seems very young to be a retiree?"

He sighed. "She's six, but was only three when we had to retire her. Halloween fireworks," he added in a flat voice when Melanie gave him a questioning look. "The noise frightened her so much, it rendered all of her training useless. She was only on the job a few months."

"Oh no, what a shame."

Finn nodded. It was a crying shame. He had been Lucy's original trainer and the two had always shared a special bond right from when he'd first brought her home to raise as a puppy, to when he'd eventually handed her over to her new partner at a graduation ceremony just like this one.

When the incident with the fireworks occurred and Lucy's partner needed a new dog and didn't have the space to keep her too, Finn decided to take her in.

The dogs worked for an average of eight years and while the centre often had a policy of finding retirees a loving home when their partners couldn't keep them on, Finn knew that he couldn't part with her again—especially given what she'd been through.

And though there was no possible way she could be re-trained, in time he'd managed to coax the frightened Labrador out of her anxieties and bring her back to the intelligent, loving companion she was.

Now, watching Lucy play happily with her equally clever and talented offspring, Finn was reminded of the comment one of his elderly neighbours had made recently.

"Honestly Finn, you'll never find someone as long as you keep that big, hairy mutt around."

And Finn thought to himself now as he had then, why on earth would he want to, when Lucy was possibly the only female on the planet who hadn't let him down.

CHAPTER 6

W HEN ABBY WOKE, a stranger's face was hovering above hers.

"Hello love, how are you feeling?"

"I'm fine–I think," she managed groggily. She tried to sit up but the stranger - a middle-aged woman all dressed in white - gently resisted her attempts.

"No, pet, lie still there for a while until the doctor gets here; he should be on his way soon. Would you like anything? A glass of water, maybe? I'm Molly by the way."

To her horror, Abby realised she was in what looked to be a hospital ward. So the woman in white with the kind face who was calling herself Molly must be a nurse.

What on earth was she doing in hospital?

"You had a little accident, sweetheart," Molly soothed, as if reading her thoughts.

"Accident?"

"You don't remember?"

Abby realised that the nurse was trying to make the question seem casual, but somehow her eyes gave her away.

"No …I …" She blinked, her eyes heavy with sleep. "How long have I been here? How did I get here?" Lifting her arm out from beneath the covers, she looked at her watch, as if this would somehow enlighten her. But there was no watch.

"Don't worry, all your things are safe and sound," said the nurse, again second-guessing her. "Your mother has them."

"Mum? My mother was here?" Now, Abby was seriously concerned.

"Ah you're awake," said a male voice from the doorway, and someone she assumed was a doctor appeared at the end of the bed. He picked up her medical chart and gave it a quick once-over. "How are you feeling?"

"I'm really not sure," she told him truthfully.

"Dizziness, nausea, anything like that?"

"No," she replied, but the truth was that she did indeed feel dizzy–with concern.

The doctor nodded and scribbled something on the chart. "Any pain or headaches?"

Well, yes she *did* feel some pressure on one side of her head but … "Will someone please tell me what's going on?" Abby asked, her voice trembling. "How did I get here? What's wrong with me?"

The doctor looked up quickly. "You don't remember?"

"Well, if I did I wouldn't be asking," she replied through gritted teeth. "What's going on?"

The doctor seemed determined to ignore her pleas and continued on with his questions. "Abby, do you know what day it is?"

"What do you mean 'what day'? It's Monday of course."

"And your phone number?"

"My phone number…" She went to shake her head at all of this absurdity, but it felt unusually heavy. Lifting a hand she discovered that the top of her head was wrapped in some kind of … bandage.

"OK, maybe we'll come back to that," the doctor said,

81

noticing her concern. "But can I just ask, what's the last thing you *do* remember?"

Confused, she tried to cast her mind back. Earlier that morning, she was on her way to work, and was rushing because ... because she'd been on the phone with Erin having a conversation about ... about a holiday, that was it. It had been after eight-thirty by the time she'd left the house, and the streets were busy...

When she told the doctor this, he nodded sagely.

"You don't remember the ladder?"

She blinked. "Ladder?"

The doctor nodded again as if she'd passed, or more likely *failed*, some kind of important test.

One that Abby didn't realise she was taking.

"Abby, you sustained a head injury caused by a falling roof tile," he explained, his voice gentle. "Initially, the force of the blow knocked you out, during which time we were unable to–"

"Afternoon everyone ..."

Suddenly another stranger appeared at the end of Abby's bed, a woman with kind eyes who looked to be in her early forties. But unlike the others, she wasn't in standard hospital attire; instead she was dressed in a smart black pinstripe suit and bright pink blouse.

"Doctor O'Neill ... I didn't realise you were on duty." The male medic stepped away from examining Abby to show her chart to the newcomer, and the two chatted in low voices for a few minutes which made her feel even more uneasy.

Eventually, they both returned to her side.

"Now where were we?" He took a tiny flashlight out of his pocket and shined it directly in Abby's eyes, after which he made another notation on the medical chart. "Ah yes, can you tell me your phone number?" he asked again, before adding jokily, "don't worry, I'm a happily married man."

Abby was far too anxious to appreciate the joke, but she quickly rattled off the digits, eager to prove to him, if not to herself, that she was absolutely fine.

"And your home address? Work address?" he went on, picking up her right arm and taking her blood pressure. She repeated both with ease, her trepidation easing a little, though she was still dazed.

"OK, we'll get you down for an MRI," he said, finally putting the chart back, "and I'll talk to you again after we've got the scans. In the meantime, just take it easy and don't move about too much, OK? You got quite the knock, and were unconscious for a while, but Doctor O'Neill will tell you all about that." He and the older woman exchanged a glance before he walked out.

Tell me all about what? Abby wondered, barely able to take it all in. *How long had she been out?*

"Abby, hi, I'm Hannah O'Neill, but please call me Hannah," the other doctor said kindly. "I'm the hospital's consulting neuropsychologist and here to answer any questions you might have."

She nodded gratefully, relieved. "So how long was I unconscious?"

"They brought you in this morning and it's now lunchtime, so no more than a few hours."

"A few *hours*? But what happened?"

"As I believe the doctor explained, you were hit on the head by a falling roof tile," she repeated pleasantly. "That's why we needed to ask you those questions. Amnesia - temporary or otherwise - can be very common after head trauma."

Or otherwise?

The nurse returned from tending to another patient. "Are you sure you don't want a drink?" she asked again.

"Actually I think I will." All of a sudden Abby was parched; unsurprising if she'd been unconscious for hours, she thought, still hardly able to believe it.

A falling roof tile ... She vaguely remembered veering across the path in order to avoid someone, but couldn't specifically recall a ladder.

Soon after, the nurse came back with a glass of water, and helped Abby sit up back against the pillows while the psychologist filled in some more of the blanks.

"Seems a workman called an ambulance, and stayed with you until it arrived," Hannah said. "You had your office ID on you when you came in, so admissions called your boss, who in turn called your family." She tucked the sheets tightly around Abby and then handed her the glass. "Your mother's been with you all morning but just popped down to the canteen. I've sent one of the nurses to tell her you're awake, so I'm sure she'll be back soon."

Abby nodded, relieved that her mother was nearby. "Any idea when I'll be out?" she asked.

But the other woman wouldn't meet her gaze, which unnerved her all over again.

"That'll depend on the results of the MRI, and we may have to do a CAT too," Hannah went on. "It all depends. Either way, you'll have to take things easy for a while."

"Take things easy?" Abby scoffed, her eyes widening. "I can't, I'm completely snowed under with work and my boss will go ballistic..."

"Abby, you sustained a serious blow to the head," Hannah spoke gently as if addressing a young child. "And until we know for sure how all affects you, everything else will need to take a back seat for a while."

"How all what affects me? What does that even mean?"

"We'll talk again when the results come back, OK?" the other woman soothed. "For the moment, you just take it easy and try not to worry."

CHAPTER 7

MINUTES LATER, Abby's mother arrived at her bedside looking concerned, but at the same time relieved that her daughter was awake and OK.

"How are you feeling love?" Teresa asked, giving her a kiss on the forehead. "I'm sorry I wasn't here when you woke up, but Molly made me go down to the canteen for a bite."

'Molly'? She had to smile. Already her mum was on first-name terms with the staff.

"That's OK," she reassured her, greatly relieved to have a familiar face by her side "and I'm OK too–I think."

Teresa patted her on the arm sympathetically. "So do you remember what happened? Before you blacked out, I mean?"

Abby explained again that she remembered everything except actually walking under the ladder.

"I was late for work, and the last thing I remember is making my way through the crowds. Next thing I know, I wake up in here." When her mother looked troubled, Abby was quick to reassure her. "Don't worry Mum, I'm absolutely fine. I can only imagine how worried you were when you got the call though."

"Well, of course I was," Teresa said. "We all were, Caroline, Dermot and Claire."

"Claire?" Her eyes widened. "Mum it's only a tiny bump; why would you bother her in New York with something like this?"

Clearly her mother thought this was a much bigger deal.

But why? Had the doctors told Teresa more than they'd told her? While her mum was a bit of a worrier normally, there was no denying that she now seemed troubled by something - something more than a bump on the head.

"Mum? What is it?" she urged. "Is there something else going on here? Something I don't know about?"

"Of course not," Teresa reassured her. "And I wouldn't have said anything at all to Claire only she called while I was leaving for the hospital, so I naturally enough I told her."

"Oh, OK." Abby's relief was palpable. All this stuff was making her neurotic ...

"So how's the patient?" came a voice from behind what looked like a colossal walking bunch of flowers, before Caroline's smiling face eventually peeped out.

"I'm *fine*," Abby replied, a little unsettled by all this fuss. "What are *you* doing here?"

"Well, that's a nice way to greet your favourite sister," Caroline grinned, reaching across to give her a peck on the cheek. "I'm here to see you, and of course to give you these."

"Thanks, they're gorgeous, but there's really no need ..."

"Ah just makes the place a little less dreary I think. Oh, and I brought some smellies too," she added, producing a couple of travel-sized Clarins, along with a bottle of Chanel No5, and Abby had to smile as her sister duly set about spraying the bed linen.

"So," Caroline said airily, once she was settled alongside Abby's bed. "Has Mum told you about Claire?"

"What about her?" Abby asked.

Her mother wrung her hands. "Well, I'm not sure if now is the right time what with you being in hospital and all–"

"Of course it is," Caroline smiled, urging Teresa on.

"Well as I said, I was talking to her on the phone earlier and … she had some good news."

"Really? What?"

"Turns out she's expecting," Teresa finished awkwardly, and Abby knew immediately that her mother felt guilty about the timing and even more guilty for being happy about one daughter's fortune while another was experiencing definite *mis*fortune. But there was little need for her to worry.

"That's amazing!" she gasped, thrilled for her older sister.

"Isn't it just?" Caroline agreed smiling.

"So, how far along is she?"

"Six months or so," her sister informed her before Teresa could reply.

"*Six* months? And she's only telling us now?" Although maybe her sister was nervous about broadcasting her happy news until she knew for sure that everything was OK–people sometimes did that.

Then Abby thought of something. "But how come she never said anything the other day? When she called to wish Mum a happy birthday?"

"Probably didn't want to take away from Mum's celebrations," Caroline suggested. "You know what Claire's like."

Abby did, though she couldn't understand how her sister could have withheld such news for so long. She was ecstatic for her though, and she'd definitely have to give her a call now. Or at least, whenever she got out of here…

"Anyway, are you sure you're OK yourself?" Caroline asked again. "Although, I have to admit you look fine to me."

"I *am* absolutely fine," Abby reiterated for the umpteenth

time that day. "I think they're making a huge fuss over nothing–not to mention wasting a bed on someone who clearly has nothing wrong with them."

But the shadow that crossed Teresa's face suggested to Abby that her mother didn't quite share her optimism.

CHAPTER 8

"I'm afraid there is indeed neurological damage," the doctor said, his tone sombre.

It was two days since the accident and Abby and her mother were at the neurologist's office for the results of her CT scan.

"What kind of damage?"

The doctor stood up and walked to the lightbox. "The blow caused some damage to your left temporal lobe," he said, pointing to a location on the scan.

Abby couldn't see anything out of the ordinary, but like most, she wasn't exactly familiar with the inside of her own brain. Still she nodded wordlessly, waiting for him to continue.

"I'll try not to get too technical, but to give you an idea of what we're dealing with, the temporal lobe houses the hippocampus which makes up part of the limbic system–the region of your brain responsible for emotion and motivation."

"But what does it mean?" she demanded, glancing at Teresa, though the calm way she was taking the news suggested that her mother already suspected further repercussions. "How will this damage to the hippocampus ... or whatever it's called, affect me in practical terms?"

"Take it easy, love," her mum said, reacting to the panic in her voice. "Best to just wait and let the doctor explain."

Doctor Moroney breathed out deeply, and sat on the edge on his desk. "To help put into context,' he began delicately, "when people develop Alzheimer's, the hippocampus is usually the first region of the brain to show damage."

Abby gasped. "I have some kind of Alzheimer's?"

He shook his head quickly. "I'm not saying that at all. All we know is that there's damage to the hippocampus, and that this will have some long-term effects on brain operation." Although the consultant was trying his best to sound offhand and even upbeat, there was no mistaking his grave demeanour. "When we got the scans back initially we weren't entirely sure what to make of them, so we forwarded the file to a neurologist in the US. Doctor Franklin's one of the highest ranking specialists in his field, particularly in the area of hippocampus injury."

Again Abby wished the doctor would just say what he had to say.

"I'm glad we did , because he noticed something we didn't–something curious."

"Like what?" Her gaze was drawn once again to the light-box.

"See here?" the doctor indicated a tiny blur just to the left of the injury. "This indicates some additional trauma–older trauma. Now, we've checked your medical records, and there's no sign of you presenting with anything here in recent years. Any idea what the wound is, or when it might have occurred?"

"No idea at all," Abby replied. She glanced at her mother who seemed just as clueless.

"You're sure?"

"Absolutely."

The doctor seemed to be watching her closely. "Our concerns are–or rather Doctor Franklin's concerns - are that this older trauma, in the same vicinity as the new one, could well have a bearing on how all manifests." He looked directly at Abby. "The only thing we can be sure of, at this point, is that your long-term memory will be affected."

She felt her heart rate speed up. "Affected in what way?"

"As I said, difficult to explain in layman's terms, but to help you understand how it all works, let me use an analogy. Think of the hippocampus as a bridge. On one side, you have all of your long term memories and on the other, your short-term memories. When your brain creates a brand new memory–a short term one–it needs to pass over the bridge for you to retain and recall whenever you need to. Are you with me so far?"

She nodded.

"But this most recent trauma has damaged the bridge a little, put a crack in it as such. So when new memories want to cross to the long-term side, some of them may ... fall through."

Her eyes widened. "Fall? Fall where?"

"As I said, this is purely metaphorical for explanatory purposes; not scientific fact," the doctor repeated, a little impatiently. "What I'm trying to illustrate is that some of your memories may not make it to the other side, or if they do, you might have trouble retrieving them."

Abby stared at the scans. She had a mental picture of an old stone bridge with a huge crack in it and her memories falling through.

"So how does the older injury come into it?" Teresa asked. "Will it make things worse ...?"

"No, the latest trauma is the root of the issue, but the older one may yet have a part to play. We're just not certain at the moment. Again, there are *no* certainties when it comes to the human brain. I really wish there were." The doctor walked round to his desk and opened a drawer. "I'm discharging you tomorrow Abby, but I need you to monitor yourself over the next while - let us know if you notice anything out of the ordinary over the next few days and weeks, any blackouts, memory lapses, things like that."

A rod of panic travelled through her. "I could have something like Alzheimer's and you want to just send me home?"

"Not exactly, more a measure of memory ... displacement ... but nothing so serious or progressive as Alzheimer's. That's the thing about the brain, Abby–it's the most complex part of the body and still the one we know the least about." He handed her a card. "You remember the doctor that came to see you before, Doctor O'Neill? She may have already told you that she's a neuropsychologist, specialising in TBI–Traumatic Brain Injury. She'll help you make sense of the day-to-day impact, and she'll also be able to monitor any changes that may occur from now on. You haven't noticed anything out of the ordinary as yet?"

"Definitely not. I'm tired and I've been getting some headaches but ..."

"Very common," he said, nodding sagely. "Just keep a close eye on yourself until I talk to you again, OK?"

Abby took the card. It was all so surreal. As far as she was concerned, she felt fine. Yes, there was a little bit of pressure in her head and she was irritated about having to miss time off work, but other than that she felt perfectly ... normal.

"But there might be nothing at all wrong with me, right?" she asked, pleading with him to give her at least a semblance of hope. "My memory might still be absolutely fine."

"Perhaps so, but ..." the doctor fudged, and Abby didn't like the grim set of his jaw, nor the very obvious doubt in his eyes.

CHAPTER 9

Sunday afternoon, Finn opened his front door to find Pat Maguire standing on his doorstep.

"Hey Dad, how's things?" he said beckoning him inside. As he did so, Lucy–who adored Pat–bounded down the hallway to greet him, her tail wagging furiously.

"Ah there you are, my darlin'" Pat bent down and ruffled Lucy behind the ears. "How was she the other day?" he asked, referring to the graduation ceremony. Like Finn, he knew how lonely she got when her pups went out into the big bad world.

"Not too bad. A bit moody initially, but much better when it was all over."

"Isn't it gas the way they know what's happening all the same?" Pat said, shaking his head. "Aren't they nearly human sometimes?"

"Better than some humans I think," Finn's expression tightened and he moved to the sink. "At least she actually gives some thought to her offspring. Cup of tea?"

"That would be grand, thanks." Pat took a seat at the kitchen table and looked at his son. "Lookit, there's no need for that kind of smart talk."

Immediately Finn felt guilty. There *was* no need, and it wasn't fair to his father– especially after all this time. But sometimes, he just couldn't help but revert to a sulky teenager instead of a grown man of thirty-five.

"Sorry, it's been a busy week and I'm a bit stressed out." Finn stood by the counter as he waited for the kettle to boil.

"Stress, stress, stress–everyone in this country is stressed these days. Whatever happened to just taking things easy?"

Finn smiled. "The one who's talking. When's the last time *you* took things easy, Dad? Sixty-eight years of age and you're *still* going up and down ladders like a madman."

Pat was a cabinet-maker by trade, but for as long as Finn could remember he'd been working as a painter/decorator and odd-job man in the area. His father could turn his hand to anything; plumbing, carpentry, electrics, a feat that thanks to him Finn could also lay claim to, and which had served him well in renovating this house.

After a stint of travelling and working abroad–mostly in the US–a few years back he'd decided to come home to Dublin and settle down.

At least, that had been the plan. He'd bought this place shortly after taking up work in the dog training centre, deciding that a run-down, crumbling old farmhouse in rural North County Dublin would suit him a lot better than the hustle and bustle of the city.

"Well, I might have to give up those ladders for a while soon," Pat said, and hearing a slight catch in his voice, Finn looked up. Suddenly realising that this was no casual visit, he stared at his father. "What does that mean?"

"Finish making that pot of tea and I'll tell you," his father replied, leaving Finn wondering what on earth was coming.

He soon found out.

"My health's not the best at the moment, son," Pat announced, having left Finn wait anxiously while he poured the sugar and milk. "I've been a bit weak in myself these last few months, which isn't like me."

His father was one of the fittest, most active people he knew. Up at dawn every day without fail, Pat would go for a good long walk in the morning before putting in a solid day's work, and then coming home to tend to the household. He'd always been scrupulous about looking after himself, and because of this tended to be fitter than even his thirty-five year old son. At least, that was what Finn had always believed.

"So I called down to Doctor Murphy who said that I was probably just low on iron and put me on some tablets. But nothing changed."

"I can't see why he thought that," Finn muttered. "You're a demon for red meat."

"Anyway, they did a few blood tests and to cut a long story short, it seems they have to keep on eye on me from now on, just in case."

"In case of what?" Finn demanded while trying his best to keep his thoughts in check.

Pat looked almost embarrassed. "Prostrate trouble – the numbers are high apparently. Lookit, don't you be worrying about me now," he said, sitting forward in his chair. "That's not why I'm telling you. The last thing you need is to be worrying about me."

"How could I *not* worry about you, you're my father."

Not to mention the only family I have. The doctors must have made some kind of mistake. But for his dad's sake, he knew he had to get a hold of himself.

"The only reason I'm telling you now is that I have to go for some more tests soon– next month in Vincent's."

"Next month ..."

"Yes. So I might need you to give me a lift in there now and again if you don't mind."

"Well, of course I don't mind." Finn would do anything for

his father, in the same way that Pat had done everything for him all throughout his life.

He felt stunned ... numb at the thought that illness had raised its ugly head. "So these tests ... what'll they achieve?"

"God only knows, but Finn these things happen to men my age," Pat was being remarkably practical about the entire situation, in much the same way as he'd been about every difficult situation he'd faced in his life. "Who knows how it'll go? What will be will be."

Not for the first time, Finn wished he'd inherited some of his father's strength of character, his extraordinary ability to face head-on any challenges life threw his way.

Whereas in the face of challenges such as this one, he couldn't summon his father's strength; instead he felt weak and afraid–pointless traits Finn knew he'd inherited from his mother.

CHAPTER 10

HE'D BEEN seven years old when she left. He couldn't remember much before that day, couldn't really remember all that much about *her*, or what is was like having her in his life.

Perhaps the memories just weren't all that strong; or perhaps he'd blocked them out intentionally. All he remembered was arriving home from school one day to find his father sitting at the big oak kitchen table, his head in his immense, callused workman's hands. Finn had never before (or since) seen his father cry.

It was very strange.

The family dog, Rex, who upon Finn's arrival had been lying at Pat's feet, jumped up to greet him.

"What's wrong?" he asked, setting his school bag down on the floor in order to pet the sheepdog behind the ears. "Dad, are you OK? Why are you crying?"

"Me – crying? Would you get away out of that," his father said, attempting a half-hearted laugh. "Haven't I gone and got something in my eye–a chip of wood, I think." Pat made a great show of rubbing one eye as if trying to dislodge something from it. "I was doing a bit of sawing in the workshop, so I had to come inside and splash some water on it."

"Oh." With some relief, Finn let go of Rex and returned the smile, although in retrospect he was convinced that he should have known that something wasn't right. He picked his schoolbag off the floor and hung it on the back of one of the chairs. "So when's dinner? And where's Mam?"

Pat stood up from the table and walked to the window above the sink, turning his back to his son. "She had to go away for a while."

"Where did she go to?"

His father was silent for a long moment, and his shoulders heaved a little before he spoke again. "Just away."

Finn frowned. This was odd. His mother was always here when he came home from school ...OK, so maybe not always, but *nearly* always. Where could she have gone to? Why would she leave without saying goodbye to him? And who would make his dinner?

Once more uneasy, Finn called Rex over, and again began softly caressing the dog's head. "But where did she go? And when will she be home?"

"Soon," Pat replied flatly, but Finn realised that throughout the entire exchange his father never once turned to look at him. "She'll be home soon."

Of course, his mother never did come home, and to this day he could still recall the sound of his father crying softly to himself at night.

Yet despite this, Pat behaved for all the world as though there was nothing unusual in Imelda, his wife of nine years, taking off and leaving him and their young son to fend for themselves.

In hindsight, Finn understood that this was simply his father's way of trying to make things easier for him, that by carrying on as normal maybe Finn wouldn't notice his mother's absence.

And for a time, it worked. In the years following her departure, he and his father did have a relatively happy and carefree life. Pat was always around when Finn came home from school, he regularly helped him with his homework and cooked him meals, and at weekends, the two of them spent long hours making things in the workshop, or took Rex out for lengthy walks in the fields surrounding their house.

For the next few years of his life, Pat did such a good job of raising him that Finn had almost forgotten his mother ever existed, but then when he reached puberty for some reason everything changed. Suddenly, Finn wanted to know more about his mother, and why the woman had just upped and abandoned them.

"It's complicated–I've told you that," Pat insisted, after Finn's repeated attempts to delve into the matter in more detail.

"What could be complicated about it? She just took off and left us to our own devices."

"It's not that simple."

"It seems pretty damn simple to me. I come home one day from school to find that my own mother has just upped and left me–no goodbye, no explanation, nothing."

"Finn that was eight years ago. Why is it such a big problem now? We've had a grand life, haven't we? You've wanted for nothing, so why get all het up about these things now?"

"Because I want to know why she left," Finn shot back. "I want to know why she thinks she had the right to abandon us like ... like a piece of dirt. And," he added ominously, "when I find her, I'm going to ask her exactly that."

Of course, Finn never *did* try to find out where she was, and in truth his periodic rants about her disappearance were more bravado (coupled with a hefty dose of teenage angst) than anything else.

His mother had disappeared from his life a very long time ago, and as far as Finn was concerned, she could stay away for good.

CHAPTER 11

ABBY ARRIVED at Hannah O'Neill's office for her first appointment, hoping the neuropsychologist would be able to shed more light on her prognosis and what to expect.

"Good to see you again," Hannah got up from her desk to shake her hand when she entered.

"You too." Hannah had made a good impression on her at the hospital, mostly because she was the only one there who'd been willing to give her a straight answer. And oddly, when Abby walked in the room just now and shook her hand, she felt a really odd sense of ... déjà vu.

The other woman smiled. "I suppose we might as well get started. Have a seat–anywhere you like," she added, when Abby looked unsure which to choose – the two purple velvet armchairs in the centre of the room, or the scarlet chaise longue by the wall. The place was nothing like she'd expected from a psychologist's office and instead of being clinical and austere, was warm and cosy with vibrant, comfortable furniture and fluffy cushions.

On the wall were funky bookshelves filled with colourful tomes and pretty knick-knacks and travel souvenirs. There were also quirky soft furnishings, like the cerise pink ostrich feather lampshade on the desk, wooden Balinese-style wall art, and huge Oriental rug on the floor.

"I know," the psychologist said, reading Abby's reaction. "Some of my other patients have compared this place to their teenage daughters' bedrooms. But I love lots of colour and warmth at home, so why should my workplace look like its been dropped in a tin of mushroom soup?"

"It's great," she said smiling. If Hannah O'Neill was anything like her office, then these visits might not be so difficult after all. She sat down on one of the velvet armchairs and Hannah took the one directly opposite.

The psychologist echoed her thoughts. "I'm glad you think so, because we'll be spending quite a bit of time together here– at least I hope we will," she added eyeing her new patient speculatively. "Would you like a glass of water or maybe a coffee?"

"No thanks," Abby shook her head. "To be honest Doctor, I'm not entirely sure why I'm here," she said, deciding it was better to be frank from the outset. "I mean, I know its because of the injury," she added with a tight smile, "but as far as I'm concerned there's nothing wrong with me."

"Good to know, and let's hope that's the way things stay," Hannah replied, her tone bright. "But–and I'm sorry there has to be a but," she added with a smile, "as explained at the hospital, the damage sustained will almost certainly impact your memory function. You got one hell of a whack on the head. Because of this, it's important we keep a close eye to see how things will go. By the way, please call me Hannah," she added affably, before kicking off her shoes and to Abby's surprise, tucking her long legs beneath her. "So Doctor Moroney talked you through the scans?"

"He tried, but it all sounded so technical I couldn't really follow."

"Well let me try to explain as best I can. Let's start with

memory – normal, undamaged memory," the psychologist began, speaking softly. "There are three main stages in memory formation and retrieval. The first is encoding– processing of initial memory–then storage, whereby our brains create a permanent record of the information, and finally retrieval, which I guess is self-explanatory."

Abby nodded studiously.

"Now, there are, within this process two distinct types of memory; short-term and long-term. For example, if I show you a random seven-digit number, you might remember it for a few seconds but then forget, because it was only stored in your short-term memory. On the other hand, people remember phone numbers for years through repetition, and these longer-lasting pieces of information are believed to be stored in our long term memory. Are you with me so far?"

Abby nodded once more, determined to understand."Sure."

"Let's break this down a little further again. Long-term memory can be further sub-divided into two more categories, semantic memory and episodic memory." Seeing her dubious expression, the neuropsychologist paused. "I can see I'm in danger of losing you now, but it's the best way to explain how the process works - or as much as we know, at least."

"OK, semantic and episodic memory," Abby repeated, trying her best to keep up, though all this technical stuff was *already* frying her brain.

"Semantic memory is concerned with the retrieval of abstract knowledge, like, say 'Dublin is the capital of Ireland'. Episodic memory then, is used for more personal memories; experiences and emotions associated with a particular time or place, OK?"

"OK."

"The hippocampus–the part of your brain that's damaged– is essential for consolidating information from short-term to long-term memory, although it does not actually store information itself. To use a common neurologist's analogy, the hippocampus is the bridge between your short and long term memory. Short term memories move across this bridge to the long-term 'department' shall we say," she said smiling. "From here, they can be usually be recalled whenever required. Does that make sense to you?"

"I think so," Abby said. "The doctor said that in my case, that bridge may have a crack in it and that some memories may fall through."

"Well, yes he's right in some respects but also, it's also a lot more complex," she said, with an apologetic smile. "The hippocampus makes up part of the limbic system, the area of the brain responsible for emotion and motivation. And I'm sure you know, emotion and memory are very closely related."

You're telling me, Abby thought wryly, instantly thinking of her ex.

Hannah continued. "For example, say you go to a party and meet lots of different people–some nice, some not so nice, others that don't make much of an impact either way. Now, when you think back on that party, who are you going to remember the most?"

Abby laughed. "Probably the woman who barely gave me the time of day."

"In all likelihood, you'll remember both the kind man and snooty woman, since each provoked some form of emotional response. In making you laugh, the man made you feel at ease, and by being dismissive, the woman provoked unease. Either way, you're going to recall both of those people next time you see them. As for the others, the ones who *didn't* engage – chances are not at all."

Abby nodded vigorously, this scenario very much striking a chord.

"But following on from this, as we discussed before, the two types of memory–long-term and short-term also come into play. Since the hippocampus is that all-important part of the brain responsible for transferring emotional memories like the ones at the party–which are eventually stored in the temporal lobe–it is in effect, responsible for *making* these new memories."

"So what you're saying is that because of the damage, I might not be able to do that, make new memories?" Abby said, panicking a little.

"No, the concern is that you may not able to *recall* these newer memories. Your short-term memory will continue to act as normal, in that it'll file away day-to-day events and send them accordingly to your long term memory. But depending on the strength of emotional reaction–and most importantly, also whether or not they are semantic or episodic–some of these newer ones may fade or become lost along the way."

"Semantic and episodic ..." Abby repeated, her mind whirling. "I still don't understand."

Hannah sat forward again. "OK, let me try and make this simpler," she said, pausing briefly before speaking again. "Tell me what you remember about 9/11."

Abby frowned. "You mean *the* 9/11, the New York terrorist attack back in 2001?"

The psychologist relaxed back into her chair again. "Yes, tell me what you remember about it."

Abby breathed out. "The first plane struck the North Tower at around 2.45pm our time. At first, they thought it was an out-of-control plane, but then they found out it had been hijacked, so by the time the second one struck they knew it was a terrorist attack. Then later, the first tower collapsed and ... what?" she broke off self-consciously. Hannah was shaking her head.

"I didn't ask you what you knew about it Abby, I asked what you *remembered* about it. For example, where were you?"

"When it happened?"

"Yes."

"Well, I'd popped home for lunch that day for some reason, I can't remember now −normally I eat at my desk. Anyway, the TV was on in the background with the sound turned down. I do remember being in the middle of making a sandwich − "

"What kind of sandwich?"

"What?"

"What kind−salad, ham ...?"

"Um, tuna possibly."

"OK. Go on."

"But what I *do* remember is looking up at the screen and seeing the smoke come out of one of the buildings. My first thought was that Claire used to work in one of those buildings. My sister lives in New York," she explained, "and when she first moved there, she worked for a company in Tower One."

Hannah considered this. "So your first reaction was related to some previous personal association with the tower, rather than what was happening at the time?"

She nodded. "So I turned up the TV, and then the second plane flew in and I watched it hit the other tower." Abby shook her head. "I was horrified because then I knew that something was really wrong and big was happening ... the news reporters were going crazy, it all seemed a bit surreal ...and even though I knew that Claire didn't work in the financial district, I started to feel uneasy."

Hannah nodded and waited for her to continue.

"I rang Mum and explained what was happening and told her to turn on the TV, but that was a big mistake really, as straight away she too started worrying ..." She exhaled deeply. "So after managing to calm her down, I told her to phone Claire and then phone me back and let me know that she was OK, which she did."

The two were silent for a couple of moments as each replayed their own recollection of the days' horrific events.

After a while, Hannah spoke again. "Abby, when I asked what you remembered about 9/11, the sequence of events you described initially was your semantic memory of events; a step-by-step account of what is by now common knowledge about that day, the timing of the crash, the fall of the first tower etc.

But what you described just now was your *emotional* recollection, not just of the event itself, but more importantly how you and your feelings were central to it. This second sequence was vivid and much more involving—yes, you couldn't remember a couple of things, such as the sandwich you made for lunch, but these trivial things were unimportant in comparison.

Your emotional reaction was particularly vivid, you immediately worried about your sister, and you very quickly reached out to the people close to you. You also outlined the empathy you felt for those involved, whereas the first time round was just a flat, emotionless account, almost as if you were reading from a piece of paper."

Abby nodded, now understanding what the doctor was getting at.

"I'm trying to emphasise the importance of emotion when it comes to memory retention. Semantic memories are *learned* memories whereas episodic memories are *experienced*, and often emotionally charged. They're felt," she clarified, pointing to her chest.

"I think I get it." Although Abby was still unsure as to what it all meant in relation to her injury.

The psychologist seemed to read her thoughts. "So because of the complex nature of the brain, and the many millions of neural pathways inside, we still have no *absolute* way of knowing how this injury will affect you long-term. The only thing we can be sure of is that it will—almost without doubt—affect your ability to recall episodic memories."

"But what about my existing memories?" Abby asked. "The ones like I just described? They won't be affected, will they?"

Hannah sighed. "It's possible but at the same time unlikely. I know that must seem very frustrating to you, but unfortunately that's just how it is. And of course, there's the issue of that older injury Doctor Franklin found on your scan. This makes things even more complicated because we could be talking about some dual-effect we can't anticipate."

"I already told them–I don't know anything about an old injury," Abby insisted, frustrated that all any of these medical people were certain about was that they couldn't be certain of anything.

"I understand. And things can take time to manifest, which is why we need to keep a close eye on your progress for the next while to see if anything … unusual happens. After an injury like this, incidental memory blips or even blackouts are common, so I need you to keep a very close eye on yourself, Abby. To start with, I suggest you try keeping a diary of your day-to-day experiences–which may help pinpoint something out of the ordinary."

"But when will this happen?" she asked, fearful now. "When might these … blips start? Will it be now, next week, next year, when?"

Hannah shook her head slowly. "I truly can't say. For the moment, we just need to wait and see."

CHAPTER 12

"HOW ARE YOU FEELING, LOVE?" Teresa asked, putting a cup of tea and some chocolate biscuits on the table in front of Abby.

It was three weeks after her release from the hospital, and since she was on enforced leave from work and had plenty of time on her hands, she called over to her Mum's for a chat.

"Most of the time, I don't know what to do with myself," she confessed. "I'm so used to having a million and one things to do at work, whereas now I have all this time on my hands ..."

"Probably no harm. You were working way too hard before all of this happened - you needed to slow down sometime."

Abby bit her lip. "And it was because I was rushing around that this happened in the first place."

"Well, it could have been much worse?" Teresa pointed out. "That falling slate could have killed you. And speaking of which, I was talking to the solicitor about the insurance and he reckons it should be sorted soon."

"Really?" Abby was taken aback that it was all going so smoothly. Though the roofing company was probably keen to get the whole thing dealt with as soon as possible–just in case the doctors discovered more serious damage in the meantime.

Just then the phone rang, and Teresa picked up. "Hello? Oh, just give me a minute and I'll be over. OK, thanks." Hanging up, she turned to Abby. "I told Mary I'd take in a delivery for her. Will you be all right here, if I pop out for a sec?"

Mary was Teresa's nearby neighbour and each woman held spare keys to the other's houses.

"Of course. Do you need help taking it in?"

"No, no, it's only a parcel. You stay there and relax, and I'll be back in a jiffy," she said, putting on a jacket. "Make a fresh cuppa and go on into the sitting room."

Switching on the kettle again, Abby did as she was bid and carried the plate of biscuits into the living room. As she had nothing better to do, she turned on the television. Nothing but ads, ads and more ads, she thought, looking around for the remote control, which she eventually spied on top of the piano at the far end of the room.

Abby approached the piano, but instead of reaching for the remote control, she impulsively lifted the lid and pulled out the small stool tucked beneath. Then she sat down and began idly running her fingers along the keys.

Some ten minutes later, Teresa returned from her neighbour's to a house filled with music, and her youngest daughter in front of the piano in the throes of Beethoven's *Ode to Joy*.

"Ah it's years since I heard that," her mother said fondly. "Actually, it's years since I heard you play at all." Then she turned and went back into the kitchen to make a fresh pot of tea.

Slightly shell-shocked, Abby stayed sitting where she was, her fingers tingling, and not just from striking the keys.

Because as far as she was concerned, she had never played the piano in her entire life.

. . .

"No need to worry, that sounds perfectly reasonable," Hannah soothed, when Abby called for an emergency appointment and she'd agreed to see her the following day.

"But I don't remember ever playing the piano," Abby insisted panicking. "As far as I'm concerned I don't know how."

"As far as your *episodic memory* is concerned, you don't know how," Hannah clarified, "because you can't specifically remember learning. Your procedural memory on the other hand, isn't concerned with when or how you learned this particular skill. It's just responsible for retaining it."

"I don't understand ..."

"Remember when I tried to reassure you that you would be able to live a perfectly normal life as far as your day-to-day activities were concerned? That you wouldn't forget how to walk or how to dress yourself, drive a car, things like that." When Abby looked blank, she continued. "OK, take for example learning how to walk. Like the rest of us, you probably learned this particular skill when you were a baby–what twelve, thirteen months old?"

"I think so yes."

"Irrelevant to your injury, I'm willing to bet that you can't actually remember learning, can you? You can't remember going from crawling on all fours to balancing upright and taking those first steps?"

"Well, no."

"But yet you still know how to walk, don't you?"

"So far, yes," Abby muttered wryly.

Hannah folded her arms. "Same as the rest of us. When it comes to learning a skill, such as walking or playing the piano, episodic memory is responsible for the recollection of 'where and when' you learned it, whereas procedural memory is responsible for the skill itself. The brain doesn't need to access the 'where and when' in order to remember the skill.

Procedural memory and episodic memory function quite separately from one another. Am I making any sense?"

She nodded thoughtfully. "I think so. You're saying that the undamaged part of my brain knows that I could play the piano, but the damaged bit couldn't remember learning how."

"Exactly." Hannah looked pleased that she was getting it. "Procedural memory is extremely durable, episodic not so much, which is why most of us can't remember learning how to walk or recall specific memories from early childhood. But in your case, because of the damage to the hippocampus, its durability is even worse."

"It was so weird," Abby said, shaking her head at the peculiarity of it all. "I just sat down, and my fingers seem to know exactly what to do."

"That's because they did know. In a way I'm glad something like this has happened." When she looked at her wide-eyed, Hannah held up his hands in a gesture of apology. "Forgive me, but what I mean is that it's a useful way to help you understand the nature of your injury and how your memory function works."

It was really happening wasn't it? No matter how much Abby tried to tell herself that the damage might not be so bad, and that she'd be OK, there was no now denying that there really *was* something wrong.

"Little things like this will be par for the course from now on," Hannah continued gently. "Some things you'll notice, others maybe not, but either way you'll need to come to terms with the fact that because of the damage, your memory will no longer function the way it used to."

After a brief pause, Abby sighed. "Well, so long as I can live a normal life, I suppose I could put up with a few small lapses now and again." When Hannah didn't reply immediately, her eyes narrowed. "What?" she demanded worriedly. "What am I missing?"

"Abby, episodic memory is only a small part of the way our brain stores memories and any changes, however small, in the way it works merely confirms the damage to your hippocampus." Hannah paused before continuing. "I'm sorry, but what happened yesterday is just the beginning."

CHAPTER 13

ABBY REALISED that over the last few years, she had very few memories–good *or* bad–that didn't include her ex.

Kieran had been there for her graduation, smiling proudly with her parents as she stood on the podium to accept her accountancy degree. She'd taken her very first plane ride with him, her hand tightly clasped in his as the plane sped up and took flight. They'd had their first foreign holiday together, he'd been at her side for Claire's wedding, and also when her dad died a few years back.

But since the breakup, those memories had become tainted so really, what did it matter if she ended up losing them?

"Talk about a defeatist attitude," Caroline chided, not long after incident at her mum's house, when she invited herself over to Abby's place. Since the accident, her sister had been unbelievably attentive. "When's the last time you got out and enjoyed yourself–*really* enjoyed yourself? It's no surprise you can't find any good memories, because lately you haven't bothered making any."

Abby stared at her, stung. "Was I that bad?" she asked croakily.

"Yes!" Caroline exclaimed. "And I'm sorry, I don't mean to upset you but I really think you need to hear this, and goodness knows I've held my tongue long enough." She looked away, and her tone softened. "Hon, I know you were at the wedding–Kieran's wedding."

"What? How could you possibly...?" Abby wanted to die of mortification.

"I wasn't going to say anything, but I think I have to now. Abs, there's no going back. You need to forget all about him and start getting on with your own life."

"You think I haven't tried?"

Now Caroline's tone was soothing. "I can only imagine how hard it's been. But the truth is, you *haven't* really tried to move on. Before the accident, you hardly saw or spent time with any of us until mum's birthday." She turned to face her, her expression remorseful. "I'm sorry and I get that you're still hurting, but you must realise by now that he isn't coming back."

"I know," Abby replied, her heart breaking afresh. "Of course I know that."

Caroline sat up straight. "So here's what I think. And you might say I'm crazy," she gave her a sideways glance, "but I reckon that blow to the head was a wake-up call. You just said yourself that life in the run-up to the accident isn't exactly worth remembering anyway," she added lightly. "So maybe now's the time to do something about it? For starters, let's go out on the town – just the two of us. A nice meal somewhere, a good old gossip and a bit of *craic.*"

Abby bit her lip. "Oh, I don't know Caroline, you know how fussy I am with food ..."

Her sister rolled her eyes. "A perfect example of what I'm talking about. You've been falling back on any excuse at all to stop you getting on with life alone - without Kieran."

"That's not true."

"Are you sure?" her sister said, eyeing her. "When's the last

115

time you went out somewhere without him? To a movie or a concert, or even as far as a bloody shopping mall. You were so used to being part of a couple it's almost as if you've stopped remembering how to function on your own–and that has nothing to do with your head injury by the way."

"That's not fair," Abby exclaimed, hurt.

But of course it was. Caroline's assessment might have been blunt, but deep down Abby knew it was correct. She *had* forgotten what it was like not to be part of a couple. She and Kieran had been together so long that since the split, she'd felt as though one of her limbs had been hacked off. Maybe her sister had a point. Perhaps she ought to get on with her life, and instead of using her injury as an excuse to retreat even further into her shell, she *should* treat it as a wake-up call.

"OK maybe you're right," she said, suddenly determined. Everyone was going to see a *very* different person to the one who'd shied away from the world, afraid to experience all it had to offer.

From now on, Abby was going to put her heartbreak and bad memories behind her, get out there and start living her best life.

WITH THIS IN MIND, a few days later she arranged to catch up with Erin.

Her friend had only recently returned from her girlie trip to Dubai, and as Abby made her way towards their arranged meeting spot–a cosy pub just off Grafton Street, she thought again about how long it had been since the two enjoyed a night out together.

Since her sister's pep talk she'd thought a lot about her day to day life in the run-up to the accident, and realised that even though she'd done her utmost to keep people at arm's length, they'd still rallied round in the aftermath of her diagnosis. And she was grateful for that.

"Hi there," Erin said, standing up and giving her an effusive hug. "You look great."

Abby raised a self-conscious hand through her shorter hair. "Don't think so," she said softly. Although it had started to grow back a little more, it would be years before she was comfortable with it again.

"Well I think it's very trendy," Erin insisted. "What'll you have to drink?"

"Just a Coke thanks," Abby said. "Doctor's orders, I'm afraid," she explained ruefully.

"You can't even have one glass of wine?"

"Not for the moment, no." The doctors had put her on painkillers for the intermittent headaches she'd been experiencing since the accident, and she was reluctant to do anything that might adversely affect her senses–particularly after the piano incident.

"You don't mind if I get something stronger?"

"Not at all, go right ahead."

"So how have you been since?" her friend asked when the waitress had taken their dinner order. "Are you feeling OK?"

"I'm grand," Abby said, not yet ready to confide in Erin about the piano incident. "I feel perfectly normal. Anyway, forget about me," she said brightening. "Was Dubai fabulous?" Then she frowned. "I'm sorry but I have to say you don't look very tanned." A fervent sun-worshipper, Erin usually turned a deep shade of mahogany following any exposure to the sun.

"Oh, the weather wasn't great," she said dismissively.

"Really? I thought it was always hot and sunny there."

"So did we," her friend groaned, before launching into a full-scale report of the girls' recent trip.

By the time their starters arrived Abby had really begun to relax and enjoy herself for what seemed like the first time in

117

ages. It had been yonks since she and Erin had got together for a natter—why on earth had they left it so long?

But Abby knew there was only one answer to that. *She* hadn't wanted to face the world, hadn't really wanted to move on with her life. A bump on the head was a pretty good way of waking a person up and reminding them what they were missing, wasn't it?

"Penne arrabiatta," the waitress announced, placing a steaming bowl of pasta on the table in front of Erin, and then a slice of lasagne for Abby.

"Thank you," she replied, her mouth watering at the sight of it. Hospital food also had a way of making you appreciate the simplest things…

"Parmesan?" the waitress enquired.

"Please," she said smiling at the waitress, who duly sprinkled some on her pasta.

Erin seemed surprised. "Well *that's* a turn-up for the books," she commented when the waitress left. "I thought you hated that stuff, didn't you use to say it smelt like mouldy socks?"

"Must be thinking of someone else," Abby commented distractedly. "Anyway - what else did you get up to in Dubai?" Judging by what Erin had told her so far, yet again she'd missed all the fun.

CHAPTER 14

FINN WAS ABOUT to begin training a new batch of recruits, which he usually found good fun but at the same time hugely challenging.

Although most of the young guide dogs had been born 'on campus' at the centre, they had spent the first year of their lives being raised and socialised in the home of one of the centre's many volunteer puppy raisers.

For the first few weeks back at base, the dogs were always a little out of sorts and Finn knew they were missing their raisers as well as the comforts of home. So for this reason, the first phase of training generally consisted of his taking them for relaxing walks around the centre and helping them get to know their trainers as well as the kennel environment and routine. But most dogs tended to settled down very soon, and the personality traits that made Labradors such magnificent guide dogs; their willingness to work, eagerness to please, and absolute adoration of praise soon became readily apparent.

Throughout the training process, Finn and his colleagues repeatedly used an abundance of rewards including physical and verbal affection, all of which built up motivation, confidence and most importantly, a happy working guide dog.

The young dog Finn was working with today, Jack, had a lovely, gentle manner, and was so far responding extremely well to his obedience training. He learnt very quickly and reacted brilliantly to all of Finn's cues, and unlike some other dogs hadn't batted an eyelid at wearing the harness. That morning alone, Finn had taught him how to walk in a perfectly straight line from A to B and almost instinctively and without any major prompting, Jack also walked Finn safely around the obstacles placed in his path. It was remarkable progress, and from what he'd seen so far, Finn was hugely confident that Jack would sail through the rest of his training and eventually qualify as a working guide dog.

But, shortly after lunch, Finn discovered Jack's Achilles heel.

Exposure to distraction was a major part of the process and for this purpose, while the young guide dogs were in training, other breeds were allowed run freely in the area–dogs who were hugely inquisitive, equally aggressive and who loved nothing better than getting close up and confrontational with larger ones. Jack Russell terriers were notorious for this 'in your face' behaviour, and the centre manager's own pet terrier was a perfect example. Small and annoyingly yappy, Rasher loved nothing better than to run up and bark at the training dogs, and do his best to try and distract them. It was the ultimate test of patience for any dog–trainee or not–and the majority, including Jack, passed it with flying colours, and much to Rasher's chagrin, ignored him completely.

For the next challenge, the trainees were introduced to an entirely different animal, one they'd been waging wars with since the beginning of time, a relentless battle that over the years had spawned a multitude of cartoons, books and films.

Not to mention one that found the prospect of trying to distract the trainees even more of a pleasure than Rasher did.

Let's see how you fare this time, Finn thought to himself, as he once again attached the harness, and he and Jack set out on a supposedly casual walk around the arena. They'd walked only a couple of yards before the harness went rigid and Jack stopped short quickly, the hair on the back of his neck standing up. Then, almost before Finn knew what was happening, the dog pulled furiously on the harness and careered off-path and in another direction. He didn't stop until he reached the boundary wall whereupon a black cat was washing herself lazily in the sun. Then, having reached the wall and dragged Finn all the way, the young dog barked wildly at the cat who determinedly ignored him and continued washing herself

"Jack, meet Sooty," Finn muttered, his tone filled with disappointment at the dog's reaction.

Despite his earlier promise, Jack would *not* be graduating as a working guide dog. After this, Finn thought sadly, he'd be lucky to get a job at all.

THAT SAME EVENING he relayed the story in full to his dinner companion.

"It's a shame–he was a great dog, and had so much promise too."

"Really." Finn's date Karina was playing with the stem of her wineglass and he realised, seemed to be only half-listening. OK, so he probably banged on a little too much about his job, but what did you talk about when you barely knew the person sitting opposite you?

They'd bumped into one another a few times at parties and social gatherings held by Finn's best mate Chris, so tonight couldn't exactly be described as a blind date, but it might as well have been. Finn didn't know a whole lot about Karina other than she was single, nice-looking and evidently wasn't all that interested in the ins an outs of guide dog training.

"Anyway, how's your starter?" he asked, deciding to change the subject.

They were in a restaurant in the centre of Dublin called *Pepe* that Chris had recommended. Finn had asked his mate for a recommendation because for the life of him he didn't know where to go in town these days.

Most of his old mates still lived and worked in the city and the cosmopolitan lives they led were million miles away from the quieter, rural pace he preferred. As the only still-remaining unattached male of the group his friends seemed to think it was their duty to fix him up with various available women, and just didn't believe Finn when he tried to tell them that he was happy enough on his own, and since Danielle, had little interest in a serious relationship.

"It's just delicious," said Karina, in response to his question about the food. "The scallops are perfectly cooked, with just the right amount of seasoning, and I'm getting a faint hint of something in the sauce that I think might be cinnamon. Yours?"

Finn gulped and looked down at his fairly ordinary looking fishcakes. "They're um …grand," he said, but Karina was still looking at him, evidently waiting for him to elaborate as if he was some kind of expert. "They taste …very nice."

"Right. Well that's good. It'll be interesting to see what the chef does with my main. The last time I had pork in a restaurant like this, it looked and tasted like something you'd get in a pub." She rolled her eyes. "Soooo disappointing."

Finn was wondering why food from a pub was such a terrible thing when in fact pubs usually dished out tasty grub in nice big portions, not like the microscopic servings he saw them putting out here—plates of food so small they wouldn't fill a sparrow, and consisting primarily of scraps of barely-cooked meat smothered in blades of green grass. And why did she have to make a song and dance about what the chef 'did' with things? As far as he was concerned it was just food, not a bloody performance.

But whatever about Karina's choice for the main course, at least he'd played it safe and gone for a nice, juicy sirloin. He'd need one what with the size of these fishcakes. Each no bigger than a fifty cent piece, Finn had consumed them in quick time, and was looking forward to filling up on meat and veg.

"I just think Dublin restaurants have a really long way to go before they can compete with those in London, don't you?" Karina was saying, and Finn realised that this was the third time in the last half hour that she'd picked up her bag and started rummaging inside it. The strange thing was that she never seemed to take anything out or put something in.

"What's the matter?" he asked, indicating the bag. "Have you forgotten something? Do you need a tissue or anything?"

Karina smiled. "Sorry–I just can't help it. It's *Chloe*, and it's just sooo soft."

Bags called Chloe…what on earth?

As Finn watched Karina's self-satisfied expression, he suddenly wanted to bolt from this shallow, overhyped, pretentious excuse for a restaurant, and run a million miles for his equally shallow and pretentious excuse for a date.

Now it was all beginning to make sense, her question earlier about his jeans and 'who' they were. John Rocha? Paul Smith? Followed by her lofty pronouncement to the waiter that she only drank 'fine wine' and could a sommelier recommend something suitable. If that was the case what did everyone else drink–shite wine?

Finn sighed inwardly. He just wasn't able for this anymore and he sorely wished he could go home to the one female who didn't care anything about designer handbags or fancy food and was perfectly happy with a tin of Pedigree Chum.

Good old Lucy rarely troubled him, even when he abandoned her to go abroad on training conventions and had to leave her in the care of his dad. And speaking of which, Pat had a consultation with the specialist early the following morning, which was a good excuse as any for Finn to go home early.

Still, since the food in this place cost a small fortune and he was absolutely starving, it would be almost criminal *not* to stay on and enjoy it, wouldn't it?

But no sooner had the thought of the cost of the food entered his head, than the waiter arrived with Finn and Karina's main course.

And when he saw on his plate a piece of sirloin steak that was no bigger than a golf ball–and covered in grass– Finn knew for certain that this was turning into the date from hell.

CHAPTER 15

"WE'RE AUNTIES!" Caroline sang down the phone line.

"What? Claire had the baby?" Abby sat up and checked the time on her bedside alarm clock. It was six am but Caroline sounded as though she'd been awake for some time.

"She went early. Zach just called Mum and he's over the moon. It's a girl, and they're calling her Caitlyn."

"Caitlyn," Abby repeated softly. "Beautiful name. I can't wait to see her."

"Well you won't have to wait too long," her sister trilled. "Better get packing 'cos we're leaving for New York on the nineteenth."

"What?" Abby blinked.

"We're all going over to see the newest member of the Ryan family." When there was no immediate reply, her sister's tone changed. "What - so you don't want to see your one and only niece? And don't you *dare* say a word about this so-called fear of flying–I told you, it's all in your head. Oh, you'll LOVE New York," Caroline insisted. "Especially this time of year."

"But ... even if I did want to go, it's so close to Christmas–there's no *way* we'd get flights and–"

"Already taken care of," Caroline said blithely. "Consider it your Christmas present."

"What? But I couldn't ..."

"Of course you can. Claire will be over the *moon* to see us—especially since you've never been. And when's the last time the whole family got together?"

"It would be amazing to see her, but are you sure they'd be able for us all?"

"I've already okayed it with Zach and he thinks it's a brilliant idea, especially having Mum around to give Claire a hand." She sniffed. "He obviously doesn't think I'd be much help." At this, Abby raised a smile. "But imagine, all the family together for Christmas in New York? Well, apart from Dermot," she added quickly, who Abby knew already had plans to go away elsewhere with friends. "Abby, it'll be fantastic."

Her sister's enthusiasm was certainly infectious and Abby couldn't wait to see her baby niece. It would be wonderful to have the family all together again, especially for a celebration.

And goodness knows she'd had little to celebrate lately...

"I'll pay you back for the tickets—" she began.

"Don't be silly, I told you—it's your Christmas present. Anyway, I put them on Tom's Visa, so he's paying for them really."

Whether he likes it or not, Abby thought smiling. "Well, I owe you both one anyway."

"Honey, you owe me nothing. So, I wonder what Caitlyn's like?" her sister went on, chattering a mile a minute. "I do hope she hasn't inherited the Ryan temperament. Otherwise our poor sis will seriously have her work cut out for her."

TEN DAYS LATER, Abby stared out of the window of the car, trying to take it all in.

New York was incredible–like something from a dream, completely out of this world.

And as she, her mother, Caroline and Tom made their way from JFK in the town car Zach had arranged, she couldn't help thinking how everything looked like straight out of a movie set.

As they neared Manhattan and the world famous cityscape suddenly came into view, Caroline pointed out the yawning gap left where the twin towers used to be, and Abby couldn't help but recall her conversation with Hannah about her own memories of that sad day.

If *this* was anything to go by, Abby was unlikely to forget her first experience of New York in a hurry. It was magnificent, awe-inspiring and totally *un*forgettable.

But boy was it cold.

Despite the temperatures, Manhattan really did look like something out of a fairytale–its streets were ablaze with sparkling trees and twinkling lights, and as they made their way along in the car, Abby marvelled at how white lights from the trees glittered in the evening light, casting a magical glow onto the pavements below.

And as she craned her neck upwards for her first proper look at the Empire State building, and saw its lights change from green to red, she realised that the famous landmark–like the rest of the city–was all dressed up and ready for the holiday season.

She'd never seen anything like it.

Some minutes later, they reached her sister's home where a beaming Claire greeted their arrival, a sleeping baby in her arms. Her sister glowed with health and her eyes shone with pride as she presented baby Caitlyn to her family.

"She's so like you," Abby said, stroking the baby's soft skin, "and there's a bit of Dad in her too, I think."

"I thought so too," Claire was pleased. "What do you think Mum?"

"She's a little stunner, that's what she is," said the proud grandmother, her eyes glistening with delighted tears. "And yes, she has your father's stubborn ould chin."

The girls laughed.

"I just can't believe how quickly all of this has happened," Abby said when they were settled inside Claire's warm and cosy living room. "It seems no time at all since we found out you were pregnant and then all of sudden, she's here."

Claire reddened. "I didn't want to jinx anything…"

Sensing she'd embarrassed her sister, Abby changed the subject. "And this place is great–huge! Sorry this is my first time coming to see you guys, but you know yourself," she shrugged, referring to her fear of flying.

But to her relief and despite her nerves, the flight hadn't been that bad at all, which may have had something to do with the fact that (unlike her first time flying with Kieran) her companions didn't seem the slightest bit stressed or worried; in fact there had been a bit of celebratory feel, helped no end by Caroline's insistence on ordering a snipe of champagne for everyone once airborne.

"We'll need to start looking for something bigger soon, or think about a move out to the suburbs, won't we Zach?" Claire teased. Her husband, a born and bred Manhattanite didn't seem too enamoured of the idea.

"Don't mention the war," he muttered, and again everyone laughed.

"So how was 'it'?" Caroline asked later, when they were all settled and little Caitlyn was back sleeping in her cot. She squirmed. "Never again, right?"

But instead of agreeing enthusiastically, Claire simply smiled and shook her head. "Most unforgettable experience of my life."

Caroline rolled her eyes. "Well, no woman forgets *that*–unless they get whacked on the head or something," she added jokingly, but then her face went white. "Yikes, sorry Abby," she cringed.

Claire turned to her younger sister as if suddenly remembering. "How are you? You look so well, I'd almost forgotten ... oh hell... I mean..."

"It's OK." Abby couldn't help but chuckle at them both. "And I'm good ... I think."

Out of the corner of her eye, she saw her mother watching closely. Teresa had been treating her with kid gloves over the last few weeks, especially since the piano incident.

"I'm grand honestly," she insisted to Claire, feeling uncomfortable that this had dragged down the celebratory mood. "Anyway, enough about me; tell us more about how you're getting on with Caitlyn."

Her sister evidently knew better than to push the topic, and Abby was determined not to dampen the mood.

Instead, she sat back and listened to Claire discuss in long and loving detail the most unforgettable experience of her life.

CHAPTER 16

OVER THE NEXT FEW DAYS, Abby and her mother spent lots of
time with Claire and the baby, while Caroline spent lots of
time shopping, often leaving poor Tom alone at the hotel to
entertain himself.

On the third evening of their visit, Claire urged Abby and
Teresa to follow Caroline's example. "You're in New York and
it's Christmas! The two of you should go out and do some
shopping, or go see the sights."

"You must be joking," Teresa scoffed. "There's no way I'm
traipsing around in that kind of cold. Anyway, it could be some
time again until I see my only granddaughter and I want to
spend as much time with her as possible." She looked at Abby.
"You should though. Caroline is heading out to Woodbury
Common tomorrow."

The thought of travelling an hour or so upstate to visit a
designer outlet mall didn't appeal to Abby in the slightest. And
as tomorrow was Christmas Eve, she really wanted to do
something a little more interesting.

"Do," Claire insisted. "I'm sure Caroline would love some
company."

"I think I'd like to do a bit of exploring around the city instead," she told them. "Don't worry–I won't go far," she added quickly, seeing Teresa's alarmed expression.

"I just don't like the idea of you wandering around on your own. What if something happens…?"

"Mum, she'll be fine," Claire interjected firmly, and Abby gave her a grateful smile.

The two had since had a good chat, and Abby confessed to Claire that Teresa's anxiousness since the accident was actually beginning to stifle her, which she suspected, was partly the reason her sister was now insisting they get out and about.

But as she'd never been to New York before and might not get the opportunity again, a few hours by herself in the city that never sleeps sounded like absolute heaven.

"That's settled then," Claire continued. "We'll all do our own thing tomorrow and then meet up back here in the evening for a nice family dinner before heading onto St Pat's for midnight mass. How does that sound?"

"Absolutely perfect," Abby replied with a grin.

ON CHRISTMAS EVE MORNING, she woke up early, eager to get going.

It was a bright, crisp but again, startlingly cold day so she made sure to wrap up well. Having borrowed a beautiful and wonderfully warm cream-coloured duffle from Claire, and teaming it with her own red bobble hat and matching red scarf, she felt and looked suitably Christmassy as she let herself out of the apartment and headed south.

Although it was desperately cold, there really was a magical feel about the place at this time of year and the neighbourhood was festooned with Christmas finest. Wreaths hung on brownstone doorways and pine boughs wound luxuriously around wrought-iron fences and as Abby neared the shopping districts, she spotted Santas on almost every corner, heard Christmas music ringing out from all directions, while shoppers bustled in and out of nearby stores and markets.

This was what New York was really about, Abby smiled and despite the cold, was much preferable to being cooped up in a centrally-heated department store, aimlessly seeking out bargains that (in Caroline's case) would probably never even be worn.

So, this was pretty special, she thought, darting out of the way of a deliveryman carrying a consignment of what looked like freshly baked bagels into a nearby café. Abby's stomach rumbled, reminding her that she hadn't yet had breakfast, and as the café looked nice and warm …

A minute later she was sitting at a table trying to choose from the café's mouth-watering menu–raspberry or pumpkin waffles, cranberry and pear bread pudding, omelettes, bagels and a whole rainbow of different flavoured muffins.

She couldn't remember the last time she'd enjoyed herself this much. It struck her again how much she'd withdrawn from life in the aftermath of the break-up, and how much she'd closed herself off from everything. When was the last time she'd spent a morning in Dublin like this, sauntering along Grafton St without a care in the world?

Eventually tearing herself away from the warmth of the café, Abby then decided to head along Fifth Avenue, hoping to soak up the festive atmosphere, and take a look at some of the department stores' world famous window displays. She also paid a visit to the eponymous Tiffany & Co store, and stared in awe at the stunning jewellery in the window, wondering if she would ever be so lucky as to own such a piece.

The shops were magical as well as suitably festive and Christmassy, but all too soon the incessant crowds became a bit much, so Abby decided to head for quieter surrounds. She left the busy shopping area and continued walking along the avenue for a while before eventually reaching Central Park South.

Despite her hearty brunch earlier, she was once again quite peckish, so a sandwich and a coffee would be good. She'd grab something from a coffee cart, take her lunch into the park, and maybe do some people-watching.

Having picked up some food, Abby went inside and found an unoccupied bench near the lake further up. She sat back, sipped her coffee and allowed herself to simply relax and take it all in. She could see why New Yorkers loved Central Park, but at the same time, she hadn't anticipated the sheer size of the place, or the strangeness of having such a huge green area amidst all these soaring skyscrapers.

As Abby struggled to open her sandwich packaging through her heavy woollen gloves, she noticed a couple of nearby grey squirrels, who sensing the promise of food, were gathering cheekily round her feet.

"Go and get your own," she scolded playfully.

Then she coloured a little, realising that someone else had sat down on the bench. And here she was yabbering away to herself.

"Yeah Phil here," she heard the guy say into his mobile. "No, I'm still here, bloody flight got cancelled ... No, it's not great, but ..."

Sensing her distraction, the squirrel at her feet saw his chance and before Abby realised what was happening, he hopped up onto the bench and snatched her sandwich.

Abby's eyes widened. "Divil!" she cried, amazed.

"Cheeky," the guy chuckled, putting his phone into his pocket.

"I didn't even know they could *do* that."

He shrugged. "Same happened to me one time in Thailand, except this time it was monkeys doing the stealing."

"Really? What did they take?"

He chuckled. "My dignity for starters. It was a tourist hotspot, and went to get them some bananas. While I was in the store I picked up some snacks too." He smiled at the memory. "I came out and held out the banana to a baby monkey, but this guy had *no* interest in bananas. Before I knew it, he reached up and grabbed my entire haul ...nachos, chocolate, everything. Leaving me standing there with a bloody banana."

Abby laughed, unable to pinpoint his accent. He was nice, she thought. Cute, in that clean-shaven American way. He looked to be about the same age as she, possibly a bit older, and had dark but rather unkempt hair, a strong jaw-line and striking mahogany eyes.

"Was Thailand nice?"

"Amazing. Granted, it's been a while since I was there, and I keep promising myself I'll go back, but I just haven't got round to it."

Abby understood. There were lots of things she too wanted to do too, and since she got here she'd been thinking about them more and more.

"Vietnam is great too–really friendly people there," he continued. "Actually most of South East Asia's great."

"Wow, you really *have* travelled," she said, feeling unadventurous and provincial.

"Not lately, unfortunately," he added grimacing. "Duty calls. Family, work–you know the story." Then her companion sat forward and looked at his watch. "Speaking of duty... I'd better get going." He stood up and put his hands in his pockets. "Enjoy the rest of your day, and watch out for those squirrels," he added winking.

"I suppose I'd better go and get myself another sandwich," she groaned.

"You should try the cafe at the Boathouse," he said pointing to a building in sight of the lake. "I'm meeting a friend there now. It's warm, they do great coffee, and even better there are no squirrels."

"Sounds good, thanks for the tip."

"Enjoy your day," he added with a grin. "And Merry Christmas."

CHAPTER 17

ABBY REMAINED SITTING on the bench for a little while longer, heartened by the unexpected encounter. But since the squirrels had made off with her lunch, she really did need to think about finding something else. The thought of somewhere cosy and warm appealed enormously…

The café area the friendly guy mentioned was busy, and to her disappointment there were no tables free. But just as she was about to leave, out of the corner of her eye she thought she saw someone waving in her direction.

"Hello again," Phil from the bench smiled. "Feel free to sit here, there's plenty of room. My friend just cancelled."

Abby went to say no, but then decided against it. Feck it, what harm? He was nice, there were no other seats and it really *was* freezing out … "You're sure you don't mind?"

"Not at all. What can I get you?" He signalled to a waitress.

Again, Abby was taken aback at how friendly he was. "A coffee and tuna sandwich thanks."

They chatted easily for a few minutes while waiting for the food, Abby marvelling at the odd liberating effect New York was having on her that she'd ended up having chats and coffee with total strangers.

"So you said it's your first visit to Manhattan?" he enquired and she nodded, explaining about Claire and the new baby.

"You guys here long?"

"Just a few more days, more's the pity." She sighed wistfully. "I had no idea there was so much to see and do. I don't think you could do it all in one lifetime, let alone a single visit."

"I know what you mean. Every time I come to New York I find something new."

"Oh," Abby's head snapped up. "I assumed you lived here."

"You mean you don't recognise the accent?" he chuckled. "Well OK, maybe there is a bit of twinge from my time here when I was younger, but I'm Irish–same as yourself."

She was happily surprised to learn that Phil was from Dublin too, and here on business.

"I was due to fly home this morning but the flight got cancelled. Another going out later but figured there was no point in sitting around JFK all day."

Abby nodded, unwilling to admit that she'd learned as much from his earlier phone conversation.

"It's an incredible city," she said, shaking her head in wonder. "I don't want to go home, not when there are so many things I want to see and do–especially at this time of year. You know, all the Christmassy stuff like the Rockefeller Tree, Macy's window ... what?" she asked, seeing him grimace.

"While you're here you should try and take in some things off the beaten track - less touristy stuff." He looked at his watch. "Tell you what, why don't I take you on a whistle-stop tour of some of the good stuff... if you're up for it?"

Common sense should have told her there was no way she should even *think* about wandering around New York with a complete stranger, but for some reason, Abby's intuition was telling her to go right ahead.

There was just something about Phil that made her feel relaxed and comfortable—and as today was all about getting out and exploring, why the hell not?

"Sounds good. I'm due back around seven for a family dinner. But I don't want to put you out ..."

He rolled his eyes and took another sip of coffee. "Putting it mildly, today hasn't worked out so well for me so far. I'm looking to kill time, that is, if you don't mind the company."

"I'd be delighted," Abby grinned, meaning it.

FINISHING LUNCH, they left the park, Phil leading the way and keeping up an endless stream of chatter, pointing out various sites and interesting bits and pieces of Manhattan-related trivia as they did so.

"Did you know that it took seven *million* man hours to built that?" he said, pointing to the Empire State Building, which was easily visible above the other skyscrapers. "And fifty seven thousand tonnes of steel."

"Cool."

Fully determined to slot into his tour-guide role, he followed this up with an equally detailed analysis of the construction of the Chrysler Building, before eventually they ended up outside a large ornate building which at first Abby didn't recognise.

"What's this?" she asked.

"You don't know?"

Abby looked up at the clock surrounded by statues and sculptures and all too soon, the penny dropped. "Grand Central Station," she realised, again having seen this building a million times on TV, but still it was no substitute for the reality.

He smiled. "Grand Central *Terminal* to give it it's proper

name, but yeah you're right. There's something here I think you'll like."

Going inside, they passed through the building's main concourse, packed with people dashing to and fro and up and down the escalators at dizzying speed.

Enthralled, Abby gazed open-mouthed at the stunning marble grand staircase, huge chandeliers and immense arched windows. In the centre of the building stood the marble and brass information booth and its famous four-faced clock–another instantly recognisable New York icon.

Then following his lead, she moved out of the way of the frantic commuters and went to stand alongside him against a nearby wall.

"Let's just wait here for a minute," he said, glancing at his watch.

"OK." Abby was silent, wondering what on earth they were waiting for but only a few seconds later, she found out. Out of nowhere, there was a blast of classical music. Again, taking her companion's lead, she looked upwards and for the first time noticed the magnificent blue and gold mural of stars and constellations spread out all over the ceiling.

"Wow, look at that," she gasped. A laser light display had just begun; multicoloured lights and different shapes moving across the ceiling in tandem to the music.

A delighted thrill ran up her spine as she watched the lights dancing across the mural. They and lots of others–tourists probably–stood watching the impromptu show, while all around seasoned New Yorker commuters continued on oblivious.

"Fantastic," she enthused when the display finished and the music stopped.

"Thought you might enjoy it. They do it every year for Christmas, every half-hour to different pieces of music."

"Amazing."

"It is, but not what I brought you to see. Though while we're here, do you notice anything strange," he asked, looking upwards again. "Strange about that mural."

Abby's brow furrowed as she peered up at the blue and gold coloured ceiling. "No – what?"

"Well, you know it's the Zodiac yes?"

She hadn't actually, but she wasn't going to admit it. "What's so strange about that?"

"The fact that it's back to front, for one."

She looked again. "Back to front?"

"Yep. Most people reckon it was a mistake by the artist, but the real reason is that he was inspired by a medieval manuscript that showed the heavens as they would have been seen from *outside* the celestial sphere." He looked at Abby and grinned. "A present day Michelangelo, eh?"

Well, that was a mouthful.

"Cool," she said, unable to think of any other reply. Still she loved the fact that he seemed just as excited about these little pieces of trivia as she was.

"Notice anything else out of the ordinary?" he asked then, which made her suspect there was more to come. She screwed up her eyes for a better look.

"Other than the back-to-front Zodiac and the lasers, I don't think so."

"How about that little dark blue patch?" He pointed to an irregular-coloured section of the mural on the right hand side, and as soon as she spotted it Abby's eyes widened.

"What does that signify?" she asked, knowing that no doubt a ready explanation would be forthcoming.

"When they did the renovation work on it back in the early nineties, they left a tiny patch of the old colour as a reminder of how much work was actually done. It's something like eighty-thousand square feet in here so that must have been a hell of a lot of effort - and paint."

"I can imagine." Abby shook her head in awe. "I never would have noticed. Not that I'd have noticed the Zodiac thing either; I'm no expert."

"Neither am I –someone else showed it to me initially, but I have to say I love these little snippets of history. Really gives a place character."

After, he led Abby across the room and downstairs to the dining concourse. They moved past the various eateries until they reached a particular spot amongst a room filled with low ceramic arches.

"OK, you stand there for a second," he said, positioning Abby in a spot alongside one of the arches.

"O–K." She smiled, unsure where this was going.

He then pointed to a position in the opposite corner. "I'll stand over there and when I give you the signal, I want you to whisper something into the corner."

"Whisper?" She chuckled. "What do you want me to say?"

"I don't know. Anything you want. Just don't make it anything *too* private," he added, with a playful smile, leaving her wondering.

With that he took up a position in the opposite corner and a few seconds later, gave her the signal.

Unsure what she was supposed to say, Abby took a deep breath and whispered the very first thing that came into her mind. *"Hot chocolate."*

Across the way, she saw him smile, lean forward and whisper something into his own corner.

And when she heard him reply *'Great idea– let's go get some,'* in a voice that was as clear and loud as if he was standing right next to her, she drew back in delighted surprise.

"How on earth...?" Her eyes grew wide, and her smile broadened when he returned to her side.

"Cool, isn't it?" He sounded mightily pleased with himself.

"It's incredible," she said laughing. "How do you *know* these things?"

He shrugged nonchalantly, but Abby could tell that he was secretly chuffed by her delighted reaction. "I just do. Anyway, about that hot chocolate," he added, giving her a mischievous wink. "You read my mind."

CHAPTER 18

"So what do you reckon?" Phil asked as he and Abby sipped their respective hot chocolates and stared up at the biggest, brightest and most famous Christmas tree of them all.

Ice-skaters swirled around the rink beneath, while shoppers and sightseers stopped to stare and admire. Carol singers serenaded alongside its branches, their voices climbing almost as high as the shining star on top, and children and adults alike were held rapt by the thousands of fairy lights that blanketed its limbs, glistening like fresh snow in moonlight.

"It's … incredible," she gasped, trying to take in the sheer size of the Rockefeller Tree. While she'd known it would be something special, she hadn't expected a simple tree to provoke such an emotional reaction.

Not that there was anything simple about an eight-foot-high spruce lit up by tens of thousands of coloured lights and situated above a dramatic gilded statute overlooking the crowded ice-rink.

On their way into the plaza, they'd passed a gorgeous display of wire-sculpted trumpet-blowing angels, magically illuminating the entire area, and the entranced faces of the children who stood watching them.

"What's that statue?" she asked. No doubt he would know.

"Prometheus," he said easily, before giving her a sideways look. "I studied a little Greek mythology in college, just in case you're beginning to think I'm some kind of anorak."

Earlier they'd stopped off briefly to visit Saks Christmas window display on Fifth Avenue, which had a completely different theme to the one Abby had seen earlier at Bergdorf Goodman, but with its winter wonderland exhibit, was just as impressive.

Now Phil looked at his watch. "You said you needed to be back at your sister's place by seven?"

"Yes." To her surprise, it was now five-thirty.

With all the walking around, the day had simply flown by but she was enjoying herself so much she now almost regretted having to rejoin the family.

"I'll have to head back to JFK myself soon," Phil said, "so let's just do one more thing before we go."

Abby nodded, happy to let him lead the way once again.

Some twenty minutes and a seventy-storey elevator ride, she was glad she did.

The vista from the top of Rockefeller Centre was astonishing. Seventy floors up and unobstructed for three hundred and sixty degrees the breathtaking New York landscape stretched for miles in every direction.

A panoramic view of Central Park and the northern half of Manhattan as well as the city's other famous landmarks were visible, including the Chrysler Building, Times Square, the Brooklyn Bridge, and the Statue of Liberty.

It was the most spectacular and magical view Abby had ever seen, and standing on the observation deck so high above the bustling city, she felt an incredibly wonderful sense of peace.

The air seemed to tingle with anticipation, and she felt a

sense of wonder she hadn't experienced since a young child waiting for Santa. There was something about this place that did that to you, something about Manhattan that took you back to those enchanting days of a childhood Christmas.

Tears came to her eyes as they stood silently taking in the view, and Abby thought to herself that whatever might be going on in her brain at the moment, and whatever happened in the future, she would surely never, ever forget this.

"Pretty cool, isn't it?"

Abby nodded, almost sorry that the spell had been broken. "It's amazing," she whispered, turning to look at him. "Thank you for bringing me here."

"Are you OK?" he asked, concern in his eyes, which in this light appeared almost black.

"I'm fine," she said, before adding quickly. "Well, at least I think I am." Then just as quickly, she shook her head and smiled. "Let's just say that things have been a bit ... weird for me lately and I really needed this."

He seemed to know not to push the topic. "I'm glad you enjoyed yourself," he said, before turning out again towards the vista of the city. "It's pretty special, New York. Every time I go away with another great memory."

Abby smiled wistfully at his choice of words.

"But that's what life's all about, isn't it?" he went on. "Gathering great memories."

He was right, she realised suddenly; the expression instantly capturing her imagination. But gathering memories–at least not any *great* ones–was something Abby hadn't done in a very long time.

She thought again to the way her life had been just before the accident, and how she'd had little to show for it other than heartbreak and misery.

Where was all the fun and excitement– where were *her* great memories?

But worse, was it too late to get out there and start making them? And even if she did seek out more experiences - like this - would she be wasting her time since she might not be able to hold onto them anyway?

But yet how could *anyone* forget something like this?

Abby drank in the view from the observation deck as if she might never see it again, the pulsating, glittering city beneath a Christmas Eve sky, unable to imagine how something so wonderful could be lost.

No, she thought, the realisation hitting her like a bolt from the blue; she was going to beat this memory thing, she *had* to beat it.

Because as her new friend had pointed out earlier, what was life without moments like this?

AFTERWARDS, they reluctantly returned to ground level, Abby sorry that their enjoyable jaunt around the city had to come to an end.

"I think I'll walk back," she said, when he moved to hail a cab.

"You will not," he scolded. "It's not safe to be wandering dark streets on your own, Christmas Eve or not. But if you insist," he said capitulating somewhat, "then at least let me walk you."

"But you need to get going," she protested, but he quickly waved her objections away.

"Honestly, there's loads of time. Any excuse to stay away from the madhouse that is JFK."

He was funny, and as she walked alongside him, Abby again couldn't help notice how relaxed and at ease she felt in his company.

Finally, they stopped outside Claire's building.

It was weird, but she'd enjoyed herself so much today she

was almost reluctant to say goodbye. "Thanks for a really memorable day."

"I enjoyed it too," he said, smiling, " and it was a pleasure showing you around."

Their gazes met, and as she gazed back into those fathomless dark eyes, she realised she was having difficulty catching her breath.

"So would you like to come in for a cuppa or …?" She knew he wouldn't have the time, but she couldn't think of anything else to say. Let alone the fact that her family would go apoplectic at the notion of her bringing home some stranger she'd met in Central Park.

As expected he shook his head. "Thanks but I'd really better get going," he said, his eyes not leaving her face. "Enjoy the rest of the night–especially St Patrick's. I've been to Midnight Mass there a couple of times and it really is something special. Oh, and while you're tucking into your dinner, spare a thought for me cooped-up in some tin can over the Atlantic."

Abby grinned, figuring she'd be sparing more than just a thought for him after this. "So Phil…" she began, again oddly reluctant to see him go, "have a lovely Christmas and thanks again for showing me around."

"It was a pleasure. Merry Christmas.."

Then quite unexpectedly, he reached forward and gave her the softest, gentlest peck on the forehead. The tenderness of the gesture stuck her, and when he stepped back, she looked again into those amazing eyes.

"Merry Christmas to you too."

"Oh, and by the way," he called back with a smile in his voice, before retreating into the darkness, "my name is Finn."

CHAPTER 19

"For goodness sake, where have you been?" Teresa's worried tones assaulted Abby almost as soon as she was inside Claire's apartment.

She took off her coat and scarf, her cheeks flushed and forehead still tingling with the imprint of his kiss, *Finn's* kiss. Abby couldn't believe she'd been calling him the wrong name all day. He must have thought she was an idiot.

"Out and about," she replied mildly, although inside she was walking on air.

She went to say hello to the baby before stepping past her mother and through to Claire's front room, which, like the rest of New York, was looking beautifully sparkly and festive.

The dining table was all set up and decked out in a crisp white cotton tablecloth upon which sat a gorgeous centrepiece of fresh holly and berries amid elegant gold candelabra. A selection of black and gold-coloured La Maison du Chocolat crackers lay elegantly alongside each table setting.

"Wow, this looks incredible," Abby said to her sister, who was bustling in and out of the kitchen getting things ready. "Can I help with anything?"

"No, it's all pretty much done now," Claire replied pleasantly, pausing for a second to mop her brow. "Did you enjoy your day? It certainly looks like it," she added grinning.

"Does it? How?"

"Well your eyes are sparkling and your cheeks are really flushed, although I suppose that could be the cold. Either way, you must have–you were out long enough. So what did you get up to?" Claire repeated, polishing Louise Kennedy Tipperary Crystal champagne flutes and putting them on the table. "Actually, no don't tell me, everything's pretty much ready to go here now, so why don't we wait until dinner to catch up on everything." She glanced at her watch. "I hope Caroline and Tom make it back from Woodbury on time–I did tell everyone seven-thirty, didn't I?"

Almost as if on cue, there came a high-pitched voice from the hallway.

"Hi everyone, Santa's arrived!"

Up to her armpits with shopping bags of every designer brand imaginable, Caroline bustled into the living room–a beleaguered looking Tom in tow. "Guys we've had the most *amazing* day, and Claire, you'll just *die* when I show you the baby bling I picked up for Caitlyn. *Fabulous* gold Dior bootees that will look so cute on, and a gorgeous Marc Jacobs babygro …"

Abby and Clare exchanged a glance. *Baby bling?*

Abby laughed, thinking that while she'd thought she'd had an interesting day, the evening seemed destined to turn out just as lively.

NEXT MORNING, the family were awakened bright and early by little Caitlyn's ear-splitting cries, and when Abby woke up it took her a few seconds to figure out where she was.

They'd had a lively and highly enjoyable family dinner the

night before, everyone was in great form and the jokes were flying.

Abby hadn't felt so comfortable and easy around her family in ages, and wondered why up to now she'd always shied away from family gatherings. Was it partly because Kieran usually hated those kind of things, so by default Abby had grown to dislike them too?

Midnight mass at the magnificent St Patrick's Cathedral had been special and very moving, and as they all sat together in the pew, Abby felt a closeness and appreciation for her mother and sisters that she hadn't experienced in a long time.

After an even livelier Christmas breakfast, during which Zach served Bucks Fizz and Caroline insisted to Claire that the baby should have some too 'But it's her first Christmas!' they all got together around the beautifully decorated Christmas tree to exchange gifts.

Caroline arrived laden down with gifts for the family, and as her flight tickets were supposed to have been her sister's Christmas present to her, Abby was taken aback when now she handed her a tiny robin's egg-blue box wrapped in white satin ribbon.

"What's this?" she asked looking up in surprise.

"What do you think it is?" Caroline replied archly. "Your Christmas present, of course."

Abby tentatively opened the package, thinking that her sister had already forgotten about paying for the flights and ... Then her eyes widened.

"Oh my..." she cried, opening the box to reveal a stunning silver link bracelet. Attached to this was a single heart-shaped charm that had some kind of inscription on it.

And when upon close inspection Abby read the words on the charm, her hand flew to her mouth: 'Return to Tiffany & Co.'

"Oh wow ..." she gasped, hardly able to speak.

Only yesterday she had stopped to stare in the windows of

the world famous jewellery store, wondering if she'd ever be lucky enough to own something from it.

"This is incredible – truly incredible," she said, tears forming in her eyes as she reached across to hug her way too-generous sister.

"You're so welcome," Caroline said. "I thought it might be a nice memento for your first trip here. After enjoying yourself so much yesterday, I doubt it'll be the last."

The previous evening over dinner, Abby had told the family bits and pieces about her adventures, although in the end she decided not to tell them about meeting Finn.

On the one hand, she was afraid that her mother would lecture her about the stupidity of going off with strangers (*'especially in your condition'*) but in addition there had been something so surreal and magical about yesterday that there was a side of her that wanted to keep the majority of it private– especially that kiss.

"I feel so awful now, I didn't know what to get you." Abby was horrified, and was now kicking herself for being so unimaginative. As usual, she'd bought each member of her family the obligatory, boring-as-hell gift voucher.

"It's OK," Caroline waved her Brown Thomas gift voucher in the air delightedly. "We all know how much you hate shopping, and given how much I *love* it ... this is perfect."

Soon, it was Teresa's turn to gasp as she too opened Caroline's gift; this one placed in a Christmas card.

"My goodness Caroline, Tom," she said, turning to her bashful-looking son-in-law, who typically, said nothing, "this is miles too much."

"Oh, don't be silly, you deserve it Mum. But more importantly, what do you think? Do you like it?"

"It's ..." It seemed that Caroline had once again rendered a member of the family speechless.

"What is it Mum?" Claire urged. "What's in the card?"

"Tickets," Teresa said. "Tickets to Verona to see a live performance of *Aida*."

"Wow, Tiffany bracelets, Italian operas and Baby Dior bootees, you really do have this gift-giving business off to a tee, don't you?" Claire was laughing. "Fabulous stuff Car, although it'll make our presents seem very ordinary by comparison."

"Don't be silly," Abby was quick to reassure her older sister, and slightly relieved to discover that Claire's gift was a small white envelope similar to the one she'd given her. Clearly her big sister was a gift voucher aficionado too.

Claire was still talking. "Now it's nowhere near as fancy as a Tiffany bracelet, but Zach and I figured it might be something you'd enjoy," she reiterated as Abby tore open the envelope to find what looked to be a pair of tickets – tickets for a concert to be held back home in Dublin the following year.

Caroline looked over Abby's shoulder. "Michael Buble – fantastic! Don't know why I didn't think of that," she said smiling as Abby turned the tickets over in her hand, examining them further.

"Oh good one," Teresa said happily.

"Is it OK?" Claire asked, when Abby still hadn't reacted. "I know it's probably a bit boring and obvious, but that concert sold out in minutes and Zach stayed up all right on the web to get them," she added, turning to her husband who smiled proudly.

For a few moments Abby couldn't speak.

"They're wonderful ... thank you," she replied, trying to inject the right amount of enthusiasm into her tone, but as Claire's face fell almost immediately, it obviously wasn't enough.

"You are still a fan?" she asked, frowning. "I mean, I just assumed that –"

"No of course, of *course*," Abby interjected, reaching across and hugging her older sister, all the while trying her utmost to figure out who this Michael Buble was, and why her entire family seemed to think she adored him.

AFTER, the family gathered round the Christmas tree for photos.

"Sorry sweetheart" Zach said fondly, when his newborn began to tire of her dad's continuous demands for the perfect shot, "but someday you'll thank me for this when you look back through your Memory Capsule."

"Memory Capsule ...what's that?" Abby asked, intrigued.

"One of those sentimental American inventions," Claire said, rolling her eyes.

"Hey, don't diss sentimentality," Zach scolded his wife jokingly. It's a digital archive I've set up for Caitlyn. Come into the study and I'll show you. I'm uploading these pics now."

Abby followed him through to his study where he tapped a few keys on his PC and brought up a program.

"See–this section records how her growth is progressing from week to week," Zach pointed to the screen. "Here we've got videos and photographs like the ones from today, family celebrations et cetera. It's basically a digital archive, from her first days on the planet ... the little things nobody remembers, you know?" Then he reddened. "Jeez, I'm sorry Abby, I hope you don't ... I just didn't think."

But rather than being offended or upset by Zach's comments, his idea had actually intrigued her.

An archive...

One of her biggest worries about losing her long-term memory was that she might lose stuff from her past, important things like her family, their names, what they looked like, even what they meant to her.

Something like this would be the answer to her prayers. She could set up an archive of her own and collect photographs, record diary entries, things to help her remember the things she loved in case those memories were lost to her for good.

A shiver ran up her spine. Why hadn't she thought of something like this before?

But strangely, this trip had made her view a lot of things differently. When she got home she'd go along with Hannah's suggestion of making regular diary entries and start taking more photographs, mementos of experiences she wanted to hold onto.

Essentially, Abby was going to take Finn's inadvertent advice and from now on, start laying down memories.

"Do you think you could set up something like this for me?" she asked Zach, her mind racing as the seed of an idea began to implant itself more firmly into her brain. "Somewhere for me to store information and photos and important stuff before ..." She paused briefly, struck by her own choice of words, "before I forget."

CHAPTER 20

IN THE DAYS since their return from New York, the idea began
to develop even further, and Abby got to thinking more about
what Hannah had said about emotion and memory being so
closely related.

If there was a real risk of her 'dropping' trivial things such
as learning to play the piano, or putting her hairbrush in the
fridge (like she'd done the other day), then there was a very *real*
chance she could end up dropping more as time went by.

Unless …

The more Abby thought about it, the more it made sense.
The incredible, amazing, *unforgettable* time she'd had in New
York had simply brought it all home.

If emotion and memory were so strongly linked then
maybe, just maybe, she could beat this thing?

If she spent the next few months getting out there, living
her best life and literally *bombarding* her memory with really
positive and exciting experiences, then didn't it stand to reason
that they too should be … unforgettable?

And, she reasoned her mind racing, if a negative experience–like her heartbreak following the break-up–could be so strongly imprinted on the brain because of negative emotion, then why not the other way round?

She decided to broach the subject at her mum's house. It was New Year's Day and the family were meeting up for another celebratory dinner, this time to include Dermot and make up for his absence in New York.

"That trip really was the best fun," Abby told them, her heart thumping with enthusiasm, as she prepared to reveal her plans, "so much so that it's given me an idea."

She explained about baby Caitlyn's digital memory file and how it might be a good idea for her to do something similar.

"Fantastic idea," Caroline enthused.

But then, when Abby recounted her subsequent train of thought, and her belief that she might even be able beat her prognosis, there was a rather … tense silence.

OK, so she'd expected the family to have some reservations, or warn her that she shouldn't get her hopes up, but what she didn't expect was outright negativity.

"It's just I enjoyed New York so much …" she babbled, trying to explain, "and I know it's something I'll remember for a very long time." Out of the corner of her eye, she thought she saw her mother and Caroline exchange a glance. "So I figured that if I actively sought out really memorable things –"

"Like what?" Teresa asked, but Abby knew by her tone that her mother didn't share her optimism.

"Well, that's the thing, I'm not entirely sure yet. I was kind of hoping you guys might be able to offer some suggestions. I really want to get out there and find other …unforgettable experiences, but I suppose I'm not sure where to start."

While the notion of bombarding her brain with adventures equal to New York seemed fine in theory, discussing it out loud was a different kettle of fish altogether.

"Unforgettable experiences …" Dermot mused, scraping his plate. "Like what?"

"I don't know," she shrugged. Clearly they all thought she was crazy.

Caroline seemed to be thinking it over. "Tell you what – you should make a list," she declared. "That's what I do whenever I start a project."

The entire family stared at her, each no doubt trying to remember when Caroline had last completed a full sentence, let alone a project.

"When I'm organising my wardrobe, for one," she supplied exasperated. "I make a list of the clothes I have, and then the things I need. Then I tick each item off one by one until I have them all, don't I Tom?" She turned to her husband, who true to form, nodded in silent agreement.

"A list?" Abby was turning the idea over in her head. It *was* a good idea and it also meant that she'd have a definite plan of action, something to work towards instead of just randomly trying things out.

And as the doctors seemed determined to keep her away from work, it would mercifully give her something to fill her days with.

In Caroline's words, this could be her project.

"It's New Year's Eve –the perfect time for lists and resolutions," Caroline insisted, getting carried away by the idea too. "Oh, it'll be so much fun–let's do it now." She whipped out her handbag and with typical enthusiasm, took out a tiny notepad and pen. "OK," she murmured, scribbling down something on the pad. "What's the first thing on the list?"

Dermot nudged his sister's elbow. "Erm, for one thing it's Abby's list, so don't you think *she* should be one making it?" he pointed out.

"Oh sure. Here you go."

She passed the notepad across and when Abby saw the

heading *My Best Life List* she faltered a little. The idea sounded great in theory, but when faced with a blank page and such a daunting task, she wasn't really sure where to start.

The others were all looking at her expectantly.

"Well, what's the first thing?" Caroline demanded. "Surely there's one huge thing you've always wanted to do? We all have one, don't we? I certainly know what mine is …what?" she asked, when the others looked at her blankly. "You mean you don't know?"

"We're all waiting with bated breath," Dermot drawled.

"Ugh! To be seated front row at Paris Fashion Week of course," she announced. "And papped there too– even better." When Dermot sniggered, she gave him dig in the ribs. "Laugh all you like, but we were talking about what would be unforgettable for me. We all know what *you'd* like to do."

"Do you now?"

"It would be flying one of those jet-fighter things, or something macho like that, wouldn't it?"

And by his reluctantly impressed face, Abby knew that her sister was spot on.

Caroline beamed. "And Mum, for a long time yours was going to the opera wasn't it? A proper live Italian opera."

With a slight start, Abby realised that Caroline did indeed seem to know the family well –probably even better than they knew themselves. In fact, thinking of it now, this had always been reflected in the gifts she gave them.

While all Teresa's children had known that their mum enjoyed listening to opera music around the house, Abby would never in a million years have thought of sending her to a real, live, Italian opera. Yet, Caroline had known instinctively that her mother would love this, in the same way that she'd known Abby would appreciate that gorgeous Tiffany bracelet as a memento of the lovely time they'd had in New York.

"What about me?" she asked her then. "Can you think of my must-do thing? Off the top of your head I mean."

Caroline bit her lip. "To be honest, no," she muttered, leaving Abby faintly disappointed. Was she that much of an oddball? "Anyway, we're trying to make a *list* of stuff for you– not just one ..." Then she stopped short and her eyes widened. "That's it!" she shrieked, excitedly waving both hands in the air.

"What's it?"

"Oh, it'll be absolutely *perfect*. Tell you what, Abs," Caroline said, turning to her, "why don't you spend the next few days coming up with stuff on your own for the list. But in addition, let *us* suggest some too."

"I don't follow..."

"I'm thinking that each one of *us* could suggest something memorable for you to do, or even better, we could do it *with* you," her sister proclaimed, clearly on a roll.

Abby looked at the others who seemed equally clueless. "I still don't get it."

Caroline sighed. "Hey, you're my sister and I love you lots, but even you have to admit that for the last few years, you've been an awful bore."

"Caroline!" Teresa scolded.

"No, it's OK." Deep down Abby knew all too well what her sister was talking about. "I *have* been a pain recently, which is partly the reason I want to do this."

"So let me get this straight," Dermot put in. "You want each of us to come up with something memorable for Abby, something *we* think she'll enjoy?"

Caroline nodded vigorously. "And preferably something she hasn't done before either," she added, and when Abby opened her mouth to say something, she cut her off. "Some of the best experiences are the most unexpected ones, so if we're going to do this, you *have* to trust us. Just remember how I so easily cured your so-called fear of flying," she added with a flourish, and Abby grudgingly had to admit she was right. "So," her sister asked looking around imperiously. "Is everyone game?"

"Should be fun actually," Dermot said with a wicked grin.

Caroline rubbed her hands together, a gleeful smile on her face. "Abby, you want suggestions to help you live your best life? Trust me - now you'll get 'em."

CHAPTER 21

MY BEST LIFE LIST (PROVISIONAL)

Take at least one happy picture picture every day
Visit the Grand Canyon
See penguins in their own environment (South
    Pole?)
Have an adventure
Drive a convertible.
Share a kiss with a stranger
Watch your all-time favourite movies in one
    sitting
Face your fears
Be more spontaneous

HANNAH READ THROUGH THE LIST, an enigmatic smile on her
face.

"What?" Abby asked, self-consciously. Making a bucket list
of sorts had been a lot harder than anticipated, and while it was
easier to come up with *places* she'd always wanted to visit, like
the Grand Canyon it was much harder to think of smaller, day-
to-day life-affirming stuff.

"I like the idea," the psychologist said, "and I particularly like the notion of you going along with others' suggestions."

Abby still wasn't sure about that one, which went under the heading 'Be More Spontaneous', but she couldn't back out now.

In the meantime, Erin had also come on board, and had reacted with gusto when Abby had outlined the idea to her in the meantime.

"I know *exactly* what we'll do," her best friend declared without hesitation, causing to Abby to yet again wonder what on earth she was letting herself in for.

And while buoyed by the reaction the idea had elicited from friends and family, she was decidedly nervous about Hannah's opinion on the matter.

"Do you think it could work?" she urged, sinking back further into the comfy purple armchair in Hannah's office.

The other woman paused, and to her immense disappointment, Abby suspected that she was trying to choose her next words carefully.

"Well ... I certainly don't think it can hurt. Sensory stimulation of the positive kind is always good for brain function. As to how or if it will impact on memory ... it's difficult to say."

Feeling more that a little deflated, again Abby hated the way Hannah could never give her a straight answer. But yet, she couldn't be too annoyed; a trained neuroscientist, it was par for the course.

"Happy pictures ... nice idea, and I'm glad you've finally started keeping diaries too."

Abby'd been pretty haphazard about that up to now, but as her days were about to get a *lot* more interesting, she'd decided she should keep an account of them.

"So when is all of this happening?" Hannah asked. "The travel-related elements will take some planning for starters."

Abby hadn't thought too much about the mechanics part,

she'd merely identified what she wanted to do or see and go from there. Though with the insurance money due, at least she'd have the means to pay for another trip to the States, although she wasn't sure how she'd get to the South Pole.

Hannah looked through the list again. "Face your Fears?" she read with an inquisitive eyebrow.

Abby nodded vigorously. "I've already started by getting over my fear of flying." But had this been a genuine fear, she wondered now, or was it - like Caroline had pointed out -more a manifestation of *Kieran's* anxiety?

"I see. And the other fears?"

She hesitated a little. "I kind of have this thing about dogs," Abby admitted. "I've always been terrified of them. It's hard to explain really, we never had one at home, so I don't know where it came from …"

"Dogs are wonderful –I have two King Charles spaniels myself and I wouldn't be without them."

Abby was struck by the fact that in the all the time she'd been seeing Hannah, this was the first time the doctor had offered a piece of information about herself or her life. But then she worried if this was actually Hannah's roundabout way of introducing Abby to her dogs.

Yikes. She wanted to get through the fun stuff on the list first, only then would she think about the other (scarier) elements.

"Any idea what the others have planned for you?"

"Just Mum so far." Teresa had asked Abby to accompany her on her upcoming trip to Verona at the end of April. She suspected it was the only thing her mum could think of and was happy enough to go along with it.

Disappointingly though, Abby suspected her mother thought the entire exercise was a complete waste of time. Since that incident with the piano, in Teresa's eyes Abby's memory was as good as doomed. "I'm pretty sure Dermot's will be something laddish, and as for Caroline, God only knows … "

Not for the first time, Abby wondered what on earth she was letting herself in for.

CHAPTER 22

First off, 'movie weekend' with Erin had been tremendous fun, and they laughed, cried and cheered their way through the movies she'd chosen, Abby couldn't recall the last time she and her friend had such a good time together.

While Erin didn't quite share her admiration of Russell Crowe in a skirt and sandals, or Ben Stiller's brand of humour, she was still willing to sit through each and every one of Abby's choices - especially, *Thelma & Louise* which she'd never seen.

"Aw, we've *got* to do that," her friend declared when the credits began to roll.

Abby nearly spat out her popcorn. "I know I said I wanted to be more spontaneous but there's no *way* I'm driving a car off –"

"I don't mean *that*," Erin drawled, rolling her eyes. "I mean a road trip–just the two of us. Just taking off and seeing where the road takes us."

A road trip? It *would* be fun.

"Hey and since driving a convertible and the Grand Canyon are two of the things on your list, why not do them both at the same time? We could fly to LA, pick up a rental and drive to the

165

canyon from there. And even better," Erin said excitedly, a plan now well and truly forming in her mind, "we could stop off in Vegas on the way."

A slow smile spread across Abby's face. Sin City—one of the biggest, brashest, and second to New York arguably the most exciting city in the world. Anyone with a snatch of imagination would probably have put this *first* on the list. Her initial choices now felt very dull and pedestrian compared to what Erin was suggesting.

"I love it," she enthused.

Having decided to add the road trip to Abby's list, she and Erin continued munching through popcorn, Pringles, and Ben & Jerry's.

But by the end of their movie binge, they'd gone some way towards working off the calories by joining in the final scene of *Footloose*. Boogeying deliriously round her front room to Kenny Loggins, Abby felt a sense of joyous abandon, something she hadn't in years.

Kieran would never have danced round the sofa like this; in fact, Kieran wouldn't have danced *anywhere* …

Lately, Abby found she was beginning to distance herself emotionally from him, and with distance came a greater sense of clarity. Their breakup *hadn't* been the end of the world, and slowly but surely she was beginning to understand that.

And now that she'd begun to recognise that there was lots of living to do, Abby was determined to throw herself into it whole-heartedly.

WHICH WAS WHY, the weekend after, she was open and willing go along with whatever her best friend had in mind next.

"OK," Erin announced, "you're probably not going to like this but—"

Abby harrumphed. "What do you mean I'm not going to

like this? The whole point of this is to pick something I *will* like, something I won't forget in a hurry isn't it?"

Her friend smiled cryptically. "Sometimes the most memorable experiences stem from stepping out of your comfort zone and taking chances, don't you think?"

Abby squirmed, not liking the sound of this at all.

And now, as they entered a small, charming restaurant, Abby got a sense of what was coming. The décor was all warm oranges and terracottas, and apart from the small candles dotted around wooden tables, the place was barely-lit which added to the cosy atmosphere. The girls were led to a small table for two and the waitress was friendly as she asked for their drinks order.

"What kind of restaurant is this?" Abby asked, skimming the menu and finding hardly anything on it that she recognised.

"It's where you're finally going to rid yourself of that stupid food phobia of yours."

"Erin I–"

"How can you say you don't like stuff if you've never even tried it?" she argued. "So here's the thing–I brought you here tonight because it's a great place to ease you into something new. Don't worry, I'm not going to force you," she added quickly. "What's going to happen is that we're going to order eight different dishes from this menu–four each, but you must promise me that you will at least taste–even the teeniest, tiniest piece of every single one."

"Eight? But that's an awful waste," Abby was struck by how much like Kieran she sounded.

"It's tapas; they only serve tiny portions. Remember that thing on your list about facing your fears?" Erin reminded her. "This is as good a way as any to start."

Abby closed her eyes and took a deep breath. "OK," she said, deciding to throw caution to the wind. "Just make sure there's nothing with eyes, OK? I really couldn't eat anything with eyes."

As per Erin's instructions they ordered four options each, Abby failing miserably to pronounce some of the names of her choices. But when the waitress returned with the first of their tapas, she gulped and her gaze became fixated on a small plate of something that looked like... well there was no denying that it looked just the same as baby puke.

She took a deep breath and tried to stop her stomach from churning. This couldn't possibly be a self-induced neurosis like Erin suggested, could it?

Abby suddenly picked up her fork and popped some of the puke-like stuff in her mouth. She let it sit on her tongue for a few moments, almost afraid to let herself taste it until, finally, she let her jaws move. And when she did she had an overwhelming urge to ... *die*.

"Ugh," she spluttered, having swooped on her drink and swallowed it down in the hope of quenching the fire on her tongue. "What the hell was *that*?"

"Um, the plan was for you to *ease* yourself into it, remember?" Her friend was still laughing as she explained she'd chosen to start with the spiciest thing on the menu.

"Well, you know what they say," Abby grinned, heady with recklessness, as she picked up another forkful. "What doesn't kill you makes you stronger."

CHAPTER 23

NEXT UP WAS Caroline's turn and yet again, it seemed forcing Abby to endure something she didn't enjoy was supposed to be memorable. True to form, her sister had decided on … retail therapy.

"Be ready 'cos we're starting early," Caroline ordered and true to her word, pulled up outside Abby's first thing.

"There was no need to collect me," Abby muttered, as she sank into the Merc convertible passenger seat.

"Obviously we're not going shopping *here*," her elegantly coiffed sister replied with a conspiratorial wink. As usual, she looked effortlessly stylish in black T-shirt and cropped cream jacket over skinny jeans. The city-chic look was completed with a pair of over-sized sunglasses and obligatory funky designer handbag. As usual, Abby felt (and looked) about ten years older in her ancient comfy jeans and trusty black V-neck.

"What?" Abby asked, puzzled. Caroline wasn't the type to shop in the larger shopping centres on the outskirts of the city, where designer labels were generally few and far between, so she'd naturally assumed their shopping spree would be concentrated on her sister's second home, Grafton Street.

But maybe out of respect for Abby's limited budget (and even more limited taste), her sister had deigned to visit the more affordable high street this time.

"Go big or go home," Caroline trilled, lowering her Prada sunglasses. "So little sis," she announced with a dramatic flourish, "London, here we come."

THEY REACHED the city round midday, and having checked into the luxurious hotel Caroline had booked for an overnight stay, they hopped in a taxi and hit the shops, Abby's head still whirling.

"So first things first," her sister said, leading the way inside Selfridges, a determined look on her face. Abby dutifully followed as Caroline negotiated a multitude of shoppers, weaving her way through the crowds with practised ease.

"A cocktail bar?" Abby asked bewildered, as Caroline climbed the spiral staircase towards a place called the Moet Bar.

Her sister grinned wickedly. "Yep. Today will be a long day, so we might as well kick it off in style." She picked up a menu. "So what do you want? A Julien MacDonald, or maybe an Alice Temperley ... or if you don't fancy a cocktail, we could just go for plain old pink bubbles?"

"Plain old ..." Abby had to laugh. Apart from that time on the flight to New York 'to calm her nerves' she couldn't remember the last time she'd had a regular glass of bubbly, let alone a *pink* one.

"Pink it is then," she said, giddily pleased at the flamboyancy of it all.

As the two clinked glasses and took a seat at the stylish bar, Abby felt a delicious thrill as the liquid hit her tongue.

"Just look," Caroline sighed, glancing out over the accessories department. "Chloe bags, Marni belts, Chanel sunglasses …ooh, sends a shiver down my spine just looking at it."

Abby, who didn't know her Chloe from her Chanel didn't quite get it, but if Caroline had her way, no doubt she would soon find out.

"So where do you want to start?" her sister asked, deciding to get right down to business. "Shoes, dresses, handbags …"

Abby shrugged. "There's nothing that I really need, to be honest."

"Need! Who said anything about *need*? Abby, shopping for something you need is no fun at all–is that what you've been doing all these years?" Her sister seemed to shudder at the very idea.

Then Caroline stood up and drained the contents of her glass, and again Abby was struck by how much energy her sister always seemed to have.

"Enough, drink that down," she chided. "Time you and I did some serious damage–and what better way to start than by finding you a truly *fabulous* dress."

Abby duly finished and followed her upstairs to where a truly bewildering selection of clothes in various shapes, colours and sizes awaited them. Her sister was already zooming in on rails and displays, picking up and discarding dresses skirts and tops with military precision.

"OK, daytime first," she muttered. "Diane Van Furstenburg, Victor & Rolf, Gharani Strok … what size are you–a ten, twelve at the most?"

"Fourteen by the look of some of these," Abby groaned, fingering a multicoloured diaphanous dress that would make any normal woman look like Ten Ton Tessie.

"Nonsense, that would look fab on you," Caroline replied, swooping in on the dress and throwing it on the alarmingly large pile she now held over one arm. She peered at the label above the rail. "Issa, good choice – hmm, maybe you do have some taste after all."

"Cheers," Abby mumbled, wondering who the hell Issa was and how he or she got away with charging an arm and a leg for this.

But ten minutes later, she was eating her words. The dress, made from silk jersey which Abby was certain would cling in all the wrong places, somehow managed to accentuate all the *right* ones. And with its multi-coloured butterfly print, instantly transformed her from a dumpy thirty-something into curvy and vivacious girl-about-town.

"Well?" Caroline poked her head round the fitting room door. "Hmm, just give me one sec…" she muttered, temporarily deflating Abby's early optimism, till she returned with a funky pair of Anna Sui black satin boots, which ended up working surprisingly well.

Staring at her reflection, Abby was entranced. In this outfit, she was no longer her dull and dowdy self, instead she looked glam and fashionable and dare she say it …cool?

"I love it," she cried, doing a twirl in front of the mirror. "It's just so … *not* me that I love it."

"Finally, she gets the point," Caroline deadpanned. "OK, now try the Pucci –prints really *are* you actually. I don't know why you don't wear them more often."

"Um, maybe because I don't have a rich husband to cover the cost?" Abby teased, as she tried on the colourful pink and orange silk tunic. It was actually quite unusual with its jewelled mandarin-style collar and self-tie belt. And speaking of cost … she glanced down at the price-tag and did a double take. Seven hundred and fifty *pounds*!

"No excuse, the high-street do great replicas you know," Caroline lectured, "you just don't bother looking."

It was true, Abby admitted, she'd never been any good at

this stuff, never had much of an eye for it—certainly not like Caroline's anyway.

"Not bad, not bad, although," her sister said grimacing, "you really should think about getting those legs waxed once in a while."

Waxed? She usually only bothered *shaving* her legs in the summer or that one time she and Kieran went to Spain.

Caroline was still talking. "In fairness, you've got really great legs, though you need some killer heels to go with a dress like that. Manolos would work."

"OK." As most of the brand names were going right over Abby's head, she simply nodded in agreement, and decided she'd think about maybe booking a leg-wax when she got home.

"Now try this," Caroline again sifted through the pile she was holding and held up a mid-length purple creation. "Diane Van Furstenberg – if the size twelve Issa dress works, then this should be absolutely *perfect* on you."

The dress did indeed look good on Abby, as did the petrol-blue jersey Stella McCartney mini-dress, gorgeous Zhandra Rhodes pink and purple chiffon maxi, and the floaty cotton Anna Sui vest top over Rock and Republic jeans.

By the time she got to the Whistles vintage-style flapper, which Caroline insisted she team with silver foil and black suede Jimmy Choo sling-backs, Abby was well on her way toward becoming a fashion convert.

There was no doubt these clothes really transformed her and also a guilty thrill to be had about wearing these designer names and lavish prices. So while Abby wasn't planning on actually *buying* any of these, she had to admit it sure was fun trying them on - a bit of a *Pretty Woman*, Rodeo drive moment.

"OK. So I think we now need to *seriously* up the glam stakes." Caroline seemed to be equally enjoying her stylist's role. "Hold on, I spotted something on the way in that would be the absolute *business* on you, but need a bag and shoes to complete the entire look. Gimme a sec."

"OK," Abby giggled, wondering what was coming next...

She was beginning to understand what all the fuss was about. One of these days, she was going to treat herself to a pair of Jimmy Choos, they were just so pretty and delicate and – oh... my..."

She stepped back in awe as the most stunningly beautiful gown she had ever seen suddenly materialised in the doorway of the cubicle.

"You like?" Caroline's voice was muffled, and she could barely be seen behind layers of voluminous fabric.

"I *love*," Abby gasped.

The dress was deep plum with a strapless ruched tulle corset-style bodice. At the waist a similar-coloured thick satin sash and floral corsage, which fastened at the back in a self-tie bow. But it was the full skirt, and its layers and layers of plum-coloured tulle that made the gown magnificent.

"Oscar de La Renta–isn't it amazing?" Caroline's head eventually peeped over the bodice.

"It's ... incredible..." She was almost too stunned to reply.

"Um, is there any chance you could take it off my hands? All these layers weigh a tonne."

Abby lifted up the dress and immediately hung it on one of the cubicle hooks, almost afraid to touch it; it was so beautiful.

"I think these will work well, what do you think?" Caroline had also procured a pair of dusky pink satin heels, and a gold beaded evening bag to accompany the dress. She looked at Abby, frowning. "Well–are you going to try it on or what?"

She wanted to try it on, of course she did, but it was so beautiful Abby worried she wouldn't be able to do it justice.

But within a few seconds of stepping into those acres of soft material and zipping up the corset, her fears were appeased. The dress seemed to fit like a dream and when Abby slipped into the three-inch-heels and eventually turned to face her reflection in the mirror, she felt a lump in her throat.

Oh my...

For once, even Caroline seemed lost for words.

"Wow..." her sister said eventually, looking her up and down. "You look... stunning. It's weird, but I actually feel emotional, almost as if you're trying on your wedding dress."

Abby turned to her, eyes glittering. Somehow, Caroline had managed to pinpoint her own feelings exactly. She wasn't sure why she felt so overwhelmed at that very moment. It was just a dress, after all.

But what a dress. And despite herself, Abby couldn't help but wish that Kieran could see her now...

"Thank you," she whispered, softly. "I don't know how you managed it but this is just ... perfect–this whole thing is just perfect. I'll ... I'll never forget it."

Caroline nodded solemnly, understanding that this was about more than just the dress.

"Wait a minute," her sister said then, rummaging through her handbag before eventually producing lipstick and a hair-brush. "Here, put some of this on and then use this to give your hair a quick going over. "

Abby laughed, confused. "Why?"

"Because we're going to make sure you *do* remember it, that's why." She fished out her mobile phone before making Abby move out of the cubicle, and then pose by a nearby store floral arrangement.

"Can I help you Madam?" a shop assistant said imperiously from behind Caroline, who was busy snapping away on her phone.

"You can actually." Without warning her sister thrust the device into the assistant's hands and ordered her to take shots of them together, all the while directing proceedings with typical aplomb.

As they grinned at the camera, Abby in her 'you shall go to the ball' Oscar de la Renta dress, she hugged Caroline tightly and decided that this truly had been one of the best times the sisters had ever spent together.

CHAPTER 24

Later, they decamped to a restaurant for a late lunch where-upon Caroline immediately ordered more champagne and the two toasted their Selfridges exploits.

Abby was still slightly dazed by the whole experience, not just by exhilaration from trying on that amazing dress, but what had happened afterwards.

While she was in the cubicle changing out of the ball gown, Caroline was outside getting ready to put back the other clothes she'd tried on.

Or at least that's what Abby had thought.

"OK, so definitely the Issa, the DVF, that Whistles skirt and those jeans?" Caroline called out. "And the silver Choos of course. But I'm not entirely sure about the Pucci, would you get any wear out of it?"

"What?" Still half-dressed, Abby shot her head out the door. "Car, you know I've no intention of actually buying anything, don't you? I mean these clothes are gorgeous but I couldn't possibly afford – "

"Oh for goodness sake, who said anything about *you*?" her sister said breezily. "This is my treat."

Abby blanched. "Caroline no, no way. There must be at least a couple of grand's-worth there, I couldn't *possibly* let you spend that much on–"

"You can and you will. This is supposed to be a memorable experience, isn't it?" she reminded Abby. "Something you'll remember for a long time to come. So how on earth will you remember if you don't take home the clothes? If you're living your best life, you need the best gear." She winked.

"Caroline, no– "

"Abby, please, it's what I had planned all along when I suggested this. And after seeing your face when you tried on the De La Renta, I'd really love to get that too, but my credit card would explode and Tom would surely leave me." She grimaced. "But the rest is my gift to you, so that every time you wear those clothes you'll remember how this and how *great* you felt in that dress."

"Caroline …"

"Say no more. I'm getting them and that's it. Don't worry," she reassured her mischievously. "I'm gonna pick out a few bits and bobs for myself too."

Those 'few bits and bobs' turned out to a bewildering amount of items including a zebra Jimmy Choo handbag, Grecian-style Vera Wang dress with gold sequin embellished straps, ('for the Marbella ball'), and stunning leopard print Manolo Blahniks heels so high that made Abby dizzy just looking at them.

Now, as they sat in the chic Covent Garden restaurant, both *buried* in shopping bags, Abby marvelled at her sister's life. The restaurant they were in boasted a Michelin star chef, with resultant menu prices to make your eyes water, yet Caroline seemed totally at ease in such sumptuous surroundings.

With the champagne, designer clobber and fine dining, Abby felt like a celebrity for a day, and when she confessed this to Caroline, her sister laughed.

"That was the idea," she said. "Believe me, I don't normally go this crazy, but I wanted to make today particularly special."

"Well you've certainly done that," Abby gave a passing waiter an appreciative glance. She giggled, the champagne obviously going to her head again. "Did you hire male models to work here for the day too?"

Caroline grinned, following her gaze. "Nope, luckily for us that's all part of the service." Then her expression quickly turned serious as the waiter in question approached.

"Ready to order Madam?" he asked with in a heavy French accent that made Abby swoon.

"Sure. I'll start with the lobster bisque, and the lamb and walnuts, thanks. And we'll also have a bottle of your Montrachet."

"Certainly. And for you, Madmoiselle?

Abby was still staring at the menu, unable to make up her mind. But in the true spirit of item number nine on the list, she decided to once again 'be more spontaneous'.

"I will try the ... artichoke risotto, and the Cornish brill please," she told the waiter, and smiled when Caroline glanced up in surprise.

"I know," she said sheepishly, "I'm as surprised as you, but why the hell not ...."

Caroline reached over and squeezed her hand. "Good for you." Then she topped up their champagne flutes. "It's about time you started truly enjoying life Abby, you so deserve it."

Struck yet again by her generosity, she looked at Caroline's perfectly coiffed blonde curls, her expensive designer outfit and extravagant jewellery - and instead of the pretentious, self-centred, airhead Kieran always insisted her sister was, Abby finally saw her through her own eyes.

She was actually incredibly generous, warm and kind-spirited, she realised now. Until recently, Abby felt alienated and slightly intimidated by Caroline's wealth and lifestyle, and as a result had distanced herself from her, convincing herself that they had little in common.

But *she* (and most likely her ex's opinion) had erected that barrier, Abby admitted now, and as a result they'd grown apart.

Since her accident and subsequent diagnosis, Caroline had been magnificent, trying to boost Abby's spirits at every opportunity, arranging the trip to New York for the whole family in order to lift her out of her misery, and even coming up with the idea of making the list.

And then to top it all off, now she'd arranged this wonderful day out, buying her all those gorgeous clothes, a posh lunch, a stay at Claridges …how could she have ever believed her to be self-centred?

Suddenly she felt another lump in her throat. "Thank you," she said, her voice hoarse.

Caroline went to wave her away "It's nothing–"

"No, I mean it," Abby interjected. "This is truly incredible. I'm enjoying myself so much I can't even explain it. And I'm not just talking about today, I'm talking about all the things you've done for me over the last few months, all the times you've been there. I don't know how to thank you."

"You're my sister," Caroline said with a smile. "And you've been through the mill. Why wouldn't I be there for you?"

CAROLINE SUGGESTED they drop their shopping bags back at the hotel before their next stop, and when their cab eventually pulled up outside a four-storey, innocuous-building, Abby was dubious.

Her sister seemed to read her mind. "Don't worry nothing to be afraid of," she said before announcing, "Two for 'Chocolate Heaven Experience'," to the receptionist.

"Chocolate?" she queried as they took a seat in the waiting area of what was clearly a high-end spa.

"Plenty of it," Caroline winked, refusing to elaborate further.

She hadn't been joking. Their experience began with a one-hour silky smooth skin-conditioning body wrap. Following this, the two relaxed side-by-side in the treatment room, both covered from head to toe in luxurious chocolate fondue and surrounded by scented candles, their delicious chocolate aromas filling the air.

"Mmm…talk about living up to the name," Abby said lazily. "I really do feel like I've died and gone to chocolate heaven."

She felt guilty though. How much must all of this be costing? When she again tried to thank her sister for her unspeakable generosity, Caroline simply waved it away.

"Don't be silly–it's nothing really. You know Tom is loaded. Now, don't get me wrong, every year we donate at least ten percent of our earnings to charity, so my conscience is squeaky clean when it comes to spending 'frivolously.'" She laughed putting additional emphasis on the last word. "But we have the house we want and the cars and all that, and since we have only have ourselves to spend it on …"

Abby ears pricked up at the slight catch in her voice as she said this. She'd always assumed Caroline wasn't remotely maternal and way too busy enjoying life to bother with children.

It wasn't something that they'd ever spoken about but then again, when would they have had the opportunity? It was only very recently that they'd even become close, despite Caroline's best efforts Abby thought guiltily. So given that she'd already been wrong in her assessment of her sister's personality, perhaps she'd been wrong about that too?

"Do you think you'll ever decide to have any?" she asked hesitantly.

Caroline chuckled. "We decided to have them from day one–unfortunately things just didn't work out."

Abby sat up and looked across at her. "What? You mean you can't ..."

"No." Caroline said smiling easily, her eyes still closed. "I'm sorry, I thought you knew that, that maybe Mum had ... Anyway, don't worry and *please* don't start spluttering with embarrassment like everyone else seems to do. It's a pity, but we're fine with it."

Abby's thoughts raced, a million questions running through her mind. "But are you absolutely sure that –"

"Oh yes, we're absolutely sure, and we have all the medical results to prove it."

"Caroline, I'm sorry, I had no idea –"

"Hey, don't sweat it, honestly. Yes, it was a blow and a shock to the system for both of us at first, but we've got lots of other great things in our lives. I never buy into negative stuff Abby. So, Tom and I can't have kids but we've got a great life, piles of money, and we love one another to bits. Why ruin all that by driving ourselves crazy over what we *don't* have?"

Abby had to admire her philosophy. It was no wonder she'd never picked up any uncomfortable vibes about her sister's personal life because Caroline refused to allow any.

The conversation came to an end when their respective therapists returned to the treatment room to carry out the next part of their 'Chocolate Heaven' experience.

Next came a luxurious, exfoliating chocolate mint body scrub (which Abby didn't mind at all), then a pampering manicure where the girls' hands were dipped in a chocolate milkshake soap, massaged in chocolate whipped cream, and then sealed with heated chocolate paraffin. Afterwards was the pedicure – a warm milk foot bath and hot vanilla and brown sugar scrub which left Abby's toes tingling. Finally, she and Caroline each had a full body massage with warmed cocoa butter oils, making their skin feeling silky smooth and smelling out-of-this-world gorgeous.

The entire experience was topped off with a mouth-watering glass of hot chocolate and biscotti, and as the girls relaxed in white robes with their treats yet again Abby marvelled at the huge amount of trouble and effort her sister had gone to in order to make this day special.

"I have never, ever experienced anything like that," she said, when later that evening, they finally returned to hotel Both shattered from the day's adventures, they'd decided to stay in and order a light snack from room service rather than head out, and Abby was lazing around on one of the room's comfy beds watching Caroline try on her newly bought clothes.

"Well, maybe you should treat yourself now and again," her sister replied, before muttering quietly. "Hell knows nobody else did." Then turning away from the full-length mirror, she bit her lip. "I'm sorry, I promised I wouldn't … after all today is all about spoiling you …"

"Caroline," Abby said. "Just spit it out, I won't be annoyed, I promise." Or at least she *hoped* she wouldn't be annoyed.

"Well..." her sister sighed. "I just felt that when you started going out with Kieran that you lost some of your … spark."

"When I *started* going out with him?" Abby repeated, confused. She knew she'd turned into some a dreary hermit by retreating into herself *after* she and Kieran finished, she realised that now, but what was all this about beforehand?

"I'm sorry, and it's not really my place to say but… I never really felt that you two were well suited"

"Evidently you were right." It still hurt to hear it though.

"I'm not trying to make you feel bad or anything, and please don't take this the wrong way, but long before you two broke up I felt that he'd taken away a lot of your oomph and zest for life." Caroline paused before adding quietly. "He was quite … controlling, wasn't he?"

Controlling? Kieran was just more of a…perfectionist

really. Which was why he'd left Abby for a prettier and much more together partner.

"I'm sorry I brought it up," Caroline said again, when she didn't answer. "Now really isn't the time for this, not when we're having such a lovely day. But to be honest, Abby, since the accident I've begun seeing a side of you I thought was lost, the more fun-loving, optimistic, game for anything side. And there's a part of me that can't help thinking that maybe that bump on the head did you some good too."

Abby smiled. "Funnily enough, I'm beginning to think the very same thing."

CHAPTER 25

"So a good time all round then?" Hannah said, when Abby finished telling her all about her recent exploits.

"It was great," she said smiling.

"Well, your sister certainly sounds like a very generous person, all those clothes and your Tiffany bracelet."

Abby dangled it on her wrist. "I feel so awful now for misjudging her." She'd also explained to Hannah how she'd been wrong in assuming that Caroline was showy and insensitive.

"It happens in families, don't beat yourself up about it. So besides all this recent activity," she said, sitting forward in her chair, "how are you otherwise? Any more headaches or changes from day to day?"

"Nope." Abby wasn't going to mention the recent hair-brush-in-the-fridge incident because she honestly didn't think that it was anything other than a case of simple absentmindedness. Like searching for car keys when they're already in your hand, or sunglasses when they're on your head.

"Nothing at all?" Hanna sounded sceptical.

"The headaches come and go and still I get tired when

185

reading but other than that nothing. And I was thinking..." she began, deciding this was as good a time as any to broach the subject. "I was thinking that since I am OK, we don't really need to keep doing this, do we? These meetings I mean."

"You want to give up our sessions?"

"Pretty much." Hannah was lovely and it was nice to be able to talk to someone, but Abby wanted to put the injury and more importantly, talk of it, behind her.

"Well, it's only been a few months – " She paused a little, "since your injury. Medically, it's still very early days. While I'm pleased that you don't seem to be experiencing any problems, at least none that you can identify – "

"What do you mean?"

"You seem so determined that there's nothing wrong that you may very well be ignoring the signs. Don't worry, this is perfectly normal and I see it all the time with my patients and sometimes – even their families. Nobody likes to admit to questionable issues regarding mental capacity or brain function, which is understandable, but also can be very dangerous." Then her voice softened. "Abby I'm not implying that this is deliberate on your part, I'm just concerned that the situation is still very fragile. We don't want to run ahead of ourselves until we know exactly what we're dealing with."

Abby tried hard to fight back her frustration and disappointment.

"I know what you're thinking and I'm sorry. But as your neuropsychologist it would be irresponsible of me to agree to discontinuing our sessions. I can't force you to attend them either, but in order for us to grant the necessary approval for your eventual return to work, we need to be one hundred percent confident of your capacities." This was all said in the kind, friendly tone she always used, but Abby recognised the covert warning in there too.

While she was disappointed that Hannah wasn't willing to

let her off the hook just yet, she wasn't too surprised. Like her mother, the doctors were convinced that her prognosis was inevitable.

They simply didn't share Abby's faith and utter determination to overcome and fight it every step of the way.

A FEW DAYS LATER, she was sitting at home and trying to find something more interesting than cleaning or watching daytime TV, when she got a call.

"Hey, it's Tina from American Holidays Travel Centre calling in relation to payment for your trip to California."

Abby had wasted no time in booking the flights, hotels and of course, the all-important convertible. She and Erin would be leaving mid-April.

"I sent a cheque last week," she told her. "Didn't you get it?"

"We did and that's why I'm calling. It's just .. the cheque was returned by the bank. I had a look and the date was wrong. Easy mistake, but you know how fussy the banks are these days."

"Oh." Abby felt a prickle of anxiety running down her spine.

"So I'm putting it back in the post to you today, and if you could just cross out the mistake and then initial the change, it should be fine. I've made a note on the file so there won't be any issue with late payment or anything. Is that alright?"

"Sure." Having promised to send back the amended cheque, Abby hung up the phone, unsure what to think.

Probably just another case of absentmindedness, she decided, swallowing.

CHAPTER 26

HER BROTHER'S idea for a memorable experience wasn't something Abby was particularly looking forward to, so when she found herself zooming around a racetrack doing over a hundred miles an hour in a bright red Ferrari–and loving it–she was completely taken by surprise.

"I know what you're thinking," Dermot said, when explaining what he'd planned, "but trust me, it'll be great."

And although initially she'd been underwhelmed by her brother's predictably laddish suggestion, by the time they reached the racetrack and spied the impressive selection of high-powered cars lined up, she began to think that this wasn't such a bad idea after all.

While she wasn't prohibited from driving, the doctors had recommended she stay off the road other than when absolutely necessary. Apparently though, Dermot had had the wherewithal to consult Hannah about his plans and the psychologist had given the idea her blessing.

Abby and Dermot each had a trial run doing three laps of the track in a lowly Subaru. While her little brother was happy to tear around pushing speeds of up to a hundred miles an hour, Abby was more sedate, preferring instead to simply get her bearings on the track before the main event.

Then the famous Ferrari 360 was wheeled out and when Abby lowered herself into the driving seat normally reserved for Formula One racers or the rich and famous, she couldn't help but feel a little over-awed and very cool (although this effect was slightly spoiled by Dermot grinning maniacally at her from the sidelines).

Then, when she'd been belted in, and the instructor directed her to rev the engine and she heard (and felt) the famous Ferrari howl, a vicarious thrill ran down her spine.

Still, this was nothing compared to the thrill she felt when putting the car through its paces on the open road.

Barely a *brush* with the accelerator sent the car zooming straight down the track, and trying to control the speed on the tight corners was terrifying but at the same time heart-thumping fantastic.

Abby was sure the instructor in the passenger seat could hear her laughing uproariously through her safety helmet as the car zoomed along the tarmac. She didn't care. This–this hair-raising but at the same time, amazingly liberating feeling of almost complete and utter abandon–was *incredible.*

Yet again a member of her family had got it right and as she took the Ferrari around the track for the fourth and final time, Abby wondered again if they truly knew her better than she knew herself.

Her heart was still thumping wildly when she hauled herself out of the driver's seat and she hoped against hope that Dermot had remembered to take a picture of her zipping along in the Ferrari.

On the way back to Dublin they stopped for lunch in a service station off the motorway.

"That was brilliant!" Dermot was just as dumbstruck from his own experience, which took him to max speeds of one hundred and eighty miles per hour. "Told you you'd enjoy it."

"I definitely wasn't sure about it at first but yes, it was really, really great," Abby enthused. "Delighted you got photos, though if I do forget this, I've no idea how I'm supposed to remind myself from a blurry red strip!"

Dermot was silent for a moment, and when he spoke again, his tone was gentle. "It must be strange to think you might ... forget these things I mean."

Abby shook her head defiantly. "*Not* going to happen. Think about what we did just now. How could *anyone* forget that?" She grinned. "As far as I'm concerned living my best life really is working–I'm fighting this. I had a brilliant day out with Caroline, I've got the road-trip with Erin coming up, and then I'm off to Italy with Mum." The list had since lengthened considerably.

"I can't believe you're going to do Vegas, lucky cow." Then Dermot gave her a sideways look. "To be honest, you're the last person I thought would go somewhere like that."

She looked up. "Why?"

"Dunno, I always thought you felt you were a bit...beneath that kind of stuff."

"*Beneath* it?"

"Yeah, you and ..." Then his face reddened, and the rest of his sentence trailed off.

"And Kieran?"

"Yeah. Sorry, but you've probably guessed by now that me and him never really ... gelled. I'm sure he was a great guy once you got to know to him, but I always felt he was a bit...superior."

Abby sighed, realising she was hearing this kind of thing a lot lately. "I'm sorry."

"I suppose he reckoned a lowly grease monkey isn't the same as a high-flying taxman."

"How many times do I have to tell you? He wasn't a taxman, he was a tax *inspector*– and I'm sure he still is," she added wryly.

"Anyway, this might sound stupid but I just wanted to tell you that I think you're much better off without the guy."

"Yes, well …" Abby wanted to change the subject. "What about you? Anyone interesting in your life these days?"

When Dermot reddened slightly, her eyes widened. "There *is?* Tell me more!"

"It's nothing really," her brother said, inwardly squirming. "I've known her for a while so… nothing really."

"Nothing my ass. You should see your face." Abby couldn't resist milking this. It was obvious her baby brother was smitten. "What's her name and when do we meet her?"

"Ah no, like I said, it's just a casual thing. But look, don't go blabbing to Mam about it either."

"OK." Abby nodded, gratified that he'd confided in her at all. "But if it becomes more than a just casual thing, I want to meet her."

"I'll think about it," Dermot grinned before deftly changing the subject. "Fancy a coffee?"

"Sure." Abby was enjoying their chat and was in no rush back.

This had been such a great idea, this whole exercise had been such a great idea actually. She was only a little way through the list and already her attitude and spirits had improved no end. And to think it had all started when she'd finally cast aside *one* of her neuroses and got on a plane to New York.

The trip was still so fresh in her mind, she could almost picture it. All the family together and having a laugh around the dinner table on Christmas Eve…Claire's beautiful

Christmas tree, little Caitlyn's gummy smile... it had been brilliant.

"It just seems so weird," Dermot was saying now. "I don't know what I'd do if something like that happened to me. And I think you're right to do what you're doing, dive-bombing your head with all this great stuff. Don't tell her I said this but it was a brainwave of Caroline's to have us arrange things for you too. Now I'm half thinking of making my own list. "

"You should, it's lots of fun."

"It's given you such a new lease of life too. Everyone was so worried when ..." then he reddened and the rest of his sentence trailed off.

"I know, I know," Abby said, "you might have been worried when Kieran dumped me, but don't pretend that you weren't relieved too."

He exhaled. "It wasn't that we *hated* him or anything, it's just that he ... well he was a bit square, really. And you guys never seemed to do anything except sit in and watch TV."

"And look down our noses at the rest of you, of course."

"Ah, don't be like that ...I only meant– "

"It's OK, joke," she reassured him and he smiled.

He'd really grown up in the last while, Abby mused. While he was still a messer and very much one of the boys, there was now a faint maturity that she'd never noticed before. Then again, wasn't she noticing lots of things about her family she hadn't previously, or more likely, had never bothered to?

She picked up her coffee mug and drank from it. "It's a good thing the insurance money is coming through soon, otherwise I'll be broke by ... ugh."

"What's the matter?" Dermot asked.

"This coffee is awful."

"Sugar might help," her brother said, waving a packet in front of her. "Two is your usual isn't it?"

At this, she felt a bead of trepidation. But she didn't ... take any - did she?

"Better?" Dermot asked, once she'd added sugar and tasted the coffee again, and Abby just nodded, afraid to say another word.

CHAPTER 27

FINN KNOCKED SHARPLY on the door of his old home, and getting no immediate reply, let himself in with his own key. Although he'd grown up in this house, he didn't believe in just barging in whenever he felt like it–despite Pat's repeated protests: "Sure 'tis your house too."

But since the discovery of Pat's health problems and the prospect of old age had raised its head, Finn couldn't help but worry about his dad and made sure he checked in on him at least every other day.

He hadn't been comfortable leaving Pat for the few days in New York that time either, even though he knew that Nora and other neighbours would be checking in, and of course he had Lucy but still …

"Will you ever go away and stop treating me like an 'oul fella?" Pat joked.

Today though, Finn wasn't just checking in, he was heading to a DIY shop and calling to see if his father needed anything. The two of them had recently installed some decking at the rear, probably where Pat was at that moment, he thought, and why he hadn't heard the door. His father loved having breakfast out on the decking; for an outdoors man, no great surprise and since it was a fresh spring day…

Heading in that direction, Finn heard voices. Nora must be there too, he thought. Their sixty-odd year old neighbour and long-time friend was great for fussing over Pat, especially since her own husband passed away a few years back.

The back door was ajar, so Finn bypassed the kitchen, planning to go straight out, but just as he was about to announce his presence, something Nora said made him pause.

"I really think you should tell Finn."

He stood rooted to the spot and frowned. *Tell him what?*

"Ah, I don't know, he's bad enough as it is, fussing over me left right and centre."

"Reason enough for to him to know."

Icy fear crept down Finn's spine. Evidently, Pat was a lot sicker than he was letting on.

"No, the timing isn't right," his father was saying now, as Finn remained in the hallway, immobile.

"When will it ever be right? Pat, he's a grown man, well able to handle anything."

"Ah he is and he isn't," his father said, which made Finn wonder ever more. "I know he's still a bit cut up over Danielle."

His eyes widened. Well, that might be true but he didn't think he'd ever given his dad that impression.

"You don't think it's strange that a fella his age isn't out on the town enjoying himself?"

Nora chuckled. "And surrounding himself with women instead of dogs, you mean?"

Cheers Nora…

"I'd like to see him settled all the same. There was a bit of a spring in his step when he came back from America, which made me wonder."

Finn's eyes widened, amazed his father could read him so well.

"Still, I think you should say something. Will we go in? It's still only March and the wind is going through me."

Finn heard the two make their way back inside, and deciding to avoid any potential bad news announcements, sneaked back up the hallway and out the front door.

CHAPTER 28

15ᵗʰ April, Las Vegas, Nevada.

Viva Las Vegas!

So surreal to drive through the desert at night and watch this huge neon metropolis appear out of nowhere. I'd seen the Vegas skyline so many times in movies that somehow it didn't feel real.

Erin and I are LOVING the convertible. There's nothing quite like driving along, the wind in your face, and a blanket of blue sky above. Major downside is that the wind is playing HAVOC with our hair. So much for getting my curls back, at the moment it's just a ball of frizz. Late last night, we arrived in LAX before picking up the car this morning. Then it was straight out of the city (scary sixteen-lane highways which Erin just breezed through) and straight on to Vegas.

Stopped off at loads of different places along the route, and driving onto the South end of The Strip, immediately spotted our hotel, the Luxor, a huge black pyramid and on top a tall beam of light so bright it can be seen from space, apparently.

Right alongside it were the colourfully-lit skyscrapers of New York, New York, which (much to my relief!) immediately triggered memories of Manhattan.

Another sign that all of this REALLY working.

Anyway .... difficult to describe how big, brash and utterly MAD this place is – I suppose you could say it's like visiting another planet. For example, when we pulled in for fuel on the outskirts, we were greeted by the sight (and sounds) of slot machines – at a gas station! *Why anyone would drive all the way out into the desert to just spend their time gambling in a service station ...*

"Well it is Vegas," Erin kept saying over and over, as if either of us could forget. (Though, in my case, very possible- ha!).

The hotel was simply jaw-dropping–a humongous thirty-storey black glass pyramid with a huge sphinx guarding the entrance. And inside statues of various Egyptian Pharaohs. It was big, bold and so unbelievably touristy that I fell in love with it on sight. Even the elevator travels on a pyramid-slanted incline!

We dropped off our bags and freshened up a little, and were just getting ready to head straight back down to the casino, when Erin said she needed to make a phone call.

And things got a teeny bit weird.

"Um, actually," she said blushing, "It's kind of private."

I thought again about how bubbly and happy she's been over lately, and I started to wonder if maybe she's started seeing someone?

So the casino – wow. Massive area about the size of a football pitch, all bursting with slot machines, roulette tables and poker rooms. To be honest, at first I felt a bit intimidated and disorientated by all the flashing lights, dinging bells and brightly patterned carpets.

Before we left, Dermot told us the hideous carpets are part of a psychological ruse to ensure your eye is drawn away from the floor and upwards to the slots, which I suppose makes sense. Also there are no windows so gamblers have no idea what time it is – day or night – another trick to keep them spending more.

When Erin came down, we decided we'd try the slots, since the gaming tables looked too intimidating.

But unfortunately they turned out boring and I felt like a bit of a drone pressing buttons and hoping for the right combination.

So I left Erin to it and wandered across to the gaming tables where a roulette game was in full swing. Players were piling their chips high on red and black, and I was trying to figure out how the game worked when some guy elbowed his way past me and randomly placed a hundred-dollar bill on the table.

A hundred dollar bill!

Seemed a real 'Vegas' thing to do – so I decided to do the very same thing myself, cool as you like.

Imagine my delight (and relief!) when the ball landed on black seventeen and the croupier calmly placed two hundred dollars worth of chips in front of me.

Just like that, I'd doubled my money.

Erin's eyes nearly popped out of her head. Needless to say it wasn't long before she joined me and the two of us were laying chips and bets like a couple of high-rollers.

In the end, I think I lost something like five hundred dollars, but it felt like the best five hundred I ever spent. I kept telling myself that gambling in Vegas is less about the money and more about the experience, although I can't deny the thrill I felt every time the little white ball fell on one of my numbers, or the disappointment when the croupier took back every penny of my hard-earned winnings.

House always wins.

First night, I slept like a baby, the combination of jetlag and euphoria proving a great sleeping pill, not to mention the never-ending glasses of complimentary alcohol the hostess kept serving us at the table.

Now I understand why people love this place.

From then on, the slots didn't get a look in. For the next few days, we tried our luck at roulette tables in the different casinos, marvelling at how each place seemed even bigger and more extravagant than the last.

At the MGM Grand, real live LIONS watched us from their glass-fronted habitat area right on the casino floor (a bit cruel I thought) but they seemed to enjoy the attention and it all looked pretty spectacular. At New York, New York we took a ride through 'downtown Manhattan' on the hotel's huge roller coaster before blowing another couple of hundred in the casino.

Then, on the last night, (having gambled almost every penny we had and enjoyed every second) we went for a walk along the Strip to take in some of the hotel's evening attractions.

At the Mirage, scores of people gathered outside on the street waiting for the hotel's famous volcano to erupt. After a few moments of foreboding silence, cascading water began to churn and a low rumble emerged from the heart of the volcano. Then, to the crowd's delight, eruption kicked into high gear as bright orange flames dramatically leapt about a hundred feet above the water, illuminating the night sky. Tack, but great fun.

But for me, the highlight (other than my brilliant first-night never-to-be-repeated winning streak) was the Bellagio fountains.

On our final night, we took our places amongst the hordes gathered by the lake in front of the famed Italian-themed hotel. And as the first bars of Sinatra's 'Fly me to the Moon' began, time seemed to stand still as the fountains came to life, and shot high into the air in time to the music.

"Wow," Erin whispered. "Breathtaking."

It was truly stunning and yet another highlight of my quest. A memory I will treasure.

Next up, the Grand Canyon. I really, really, can't wait. Honestly, if my brain lets fantastic memories like these just fade away and die, then there really is no hope. But I'm pretty confident.

Watch this space ...

ABBY RETURNED from her latest US trip brimming with enthusiasm, adrenalin, and pages upon pages of diary entries.

She was really getting into the swing of journalling now and while in the beginning, she'd tried to break events down the minimum (and end up diluting the experience), she was gradually learning to be less self-conscious.

Now she pretty much wrote on the fly about things as they happened and more importantly, how she felt about them.

She'd also taken tonnes of photographs throughout the trip, her and Erin in Vegas, the two of them at the Grand Canyon and in LA and transferred all of the information into the digital programme Zach had created.

And while Erin, Caroline and Dermot were a hundred percent behind her efforts, Abby knew she still hadn't managed to convince her mother that any of this would help to fight her diagnosis.

So she was a little less than enthusiastic about the next thing on her list; a trip to Italy with Teresa.

"Make sure Mum enjoys herself, won't you?" her sister reminded her as she dropped them off at the airport. "This trip is a big deal."

"Of course." She wasn't quite sure what Caroline meant, but supposed she was in a roundabout way asking her to go easy on Teresa.

And while Abby had known that Italy was famed for its stunning architecture and cultural attractions, nothing could have prepared her for the picture-postcard beauty of Verona.

Second only to Rome in terms of well-preserved monuments and ruins, the place was steeped in history, from the immense Porta Borsari, an archway which once made up part of the original city wall, to the mind-blowingly picturesque Piazza d'el Herbe, one of the most charming town squares she'd ever seen.

A busy tourist and bustling commercial area, the piazza was teeming with old Roman monuments and beautiful sculptures. The hotel that Caroline had arranged was just a short walk away from the piazza and when they'd settled themselves in the charming boutique hotel, they decided to wander around and find somewhere nice to eat.

"Isn't it gorgeous?" Teresa seemed just as taken with it all. "Ah your Dad would have loved this."

Abby smiled. Who wouldn't love Verona? It was romantic, historic, not to mention that it was also the reputed setting for Shakespeare's Romeo and Juliet. On the way in from the airport, their taxi driver, (who by his hair-raising carry-on *must* have been in training for Formula One) advised them to pay a visit to Juliet's balcony and the thirteenth century home of the Capuleti family.

They had an unhurried and enjoyable dinner in one of the many trattoria dotted around the piazza, and relaxed over delicious lemon and bergamotto sorbets their waiter had recommended. Abby noticed her mother seemed quiet over the meal and suspecting that Teresa might be tired after the travelling, suggested they head back to the hotel after and delay exploring until the following day.

"Do you mind, love?" She seemed relieved.

"Not at all. An early night will do us both good—set us up for the big day tomorrow."

Although in truth, Abby'd love the opportunity to look around further, daylight was fading and she knew her mother wouldn't be comfortable with her wandering around on her own. But here would be lots of time to see everything tomorrow before the opera performance.

Back at the hotel, again she noticed how tired and uncommunicative her mother was.

"Are you feeling OK, Mum?"

"I'm grand love, a bit tired, but excited about tomorrow. I know it's probably not really your thing, but since I had a ticket, I thought it might be nice. I'm sorry I couldn't think of anything more exciting for you."

"Don't be silly, of course this is exciting. I've never been in

Italy before and," she added with a grin, "we've never been away anywhere just the two of us either, have we? It'll be great," she assured Teresa.

The following day, they went on a walking tour round the city and took a closer look at some of the ancient Roman buildings. Abby had never really had any great interest in history, in her schooldays she loathed it, but it was impossible to be in a place like this and not feel the weight of history bearing down upon you, nor the power and grandeur of the Roman Empire in its heydey.

Wandering along the tree-lined Via Alfresco Oriani they eventually arrived at the main drag, a wide boulevard called Corso Porta Nova. From there they headed for Piazza Bra, where the Arena was located.

Entering the square beneath a magnificent double arch, Abby's attention was immediately drawn to an immense roman amphitheatre right in the centre.

"That's where we're going tonight?" she gasped.

While she was aware that the opera performance would be held outdoors, she had absolutely no idea of the sheer scale and magnificence of the amphitheatre. For some reason she'd been expecting something small and quaint, rather along the lines of the movie-theatres they had back home. The place looked like it had come straight off the set of *Gladiator,* so she was completely blown away. The Arena was in a word massive, the third largest in Italy apparently, according to Teresa's guide book. "My goodness, can you imagine what it'll be like tonight?"

But Teresa didn't reply, and when Abby looked around, she saw her mother still standing in the middle of the square, gazing at the magnificent structure, lost in a world of her own.

"Mum?" she prompted. Considering this was something her mother had always wanted to do, she'd been strangely off-form since they arrived here.

Teresa smiled tightly. "Your father would have loved this."

Abby frowned, realising that this was the second time her mother had said this. "I'm sure he would." She went to move off again, before all of a sudden a thought struck her.

"Mum," she whispered gently, her heart melting as she laid a hand on her mother's arm. "Was this something that you and Dad ... something you planned to do together?"

Teresa nodded quickly, trying to hold back tears.

"Oh Mum..." Now she understood why she'd been so uncommunicative. Putting an arm around her, she gently led Teresa away from the crowds toward a quieter spot on the edge of the square.

"We always said we'd go somewhere special on our fortieth anniversary, somewhere romantic. T'was your dad who suggested here, and the opera because he knew how much I loved it. We had it booked and everything when ..." She looked away, biting back tears.

Abby felt a huge lump in her throat. While she knew that her parents were due to celebrate a landmark anniversary the same year that Jim died, she had actually forgotten amidst the grief and suddenness of his death.

But of course her mother wouldn't, and remembering that she and Jim should have been together in a place like this must have broken her poor mum's heart.

Now, Abby felt ashamed. To think that she had initially treated the invitation so casually, when this trip meant so much to her mother ...

Again, she was taken aback by how estranged she'd become from her family, and how little she truly knew about them.

"Why didn't you tell me?"

"Ah, I didn't want you to feel obliged, or think that you had to hold my hand or anything," Teresa said. "And if I was going to come, I wanted someone I loved with me, someone who'd understand."

"I'm glad– no–" Abby corrected herself, "I'm *honoured* you choose me, and I'm so glad I'm here."

Teresa smiled and squeezed her daughter's hand. "So am I, love."

Later, having toured the majority of Verona's wonderful sights–including Juliet's balcony - Abby and Teresa donned their finest garb and made their way back to the Arena for the performance of Verdi's *Aida*.

Inside, the amphitheatre pit was surrounded by forty-four tiers of steps which soared high above the stage area. It held up to twenty-five thousand spectators, most of whom were now taking their places on the stalls at ground level in the pit on numbered seats along the steps, or on the bare steps themselves. Abby was pleased they didn't have seats, the steps that made the whole experience much more authentic. It was a wonderfully warm, balmy evening and the fading light, coupled with the beautifully-lit ancient Arena made for an electric atmosphere.

Then, the first act was announced, and immediately the hum and activity died down to complete and utter silence. And when the orchestra finally began, Abby felt a shiver down her spine. She couldn't believe she'd been so offhand about attending originally–it was without a doubt, once-in-lifetime incredible.

She smiled at Teresa who was held rapt by the atmosphere and the sheer magic of the whole experience too. And as the first act began in earnest the two sat back and settled in to enjoy the performance.

By the end of the third act, Abby was an opera devotee. This was nothing, *nothing* like she'd even seen, heard or experienced. The way the performance was capable of arousing and enrapturing the audience was little short of astonishing. And although she didn't understand a word of what was being sung, she could feel every ounce of emotion come through the performer's voice.

At one stage, in the darkness, she looked across and saw tears running down her mother's cheeks. This was hair-on-the-back-of-the-neck stuff, an intensely emotional experience, and as the singer's incredible voice built to a stunning crescendo, Abby could feel the anguish in every note.

Knowing that she was undoubtedly thinking of Jim and how he should have been here too, she reached across and took her Mum's hand in hers.

It was hard to imagine your parents as a couple in love, with the same hopes and dreams of any other. But hers had been truly devoted to one other, and now almost three years later her mother was still grieving heavily for the love of her life - a man with whom she'd spent almost forty years of her life, and still loved with all her heart.

It was heartbreaking yet massively touching, and Abby prayed that someday she would experience love like that.

She'd been so sure after the break-up, that nobody could understand or appreciate what she was going through, but of course her mother would've understood only too well. Teresa had lost love too, although what she'd shared with Abby's father had been very different.

Now Abby realised that it hadn't been that way for her and Kieran; it had been *nothing* like it. Things had been one-sided in that relationship. His rejection of her still hurt–hurt massively, and as much as she'd tried to convince herself that he'd made a mistake and would eventually realise the error of his ways, she now finally realised that she didn't want that.

She'd always blamed herself for his leaving. Always felt that if she was that bit more glamorous, lost that bit more weight, made more of an effort, then maybe then he wouldn't have left.

Yet now she realised that so much had been about trying to satisfy him and keep him happy. The moods and sulks, not to mention unpredictable temper … it hadn't been right at all, had it?

But what she *did* know now was that as much as her mother was hurting, as much as Teresa was grieving, she was grieving for a love that had been mutual, honest, and enduring.

And Abby had never experienced love like that.

CHAPTER 29

A LITTLE AFTER her return from Italy, Abby thought again about going back to work.

It was now six months since her accident, and in that time she'd experienced some incredible things–some she'd always wanted, others not, but in the end all equally enriching.

The list had helped her formulate some fantastic experiences and memories, and there was no doubt that throughout the process she had reconnected with and become much closer to her family.

She was hugely grateful for the effort everyone had gone to in helping her through the worst, and realised just how important they were and how lucky she was to have them in her life.

But perhaps, best of all, she'd finally begun to *really* start getting over Kieran, putting his betrayal behind her, and although she couldn't say she'd completely forgotten him, Abby knew for sure that she was capable of moving on without him.

Since she hadn't had any recent lapses or blips, it also seemed that her plan to defeat her prognosis was working.

"We'll just have to wait and see," Hannah trotted out her

usual mantra at their most recent session. "With these things, you just never know."

The idea of going back to work, back to some form of normality, was especially heartening, so the day before she'd given her boss a call and asked for a meeting.

It felt been ages since she'd set foot in Duffy Masterson and although Frank had been amenable to the idea of her return he had a few reservations about her abilities.

A detailed report from Hannah should allay these worries, lthough Abby knew that if he *did* let her come back, her performance would be under the spotlight for a while.

But that was the way things were going to be from now on. Everything she said and did would be assessed and examined for signs of anything out of the ordinary.

She should be used to it by now ...

The meeting went reasonably well, all her old colleagues greeted her enthusiastically upon her arrival, but for some reason Frank still seemed reluctant. "I'm just not sure Abby," he said. "This business can be very stressful as you know."

"Maybe instead of being reassigned to my usual clients, I could start by working on some of the smaller stuff?"

By this she meant the more straightforward accounts, clients usually pawned off on trainees. She supposed she couldn't blame him for being wary – until she'd proved herself up to the task she herself couldn't be sure how she would perform.

"Abby, I'm sure you'd be fine with the numbers, but it's only been six months and the doctors recommended at least a year, didn't they?"

"I know, but I'm going out of my mind with nothing to do." The list had kept her occupied for the last while, but now that she'd come back down to earth, Abby was bored.

Frank looked guilty. "I'm sorry," he said again. "Believe me, I'd like nothing better than to have you back, but at the same

time I don't want to be responsible for … well you know …
anything going wrong."

She supposed she could appreciate his position; still, it was
disheartening to think people were still suspicious of her capabilities, even though she'd proved time and time again both to
herself and everyone else, that she was *fine*.

"If you don't mind my saying so, I think that old bump on
the head might have done you a bit of good actually," Frank
joked. "You seem way more relaxed these days."

"In all honesty, you're not the first person to think that. I
know I probably wasn't the most fun person to have in the
office." She smiled. "If anything, it's taught me that I shouldn't
take life so seriously, so yeah."

"Sure come back to me in a few months time and we'll see
how you are then, how does that sound?" Frank smiled, giving
her the elbow once and for all.

"OK then," Abby agreed with a sigh, wishing that everyone
would just have a little more faith.

AFTERWARDS, she grabbed a takeaway coffee and bagel,
deciding to go into Stephen's Green for lunch.

She and about a hundred others, Abby thought ruefully, all
trying to make the most of the rare sunshine. She was just
about to choose a patch of grass to sit on when she spotted an
elderly couple vacate a bench.

Glad of the opportunity to eat in comfort, she was just
about to claim it when she spotted a blind man and his guide
dog about to do the same. Hesitating a little, she let him take
the seat instead.

"There's plenty of room," the man offered, evidently sensing
her presence, or perhaps he was only partially blind.

Slightly thrown, Abby wasn't sure what to do. "Oh, it's fine,"
she began, not entirely comfortable with the dog's proximity,

although this one seemed quiet. Course, assistance dogs were known for their calm temperament. "I I can always sit on the ..." Her voice trailed off when she realised the man was looking at her strangely. And yes, he was definitely looking, not just in her direction or straining to make her out. He was *looking* at her and he was smiling.

"Well hello," he said with a broad grin. "Fancy bumping into you here."

He seemed so sure he knew her that Abby didn't how to respond. "Um, I'm so sorry," she began, mortified, "but I think you've mistaken me for someone else. It's understandable, of course ... I mean ..." she babbled on, wishing the ground would open up and swallow her.

But at this, he started to laugh. "No, this isn't ... I'm not blind," he chuckled, glancing at the dog who dutifully wagged its tail.

Abby frowned. "You're not?"

"No. This isn't my guide dog, well she *is* mine but," he broke off, shaking his head. "Sorry I can see why you're confused. There's nothing wrong with my eyesight and," his voice dropped to a whisper, "she's not actually a guide dog."

He grinned conspiratorially and again Abby was struck by the familiar way he spoke, as if they'd met before.

But had they? She didn't think so. He was very good looking with dark brown hair and even darker eyes, and she was pretty certain she would've remembered someone who looked....

Then all of a sudden, her heart skipped a beat, and a trickle of fear began to crawl along her spine.

"I'm sorry, where did you say you knew me from?" she asked, somehow managing to find her voice.

"Well, New York of course," he replied, as if this was a stupid question. "On Christmas Eve? We met in Central Park when the squirrels made away with your sandwich ..."

At this, something niggled in the corner of Abby's mind–something she couldn't quite get a handle on. When there was no immediate recognition on her part, he continued on. "I spent the afternoon showing you round the city, we did the whispering thing in Grand Central Station and went up to the Top of the Rock? Don't tell me you can't remember?"

Heart hammering, Abby racked her brain, trying furiously to figure out where all of this was coming from. She remembered being in New York of course–remembered staying with Claire and Zach in their apartment. And she remembered the family having a really nice Christmas together and going to St Patrick's Cathedral for Midnight Mass, but that was about it.

She certainly had *no* recollection of meeting some strange guy, let alone spending an afternoon with him on Christmas Eve. So clearly he *must* be mistaken–

"Abby?" he queried, and at the mention of her name, her entire world began to spin. He really *did* know her. Which could only mean …

"Are you all right? Bloody hell, you've gone as white as a sheet."

Those were the last words she heard before her head filled with stars, and Abby's world went black.

CHAPTER 30

THE DAY HAD STARTED REASONABLY WELL.

The weather was warm, the skies clear and bright and since today was Finn's day off he'd decided to head into town, taking Lucy along for company.

The two had taken the bus into the city, and disembarked at O'Connell St. Despite the crowds, Lucy weaved through the throngs, negotiating their route with practised ease. Finn was gratified that she hadn't forgotten any of her previous training.

Once a guide dog always a guide dog, and speaking of which… He reached into his rucksack and strapped a visibility vest on, a cheeky little trick that ensured the two got access to every public amenity and retail premises in the city. OK, so he knew he was being brazen, but it was almost lunchtime, and it wasn't fair to keep her tied up outside while he ate.

Having enjoyed a hearty fry-up in one of his favourite café's, he and Lucy eventually continued walking across O'Connell Bridge and onwards to Grafton Street.

"Good girl," Finn praised, proffering a treat when they reached the gates of the Stephen's Green.

Lucy dutifully led him into the park, across the low stone

bridge above the duck pond, and out towards the main seating area where there were lots of people sitting on the grass and park benches, reading newspapers, drinking takeaway coffees and idly watching the world go by.

"Not much chance of a seat around here," he murmured.

Just as he was about to give up, he saw a couple leave a bench nearby. He and Lucy quickly went to claim it at the same time as a woman coming in the other direction.

"You're welcome to sit, there's plenty of space," he said, when she stepped back to let him take it.

"No it's fine ..."

Finn looked up quickly, instantly recognising the voice and trying to get a better look at her face beneath the mane of mid-length curly blonde hair. "Well hello again," he exclaimed, smiling. "Fancy bumping into you here."

To his immense embarrassment, she didn't seem to register any recognition whatsoever, so much so that for a brief second he worried that he'd made a stupid mistake. But no, it definitely *was* her; he would recognise those huge eyes anywhere. He hadn't changed that much since, had he? OK, so today he looked a bit shabby and was in badly need of a shave but ...

Then spotting she was staring uncomfortably at Lucy, he understood. Of course!

Finn chuckled, explaining about the dog and the fact that he wasn't actually blind. But when he tried to jog her memory about how they'd met in Central Park, something very strange happened.

The girl (Abby, he remembered) suddenly looked frightened out of her wits. "Are you OK?" he asked.

And to Finn's complete and utter astonishment the poor girl out-and-out fainted.

· · ·

ABBY OPENED HER EYES, feeling something wet and cold on her face. She sat up quickly, wondering how she'd ended up on the ground and why a huge, scary-looking dog was resting alongside her, watching her intently!

Then she noticed a man standing over her holding a bottle of water, and in an instant remembered what had happened. She'd fainted, she realised, mortified.

"Are you OK?" the man asked, his dark eyes full of concern. "I tried to catch you, but you slid off and onto the ground before I even realised."

"Sorry," she said, trying to stand up and get some distance from the scary mutt.

"Here," He held out his hand, and still keeping a wary eye on the dog, she took it, glad of the assistance. "Just sit there and take it easy for a while," he said, helping her onto the bench. "Do you want a drink of water or anything? I used a few drops on your face to try and wake you up, didn't have any smelling salts on me today sorry," he added with a grin. "Or if you want to wait there, I can always nip across for some hot chocolate?" He smiled. "Won't be half as good as that stuff we had in New York, but ..." he shrugged easily.

It was all so ... so surreal having a complete stranger come up to her in the park and start chatting as if he knew her well, talking about things of which Abby had absolutely no recollection.

Could it be some kind of joke? Or worse, she realised now, her stomach plummeting, was it simply proof that the doctors had been right all along ...

The thought was too much to bear and without warning, Abby began to sob. As she did, the dog moved to rest its large head on her lap and she jumped back, terrified.

"Don't be afraid, Lucy's only trying to trying to comfort you."

"I'm just not ... I'm kind of scared of dogs actually ..."

215

"Oh, sorry." He instructed it to move away, and to Abby's relief it did. But even so, she still couldn't stop sniffling. "It's OK, I promise," he reassured her.

Brushing away tears, she eventually found her voice.

"I'm sorry," she said, with a shake of her head. "You must think I'm some kind of psycho, fainting and crying, but the thing is, I really *don't* remember any of what you're telling me. I don't remember you, or meeting you in New York. To be honest, now I'm not entirely sure if I actually remember *being* in New York." With that, the tears started again.

He frowned, perplexed. "I don't understand ..."

"I'm not sure that I understand myself," Abby went on. "I mean, I *think* I do but ..." She bit her lip and shook her head. The realisation that she really was losing her memory was hard enough; let alone having to deal with it in front of a complete stranger.

Although as far as he was concerned, he wasn't a stranger at all, was he?

"Hey, you've obviously had a shock," he said kindly. "Why don't I go and get us a couple of coffees, and maybe you can tell me all about it."

Which was how, in the middle of St Stephen's Green with a strange but gentle dog at her feet, Abby spent the rest of the afternoon spilling her heart out to a man she was absolutely sure she'd only just met - but was so understanding and sympathetic it felt as though she'd known him for years.

CHAPTER 31

FINN'S HEAD WAS SPINNING. It was a crazy story, and while it certainly didn't seem as though she was lying, it was incredible and in truth, a bit disheartening that she could have forgotten him.

Disheartening because since that time in New York, he'd hardly been able to forget *her*.

He'd been there for a training seminar held by *Guide Dogs of America* and recalled how pissed off he'd been about his return flight home being cancelled. And while he'd been able to arrange another for later that evening, it wasn't much fun having to wait at JFK for hours, especially on Christmas Eve.

So instead of hanging around, he'd decided to take a cab back into central Manhattan and spend a few hours killing time there, maybe arrange to meet up with an old friend of his who worked on Park Avenue.

But while his mate had originally been all for meeting him for lunch, he'd had to cancel, which was how Finn had ended up having lunch with Abby, who for some reason, thought his name was Phil.

Back then, he'd taken it exactly for what it was—two

complete strangers brought together unexpectedly amidst the charm of a New York Christmas. But since his return, his thoughts had more than once strayed to the girl he'd bumped into, the one who'd laughed at his jokes and had been almost childishly impressed by everything he'd shown her.

So when today they'd run into each other and she hadn't the faintest iota who he was, well there was no doubt it had an effect on the old ego.

Though any disappointment he might have felt couldn't be anywhere close to the anguish and worry she was experiencing now.

"The doctors were right in the end," Abby said finally, having relayed to Finn the events of the past six months. The defeated look on her face and utter hopelessness in her tone almost broke his heart in two. "I was an idiot to think I could have prevented this."

"You don't know that for certain," he replied, not entirely sure how to handle this but at least wanting to try. "You've remembered everything else that's happened since then, haven't you?"

She crumpled up her empty coffee cup and shook her head sadly. "I don't know ...I *think* I have, but I've been keeping records of everything...so now I can't tell if it's my own memory, or the digital memory that's storing them for me."

Finn sat forward on the bench. "Does it really matter?"

"What do you mean?"

"I'm not trying to be flippant but does it really matter how or where these memories are stored as long as they're *some-where*? If your own memory is fading, but you're backing up albeit digitally, then you'll still be able to recall stuff whenever you like, won't you?" He shrugged his shoulders. "Honestly, I wished *I'd* thought of doing something like that, keeping a record of my experiences as they happened. I've travelled all over the world, but can only really recall some things now–

like those monkeys in Thailand." When she looked blank he quickly realised that if she couldn't remember meeting him, she'd hardly remember his thieving monkeys story. "Anyway, what I'm trying to say is that by keeping an account of this stuff, you really do get to hold onto it forever."

To his satisfaction, Abby seemed a bit heartened.

"I suppose I've never thought of it that way," she sighed. "Maybe that's exactly why stuff feels so vivid in my mind. And why I got such a shock when I met you. As far as I was concerned, New York was *also* still fresh in my mind, but seems it's only the bits I wrote about." She looked away, trying to blink back tears.

"You didn't think enough of me to write about it?" he teased, and to his relief, she raised a smile. "Look, you've had a shock, and I'm sure you have a lot to think about. But try not to be too hard on yourself Abby. So what if you don't remember me, big deal. It's nothing compared to all the amazing things you've seen and done recently." He breathed out. "I suppose what I'm trying to say is, don't abandon all hope. This could just be a tiny blip like those others you described, nothing major. So, go home, take it easy and have another chat with your doctor. But don't let this set you back. From what you've told me, you've been having a blast. What's to stop that continuing?"

She smiled. "Thanks but maybe I knew deep down that something like this was going to happen. There were a couple of other things … little things, but I ignored them, I wanted to ignore them." Then she looked at her watch. "I really should be thinking about heading home. I've already taken up enough of your time."

"I'm only sorry that meeting me was what brought this on." As much as he'd wanted to bump into her again, Finn now had mixed feelings about it.

"Please don't be. I'm glad I met you, honestly. You've been

great, and probably the only person who hasn't looked at me like I'm crazy for even thinking I could beat this."

"Crazy is the last word I'd use," he replied softly. "To be honest, I think you're very brave."

The two were silent for a moment before Abby spoke again. "I know this might sound weird, seeing as you hardly know me..." she said, her voice trembling, "and you can tell me to get lost if you like ... but the thing is I really need to know if– "

Oddly, he understood immediately. "You want to find out if you can remember me again after today?"

"I'm sorry, I know I have no right to ask..."

"Of course you do and for my part, I'm very glad you did."

"Are you sure? I don't want you to feel as though you're part of some weird experiment."

"It's not like that. Actually, it cuts both ways because I'm interested in finding out if I've made a lasting impression *this* time round," he joked, and this time she actually laughed. "OK then, so how do you want to work it?"

This was important to Abby and he wasn't going to minimise it. Hell, it was important to *him*.

Having finally met a woman who'd roused his interest, wasn't it just Finn's luck that the next time they met, she might not know him from Adam ...?

CHAPTER 32

EXACTLY TWO WEEKS LATER, Finn rang the doorbell.

"Hello?" A friendly voice that definitely wasn't Abby's drifted out of the intercom.

"Um, hi," he said, speaking nervously into it. "I'm here to see Abby."

"Oh. OK, just a sec, I'll buzz you up," the girl replied in a breezy tone that buoyed his confidence somewhat.

But then upstairs Abby opened the door, and spotting the completely blank look on her face, Finn's heart sank to the floor.

"Hello ..."

They'd discussed it of course. What would happen if their experiment failed, and Abby didn't appear at their agreed meeting point. He'd waited there for a full hour past the time, all the while stupidly trying to convince himself that there might be a perfectly normal explanation for her non-appearance.

He'd also arrived a half hour early, just in case. But when eight o'clock came and went and Abby still didn't appear, Finn knew that her worst fears had been realised.

She'd forgotten the meeting, which meant that she'd forgotten him too.

Worse, it also meant that as far as she was concerned, their conversation in the Green had never happened, so in effect, she still believed her memory was fine. This was the bit that had worried him the most and what had almost stopped him from following through with the second part of their agreement.

Though they both knew that this was the only way it could work.

She looked at him now, her expression so untroubled and innocent of what was to come that he almost turned and ran.

But he knew he couldn't; he'd made her a promise, and whether she knew it or not, she was depending on him.

"You were looking for me?" she urged politely.

"Abby, hi. My name is Finn and I'm here because I have something very important to tell you." They'd rehearsed what he'd say if things didn't work out, and while it sounded reasonable at the time, now he thought it came across a bit melodramatic.

As expected, she was taken aback. "What? What's all this–"

"Everything all right?" The other girl appeared in the doorway. "What's taking you so …oh hello," she said.

Finn swallowed, suddenly at a loss, though it made him feel a whole lot more comfortable having somebody Abby trusted. Then he remembered Abby mentioning her best friend.

"You're Erin?"

"That's me," she said, and there was a brief silence as she looked from him to Abby, evidently seeking an introduction.

"I'm Finn," he told her. "Um, this is kind of difficult to explain, but I'm sort of a friend of Abby's…" his voice trailed off when he saw her staring at him in bewilderment. "If you could just – "

"For heaven's sake, come in," Erin ordered, much to Abby's chagrin.

"I'd better not, thanks."

"I'm sorry, but what do you want?" Abby asked, her tone suspicious now. "And how do you know Erin?"

Finn cleared his throat yet again.

"Abby, this is going to sound strange, and I know you think you don't know me, but just hear me out." He took a deep breath, trying to remember all word for word. "I know about your accident and that you've spent the last few months trying to live your best life in the hope of overcoming your prognosis." The fear in her eyes was enough to stop any man in his tracks, but still Finn refused to break stride. "I know you lost over a grand on roulette in Las Vegas, most of it on black 17. I know that you really wish you'd had the guts to hit one-hundred-and-eighty in the Ferrari. I know you never felt as close to your mother as when she took your hand at the high notes in *Aida*. I know that you when you tried on that ballgown in London, you wished that ..." He looked down at his notes, "that Kieran could have seen you in it, just so you could prove him wrong." Finn gulped, as all at once he saw her expression change from wariness, bewilderment to outright panic. "I know all of these things are deeply personal. But I only know about them because you told me about them last time we met," he blurted, eager to get it all out now. "You told me to help gain your trust in telling you something else you already know."

"Who *are* you and why are you doing this?" Abby cried, her eyes filling with tears. "Get out of here!"

"I'm sorry, but I had no choice ..." Finn went on, troubled by her despair. "We both agreed that this was the only way ..."

At the sound of raised voices, Erin reappeared, her friendliness of earlier quickly displaced. "What the hell is going on?"

Abby turned on her heel and raced back inside.

"I'm so sorry, I didn't mean to upset anyone," he said, with a despondent shake of his head. "Well, I guess I knew it would upset her of course but ..." He struggled to explain then trailed off, realising how outrageous it sounded.

"Hold on, you're telling me Abby *knew* there was a problem?" Erin frowned. "But she never said a word."

"She didn't want to in case it was just a one-off, a freak occurrence. So she asked me to help."

"Which was how you knew my name."

"Yes, she told me all about your road-trip to California, lots of personal things. We thought it would help her take what I had to say in good faith."

Erin was silent for a moment, and seemed to be considering this. "So you two met on Christmas Eve, and she didn't remember a thing?"

"Yes ... wait, how did you know it was Christmas Eve?"

She sighed and Finn couldn't decide if it was one of resignation, or relief. "Because we've *all* known that things weren't right with Abby, but none of us had the heart to break it to her."

CHAPTER 33

"An interesting development," Hannah said, which Abby thought was putting it mildly.

She'd spent the entire weekend holed up at home with Erin. She couldn't believe that after everything she'd done, how hard she'd tried to defeat it, her memory really was failing.

She hadn't done anything to make it better, it was pointless even trying. And to make things worse it seemed everyone else had known that too. Erin confided that they'd all been aware of some 'blips'.

"They knew you didn't remember who Michael Buble was when you got those tickets," she confessed. "And Dermot mentioned something about sugar in your coffee?" She put a comforting arm around her friend. "I noticed a few things in California myself too, like a blank look you'd sometimes have in conversation. To us they were red flags but because you were so determined, we didn't have the heart to shatter your illusions."

Now, sitting in Hannah's purple armchair, her arms wrapped tightly around her body, Abby looked at the psychologist.

"I can't believe it," she said croakily. "I just can't believe that this is really happening."

"I know you don't want to hear it but this was what I was trying to tell you all along. But there are also some positives. Now you know you can't rely on your memory for everything, but since it's episodic memories you're losing it's not the end of the world."

"Not the end of the world? Hannah, I have absolutely no recollection of meeting that guy before yesterday. But I *do* remember New York."

"Remember, back at our first meeting when I explained the difference between episodic and semantic memories, and I asked you to tell me what you remembered about 9/11?"

Abby nodded.

"Well, let's use that to make sense of what's happening here. You remember being in New York with your family because you've all spoken about and shared the experience since. But, what you actually remember is the semantic version of events, not the episodic. And through talking and reminiscing with your family, you reinforced the experience."

"You're saying that my memories of New York aren't real?"

"Of course they're real Abby, it's your recollection of them that's important. Cast your mind back now to Claire's apartment and tell me what colour her front door is, or precisely how the dining table was decorated for Christmas dinner."

To her dismay, Abby realised that no matter how hard she tried, she couldn't do it, couldn't actually put herself back in Claire's apartment. She couldn't remember any of the specifics, other than the dinner, the Christmas presents and all the other things that the family did together. It was weird and very scary, but at least it gave her some idea of what Hannah was talking about.

"Abby, I know it's hard, but try to take some positives out of this. OK so most of it has faded but yet you did in fact retain a lot of that visit, which us tells that your memory can cope through continuity. And as I said, reinforcement is obviously hugely important too."

"I don't know what that means."

"Well, because your family remembered their own recollections of it reinforced your memory. Your memory of it is essentially anchored by theirs. While you appear to have no recollection of wandering around by yourself, because this memory hasn't been reinforced –you were on your own for most of it. The only person that could have reinforced it was Finn. Yet by the time you bumped into him, the memory was lost." She paused slightly, trying to make things as simple as possible. "I suppose it's a bit like studying for exams. We take in a huge amount of information just for the exam, but unless this information is reinforced, our recollection of it tends to fade. It's not quite the same thing as what's happening here, but it's a reasonable comparison."

"OK." Abby nodded but it didn't make her feel any better. "But I don't see how knowing this is supposed to help me."

"Well, for one thing we now know that the quality of your memories are dependent on continuity and reinforcement. And Abby, you've already come up with a means to supply both of those things."

"I have?"

"Yes." Hannah declared, as if it was the most obvious thing in the world. "With your diaries and photographs and all the mementos you saved. Abby, by making a digital backup of day to day life and bigger events as they happen, you've actually given yourself the means to hold onto them–and ensure that they're never really lost for good. While we all do this to a certain extent, you've actually taken it to another level."

"So you're saying that it's OK if some of my memories fade, because I've backed them up elsewhere?"

"I'm just saying that's one way to look at it. While your

memory will inevitably end up losing some things, you have the means to hold onto the more important ones too."

While the notion made Abby feel a little better, it still raised other, perhaps more troubling questions. For one, was this the worst it was going to get? That she'd be able to retain stuff for about a week, but unless she kept a backed-up account, the memory could fade away forever.

Would she need to spend the rest of her life living vicariously through digital backups?

CHAPTER 34

June 14th, Dublin

Hard to believe how close Finn and I have become now. And while I truly honestly can't recall meeting him those other times, it now feels as though I've known him forever.

Clichéd I know, but in this case true.

After a long chat that first (or should I say third?) time we met, he called over a few days later to help me, as he described it 'fill in the blanks'.

I'm so sad I can't remember our day in New York – it sounds wonderful, especially the Christmas tree and the lunch in Central Park. It all comes across like such a fairytale that if I didn't know better, or trust him so completely I don't think I would have believed it. Still, I think he's probably embellished a few things here and there – just to make himself sound better.

Not that he has to try too hard.

But one time, he gave me an awful shock. I opened the door to find him with a huge dog. Nearly had a heart attack, but then, a very weird thing happened.

The dog just sat down patiently on its hindquarters and I felt an unbelievably strong sense of déjà vu.

229

"This is Lucy," Finn said. "You two have met before and I know she's anxious to make sure you're OK."

"We have?" But some instinct told me that there was no need to be afraid, and he must have been telling the truth because somehow I knew I could trust this dog.

And Lucy is kind of cute, especially the way she so obviously dotes on Finn. The second time he brought her for a visit, she moved to where I was sitting and nudged me. "She wants you to pet her," Finn informed.

So sure enough, I moved my hand down to rest on the back of her head. And as I did, I was amazed (and actually quite pleased) to see her huge tail thump from side to side.

So I think Lucy is definitely growing on me.

How do I feel now that I know my memory is really banjaxed? Terrified mostly, but as Hannah keeps saying, at least I've established a way around it. It is a bit surreal having to take time out every day to keep thorough accounts of ordinary stuff like now.

When I was doing it for Vegas and London and everything it didn't seem so ... necessary.

And if this is all I need to do to lead a normal life then is it really too much to ask ...

"CAN I ASK YOU SOMETHING?"

Since Abby discovered the truth about her prognosis, Finn had spent almost every waking moment by her side.

Now she was making coffee at her place when he broached a question. "Did you remember to put the sugar in?" he asked and with a start, Abby realised that maddeningly, she hadn't.

"What did you want to ask?" she prompted, adding the requisite sugar before joining him on the sofa.

"Tell me if I'm being nosy, but remember that time I came to tell you about ... everything?"

Sweet that weeks later he was *still* embarrassed about

having to put her through that, when the truth was, he'd done her a favour. Granted it didn't feel like that initially, but subsequent sessions with Hannah, and the psychologist's insistence that she had a workaround, had lifted her spirits.

As had Finn's visits.

"OK, bad word choice." He chuckled. "That list you gave me... of stuff to tell you, personal stuff. Do you mind my asking who is Kieran, and what exactly did you want to prove him wrong about?"

Abby bit her lip. "My ex," she said quietly, and he nodded as if he'd guessed as much. "Things ended pretty badly between us, well bad for me anyway. We were together for over five years, and within a year of our break-up, he'd married someone else."

Finn sucked air through his teeth. "That's tough."

"Not as tough as finding out that while I'd always assumed we were heading for happily ever after, he was just filling in time waiting for something better."

"Oh, come on," Finn began to protest. "I sincerely doubt that –"

"I'm not just surmising," she interjected firmly, a knot in her stomach as she thought about it. "I know this because he told me."

"What?"

She nodded. "One day he came home from work and out of the blue told me that he wanted to finish things, that he'd found someone else. But out of respect for me, apparently," she added rolling her eyes, "he wasn't going to take up with her until it was over. I know what you're thinking," she said, when Finn went to say something. "It sounded lame to me too but he was always straight up like that, too straight sometimes." Apparently he'd been biding his time for ages, waiting for the right moment. "So after I'd picked myself up off the floor, I tried to figure out where all of this had come from, how he found it so easy to cast me aside." She looked down and began to study a piece of carpet. "And he said, surely we both knew you were never the kind of woman I'd marry?'"

Finn seemed appalled. "Arsehole."

"I've never told anyone that, you know; what he said. It was too embarrassing and worse, all too easy for me to believe. I've never been good at the whole fashion and dressing up thing," she told him wryly. "So then in London, when I tried on that dress…"

"For goodness sake, the guy was an idiot," Finn muttered. It was endearing, but it was what he said next that really made Abby smile. "And you don't need some posh dress to prove him wrong, not when you'd look great in a bloody bin bag."

Spontaneously, she threw her arms around him. "Thank you. You don't know how much better that's made me feel."

He hugged her back at first but then broke away. There was a brief tension-filled moment as their eyes met and, before Abby knew what was happening, they were kissing.

He tasted of fresh coffee and his skin smelt of soap and she felt the prickle of his stubble at the corner of her mouth, while her hands ventured under his arms and down to the small of his back. She didn't stop to think about whether or not this was a good idea.

All she knew was that she was kissing Finn, someone she'd only known a few weeks at the most, practically a stranger … and it felt amazing.

CHAPTER 35

July 1st, Dublin.

So Mum met's Finn now, and to say it was a tense affair would be
an understatement.

When we first arrived she and Dermot did their best to make him
feel comfortable. Dermot chatted to him about football and Caroline
asked him all about the dogs, while Mum just flitted around the place
looking tense and uncomfortable.

"How can something like this possibly work?"

Honestly I think that's part of the reason I've become so close to
Finn so quickly; he never tries to pretend.

It's like he understands me. I don't know, maybe it's because he's a
dog trainer and is used to people coping with all kinds of challenges?

It is a bit hard for me to believe that I could feel this close to
someone I've just met (I know it was actually longer but I'm still
drawing a blank on that). And after all this time, I think I've finally
managed to forget all about Kieran. Forget him? Ironic, huh?

"Well, you've certainly landed on your feet this time," Erin said. "I'd take a knock on the head any day if it meant a guy like that turned up at my door."

She still hasn't made mention of anyone new, although I still suspect there's something she'd not telling me. But maybe it's still early days, so she doesn't want to jinx it?

Anyway, back to dinner.

Mum was being Mum, making a huge hoo-ha about dinner and who should sit where, so much so that she barely managed a quick hello to Finn when we first arrived.

At times, I get the sense he seems more comfortable around dogs than people, and seeing him visibly relax when telling my mother all about the work they do at the centre makes me certain I'm right.

All the talk about the dogs seemed to soften my mother up a bit too, and for a while it looked as though Finn had charmed her in the same way he had the others.

But after dessert, he put the kibosh on it. Just as we finished up eating, I sat back in my chair and said to Mum. "That was fab, the nicest meal I've had in ages."

"Not sure if that's a compliment," Finn piped up, grinning. "Most of the time poor Abby can't remember what she's had for breakfast."

FINN COULDN'T BELIEVE IT. He'd been so sure Pat would be thrilled he'd finally found someone.

"Lookit, she seems lovely, but who knows what could happen with her in the long run? It's bad enough that she drew a blank on meeting you in America, let alone again here. I know you think you were only trying to help Finn, but really you should've run a mile."

"Abby's fine. OK, well not *fine*, obviously, but she's learning to come to terms with this, and I'm helping her."

"Bloody hell Finn, thirty-five years of age and you're still rescuing things."

His head snapped up. "I can't believe you just said that."

"There's more than a grain of truth in it too, and you know it."

He understood the point his father was trying to make, but this time Pat was wrong. While of course he wanted to help Abby and would do anything to make things better for her, it wasn't just about that. He'd felt something for her in New York and again when they met in the Green–back when he'd known nothing at all about her head injury or the damage it caused. And while the look on her face when he had to break the news was enough to break his heart, it wasn't the reason he was with her now.

"It's not about rescuing Abby," he told his father now. "I care about her."

"Like you cared about that Danielle one, and look what happened there?"

From day one Pat had never accepted his ex but in fairness to him, he'd kept his mouth shut and his oar out, until the day Danni packed her bags and left.

"There are plenty of nice, normal women out there, Finn. Why go for the one that's damaged?"

"Dad that's a terrible thing to say," Finn said, raising his voice. "So she has some problems, big deal. She can get around them, *we* can get around them."

Pat gave a deep sigh. "That's what *I* thought," he said eventually and in the same instant Finn realised he was referring in some way to his long-absent mother.

Something Pat never did.

"What are you talking about?"

Pat sat down on the sofa, and leaned against his walking stick. "I think you know" After a brief pause, he went on. "When I married your mother, she had a problem too."

"What kind of a problem?"

His father sighed. "The same one that stalks the length and

breadth of this country and always has. The demon drink, Finn."

"Mam was an alcoholic?"

"A chronic one," Pat said nodding. "Oh, she wasn't too bad at the beginning, at least not that I knew of. I was aware she liked a drink, sure we all did, but usually on a Saturday night when we were out, but not in the middle of the week with a baby crying in the other room."

Suddenly the significance of what his father was saying hit home. "She drank when I was a baby?"

Pat nodded, his eyes weary. "And every day when you were growing up. You don't remember any of it at all, Finn? Her fast asleep on the kitchen table in the middle of the day, or not being there sometimes when you came in from school?"

Finn now cast his mind back to the day he found out his mother had left, and the broken pieces of glass on the floor. He remembered thinking that Rex must have bumped into the table or something, causing havoc like he usually did. But now, he also recalled noticing a funny smell, a bitter smell that he'd always associated with his mother. One that he now understood must have been whiskey.

"So what happened?" Finn wanted to know now. He'd wanted to know all his life, but had never been able to get Pat to even talk about that day, much less explain it. "What happened to make her leave?"

Pat sighed. "I came home earlier that day to find her passed out on the kitchen table – again. Although I loved the woman dearly, by that stage I was sick to the teeth of what was she doing, to us and our marriage, but more importantly to you. So many times I'd come home from work and find her holed up in her bedroom drinking away while you were downstairs on your own with nothing to eat and no company but poor old Rex. I'll tell you, you got more encouragement and attention from the bloody sheepdog than you ever did from your mother. Sure, you didn't start talking until you were gone two." Pat looked pained. "Imelda might have abandoned me and our marriage long before, but I wasn't going to let her do the same to you. So a few months before that I'd given her an ultimatum, either she stopped drinking or I would insist she leave."

Finn was horrified. "What? How could you do that? She needed help."

"She got help and plenty of it many times through the years," Pat told him in a flat voice. "I told her she had to choose between us–you and me, her family–or the bottle. But as always, Imelda chose the bottle."

Now he looked at Finn. "Son, don't think for a second that it was easy for me. I loved that woman with all my heart–still do. But she had love for one thing and one thing only. And while she'd already ruined our marriage because of it, I couldn't let her ruin our son.

So as I said, I'd told her that this was her last chance, that if she touched another drop, she'd have to leave. I had to, Finn–there was no other way. So when I came home that day earlier–I'll admit I was spot-checking, that's a way of life with alcoholics–and I saw the half-empty bottle of whiskey on the table."

Finn said nothing, and waited for him to continue.

"I sat down in front of her, poured out my heart and soul to the woman, told her what she was doing to our family, and what she would end up doing to her life. But I knew she wasn't taking any of it in. She never did. While she'd promise you the moon and the stars and you'd believe her, the next day she'd be holed up somewhere again. So finally, I put both the bottle and a picture of the three of us together on your Communion day down on the table. And I made her choose."

His voice broke then, and he looked away.

"I'm sorry son, I know it hurts you to hear this now, and it hurts me to have to talk about what I did back then, let alone *do* it. But it was the only way I could ensure you had the best possible chance in life. She was no good to you as a mother. She couldn't handle responsibility like that. So, in the end, as you probably know, she chose the bottle."

Finn ran a hand through his hair, unable to believe what he was hearing. "But where did she go after?"

"She has relations in England, a brother, so I presume she went there initially. I thought the fact that I'd followed through with my threat might be enough to make her realise the significance of it all. But no, she just walked out the door and I haven't heard a word from her since. I thought maybe a birthday or a Christmas card, but nothing."

Finn didn't know how to feel.

"And in case you're wondering, yes of course I tried to track her down, many times over the years, just to make sure she was OK. I loved her Finn, even with everything she'd done. I got in contact with the brother but to be frank, I got the impression he'd washed his hands of it too. So if at any stage you think about the doing the same, just keep in mind that what you find might not necessarily be what you're looking for."

"But why didn't you tell me this before? Why tell me now?"

"Because I knew you'd probably go off on some mad search for her and try to save her, that's just your way. And it would be pointless because I'm sure you've heard said many times before, no one can cure an addict that doesn't want to be cured. So no, I didn't tell you and I still stand by my decision."

Finn cast his mind back to the conversation with Nora he'd overheard that time. Was this what she'd been trying to convince his father to tell him?

"Nora...did she know anything about this?"

"She's been living next door for as long as we've been here, Finn. Of course she knew. Why do you ask?"

Finn went on to explain about what he'd heard and how he'd worried it had been something to do with Pat's health.

"Ah, go away out of that, sure you know I'm fine," his father said, waving an arm in protest. "Anyway," he continued, after a brief pause. "So now you know."

Thinking about it now Finn should have guessed. It was tragic that his father had sacrificed everything to try and ensure he had a better life without her. And Pat was right, had he known the truth then yes, he *would* have moved heaven and earth to try and help his mother, to try and 'save' her, as Pat put it.

But then he remembered the reasons this discussion had come about in the first place.

"It's not like that," he told his father, when Pat again tried to point out the comparisons. "Abby doesn't have an addiction, something that can ruin lives. There might be challenges ahead, but we can get through them, I know we can."

His father didn't seem convinced. And Finn didn't need to read the other man's mind to know that Pat was thinking. *I thought the very same thing.*

But the opportunity to further discuss it was lost, when just then, the phone rang.

"Hey there buddy–still good for the hanging next month?"

Finn had to smile. It was his mate, Chris, whose wedding was coming up. He'd asked Abby to be his plus-one and she'd agreed.

"Of course, looking forward to it. How are you? Not getting cold feet I hope?"

"Nah, nah, nothing like that. Listen, just a quick call really," Chris said, his voice growing serious. "I wasn't sure if you already know, but I thought I tell you that Danielle's coming to the wedding too."

Finn exhaled, not sure how to feel about this. He hadn't

seen his ex in years; and now just when he'd finally found someone else ...

"And," Chris continued, interrupting his train of thought, "there's something else ..."

CHAPTER 36

ABBY STARED AT HER REFLECTION, more nervous about this wedding than she cared to admit. Not only would she be meeting the majority of Finn's friends for the very first time, but she'd also be coming face to face with the famous Danielle.

Maybe she had nothing to worry about, she thought, sitting on the edge of the bed and fastening her shoes. Maybe Danielle was small, cross-eyed and overweight and bushy-haired. And seeing as Abby herself was small, overweight and *frizzy* haired they'd get on like a house on fire. The cross-eyed bit would be the only difference between them and should give Abby a clear advantage over the girl who'd broken her beloved Finn's heart.

As if. From what she could gather from Finn, who really didn't go into too much detail other than the fact that the relationship had ended two years ago, Danielle liked the more glamorous side of life, which was one of the reasons they'd broken up.

On the one hand while she was glad that he'd let her know in advance that his ex would be at this wedding, on the other it made Abby even more nervous about the day than she would have been otherwise.

"Ready?" Finn asked, popping his head around the bedroom door. She'd stayed over the night before so it would make it easier for them to drop off Lucy at his dad's before heading to the wedding.

"As I'll ever be," she replied, exhaling deeply. Thanks to Caroline's shopping spree, Abby–dressed in her Whistles sequinned skirt, satin bodice top (and her beloved Jimmy Choos)–looked considerably better than she felt.

"This should be fun," Finn commented as they climbed into the Jeep–and was it her imagination or did he sound nervous too?

Having dropped off Lucy at Pat's, they arrived at the church and as they pulled into the car park, Abby was vividly reminded of the last time she'd shown up at a wedding.

She grimaced. Ironically, Kieran's wedding was something she could still recall in vivid detail.

Had she really been that much of a lost cause that her only clear memory from before had been such an embarrassing one?

Finn parked and the two headed towards the front of the church to where some guests were standing outside chatting amongst themselves. They were about to go in, when they heard a male voice from nearby.

"Finn Maguire – talk about a blast from the past."

Finn's expression broke into a smile, and taking Abby's hand, he approached a group standing to the right of the doorway. She gulped, now feeling horribly uneasy about the prospect of meeting his friends, or worse his ex.

"Where have you been hiding?" asked a woman, greeting him with a hug and when they'd all finished saying their hellos, he turned and introduced them.

To her relief, Danielle didn't seem to be amongst this particular group and when it was time for everyone to go inside, Abby and Finn entered one of the pews on the groom's side of the church. As they took their seats, she got the distinct impression that he seemed a bit self-conscious, almost as if on the alert for something. Or someone.

Abby was almost sorry she'd agreed to come. If he was this on edge now, what would he be like when his ex was actually in the same room?

"Are you OK?" he asked, when the ceremony was over and everyone began to pile out of the church and back into the sunshine. "You seem very quiet and – "

"Hello Finn," said a throaty female voice from beside them.

It was as if every single one of Abby's nightmares had come true.

Far from the pudgy, cross-eyed munchkin she'd hoped Danielle would be, instead stood a tall, tanned beauty with stunning aquamarine eyes, perfect skin and an even more perfect body, dressed as she was in a wispy chiffon dress whose designer creator Caroline would be able to pinpoint instantly.

Abby didn't care or didn't need to; Danielle was the kind of woman most designers had in mind for their creations–elegant, classy, sexy–and certainly not short, pale, spare tyre-carrying women like Abby.

Finn seemed a bit dazed too; as if over time he'd forgotten how beguiling she was.

"Good to see you," he greeted formally, leaning over to kiss the former love of his life on the cheek and as he did, Abby thought about just slipping away, grabbing a cab home and forgetting all about him.

It wasn't as if it would be that difficult …

But then he surprised her by turning away and reaching for her hand.

"This is Abby," he said, and despite his efforts she still couldn't help but feel like a spare part in the middle of the two, so palpable was the history between them.

"Hi," she said feigning what she hoped was a friendly and confident smile.

"Well, I guess I'll see you both back at the hotel later?" Danielle was saying, and Finn nodded.

"Looking forward to it."

I'm sure you are, Abby thought despondently as she saw the look on his face while he watched her walk away.

She'd been wrong to come here today, and Finn had been wrong to ask her.

Because any fool alive could tell that he was still in love with the woman who'd obviously broken his heart.

FINN'S STOMACH gave a little fillip as he watched Danielle walk away. She was still as stunning as ever, still graceful and elegant. Looks were everything to her, always had been, another reason she'd found living in the country so difficult and so 'pointless' as she used to put it herself.

He'd tried his best, tried to make her feel loved and secure, but she was the kind of woman who could only feel secure if everyone's eyes were on her.

And right then, she was getting her wish. Notwithstanding the bride who should have had all the attention, Danielle was still the show-stopper.

"She seems nice," he heard Abby say from alongside him which quickly brought his mind back to the present and his gaze away from Danielle.

He tried to think of something light-hearted and off-hand to say, something to try and conceal the mixture of emotions he was feeling just then, but nothing came to hand.

"She is," he said simply, as he and Abby headed back to the jeep and followed the rest of the wedding party out of the church grounds.

"I suppose it must be strange seeing her again," she continued, and again Finn couldn't do anything other than agree.

As they drove to the hotel, Abby grew silent, much to Finn's relief. Evidently she understood that he wasn't interested in making idle conversation, and he appreciated it.

In truth, chit-chat was the last thing he wanted just then. He was too busy thinking how he was going to get through the rest of the day with his ex in the same room.

CHAPTER 37

THE DAY WAS TURNING into a nightmare.

Finn had barely said two words on the way to the hotel, and Abby sensed he was completely preoccupied.

When they arrived at the old country hotel where the reception was to be held, she couldn't relax until she'd studied the seating plan and discovered that Finn's ex was mercifully seated at a different table.

She didn't know any of his friends and it was very difficult to get to know them when it was obvious they saw her as something of a curiosity.

"So you really don't remember anything unless you make a record of it?" Jayne, one of the wives probed. All the women were left seated together around a table in the lounge while the men were up at the bar.

Abby shifted self-consciously in her seat. Her situation wasn't easy to explain at the best of times, let alone to a group of strangers.

"It's a bit strange I know, but I've just had to learn to live with it." She didn't elaborate any further, hoping that they'd understand she was uncomfortable talking about it.

"So you might not remember meeting *any* of us today?" another woman said, with a hefty dose of scepticism.

Abby went on to explain Hannah's 'reinforcement' theory but could sense that most of it was going right over their heads.

"It must be really tough for Finn," another persisted and Abby tensed, wishing they could change the subject, and because such a comment had understandably touched a nerve.

"Finn's not *that* easy to forget," joked someone, whose name Abby couldn't recall. Lyndsay? "I think it's great that you guys are managing to work it out," she said, evidently sensing her discomfort. "We're all thrilled to see him happy again."

Jayne nodded. "Yes, to be honest, after Danni we were all worried he might never...well, you know."

Abby just smiled, unwilling to betray her insecurities.

"Doesn't she look amazing today too?" another commented.

"Stunning," Jayne nodded vigorously. "That dress really suits her, although I have to say I thought the plunging neckline was a bit much."

"So soon after the surgery?" Frances enquired, and at this, Abby's ears pricked up. Hmm...evidently the paragon's beauty wasn't completely natural? "You know Danielle, always likes to make a statement."

It was bad enough having Finn going all gooey-eyed over his ex, let alone his friends rubbing it in about how amazing she looked.

"Well it's about time..." The girls' husbands eventually pulled up seats at the table, Finn having been waylaid by another guest on the way. "I thought you lot had abandoned us."

"Abby, I was just telling Finn I think he really landed on his feet with you," Frances' husband, Ray piped up.

She smiled, relieved that at least *one* of Finn's friends didn't seem to think he'd made the mistake of his life by walking away from the wonderful Danielle. "Really, why's that?"

"Because if you two have an argument, he doesn't have to put up with all the sulking and pouting afterwards." Ray chuckled and winked at Abby, clearly delighted by his own wit. "Sure, won't the whole thing be forgotten about in the morning?"

As THE NIGHT wore on and wine started to take effect, Abby gradually began to relax and enjoy herself.

She and Lyndsay were quick onto on the dance floor when the happy couple finished their first dance and the band ramped up the tempo.

Finn had disappeared somewhere after the meal and hadn't returned to the table since. Abby tried to convince herself that there was nothing strange about this; it was his friend's wedding after all and there were plenty of people he hadn't seen in a while.

Around midnight, she agreed to accompany Lyndsay outside to the terrace for a cigarette.

"I can't help it, I've been off them for months but the drink is wearing me down," the other girl persuaded. "Roger would kill me if he caught me. Come on, you can keep a look-out."

If Abby hadn't agreed, she would never have spotted Danielle and Finn sitting together on a bench nearby.

Engaged in deep conversation, the two seemed oblivious, immersed in their own private cocoon. Abby would never have spotted the way he looked at his ex, his head inclined closely towards hers, the way he shook his head and smiled at whatever she'd said. Then Danielle was tracing a finger along Finn's cheek...

Lyndsay's words swam out of focus as Abby stared wordlessly, unable to believe what she was seeing.

Why would he do that? And in front of all these people?

"I have to go," she muttered, rushing inside before the other woman could react. What did it matter?

She hurried back to the table to retrieve her things, barely registering the inquiring looks on the others' faces, before going outside to reception to call a cab. She'd been a fool to think that Finn would choose someone like her over Danielle, someone like her over *anyone* else Abby realised, pacing out front as she waited for her cab.

A true case of deja vu as she got into a taxi and rushed away from another wedding.

Still, she realised, her thoughts racing; this time Abby had a sure-fire way of ensuring that Finn's betrayal wouldn't hurt as much as Kieran's.

That the image of Finn and his ex together wouldn't keep replaying itself over and over in her mind the way the image of Kieran marrying someone else had.

Thank goodness that this time, she had foolproof way of ensuring she'd never have to experience that kind of pain again.

CHAPTER 38

A LITTLE WHILE, Finn appeared at her flat.

"What's going on?" he demanded. "Why did you just leave? I thought something might have happened, that you might have had some kind of ... episode maybe."

"As if you'd care," Abby shot back, overwhelmed by the intensity of her feelings. She'd shared everything with him, her fears and worries and insecurities. She'd fallen heavily for him and he'd thrown it back in her face.

What else was new?

"Why wouldn't I care?" he asked, frowning. "Why are you being like this Abby? What the hell happened?"

"What the hell happened?" She couldn't believe he was even asking her that. "You and Danielle sitting and cuddling in a corner happened. You not being able to take your eyes off her all day happened. Why bring me to that wedding when all you wanted was to get close to your ex?"

"Abby calm down, you've got it all wrong."

"I might have a head injury but I'm not stupid. Don't patronise me. I saw the way the two of you looked at one another.

She was stroking your cheek, and the two of you were holding hands …"

Finn breathed out heavily. "You have it wrong. Yes, Danielle and I were sitting together, and yes it felt a bit strange seeing one another again. I told you before that things didn't end well with us and…"

"End? To me it looked like nothing at all had ended, in fact, it looked like everything was about to begin all over again. What I can't understand is why you thought you felt it was OK to string me along all this time, when you were still in love with her," she said, her voice breaking. "Or were you just planning to carry on regardless, because even if I did find out you were sneaking around, I wouldn't remember anyway?"

"Abby, please calm down…"

"Actually I'm perfectly calm. And it doesn't matter, because unlike what I told your friends, I have absolutely no plans to make a record of today; in fact I have no plans to keep a record of *anything* about us." She looked away, and tried to blink back tears.

"What are you talking about?"

"We made a mistake thinking we could make a go of this, so there's no need for you to feel guilty about it. In time I'll have forgotten you anyway. So go on back to your precious Danielle. I won't stop you."

"I don't understand," he said frowning. "What are you saying?"

Her jaw tightened. "It means that I got rid of it all - the archive it's all gone."

He looked horrified. "You deleted the files?"

"Yep." Her mouth was set in a firm line.

It was liberating in a way; it meant that instead of spending months mourning Finn's absence, she could do it with the flick of a switch. What broken-hearted woman in the world *hadn't*

251

wished for that? A way to magic away all the hurt and pain of a broken relationship?

"I don't believe you," he was saying. "You would throw away all we have just because you think you saw something between me and an ex?"

"I *know* what I saw."

"No, you don't. What you saw was two people who hadn't spoken in a very long time catching up."

She stared at him. "Do you normally catch up with people by crawling all over them?"

"I wasn't crawling all over her. It was emotional, yes, but you really don't know what you're talking about."

"Clearly I don't. But I know what I saw. And goodness knows your friends kept going on about how well she looked and how affected you were."

His head snapped up. "What? Who said that?"

"Frances - and Jayne, talking about how wonderful she looked. It's obvious they think you're still in love with her, so I know it's not just me being paranoid."

"Abby–"

"Did you think I wouldn't notice that you went all quiet and unresponsive after bumping into her outside the church?"

"Abby stop it please," Finn said, his voice rising in frustration. "You've got it all wrong."

"How could I - ?"

"Danielle's sick," he cut in flatly.

"What?" she frowned, looking up. "What are you talking about?"

"She got breast cancer. I found out from Chris a week ago. He thought he should say something before I bumped into her at the wedding."

Instantly, Abby's mind flashed back to Frances and Jayne's comments about Danielle's low neckline and the mention of surgery. She'd immediately assumed they were talking about cosmetic surgery; she certainly hadn't considered for a *second* that it could be anything else…

"That's why I went quiet after meeting her outside the church," Finn went on. "I just didn't know how to react. I knew I'd have to say something …" He shook his head. "Abby, I spent three years of my life with Danielle and I cared about her a lot–I still do–but not in the way you think," he added quickly. "I wanted to express support, let her know that if she needed anything …"

Abby thought back again to the two of them on the terrace, how intimate they'd looked. Straight away she'd assumed they were being flirtatious but thinking about it now …

"I'm sorry …I had no idea…I couldn't have imagined …" She shook her head, ashamed. "When I saw you two together, I just assumed…she's so beautiful… and you'd been acting so strangely…"

"Abby, what Danielle and I had is long gone. I'll admit that hearing about it from Chris and then seeing her today knocked me for six. I wanted to let her know that we're all rooting for her, that we're all hoping she comes through it."

"And how is she?"

He shrugged. "Same as anyone would be. It's difficult to explain but for a woman like Danielle…" he shook his head. "She's always been very insecure about her looks."

A woman like that insecure? Abby couldn't comprehend it.

"I know what you're thinking, but believe me it's one of the reasons we split up. Danielle needs to be reassured of how wonderful she is and how amazing she looks. That's why she hated moving to the sticks. It was a world away from the bright lights and glamour of Dublin. Here in the city, she got all the reassurance she needed, but way out there…"

Abby didn't know what to think. If such a beautiful woman wasn't comfortable in her own skin then what hope was there for anyone?

"Before you ask, I don't know *why I didn't tell you. I suppose I just wanted to get my own head around it first. I got such a shock, and then to think that I'd be seeing her again after all this time and in those circumstances...to be honest, I just didn't know how to feel. But if I'd known you'd mistake my actions today for something else entirely, well then of course I'd have said something. But I just wasn't thinking straight to be honest. I'm sorry."

Abby moved across the room, and put her arms around him. "No, *I'm* sorry. I shouldn't have been so paranoid, and I shouldn't have doubted you." Standing in his embrace, she looked away guiltily. "But when I saw you two sitting together like that, and you holding her hand..."

Finn kissed the top of her head. "I really thought you'd know I'd never dream of hurting you. My heart went out to her today, but not in the way you thought."

"I know and again, I'm so sorry."

"And the others kept talking about how she looked?" He rolled his eyes. "No wonder women are so paranoid."

They went to sit together on the sofa.

"Were you that mad at me that you were really planning on getting rid of everything?" Finn asked then. "The diaries, letters and photographs, the entire file?"

Abby nodded, a lump in throat.

"You were willing to just wipe me out of your life, without giving me a chance to explain? Abby, I love you, surely you know that?"

Her heart leapt. He *loved* her?

"I've made such a mess of everything." Now she had no choice but to admit the truth. "I really did delete the entire file Finn," she said, afraid to meet his gaze. "It's all gone."

He jumped up from the sofa. "Show me."

Going to her computer, he pulled out a chair and sat in front of it while Abby bit her lip.

What had she done?

But instead, Finn smiled. "You just deleted the file?"

"I know, I'm sorry, but I was so angry and I just wanted to–"

"No, no, it's OK," he said, cutting her off. "You didn't remove it completely; it's still in the recycle bin–look."

"What?" She stared in amazement as he clicked on the desktop icon, where inside the relevant archive was still intact. And within a few clicks keys, fully restored.

"I never even knew that existed," she gasped, now feeling like she'd won the lottery.

She *hadn't* deleted their time together, hadn't thrown away some of the very best memories of her life.

It was still all still there, every last moment.

Finn grinned, and kissed her on the forehead. "You ain't getting rid of me that easily."

CHAPTER 39

THERE WAS no room for mistakes. This had to be perfect–*better* than perfect.

Finn had gone over the plans so many times, he was now seeing it unfold in his sleep.

What had happened at the wedding had galvanised him into action. He loved Abby and needed her to believe that. Given all that was happening he knew she was hesitant and insecure about his feelings and their relationship in general.

"Are you absolutely sure about this?" Pat had said, dubious. "Because this is something you need to be in for the long haul."

"I know that Dad, and it holds no fear for me." Finn didn't intend to make this sound as though he was getting at his father for not being in it for the long haul with his mother, but he couldn't help it if Pat decided to take it that way.

As for his mother, now that he knew the truth he was sure he'd try and locate her at some stage, but not just yet. There were too many other important things going on in his life at the moment and he didn't want to make it any more complicated.

Finn's intentions now were to remove any uncertainty where Abby was concerned and make life a whole lot simpler.

And with any luck, memorable too.

PARIS! Abby couldn't wait. She was so looking forward to getting away - just her and Finn and no worrying mothers and disapproving fathers in the background.

While she was by now used to Teresa's over-protectiveness, Pat Maguire's reaction to their relationship had been hard to take. Finn had confessed about his father's reservations shortly after their heart-to-heart about Danielle.

The problem was that his dad's reaction merely highlighted Abby's own concerns, and what could happen if her prognosis got any worse.

Late Friday evening, they arrived at their Parisian hotel, a romantic Baroque building central to all the popular sights, and had a nice quiet dinner there before heading out afterwards to visit the Eiffel Tower.

Having taken obligatory tourist photos, they decided in the end not to take the elevator up to the observatory as the queues were a mile long, but to Abby the majestic gold-lit structure made the views just as good from ground level.

The following morning after breakfast Finn suggested they pay a visit to Montmartre with its cobblestone streets and maze of narrow alleyways.

Here they spent some time exploring the Sacre Coeur Basilica and its surroundings, and having savoured yet another of the most spectacular sights of the French capital, they wandered hand-in-hand before eventually strolling over to Place du Tertre.

"Oh look," Abby cried with delight. It was very touristy but at the same time so uniquely Parisian that she couldn't help but be impressed. The square was full of French painters and artists dressed in traditional Parisian garb with their striped T-shirts, neck handkerchiefs and black berets. As they ambled along enjoying the buzz and atmosphere, one of the painters approached them.

"Monsieur, Madam, I paint your portrait?" he said, in that irresistible French accent.

Certain that Finn would shush the hawker away, Abby was taken aback when he enquired about the price.

"Ten euro Monsieur," the artist told him.

"Sounds good, why don't you go for it?"

"Me?"

"Hey, you're the photogenic one," he joked.

Abby smiled, liking the idea of an unusual keepsake, so the artist—who told them his name was Pierre (what else?) —set her up on a tiny stool before sitting down at his easel and getting to work.

Pierre worked diligently for about ten minutes, throughout which Finn loitered alongside him keeping a close eye on proceedings. She wished he'd stood in for the portrait too, it would have been nice to have a picture of the two of them together, but she guessed it wasn't really his style.

"Looking good," he said, winking at her.

But when Pierre eventually turned the easel back to show Abby the drawing, she was completely taken aback—and in a good way. The likeness was amazing. Although pity really that it was in black and white; she really would have preferred it to be in colour but …oh some of it was.

"What's this?" she asked, pointing out a necklace he'd included in the drawing, even though she wasn't wearing one. A key-shaped gold-coloured pendant, it was the only detail in full colour, which was why Abby couldn't help but notice it.

"Ah thees'" Pierre explained with a smile, "thees is zee key to happiness."

"Oh OK." Abby inwardly rolled her eyes, realising that this was obviously some kind of a tourist ploy, but since her own likeness was good she wasn't going to complain.

"Merci, thank you very much indeed," Finn said, taking out his wallet to pay Pierre, who rolled up the portrait and tied it with a piece of red ribbon. Then the artist kissed Abby on both cheeks and wished her well.

She had to smile. Touristy or not she was loving this.

Having left Pierre to his work she and Finn continued through the Place du Tertre and down to another street before heading into the quieter, more peaceful Rue de Saules.

The atmosphere was wonderful and so intrinsically French with all the little shops and cafes that Abby was transfixed. A little way down the street, a brightly dressed woman selling jewellery on the pavement smiled at them and waved.

"Let's go take a look," said Finn, leading them towards the street seller, much to Abby's surprise. Evidently Paris was working its magic on him too…

"Something you like, Mademoiselle?" the woman asked, smiling at them both.

"No thanks," Abby said, not particularly blown away by any of the stuff the woman was selling. But then catching sight of something, she stopped short. "Look at this," she exclaimed to Finn, picking up a chain and pendant *identical* to the one Pierre had sketched her wearing. Attached to the chain was a small yellow gold pendant in the shape of an old-style key.

"Ah, you have good taste Mademoiselle," said the street-seller. "All my jewellery hold extraordinary powers, the promise of beauty, good fortune and especially," she added with a smile "everlasting love."

Right, Abby thought sceptically, this was *definitely* an elaborate tourist scam being carried out between the street sellers. Mysterious pendants and everlasting love my foot. Did she have the word 'sucker' written on her forehead or something?

But Finn was smiling.

"That's incredible," he said to the woman, before unfolding the portrait and pointing out the self-same pendant. "What an amazing coincidence."

Abby looked at him, surprised. Clearly he'd decided to just play along for the fun of it.

"Amazing indeed," replied the woman, looking from the portrait back to Abby. "Must be a sign." With that, she picked up the pendant and went to clasp it around Abby's neck. "Here, Mademoiselle, take it, clearly it is destined to be yours."

"Um, no thanks," Abby said, a bit wrong-footed by these intimidating sales tactics. She shot a nervous glance at Finn, who to her surprise, seemed to be finding it all very amusing.

"No, no you misunderstand," the Frenchwoman protested, continuing to hold the chain out to her, "there is no charge, this is a gift – it is yours."

"What?" Now Abby was completely baffled. She looked at Finn who just shrugged.

"She said no charge."

"Ah, but I don't really want it," Abby murmured, as the Frenchwoman finally succeeded in clasping the chain around her neck.

Finn was openly laughing now. "But she says it has magical powers," he said winking at her.

"It is yours. No charge." The seller was determined that Abby should keep the pendant whether she wanted it or not.

"OK then," she said sighing and wondering yet again what the punch line was going to be. Would she now have to buy more jewellery in order for these so-called 'magical powers' to work?

But it seemed there was no punch line; at least none from this street-seller anyway, as satisfied that Abby had accepted her 'gift', the woman smiled and moved on to another customer.

"What on earth was all that about?" she asked, fiddling with the necklace as she and Finn continued on down the street.

"I have no idea, but whatever it was, it was worth it simply for the look on your face. Talk about suspicious." He gave her a sideways glance. "I think it suits you actually."

"But why would anyone just give me a free necklace? I mean, I know its not real gold or anything but …" Then suddenly the thought struck her. Pickpockets. Abby opened her bag and began frantically searching for her purse, but to her relief it was still there. Weird …she'd been certain it was some kind of elaborate diversion to keep her and Finn occupied while an accomplice relieved them of their money.

"I can't believe what a paranoid little mind you have," Finn said, amused by her reaction. "A nice woman gives you a free gift and all you can do is jump to conclusions."

The two of them stopped off at a nearby café, and spent a lovely hour sitting outside on the pavement taking their time over delicious chocolate crepes and a couple of French roast coffees.

"It's beautiful, isn't it?" Abby said, enjoying the laid-back vibe of it all. "Now I understand why people love Paris so much. It's very romantic."

Finn laid a hand on hers. "I'm really glad you're enjoying it."

"How could I not?"

"Well, you've visited so many other amazing places this year … it must be hard to find a favourite."

Abby smiled. "There's a big difference, though isn't there?" she said slightly pink-cheeked as she spoke, "I wasn't with you." Even though he'd told her almost every day since his friend's wedding that he loved her, she kept waiting for the axe to fall and for him to realise that he was taking on too much by being with her. But so far, this hadn't happened.

After lunch, they continued strolling along the same narrow Parisian streets, Abby lightly fingering the pendant as she walked, still trying to figure out why the street-seller had gifted it to her.

Then out of the corner of her eye, she noticed an agitated-looking man running down the street towards them. He seemed to be in a bit of a panic and kept anxiously looking behind him as if afraid he was being followed.

Suddenly the man rushed up to her and Finn, and looked behind him once more, before reaching into his jacket and pulling out a … well, it looked like some kind of *box*, Abby thought, relieved. She'd been sure it was a knife or some kind of weapon.

Now she stared at him, completely taken aback as he thrust the box or whatever it was into her hands.

"For you Mademoiselle," he whispered, breathlessly.

"What …what are you doing?" Abby cried, troubled by the fact that unlike her, Finn didn't seem to find any of this at all worrying, or in the least bit surprising. "What the hell is …?" But the rest of her sentence was left hanging in the air as the man raced off again, almost as quickly as he'd appeared.

Abby stared at Finn who seemed to be having trouble meeting her gaze and, she realised now, keeping the smile off his face.

"What is all this?" she pleaded, completely lost. She looked down at the object, which was indeed a box, a kind of wooden chest. And, she realised now, had a golden lock that looked suspiciously the same size as the key-shaped pendant she wore around her neck.

"Finn, what's going on?" she gasped, feeling somewhat relieved now, as she understood that *whatever* kind of joke this was, he seemed to be in on it.

"I'm sorry," he said red-faced with suppressed laughter. "Your face … it's such a picture. Anyway, aren't you going to open that box?"

Taking a seat outside another nearby café, Abby sat the

mini-chest in her lap, all the while stealing surreptitious glances at Finn.

She removed the chain from around her neck and using the key, deftly opened the box. Upon first glance it seemed empty, until then she noticed a piece of parchment inside.

Gotcha. How does dinner and a sunset cruise on the Seine sound?
F
XXX

ABBY STARED AT HIM, wide-eyed. "This–all of this was you? The portrait and the pendant and this ..."

He smiled boyishly. "Surprise."

"But how did you...?"

"Don't you worry about that now," he said with a grin. "So what do you think?"

"You're amazing," She held up the piece of parchment and read it again. "Well yes, dinner on the Seine sounds perfect. You did all this ...just to tell me what we're doing tonight?" Abby was completely blown away.

Now he was blushing. "Hey, I have to do something to make things memorable, don't I?"

Hearing this, Abby was struck by sadness that he needed to go to such lengths because of her.

Why couldn't they be just like any other couple, able to enjoy Paris for what it was? Just enjoy being together without having to go to such elaborate lengths. It wasn't fair to him...

"What's wrong?" Finn asked, spotting her rapid change of mood. But when Abby confessed what she'd been thinking, he wasn't having any of it.

"Don't be silly, we're living in the moment. And don't

forget, these are *our* memories - what's wrong with making them memorable for us both?

CHAPTER 40

AT SEVEN PM that same evening, hotel reception called to announce that their transport had arrived.

"What transport?" Abby asked, bewildered.

"Well to the boat I'd imagine," Finn replied in a tone that suggested that he was up to something once again.

Going downstairs they found a magnificent black Bentley MK VI complete with chauffeur waiting outside.

"Wow, I'm impressed," Abby beamed while Finn just smiled and said nothing.

When they were both comfortably settled inside the car, the driver cut across the Parisian boulevards before eventually stopping at one of the quays whereupon a large yacht was moored on the wharf. Upon arrival, the chauffeur held open the door of the car and as Abby and Finn stepped out of it they were immediately welcomed by the captain before being invited aboard the luxurious teak steel and wooden mahogany boat.

"A private boat too?" Abby gasped, realising that they were the only passengers onboard

"Of course," Finn replied casually, as if renting private boats for trips along the Seine was something he did every day.

As the boat pulled away from port, they headed for the outside deck where a waiter offered them each a glass of champagne. Glasses in hand, Abby and Finn took a seat and began to relax and enjoy the magnificent show.

As darkness began to fade and the boat cruised along the river Seine, the city's most majestic and glorious buildings passed before their eyes: the Eiffel Tower, the Grand Palais, the Hôtel National des Invalides, the National Assembly ...

And as the last rays of sunshine disappeared behind the monuments, they sat together in each other's arms while the boat drifted away, and Abby recognised, a Michael Bublè number playing softly in the background.

"This is amazing," she whispered, completely overwhelmed. "I can't *believe* you managed to organise all of this without my knowing. It's incredible."

"You deserve it," he said, drawing her close, and they shared a gentle kiss before the waiter gently interrupted to let them know that dinner was ready to be served.

Afterwards they sat back for a while digesting their incredible feast, but some minutes later, Abby noticed the yacht reduce its speed and come to a gentle halt.

She raised an eyebrow. "I hope we haven't run out of petrol, not that I'd complain about being marooned here."

"Non Mademoiselle," the waiter supplied helpfully. "We are stopping at the Pont des Arts. It is considered by Parisians as the lovers' bridge."

"Oh right." Well the bridge was indeed elegant and pretty, and like most bridges in Paris had a spectacular viewpoint, of the Louvre.

The waiter was still speaking. "Two centuries ago this bridge was a real suspended garden adorned with small shrubs, flowers and benches, which is how it obtained its romantic association."

"Great thanks," Finn murmured, and was Abby imagining it or did he seem annoyed by the interruption?

Evidently deducing the same thing, the waiter bowed imperiously before retreating inside the cabin.

"What's up with ...?" But the rest of her sentence trailed off as something else caught her attention.

And to Abby's total amazement, right in front of her eyes she saw what could only be described as a *cascade* of red roses drifting gently down from the bridge and onto the ship's front deck–right in front of where they were sitting.

"Oh my ..." she gasped, turning in amazement to Finn, who had a strange expression on his face.

It was only then that Abby realised he was holding something in his hand, something small and shiny and for a second, it crossed her mind that he'd brought along the pendant he'd used to spring this mornings' surprise.

But this was no pendant.

"Abby," he said, his voice thick with emotion, his dark eyes locked onto hers. "Will you marry me?"

And there, in the moonlight on the Seine while hundreds of red roses showered down from the bridge above, Abby made her reply.

"Yes," she said, her tears falling almost as quickly as the roses. "Finn, I would love to marry you."

"You're what?" Teresa gasped, when upon their return from Paris she and Finn called to announce their happy news.

"We're getting married," she cried, joyfully thrusting out her right hand so her mum could inspect her ring, a setting of three equally large diamonds on platinum. It was *exactly* what Abby would have chosen for herself.

The rest of their stay had been magical.

That night on the boat, when she'd said yes, the waiter arrived with a fresh bottle of champagne. As the cork popped and she and Finn clinked glasses against the magical romantic background of subtly lit Parisian buildings, she still couldn't believe that such a wonderful thing was really happening to her.

She'd picked up one of the roses, determined to hold onto it as a tangible memory of this incredible night.

Back at port, the Bentley was once again waiting to chauffer the two of them back to their hotel. On the way back, Abby kept going over and over everything in her mind, trying to recall every second of what had happened, concerned that this particular memory would soon fade to nothing.

But as it happened, there was no need; Finn had thought of everything. Beforehand he'd asked the company who'd arranged the cruise (along with the charade in Montmartre) to film what had happened at the bridge, which meant that Abby now had a visual record of his proposal (and her delighted reaction) for posterity.

But later that night as Finn lay fast asleep beside her, Abby couldn't resist committing to paper the overwhelming emotions she'd experienced that night. She was terrified that what had easily been the happiest moment of her life could so easily be lost, and right then, if she could have made a deal to swap the memory of that night for every other before the accident, she would have.

If she could hold onto just one memory for the rest of her life, it would be that one.

Now back home in Dublin, her mother was staring at Abby's engagement ring with a mixture of awe and confusion.

"You're really getting married," Teresa repeated, blindsided by this development.

"We are." By his tone, Abby knew Finn was a bit stung by

her mother's unenthusiastic response. She too was disappointed by her mum's reaction, couldn't she see how happy and in love they were?

But it seemed that this time they'd both misjudged her, as without warning tears sprang to Teresa's eyes and her mouth broke into a wide smile.

"It's a beautiful ring," her mother said, sniffling, "and I'm so pleased for you–for both of you," she added looking at Finn.

Thrilled that her mother seemed to have come round, Abby engulfed her in a huge hug. " We couldn't *wait* to tell you!"

"Well," she said, looking a bit embarrassed, "I suppose you know I've had my worries about how the two of you will cope, but you seem to have managed fairly well up to now."

"Abby's the best thing that's ever happened to me, Mrs Ryan," Finn said squeezing his fiancées hand. "And we're in this together, for better or worse."

Abby looked at him then, suddenly realising the significance of that vow–especially for him. For better or worse? But what if … if things got out of hand and her memory deteriorated even more, what kind of life would they have then? Or more to the point, what kind of life would *Finn* have?

Suddenly, Abby began to get an inkling of the concerns her mother and his father had. And she wondered if for Finn's sake she might have been too hasty in accepting his proposal.

"You're a good man," her mother was saying, hugging them each in turn and Abby was so overcome by the doubts she'd just experienced she couldn't think straight. "So have you set a date yet?"

"We're thinking maybe Christmas, better get it done as soon as possible before she forgets about me altogether," he joked winking at Abby and this time, it wasn't Teresa who was appalled by his words.

"Are you all right?" Finn asked, when Teresa went into the kitchen to put on the kettle and organise a plate of biscuits, champagne not a staple in the Ryan household. "You've gone a bit pale."

"I'm OK," she said, feigning a smile, the all-consuming joy she'd felt earlier suddenly deflated by the realisation that spending the rest of his life with her might not be as straight-forward as Finn thought.

CHAPTER 41

"You're being silly," he argued, when later that evening back at the flat she broached her concerns, "you know doesn't matter to me, why would it?"

"Why *wouldn't* it?" Abby countered. "It's bad enough to think that this time next month I might not remember the best day of my life, let alone try to plan another."

She could think of nothing else all throughout their visit to her mum's, how she'd been rash and unfair to just automatically agree to marry Finn without thinking about the consequences.

He looked at her, stunned. "You mean you've changed your mind?"

Abby shook her head. "No, no, that's not what I'm saying. I'm just thinking that maybe we need to be a hundred percent sure we can cope with ...with my situation," she dropped her gaze to the ground, "before committing to one another, or at least before you commit to *me* for the rest of your life."

He strode across the room, and kneeling in front of her, took both of her hands in his. "Abby I love you, and as far as

I'm concerned that's all that matters. I want to spend the rest of my life with you no matter what."

A lump came to her throat and she sorely wished that she had the strength of his conviction.

"It doesn't bother you that without the help of stupid diaries and digital back-ups that I *might* not remember you from day to day?" she said, ashamed to have to admit this yet again, and even more ashamed that despite this, he could still love her so unconditionally. "That I don't truly remember all the wonderful times we've had together since we first met? Some things I haven't managed to hold onto, some precious moments we've shared that I can never get back."

Finn's dark eyes bored into hers. "I know that the love you have for me isn't just because of what some notebook tells you. How could it? You must feel it too, don't you? Something else—something separate from your memory must register surely?"

She locked eyes with him, the realisation hitting her like a thunderbolt. "You're right," she said and a tiny flutter of joy unfurled inside her as she realised.

That whatever about in her head, surely Finn would, without doubt, always be in her heart?

ERIN WAS OVER THE MOON.

"Will you be my bridesmaid?" Abby asked, restored to her original elation now that Finn had allayed her fears. "You can say no if you like, it's just…"

But a high-pitched squeal from the other end immediately gave Abby her answer.

"It would be an *honour!*" her friend gasped. "And are you having Claire and Caroline too?"

Abby was, much to Caroline's delight.

"Oh think of all the fun we'll have shopping for dresses. We must go back to London, or maybe even New York, see if we can get you something like that de La Renta number you liked. Wouldn't it be just *gorgeous* in white? Then again, maybe Vera Wang would be better, or even Sharon Hoey or ..."

Abby had listened patiently while her label-loving sister ran through every wedding dress designer in the book. But she supposed Caroline did have a point. If she got herself a drop-dead-gorgeous and simply unforgettable wedding dress, then afterwards it could make up part of her mementos of the day itself couldn't it? Or more likely, she thought dishearteningly, it could be a complete and utter waste of money seeing as she wouldn't remember how she felt in it anyway. Still, the dress and the day weren't just for her, but for Finn too and she owed it to him to look incredible.

Particularly as, rather than the predictably happy reaction she was receiving from her friends and family to their news, all Finn seemed to be getting was strife.

His father wasted no time in letting him know how much he disapproved of the engagement and once again Abby was taken aback by the strength of the old man's convictions. While he never outwardly disapproved of her, he seemed whole-heartedly against their relationship, despite Finn arguing that Abby had a handle on her issues.

And she had, no matter what Pat or her mother or anyone else might think. She and Finn were in love and although of course she had her problems, they'd both managed to find a workable way around them.

So what was everyone so worried about?

"YOU'VE SET A DATE?" Hannah said at their next session. "I'm so pleased for you Abby, that's fantastic."

Now that the families had been told, the wedding arrangements had begun in earnest. They'd decided on a Christmas Eve ceremony to mark a full year since their first meeting.

"You don't think I'm taking a huge risk?" Abby asked tentatively. "Or should I say, *Finn's* taking a huge risk?"

"Is that what you believe?" As usual Hannah had to answer a question with a question

Abby shrugged. "I don't really know. We've managed well up to now, but my issue will always be in the background won't it?"

"You *have* managed extremely well up to now, and from what you've told me, Finn sounds like the kind of man who knows exactly what he's doing."

Abby smiled, gratified.

"Anyway, all relationships and marriages face challenges of one kind or another, Abby. Yours is unusual, but at the same time it's evidently not insurmountable."

Then she sat back in the armchair and crossed her legs. "Now let me ask you something. Do you remember back when we first met, and you were recovering from not only your head injury, but also a broken relationship?"

"Of course." Unlike before, Abby wasn't at all self-conscious about the subject this time.

"Well, how do you feel about all of that now?"

"About Kieran?" she clarified, exhaling deeply. "Looking back, I can't believe how much of an effect it all had on me. I'd let myself sink to such a low, I never went out, never did anything interesting, was *definitely* no fun to be around ..." She shook her head. "Caroline was right. I'd shied away from living my life."

Abby chuckled softly, thinking about all the wonderful experiences she'd had over the last year, not just the travel or the time she'd spent with Finn, but also the little things, like reconnecting with her family and Erin or something as simple as trying out new food in a restaurant.

It had been a huge journey of self-discovery and through it all, she'd come to realise just how much the people closest to her mattered. *And* gained a spectacular wardrobe, a keen appreciation for fashion and was even a bit of an expert on gambling.

When she explained this to Hannah, the other woman smiled.

"And that girl–the one you just described as having shied away from life? How did she come to be like that?" she asked, her tone level and Abby thought, a bit studied? *"Was* it just a broken heart?"

"No," she replied firmly, having come to this realisation some time ago. "Kieran was bad for me, or perhaps we were bad for each other. He was strict with money, so *I* was strict with money, even though I know I wasn't always like that. Then, his food foibles gradually became my food foibles. We could never go out to eat anywhere because when we did his fickleness became so uncomfortable that there was no point. I can see all this now, even though this time last year I would never in a million years have admitted it," she admitted, feeling a bit naïve. "As far as I was concerned, he was all I wanted, the love of my life, which was why I was so devastated when he left."

"And do you still feel that way now?"

Abby shook her head firmly. "Not at all. In fact now I know he actually did me a favour." She grinned feebly. "Hindsight is a wonderful thing."

"So you now believe the relationship–ultimately–was bad for you?"

Abby was surprised by the conversation's complete change in direction. Instead of discussing her and Finn, Hannah seemed to be unusually interested in Kieran. Still, she supposed they were valid enough questions, given how badly she'd taken the break up.

"I would never have said it at the time, but yes, I would have to agree that the relationship was bad for me."

"In the sense that...?"

"In the sense that we became too dependent on one another, or should I say, *I* became too dependent on him and his approval. But at the time, I wanted to be him with no matter what. To break it all down to basics, I loved him and wanted to keep him happy."

Hannah nodded, and seemed to be pondering something. "Difficult question I know, but how does your relationship with Kieran compare to the one you now have with Finn?"

Abby smiled. "There's a world of difference. I don't know, with Finn, he kind of ... well, it's difficult to pin down but it's like he lets me be myself. I don't have to agree with his outlook or everything he says, whereas Kieran used to take offence to my not going along with what he wanted."

"Controlling you mean?"

Abby's looked up. That was the second time someone had used that word to describe him. "Well, that's a strong word, but yes, I suppose."

"So you ended up being the kind of person he wanted you to be instead of being yourself?"

"Yes, sounds sad, doesn't it? Sad pathetic I mean."

"Not really. You two were together for a long time, so naturally some form of convergence would occur –by this I mean couples often adopt each other's ways, sometimes even mannerisms. It's a form of consensus. I'm sure Kieran adopted some of your traits too."

Abby shook her head. "Nope."

"Really? Interesting."

For some reason, Abby felt once again obliged to defend him. "Look, it wasn't a fault on Kieran's part, I actually think he was just a much stronger personality."

"So he must have been difficult to argue with."

Now Abby felt a little defensive. "We didn't argue much actually," she replied, her expression closing.

"Well, that's good." Hannah smiled, almost as if she hadn't noticed the subtle change in mood, but yet Abby knew she had.

But the psychologist had another question.

"Abby, there's one thing about your brain injury that's always troubled us, and as it seems to be the very thing that's making your prognosis so unpredictable, it would be good to get to the bottom of it."

"What's that?" Abby frowned, not sure what she was getting at. She didn't think too much about the mechanics of her brain or the injury any more, now that she'd had a good handle on how things worked.

"You remember the secondary injury, the older trauma that appears to have a bearing on the newer one?"

"Yes."

"So now that some ... time has passed and you've gained emotional distance, do you have any idea, any idea at all where you might have got that older injury?" When she said nothing, Hannah prompted further. "Maybe a bump on the head from a fall or ..."

Now Abby stared at her, finally understanding what she was getting at.

"Oh my goodness," she exclaimed. "You think that *Kieran* did something? That he could have ..."

But Hannah said nothing and by the look on her face, Abby knew that this was *exactly* what the other woman thought.

"I can't believe you would say or even *think* something like that," she cried. "OK so Kieran wasn't perfect, but he would never, *ever* do anything to hurt me in the way you're thinking. No way." Abby was horrified by the notion.

"I'm sorry," the psychologist said now. "And I don't need a degree in psychology to tell me that I'm obviously very much mistaken. Forgive me, but I had to ask the question."

The two of them sat in silence for the next few minutes, Abby appalled with Hannah for even thinking such a thing. But grudgingly, she could perhaps understand. By her own admission, Kieran had had a hold on her, and the older injury still remained a mystery.

Finally, Hannah spoke again.

"Just one more question about Kieran if you don't mind. Don't worry," she added quickly, seeing Abby's wide-eyed expression. "I just wondered, given he was someone of such great importance in your life, if you happened to see him again now, how do you think you'd react?"

There was only one real answer to that.

Abby smiled. "Wouldn't affect me in the slightest," she replied confidently.

CHAPTER 42

Things to remember:

Put the rubbish out on Sunday night
Next appointment with Hannah is on Monday
    at ten
My flight's back lunchtime on Monday
Take two sugars in your coffee!
I love you
xxx

ABBY SMILED as she read the list that Finn had left on the fridge. He'd left for a work-related event in Manchester the night before.

Lately he'd taken to leaving little notes and reminders around, some tongue-in-cheek, but others a genuine effort to help her remember small but important pieces of information when he wasn't there.

And although they had the occasional hiccup now and again, for the most part things were still going great.

Her habit of detailing everything that happened day-to-day had literally saved her, and she didn't know what she'd do without those archives, particularly when it came to her and Finn.

As they now saw each other daily, her memory had necessary continuity so she was to all intents and purposes functioning normally. Something she was hugely proud of.

She smiled, recalling the video clip of the marriage proposal, which she'd watched many times since.

It was one memory Abby sorely wished she'd been able to retain of her own accord, because whatever about seeing it on film, or reading back an account, it was impossible to truly capture the overwhelming happiness she'd felt at the time. She'd give anything to be able to relive that night, the look in Finn's eyes when he asked her to marry him, the magic and wonder of it all when those hundreds of rose petals began cascading onto the boat.

But that was the way things were now.

It was stuff like this that sometimes made her frustrated and bitter. But at the same time, how could she be when her issues had inadvertently led her to Finn?

Since meeting him she'd been happier than she'd ever been in her life, debilitating brain injury or not. And she knew without question that her wedding day would be the happiest day of her life, so who cared if she couldn't record every little detail?

And as he'd pointed out, most people didn't sift through details and distil every moment down to the best and most important things like they did.

Live in the moment...

She just wished her Mum could be as upbeat. Why was she still so worried about her? And time hadn't softened Pat

Maguire's opinion either; the older man still making no secret of his belief that Finn was taking on too much of a burden, something that was difficult for Abby to take.

Because she wondered the very same thing every single day.

HAVING HAD A NICE LIE-IN, Abby got up and threw on a pair of comfy yoga pants and grey zip-up.

Today she was going to enjoy taking it easy. Not that she'd done much else lately, she thought wryly. She'd really have to think again about going back to work, *definitely* after the wedding anyway.

She and Hannah had talked about this again recently, and while the psychologist still stood by her original suggestion that she should take at least a year out, Abby was bored.

While she'd had the wedding plans to occupy her, now pretty much everything was done. The church and hotel were booked, flowers and dresses ordered so really all she and Finn had to do now was turn up on the day. Abby smiled. And book their honeymoon of course. There was one thing on her list that she hadn't yet managed, one major destination she desperately wanted to visit, and for this one, Finn would be joining her.

"All the way down there just to see a few penguins?" he'd laughed, when she'd told him she wanted to go to the South Pole.

This time last year she'd been holed up in her apartment, hiding away from the world and from all that life had to offer. Now, as a result of her head injury, she'd done the most amazing things, had seen the most incredible sights, and by falling in love with Finn, had the most unforgettable experience of all.

She picked up her keys and checked her purse before heading out to the shops for the Sunday papers.

It was a lovely, clear October day and Abby had a spring in her step as she walked to the end of the road and in the direction of the nearest ATM.

There was a small queue ahead of her and as she waited obediently in line, she began daydreaming yet again about her and Finn's upcoming honeymoon to Antarctica.

A tap at her shoulder quickly brought her out of her reverie.

"Excuse me, are you waiting to use this?"

At the sound of the voice, every single nerve ending stood to attention and Abby stood rooted to the spot, almost afraid to move.

It couldn't be … could it?

Time seemed to stand still, as numbly, Abby finally turned around and came face to face with …

"Kieran?"

"Oh," her ex replied, evidently just as taken aback. "Em, Abby," he mumbled. "I …em …didn't recognise you."

Contrary to what she'd assured Hannah and indeed what she'd believed herself, all the old insecurities came flooding back at once. Her hair was unwashed and greasy, she had no make-up on and was wearing a dowdy zip top, the first thing that had come to hand.

But her embarrassment about her appearance wasn't just brought on by Kieran's presence; it had in fact, much more to do with his companion.

Kieran's wife was watching her with undisguised interest. Abby however, barely noticed this; she was too busy staring at the buggy between them.

"This is your …. child?" she gasped, stepping backwards as she stared from the baby back to Kieran, an avalanche of emotions crashing over her, followed just as quickly by a rush of questions.

It was just over a year since her accident, so they could only be married that long, but this child … this child was–

"I'm sorry I have to go," she cried, suddenly desperate to get away from them.

"But don't you want to...?" Abby was moving so fast she barely heard him call out something about the ATM, and she knew he and his wife were probably taken aback by her sudden haste.

No scratch that, why *would* they be taken aback? It was much more likely that they were laughing at her, laughing about what she was too stupid to realise at the time.

They had a toddler ...

She'd been right all along; Kieran *had* betrayed her, despite his crap about doing the honourable thing, and breaking up with her before they got together. Honourable my foot. That child *must* have been conceived long before they split up...

"Abby wait!" Suddenly, she heard a voice call out behind her. Despite the fact that she didn't want to speak to him, didn't want to even *look* at him, her legs began to slow as if by their own accord.

Seconds later, he appeared in front of her. "Are you OK?" he asked, and the fake sincerity in his voice was the final straw.

"How can you ask me that?" she gasped wretchedly. "How dare you ..."

He looked uncomfortable. "I'm sorry ... I know it must have been awkward, but ..." he shrugged. "I know it's been a while, but it's good to see you."

Now she felt as though she'd passed into some kind of parallel universe. What on earth was wrong with him? Why did he expect her to be happy to see him out of the blue like that, especially with what she'd discovered? Or had he been so caught up in his own life that he didn't even realise the significance? Was he really that stupid, that heartless?

"Kieran, you have a toddler," she began, willing him to do the maths and make the connection.

Again he seemed non-plussed. "So?" He wrinkled his brow.

"Don't you have any idea why I'm so upset?" He seemed so clueless that briefly, Abby wondered if *he* was the one with the memory problems. "Any idea at all? You swore you and Jessica weren't getting together until it was over between you and me."

He frowned, and was it her imagination or was he now starting to back away a little? "Abby I really don't know what is wrong with you …"

She really couldn't believe she was hearing this. What did he think she was – stupid?

"Why are you doing this?" she demanded. "Why are you still trying to pull the wool over my eyes? I'm not an imbecile, despite what you seem to think. That child was obviously conceived when we were still together."

Now realised Kieran was looking at her very strangely, as if she'd lost her mind.

"Abby," he said, his voice slow and firm. "Alan was conceived on our honeymoon, two years ago."

"What …?"

But then suddenly, just like that, it hit her.

Her world began to spin on its axis as she finally understood why dates had kept confusing her. That time with the cheque; she hadn't been absentminded in writing it at all; instead something else had been at play.

Her mind reeling, Abby reached out and held onto the wall for support.

Although she'd questioned this privately a few times, she'd eventually put it down to a possible side-effect of her injury, one didn't really matter much in the scheme of things. No big deal.

But one thing she could be *absolutely* sure about was the timing of her accident, which occurred shortly after Kieran's wedding, and which he'd just confirmed was two years ago.

It could only mean one thing, Abby deduced, flabbergasted.

A whole year had passed, one about which she had no recollection, no clue as to what occurred.

A lost year.

But in order for this to have happened, she realised grimly, it wasn't just her memory that had been playing tricks on her.

Everyone else had too.

CHAPTER 43

"How long has this been going on?" White-faced, Abby appeared at her mother's door. "How long have you been lying to me?"

Teresa visibly paled.

"Love, what are you talking about–?"

"Don't lie to me," Abby cried, brushing hastily past her. "You've been doing that long enough, you Caroline and Erin, and whoever else is involved!"

After discovering through Kieran that she'd lost a year of her life and the significance surrounding it, Abby had raced back to the flat and immediately called Finn, who she suspected *must* have been involved too. But she couldn't get him on the line and had no choice but leave a tearful, rambling message on his voicemail.

She didn't know what she'd do if she discovered that Finn was in on this, if he too had deceived her in such an awful way.

Now, Teresa stared at her daughter, her expression panicked. "Involved in what?" But just as quickly her face crumpled, and now she looked resigned and fearful. "Love, why don't we both sit down and talk this over, OK?"

"How could you do this to me?" Abby insisted, fraught with terror, distrust – a million and one things were going through her mind. They'd deceived her and she wanted to find out how, where, and most importantly *why*?

"Love, we were only doing what we thought was right– "

"You thought lying and pretending and making a fool of me was right? How did you work that one out?"

"Abby please, sit down there and I'll make you a cup of tea, OK?"

"I don't want a cup of tea, and I don't want you to patronise me." Suddenly weary, she sank onto the sofa, her eyes filling with tears. "What's happening to me Mum? I don't know what's real anymore."

"Honey …" Moved by her distress, Teresa gathered her daughter in her arms and for a brief moment, Abby relaxed in her embrace. However, just as quickly, she remembered the reason she was here and she stepped back.

"Tell me what's going on."

Teresa exhaled deeply and shook her head. "What happened? How did you– ?"

"How did I find out that everyone's been messing with my head? I bumped into Kieran today - with his toddler son."

"Oh."

"Is that all you can say? Somehow I lose a year of my life and all you can say is 'oh.'"

"We never expected … we were going to tell you eventually," Teresa struggled, not sure what to say.

"You were going to tell me when? When another two or maybe three years had passed?"

"Doctor O'Neill said – "

"What?" Abby's head snapped up. "What's Hannah got to do with this?" Then it hit her. "Of course, she has to be in on it too … I don't believe this."

She slumped heavily onto the sofa. Hannah, to whom she'd confided so much of her thoughts and feelings…

Now Abby realised that this too was another charade, another betrayal. Wasn't there *anyone* she could trust anymore?

"Love, maybe it would be better if you spoke to her about it; she'd be able to explain it all much better than I could."

"For goodness' sake you're my mother!" Now the tears had started to flow, despite Abby's best intentions and again, Teresa floundered.

"They advised us to wait until after the wedding, because of the stress of it all you see…"

Abby shook her head vigorously. "Mum, you're not making sense. What's the wedding got to do with it? And what do you mean, 'they advised you to wait', who's 'they'? Please," she implored, when she saw her mother hesitate, "I really need to know."

Teresa slumped onto the sofa. "Love, this won't be easy for you to hear and I really wish you'd let me call Doctor O'Neill; she really would be much better able to explain–"

"Forget Doctor O'Neill," Abby interjected shortly. "Whatever it is, I want to hear it from you."

Teresa waited a couple of seconds before speaking, as if trying to decide the best place to start. Then she sighed.

"Love, when you woke after your head injury eleven months ago …It wasn't the first time you'd woken up," she continued, her gaze falling to the floor. "It was the fourth."

"What?" Abby gasped. "What do you mean?"

"Your accident didn't happen last year like you think –it happened well before."

She couldn't speak. Even though she'd figured out that much, it still stunned her to hear her suspicions confirmed. All those 'mistakes' she'd made about dates hadn't been symptoms of her injury at all, they really had been spot on… Which meant that a whole year of her life really had been lost.

"But how...*why?* Was I in a coma or something–what?"

"No, no nothing like that. As I said, that last time was the fourth time you came to."

"Came to from what?"

Teresa took a deep breath. "From another blackout."

"Blackout..."

"Love, I can only imagine how confused you must be. So maybe I should just start from the very beginning, and then you might be able to understand."

Abby sat down across from her, feeling dizzy. Blackouts?

Her mother sighed again. "As you know, that blow to the head caused terrible damage, especially to your brain."

She nodded, unable to speak.

"But when you woke up in the hospital the first time, the extent of that damage was plain for all to see. There was a major gash on the side of your head, and the doctors had to shave off most of your hair."

Abby's hand instinctively went to her head. "Shave it off?"

"Yes. It was completely gone. But it's grown back fairly well now, although I know it seemed so much shorter when you woke up the last time. "

"But Hannah said – "

"I know they told you they had to cut it shorter to examine the wound, but that was so you'd think it was the ... first time. And of course the wound has also healed well."

Hearing all this, and the extent of their lies, Abby was gobsmacked.

"Go on."

"As I said, you woke up that first time with a severe head wound. But everything pretty much happened the same as it did last time, the doctors sent you for an MRI to try and determine the extent of the damage, and they came up with the same diagnosis, the damage to your hippocampus and how it would affect your memory."

Teresa paused and she looked pained. "But love, you took it very badly," she told her. "You were distraught about the prospect of losing your memory, none of us could comfort you, and you wouldn't go outside for weeks on end because of your hair and the way you looked – not to mention that you were still broken-hearted about Kieran. The doctors suggested that you see a psychologist to help deal with your emotions, but you wouldn't have any of it."

Abby stared at her–unable to believe that all this had happened, actually happened without her remembering it. It was as though she'd stepped into some weird, parallel universe...

"Hang on a second," she interjected then. "You're saying that the doctors explained the damage to me, and I couldn't cope with it?"

"Pretty much, yes. It's hard to explain love, but as soon as you realised that you were indeed forgetting little things here and there, emotionally, you just couldn't cope. And you wouldn't let any of us help you. I wanted you to move in here with me but you refused and ... well we were all very worried – the doctors included – about how you were going to cope in the long term. As it happened, we soon found out."

"What? What happened?"

"It was a couple months after the original accident. You were found unconscious on the street near your flat. The doctors told us you'd had some kind of epilepsy attack, which they said is often a side-effect of traumatic brain injury."

Abby was stunned. "Epilepsy?"

"Yes." Teresa shook her head, and she could only imagine how terrifying it must have been for her mother to learn of this, to say nothing of how she herself felt hearing about it now.

"The attack was severe and apparently caused a blackout of some sort ... I don't really know." Teresa's hands were clasped tightly in her lap, and Abby could see it on her mother's face that the burden of explaining all this to her was taking a lot out of her.

But hearing it was taking a lot out of her too.

"How long ... how long was I out for?" she asked then.

"Maybe a couple of hours or so between the time you blacked out and when you woke up, the doctors said. But love, the crucial thing is that when you woke up that second time, all you could remember was leaving your flat that morning. It took us a while to figure out that you weren't talking about leaving it *that* morning–the morning of your blackout–but the one of the original accident–the day you first got hit. It was as if the previous few months had never happened."

"I don't believe you," Abby cried. "My entire memory wiped clean, just like that?"

"The doctors said it must have been all the pressure you were under in trying to come to terms with it. You were under such an incredible amount of stress trying to cope with all this on your own, which must have been so overwhelming ..." Her mother's guilt about it all was plain to see. "But you wouldn't let any of us help you, you just insisted on locking yourself away from us all like you did after Kieran and eventually I suppose it just became too much ... But then when we found out that the seizure had caused your memory to ...reset itself almost, we knew that the doctors' fears were realised and the damage was real."

Abby was still struggling to comprehend all this. "So what about the other times?" she urged. "You said that the last time I woke up was the fourth time, so what happened in between?"

"Again the doctors went through the process of explaining the memory loss to you except this time they could tell you for sure that there were no maybes about it, your blackout had proved that. At first you didn't believe that so much time had passed, until you discovered the date and admitted to yourself that you couldn't account for the months that had gone before. So this time, after lots of convincing, you agreed to take their suggestions on board, and agreed to meet with Doctor O'Neill to talk things through and try and ensure that the same thing didn't happen again."

Which explained why Hannah was in on it too, Abby realised now.

"Unfortunately, barely a month later you had another attack, this time in front of my own eyes here at the house. You had another seizure– except this time you were out for four or five hours." She bit her lip and tears came to her eyes. "It was an awful time."

"And again, when you woke up, all you could remember was leaving your flat that morning, same as last time, despite the fact that by then almost four months had passed since you first got hit."

She paused then, as if to give Abby time to let it all sink in.

"And I remembered nothing at all again, not a single thing?"

Teresa shook her head. "No, we were right back where we started, and had to explain everything to you all over again. You reacted the same but agreed to see Doctor O'Neill."

"So what happened to cause the latest seizure? The one I woke up from …a year ago?"

"We're not sure love, as this time it happened when you were out and about. The doctors seem to think that maybe stress brings the seizures on, but because you can't remember what happens beforehand, we've no way of knowing."

The neurologists had been right all along, Abby admitted terrified. Her long-term memory was in fact useless, which meant that all the time and effort she'd spent trying to cope with this had been a complete waste of time.

"But why did you decide to keep me in the dark this time?" she asked then. "Why trick me into thinking the accident happened last year, instead of long before? What was the point?" Then to her horror, she started to sob. "Why give me all that false hope, and let me think that I could actually get through this, when you knew that there was no chance, and I was only kidding myself. Why did you do that, Mum? Why give me false hope when you knew – you *knew* – it was all in vain?"

"It wasn't my decision – "

"But you're my mother!" Abby was inconsolable, the realisation that all was lost well and truly hitting her. "Surely you couldn't agree to such a horrible and *hurtful* deception, no matter whose decision it was. How stupid do you think I feel?" Tears were racing down her cheeks. "I don't know what to believe, don't know who to trust ... you're my mother, how could you possibly agree to do something like this to me?"

"Love, of course I didn't agree with it, but in the end I had no choice. The decision was made and although I didn't like it one bit, everyone else agreed it might be for the best and– "

"But what gave Hannah or the doctors or whoever ..." she said, deciding that this was the most likely scenario, "what gave them to right to mess with my head. And for Christ's sake *why?*"

Teresa's hands were shaking. "I don't know... I –"

"What do you mean you don't know? Mum, why can't you just tell me why you did this, why you decided to turn my life upside down by lying to me like this? Why?"

Teresa looked at her, a world of hurt and regret in her eyes. "Love, only you can answer that," she said in a small voice, "because the decision was all yours."

CHAPTER 44

ABBY STARED AT HER, stunned. "What? What are you talking about? Why would *I* ... *how* would I – "

"This is why I wanted you to speak to Doctor O'Neill," Teresa went on quietly. "She knows more about that than I do. You broached the idea and discussed it with her before you came to us."

"*I* asked you to pretend that the accident had just happened, to pretend that all this time had gone past without my noticing it? Why would I do something like that? As if I wouldn't notice." Abby was flummoxed. But of course, she *hadn't* noticed, had she? And whenever she did feel slightly wrong-footed or confused about a timeline, she automatically put it down to side effects and never even entertained the notion that her instincts might be right.

"As I said, Doctor O'Neill is the one to talk to. All I know is that you came to me and begged me to go along with it. You told me you had your reasons, so how could I say no? I would have done anything to take away the worry and stress you were under." She paused. "And love, you have to admit it worked.

Instead of being upset, you came out fighting and making that list seemed to give you a new lease of life. You were a different girl, positive, optimistic and so determined to live your best life. I hadn't seen you so vibrant and so ...happy for a long time. Instead of being depressed and defeated, you picked yourself up and went out and grabbed life with both hands. It was working. You hadn't had an attack since, and you seemed happy we weren't going to risk your progress by telling you and stressing you out all over again. But of course, we could never have anticipated your meeting Finn."

Abby was so caught up in the explanations that she'd almost forgotten that Finn had been the one to tell her the truth.

"Was he in on this too?" she asked carefully, although at the same time she was now pretty sure she knew the answer.

"No, of course not. You bumped into him that time in New York and none of us knew anything about him. No," Teresa went on, seemingly upset by the very notion. "He had nothing to do with that and wasn't he the one who helped you realise that there was actually something wrong?"

Heartened by the fact that there was still at least one person she could count on, Abby went on. "But when I found out from Finn that I was in fact losing memories, why didn't you tell me then? Why continue with the charade?"

Teresa sighed. "We talked to Hannah about it, and she felt that it was all still too fragile, and that if anything might set you back even further. As it was, you were so taken with Finn and he with you that we also didn't want to risk ruining the relationship. The two of you have always been so determined you could make this work and ... you have. You know I was very worried at the start, and I really wanted to tell you, but I couldn't run the risk. What if you turned against us? In a way, I'm glad it's all out in the open now."

But Abby couldn't share her mother's relief as the actual

significance of everything she'd told her hit in the solar plexus. And all her worries and insecurities about marrying Finn came rushing right back.

How could they have a future if she could black out at any given moment and draw a blank about him and their relationship? In spite of Finn's protests, she now knew for certain she that she couldn't fight her prognosis, had never fought it, despite them both foolishly believing otherwise.

Abby knew deep down that Finn was banking on her being able to fight this, that he'd convinced himself that the backup diaries and archives they were keeping would be enough to maintain her missing life.

Yet it had all been utterly pointless.

ABBY ENTERED Hannah's cosy and familiar office, understanding now why she'd felt that very strong sense of déjà vu the first time she came here (or what she'd *believed* was the first time).

From behind the desk, Hannah studied her carefully.

"So you know," she said evenly.

Having learnt only some of the background surrounding the deceit from her mother, Abby had immediately called Hannah and asked to see her. And despite the fact that it was Sunday and out of hours, the other woman agreed.

"Now I know," Abby said, her mouth set in a hard line, "and I want answers."

"What kind of answers?"

"Well for one thing, how? *Why?* Why did you and everyone else agree to lie to me and let whole chunks disappear from my life? What was the point?"

"What do *you* think was the point?"

"Hannah, just answer the question for once–please!" Abby

collapsed into her usual armchair, except this time its warmth and softness didn't give her any comfort. Her eyes shone with tears. "I'm going out of my mind here."

"I'm sorry," she said. "Believe me, the last thing I wanted was for this to happen."

"Then what *did* you want? What were you trying to achieve? Was it some kind of psychological experiment? A lab rat—what?"

"Of course not." Hannah took her usual seat directly across from Abby. "You said your mother explained about the previous blackouts?"

"In a way. She said that every time I had one, I would lose everything that happened since the accident."

Hannah nodded. "We couldn't figure it out at first. It was only when they sent the scans to the States that we became aware of the other injury—that older one," she added eying Abby steadily, "and the Americans concluded that this must be having some knock-on effect."

Something that they'd been trying to tell her all along, Abby thought.

"Back then, Doctor Moroney mentioned the case to me initially in passing. He was understandably concerned about your emotional state, and after the first seizure, he insisted on your seeing me."

She met her eyes. "Abby, you wouldn't believe how angry and resistant you were back then. You were suspicious of the doctors of me, your family—everyone. It's such a horrible, scary thing to happen to someone, losing chunks of memory, and naturally enough you were finding it difficult to cope. But eventually, you started confiding."

Again, Abby found it difficult to get to grips with the fact that she remembered absolutely nothing about any of this. It was terrifying.

"Your prognosis intrigued me from the very beginning, and eventually, it got to the stage where I almost looked forward to our sessions. The damage to your brain was–*is* " she clarified, meeting Abby's gaze, "so unique that none of us knew what you might fail to remember from one day to the next."

"So I *was* a lab rat then ..."

"No, of course not, that's not what I meant. We'd become very close you and I. In a word, I'd say we'd become friends. I worried when you worried. I tried to be there for you and give you as much emotional assistance as you needed, but then, when you had the second seizure, we had to go through the same process all over again.

Once more, you were distressed and distrustful when you learnt from the doctors and your family what had happened, and that you'd lost all memory since the accident, not once, but twice. You were of course wary around me too–I had to regain your approval to the point that you were comfortable discussing your feelings with me.

But then, when you had the third seizure, and discovered that it *was* the third one, you started to lose hope altogether. Up until then, you'd started talking about maybe fighting it, trying to find a way to beat it. But the third one took every ounce of fight out of you. As far everything was futile - what was the point in trying to overcome it? What was the point in doing *anything*? You became depressed, and eventually you stopped coming to me altogether. As your psychologist I was concerned, but as your friend, I was worried and all I wanted to do was help."

"So you decided to lie to me the next time I blacked out? And when I woke up, pretend that it was the first time it happened? How did that help anything?"

"No, we decided that together."

"But why Hannah?" Abby said, shaking her head in bewilderment. "That's the bit I truly can't understand."

The psychologist took a deep breath. "Abby, how did you feel up to this morning–*before* you discovered the truth? Be honest, what would be your assessment of the last year?"

When Abby said nothing, Hannah decided to fill her in.

"Wouldn't you say that it's been wonderful? The best year of your life, possibly? You did so many amazing things, saw so many wonderful sights, reconnected with the people close to you. Unlike the aftermath of the break-up, you let them in, allowed them to help you get through this. But most significant of all–"

"I met Finn," Abby added quietly.

"Yes, but furthermore you truly believed there was a chance you could beat this," Hannah went on. "You were *sure* you could beat it."

"Yes, but that's because I didn't know the damage was permanent..." Abby argued, feeling really stupid now.

"But wasn't this something to cling onto, the thought that you could live a normal life, that you could learn to live with it?"

Abby shook her head. "I'd *fooled* myself into believing in hope, you mean."

But then, almost as soon as those words were out of her mouth, the realisation hit her and she understood. She looked up and realised that Hannah was wearing a satisfied expression on her face.

"That was it?" she asked, things finally beginning to make sense. "That was why it came about? To give me hope?"

The psychologist nodded. "How else can anyone deal with the dark times in life? There has to be some light at the end of the tunnel. You might call it fooling yourself Abby, but didn't it indeed nurture optimism? The belief that you might be able to beat this thing fuelled everything you did this year. You went out and lived your best life."

Maybe that was true but what did it matter when now she was right back at square one?

"Are you?" Hannah replied when she put this to her. "Are you really? It's been a year since your last seizure, you've been living life with gusto and at the same time, you've even managed to find a failsafe way of holding onto memories. Abby, whether you admit it or not, hope *has* given you a way to beat this thing, and not only that but through meeting Finn, you've also found happiness."

At this, Abby looked away guiltily.

"What?" Hannah queried, seeing her expression.

"Not any more." Although her tone was hard, her eyes filled with tears and her voice croaked.

"What do you mean?"

"I'm going to end things, Hannah. I have to. When he finds out that all of this has been a big lie."

The other woman's eyes widened. "But you haven't lied to anyone. Other than yourself of course, but– "

"I can't expect him to live with this, with the knowledge that I could black out at any time, and end up losing all memory of our time together. It isn't fair."

"But Finn loves you, and if he knew– "

"It doesn't matter." Abby interjected. "I've made my decision. I'm not going to be a burden on him–I can't be."

"Well, as your fiancé, don't you think he should have some say?" Hannah pointed out.

"But *I* would never know," Abby cried. "I would never know if he was staying with me out of pity, knowing that I'm a ticking time bomb. What kind of a marriage could anyone have in a situation like that?"

"But Finn's partly the reason you're doing so well, probably the *main* reason you're doing so well and –"

"Exactly. So how is it fair to expect him to live with the obligation of being entirely responsible for my well-being?"

"I can't believe you would be so willing to throw it all away–"

"I'm not willing Hannah, as far as I'm concerned I have no choice." She bit back tears. "Knowing what I know now - about my missing life … there's no future for us – there never has been."

CHAPTER 45

FINN CALLED AGAIN first thing the next morning, when Abby had sent him a reassuring follow-up text the day before, telling him she was out and about with Erin. Given the enormity of what she'd discovered, she knew she couldn't bring herself to talk to him.

"Hey it's me, what's going on?"

Now her heart twisted at the sound of his voice. She hadn't slept a wink, instead tossed, turned and fretted until daybreak. While last night she'd convinced herself beyond doubt that she was doing the right thing, hearing him on the other end of the line was now seriously testing her convictions.

"Hi," she replied quietly. "Nothing much."

"Well what about that voicemail you left yesterday? You sounded really upset."

Abby swallowed hard. "I was, but I'm OK now."

"You're sure?"

"Yes, it was nothing honestly."

"I'm not sure if I heard right 'cos you were speaking so fast, but did you mention something about bumping into Kieran?"

"That's right yes." Abby tried to keep her tone even and there was a brief pause before he spoke again.

"OK. So how did that go?"

"It was … strange," she said hesitating a little. She'd thought about doing this over the phone, but it wasn't fair and in any case, she knew he wouldn't accept it.

"Strange …" he repeated and Abby knew he was waiting to hear more.

"Let's talk when you get back," she said, trying to keep her voice upbeat, although in reality she was shaking.

"OK. So all going well I should be home by three. I'll pop over to Dad's to collect Lucy and – "

"Better not," Abby interjected. "Um, I've just cleaned the carpet and I don't want hairs all over it."

Finn hesitated a beat before replying. "OK, I'll leave her at Dad's."

"If you wouldn't mind."

"Fine." Now he knew something wasn't right. "See you later."

ONE LOOK at him told Abby that this was going to be even harder than she'd thought. There was a dark covering of stubble on his jaw, and those liquid brown eyes bored heavily into hers.

"Hi," she said levelly. "How was the trip?"

"It was fine. Look, what's going on?" he asked, leaning on the back of the armchair. "You sounded really strange on the call yesterday. What's happened? And why didn't you want me to bring Lucy?"

Abby looked away, unable to meet his gaze. "Something's happened," she told him in a broken voice.

"Well, I kind of guessed that much." He gave a short, humourless, laugh. "So what's up?"

303

"Maybe we should sit down …"

He came round and sat down on the armchair, but instead of relaxing into it, perched on the edge, his pose tense and rigid.

Again, Abby was struck by how much she really loved this man, how she adored every inch of him. But oddly, rather than make things even harder, it actually reiterated how necessary this was, and gave her the strength to see it through.

This was no longer about her feelings; it was *entirely* about his. Summoning every ounce of courage she had, Abby swallowed hard.

"So I bumped into Kieran yesterday."

"I know–you said."

"And … well, it was a bit surreal."

He said nothing, waiting for her to elaborate.

"Finn, I don't know how to say this but …"

Now he frowned and his expression became more guarded. "Say what?"

"We've had a wonderful time together, and you've helped through so much, but …"

"But … ?"

"I'm really sorry," Abby fought back tears, "but I realised I'm still in love with him." The lie came out a lot easier than she'd anticipated.

"With Kieran?" Finn was staring at her with a mixture of horror and confusion. "What? But he's married."

Abby shook her head. "Not for much longer, the marriage failed, he doesn't love her, they're getting divorced, he made a big mistake." Somehow lie after lie gushed out of her mouth, but she couldn't help it. She had no other choice.

"He made a big mistake," Finn repeated sarcastically. "And when did he discover this? Was it before or after he'd dumped you for someone else? Or was it when he realised his new wife wasn't as easy to control, or didn't bow to his every need like you did?" His words were cruel but Abby knew she deserved them.

"It wasn't like that," she protested. "We had a very long chat and I now understand exactly where he's coming from. Apparently, the marriage was over before it had even begun. Anyway, that part doesn't really matter. What matters is that I found out that the feelings Kieran and I had– *have*–for one another are still very strong. And I can't just ignore that."

"Oh, I see. But you seem fully prepared to ignore *my* feelings, and what *we* have, not to mention everything we've been through over the last few months," he spat, and she knew that this wounded him more than anything. "But then again that's nothing new, is it? Most of the time I'm lucky if you remember from one day to the next who I actually am."

Each word felt like a dagger through her heart but merely brought home how difficult their situation already was, let alone what it would be like if they carried on. No, this might be agony now, but at the end of the day it was the best possible thing - for both of them.

"I'm sorry," she said mutely.

"You're sorry? Is that all you can say? You're telling me you're dumping me for some guy who sounds like a controlling, penny-pinching arsehole who couldn't be more wrong for you, and certainly doesn't deserve you. Does he know about you? About your injuries?" he asked.

"He knows what to expect, yes."

"You're actually–*seriously*–considering going back to him?" Finn gasped, shaking his head in amazement. "You're seriously prepared to throw away everything we have for some guy who treated you like dirt?"

"It wasn't like that, we were both at fault and– "

"Oh, don't give me that crap, Abby. If you honestly believe

that then you have bigger memory issues than you thought. Kieran was so wrong for you; you admitted that yourself. What's changed?"

"I don't know, it's difficult to explain. Please don't make this any harder than it is," she cried and now the tears were genuine. She couldn't keep this up much longer; it was bad enough that she had to lie to him at all, let alone having to hear home truths. "I can't help how I feel."

"So you're breaking up with me. Now that the wonderful Kieran is back you've decided to just cast me aside."

"It's not like that. I care a lot about you, but when I saw him again I– "

"I don't believe this," Finn ran a hand through his hair. "You're really considering going back to him?"

"I'm not considering it," she said, landing what she hoped would be the final blow. "I've already decided. I love Kieran, have always loved him and I just can't help how I feel. Look, we had a fantastic time together and I'll always care for you–"

"Is this some kind of a joke Abby? We're engaged for goodness' sake!" He looked at her finger and seemed to realise only then that she was no longer wearing her ring.

"I'm sorry, but you have to understand that I can't marry you now, knowing what I know. It wouldn't be fair." It was the only piece of truth she'd uttered since he arrived.

"Abby, come on, you can't be serious." Those intense brown eyes seemed to penetrate her very soul and again she had to look away. "After all we've been through?"

She nodded, her face impassive. "I'm sorry. Please don't try and change my mind," she added, trying to make her tone hard and devoid of emotion, "it's no use."

At this, Finn's bewilderment finally turned to anger. "So now that lover-boy's back, you want me to just turn tail so you can get on with your life as if I never even existed?" he bellowed. "Well, I suppose *that* will be easy for you – hell knows you wouldn't have a clue who I was if it weren't for the archive." Abby had never seen him so upset and was forced to remind herself yet again that she was doing this–*had* to do it–for his own benefit.

"OK if that's what you want fine–let's do that." Finn fumed. "Let's end it all here and now. While we're at it, why don't I do the job for you?" Following that, he got up and stormed into her bedroom.

"What ... what are you doing?" she asked, shocked by the ferocity of his anger. She went after him into the bedroom to find him standing in front of her laptop, furiously tapping on the keyboard. "Finn, what are you doing?" she asked again.

"What am I doing?" He turned to look at her, and Abby didn't think she'd never forget the look of pain and betrayal in his eyes. "What do you think?"

She looked at the screen and realised that he was deleting the archive; all the diaries, pictures and video clips–all the memories–of him and their relationship over the last few months. Wonderful, happy memories ... photos of the two of them together and with Lucy, with her family and his dad just after their engagement, the film clip of his amazing proposal...

"I'm taking myself out of the picture, out of your life, just like you want," Finn went on. "Hey, you tried to do all this yourself once remember?"

Abby could do nothing but stand and watch as his fingers moved over the keys with alarming speed, as he erased every item–every last trace of her missing life.

Delete selected items permanently? the computer prompted.

"Hell yeah," Finn grunted, stabbing the *'Yes'* button with added determination.

Finally he stood back and turned to meet her gaze for what Abby now knew for sure would be the very last time. As he did, she saw that his eyes were red-rimmed.

"There you go," he said resignedly. "Clean slate- just like you wanted."

Then without another word, he marched out of the room and out of her life.

CHAPTER 46

One month later

"It's been so long since I was here, I'd almost forgotten how *huge* this place is," Claire gasped, marvelling at her sister's luxurious home.

It was late November and she, Zach and baby Caitlyn were home for a visit. Tom and Zach had gone out for a game of golf, and as Teresa insisted on spending some quality time with her only grandchild, the three sisters decided to get together for a catch-up at Caroline's.

Abby's sister had the kitchen redesigned for what must have been the third or fourth time in as many years, and now she marvelled at Caroline's bravery in going for bright red kitchen units along with a stark white tiled floor. It wasn't something she would have chosen for herself, if she ever had a house of her own that was, but in this huge open plan room it really worked.

It was great to have Claire home too; notwithstanding the

fact that she hadn't seen her since last Christmas, having her here also helped take her mind off her own situation–at least temporarily.

For some reason Abby felt a dull ache in the pit of her stomach at the thought of Christmas. She wasn't sure why– after all, she'd had a lovely time at Claire's last time. But maybe that was it, she decided, an ordinary Christmas at home couldn't hold a candle to a New York one.

Now, as the three shared a bottle of wine beneath the patio heater on Caroline's decking, she listened distractedly to her sisters discussing the merits of red kitchen units over wooden shaker ones, and wished she could summon up the enthusiasm to do the same.

She didn't know what was going on, but lately she just felt … numb. She supposed it was inevitable but at the same time, she knew she had to at least try and come to terms with the truth about her prognosis.

"You haven't had a seizure in ages, so there's no reason to believe they'll continue," Hannah had tried to tell her at their last session, but now Abby could no longer bring herself to care.

Having discovered the depressing truth of her prognosis she'd decided that it was best to end her sessions with Hannah completely. The psychologist had tried her utmost to convince her not to, but there seemed little point in carrying on.

Abby knew the truth and now she had to try and learn to cope with this on her own. While she believed Hannah that she herself had *insisted* upon the idea of the deception (and the psychologist had shown her a signed release testifying same) Abby no longer felt able to trust her.

In truth, it was hard to trust anyone now, and in the meantime, she'd pleaded with Erin and her family to stop hiding things.

"No more secrets, please," she'd implored suspecting that

such an elaborate deception would've been considerable strain on them too.

"Trying to work around Claire's pregnancy was very tricky," her mum confessed, "particularly as she was so far along when you had the last blackout. We had to pretend she wanted to keep it under wraps, whereas the truth was that all of us–including you–had known for months."

"And we couldn't celebrate Tom's fortieth either," Caroline chipped in.

But the hardest thing of all (and the one Abby felt most guilty about) was the fact that Erin had indeed started seeing someone.

Dermot.

"We couldn't admit that we'd got together while you were ill," her best friend informed her sheepishly, and Abby immediately thought back to how her brother had almost let it slip that day in the service station, and how strangely reluctant Erin had been to confide in her.

"We got chatting at the hospital one of the times and I suppose things just went from there."

Abby was thrilled for them, but felt awful that they'd had to keep their relationship under wraps.

And of course, there were some other things Erin had had to keep hidden too.

"I nearly had a heart attack when we met up that time after you got out of the hospital, and you commented that I didn't have much of a tan," she said. "I'd completely forgotten that you'd naturally assume I was just back from Dubai ...

So many secrets, so many lies ... Although the truth had been devastating, Abby was in a way glad that they'd all stopped treating her like a special case. Much better to have things back to normal–although she didn't think that the word could ever be applied to her situation ...

Just then there was a loud rustling from the bottom of the

garden, and all three sisters jumped backwards in fright when, from behind thick bamboo, a small Jack Russell terrier emerged. The little dog sniffed around the area for a while, and evidently oblivious to his surprised audience, eventually sat back on his haunches and pooped all over Caroline's perfectly manicured lawn.

"Go and poop in your own garden, you little fecker ..." Caroline jumped up and went to shoo her neighbour's dog away.

Claire looked at Abby in surprise. "Well, I never thought I'd see the day," she laughed. "I was sure you were ruined for life."

Abby looked at her. "Ruined for life?"

"After the dog that knocked you over when we lived in Woodbrook?" she said, referring to where the family lived when they were kids. "I figured he was the reason you were always terrified of dogs. Though I wouldn't blame you; hit yourself a hell of a whack on the kerb."

Having heard the tail end of the conversation, Caroline sat back down. "Hell of whack where?" she said, and as her sister met her eye, Abby understood what she was getting at.

"Here," Claire said, pointing to the left hand side of own head. "I'm surprised it didn't knock you out altogether, although maybe it did, I can't really remember. Either way, I wasn't going to say anything to Mum about it; you were only six and I was the one supposed to be looking after you and ... what?" she asked frowning, as Abby and Caroline looked at one another.

Her older sister had not only given Abby the reason behind her long-held doggy phobia, but also solved the mystery of her earlier, unidentified brain injury.

LATER THAT EVENING, when the others went back to Teresa's, Abby and Caroline chatted some more.

"I think you should tell Hannah," her sister said.

"What's the point? It doesn't matter now, does it?"

"Well, for what it's worth, I think you made a mistake giving up seeing her. She was only doing what she thought was right– we all were. And you have to admit that keeping you in the dark did you nothing but good in the end."

"If it did me nothing but good then why I am so low?" Abby sighed. "Why do I feel so … I don't know … miserable?"

Caroline seemed to want to say something, but then decided against it.

"You've been through a lot emotionally," she soothed. "But try not to let it get to you too much - it's stress that triggers the seizures in the first place, remember?"

"I know, I know," Abby was worn-out from hearing this. "Maybe I'm just feeling down because I no longer have my Best Life list. Should I make another?"

"Sweetheart, while the list was a wonderful idea at the time, I think it's probably served its purpose now," her sister said gently. "It was great that you managed to do all those things and you know we loved doing them with you, but now it's probably best for you to try and get back to some kind of reality." She looked sideways at her. "How *is* your memory these days? You're still backing everything up?"

Abby was, but not with the same enthusiasm. It was hard to see the point. And the significance of her discovery had sent her into such a tailspin that she didn't particularly *want* to remember what she was feeling these days.

While she'd diarised bumping into Kieran, and having it all out with Hannah and her mother, after that she hadn't recorded much else. It just seemed pointless.

Yet deep down, Abby got the sense that something else of great significance had happened; something she didn't particularly want to remember, and hadn't made a record of it on purpose.

"I'm doing my best, but I find it all a bit futile to be honest," she said.

"Well, I don't. If you do black out again, the archives will keep you up to speed."

The truth was, Abby wasn't sure if she even cared anymore. *Everything* seemed pointless and hopeless at the moment.

She just couldn't figure out why.

CAROLINE WAS in Dundrum Shopping Centre immersed in her favourite pastime. She'd just dropped a *fortune* in Mamas and Papas on baby gear for a friend who'd recently given birth, and she decided to stop off for a quick bite to eat before heading into Harvey Nicks to do even more damage to her credit card.

All the Christmas party stuff was in now, and as well as updating her own wardrobe, she was planning on buying Abby a brand new handbag or perhaps a killer pair of heels; something that might help cheer up her little sister.

While their mum had initially been completely against the recent deception, Caroline had to admit that Abby's idea had some merit.

Unlike Teresa, Caroline didn't need a psychologist to put her mind at ease, as far as she was concerned if it helped Abby, that was all that mattered.

But despite this, she was now relieved the fantasy was finally over. Oddly the longer things went on and the better Abby managed, the easier it became to keep her true prognosis a secret.

"I don't bloody *believe* this!"

She turned around sharply at the sound of commotion coming from the hot food queue a little way across. Two men were squaring up to one another over what seemed to be a spilled bottle of Coke, and speak of the devil ….one of them was Finn.

Although he had his back to her, Caroline would recognise the voice anywhere, not to mention the worried-looking Lab by his side.

"Aren't you going to apologise?" Finn snarled at the customer who'd evidently been trying (and failed) to balance two bottles of Coke on a tray with one hand. Both had crashed to the floor and exploded all over Finn, who was ahead of him in the queue.

"It's an accident–what's your problem?" the man replied, gruffly.

"My problem is that I'm covered in goddamn Coke," Finn retorted angrily "Accident or not, you could at least bloody apologise."

Caroline was taken aback - he was usually so mild-mannered. Poor Lucy, was looking very sheepish alongside him and gently nudged his leg in an effort to calm him.

"Ah piss off– you shouldn't be out on your own anyway," the man said derisively.

"People like me…?"

As both men continued to stare each other down, Caroline could see Finn's jaw working furiously, and realising that the situation was about to explode, hurried over to his side.

"Hey, long time no see," she greeted Finn, quickly putting herself between the two men. Lucy looked up and gratefully wagged her tail.

"Caroline…" Finn said. "What are you doing here?"

The other man grunted, moving away and when Finn went to follow him she put a hand on his arm.

"Don't," she soothed. "He's not worth it. I was just getting something to eat, why don't you and Lucy sit down and I'll get some paper towels. And maybe a drink?"

Finn looked at her warily before nodding.

"All right," he sighed eventually, "just a coffee, thanks."

As he trundled away from the waiting area, Caroline couldn't believe how dishevelled and ... despondent he looked.

She knew that this wasn't all to do with the recent fracas; given his bloodshot eyes and irritable behaviour, Finn clearly wasn't himself.

So he was taking the break-up badly too, but unlike Abby was all too aware of the reasons for his broken heart.

Right, she thought, as she watched a clearly defeated Finn slump heavily into a seat nearby (rather reminiscent of the way Abby had looked the week before at her house) enough sanctimonious nonsense.

Time to make things right.

THE HEAVY, leadenness in her head still wouldn't go away, no matter what Abby did.

Today, she'd arranged to meet Erin for lunch in the Italian Quarter. Her friend was apparently eager to try out a new restaurants, although Abby suspected it was probably just another ruse to cheer her up.

Everyone was trying hard to keep her spirits up, but since she'd discovered the truth, Abby no longer had the same enthusiasm, despite how far she'd come this year.

There was still no getting away from the fact that one single slip, and it would all be gone and she'd be right back at square one. This year had been the best of her life and she'd never been happier, but try as she might she couldn't rise out of the fog.

It felt a lot like those early days after her break up with

Kieran, when she felt that everything in the world had turned bleak and horrible.

Except this time, she got the sense deep down that she was missing something - something important.

Difficult to explain, especially now, but it felt like almost hiding something from herself. Strange feeling, knowing that you couldn't trust yourself, let alone others.

She had expected to feel more upset and paranoid, but the truth was she just didn't have the strength. Probably understandable given her setback – like someone running a marathon to discover that the race finished the day before.

Spent, drained and numb that such immense effort had gone to waste. One more seizure and she'd be right back where she started. Must be a little bit what purgatory was like.

As Abby continued down the street, a handwritten poster on a nearby lamppost briefly caught her attention.

Your favourite colour is purple.

Some new marketing thing, she mused as she spied another sign further along the path.

You take two sugars in your coffee.

Huh.

By the time she passed the third sign, her curiously was piqued. Was there an election happening soon or …? Interesting way to catch people's attention.

Your favourite book is 'To Kill a Mockingbird'

That was her favourite book.

Your favourite song is 'The Long and Winding Road'

Abby looked further down the street and saw that every lamppost along her street adorned with these strange posters.

This was weird….

Your favourite film is 'Gladiator.'

It was almost as if these things were personalised. Just went to show how commonplace her own tastes were, didn't it? she mused. And how incredibly well targeted these campaigns could be.

Your favourite number is 17, even though it lost you $1k in Vegas

Hold on …Now Abby was feeling spooked.

What was going on? Each one of these signs had relevance; in was like they were referring *precisely* to her and her life. Surely there weren't that many others who ate chocolate out of the freezer, loved *Gladiator*, or bet 17 in Vegas?

Abby moved on, agog with confusion while other passers-by seemed to be moving on without interest–or concern.

Your hardest memory was your dad's death

Now Abby was totally wrong-footed. What *was* all this? She might be paranoid these days, but this stuff really was personal to her. She quickly moved on to the next sign.

Despite what you think right now, your best *memories are yet to come…*

Tears came to her eyes then, but not borne from fear.

Looking ahead to the final sign, Abby saw someone standing alongside it–someone watching her as she approached.

You ….

And to her trepidation she realised it was someone she recognised, although how she knew this or who the person was, she honestly couldn't say.

All Abby knew was that when she'd first laid eyes on him, her heart leapt into her stomach, and she had the clearest sense of déjà vu.

Except something told her that it wasn't quite déjà vu.

Temporarily shifting her gaze away, she read the final sign.

And I want to be there for every last one.

"I REALLY DON'T KNOW where to begin ..." the guy said uncertainly as they faced one other. "You've probably guessed that we kind of ... know each another."

She nodded wordlessly. His eyes, dark brown, almost mahogany - but more than that she realised, her heart hammering - they were *familiar*.

"I suppose I might as well start from the beginning– "

"No need," Abby interjected, her voice a whisper. "I know."

His eyes widened as he clasped her hands and held them. "You mean you ... remember?"

"I just know," she gulped. "It's the reason I've been carrying around this ... weight in my heart – you're the reason. I'm certain of it."

"Abby, why did you do it?" he asked gently. "Why didn't you tell me - why push me away? When Caroline told me the truth I–"

"Because it isn't fair," she said, not needing to know the details; not when it was so obvious that this man's absence was what was causing her so much pain.

Why *wouldn't* she have pushed him away, when it was so clear she was in love with him?

"We can deal with this," he spoke quickly. "We've dealt with it before. Even without all the stuff I erased, we'll start again."

Now Abby understood why she had no memories of him (at least not any tangible ones), nothing to trigger the time they'd spent together. "Ah."

"I'm sorry …I was so angry. But we can build it all up again, make more memories - together. I meant what I said –the best is yet to come."

Her heart soared, but still she was unsure. "I so want to believe it, but you don't know that."

"I *do*," he argued. "And I know that I don't give a damn if every morning you wake up beside me and don't recognise me–just as long as you *do* wake up beside me."

"You don't really mean it."

"Abby, I love you and I want to spend the rest of my life with you. Don't push me away again. For better or worse, remember?"

She couldn't help but laugh. "The word is meaningless when it comes to me, you know that right?"

"Don't I just?" he replied, chuckling too.

Abby looked into his eyes and studied every contour of his face, all the while furiously trying to recall a memory, some tangible recollection of this man who was of such immense importance, but it stayed out of her grasp. There was nothing but a feeling.

Muscle memory? After all, most crucial of muscles was the heart.

She tentatively lifted a hand to his cheek. "You do realise what you're getting into …"

"You'd better believe it," he replied, drawing her close and into his arms.

The two of them stood like that for a long time, wrapped together, gazes locked, both willing the memories to return.

But Abby didn't need memories to to know that she was deeply in love with this man, and knew instinctively that she could trust him with her life.

Finally, and without breaking eye contact, he inclined his head towards hers.

"Oh and by the way ..." he murmured but Abby could barely hear him over the beating of her own heart. "Just in case you're wondering ..." He managed to get the rest of the words out right before his lips met hers, "my name is Finn."

SNOW PINE CHRISTMAS

ADAPTED AS THE HOLIDAY MOVIE 'CHRISTMAS
ON THE ROCKS'

CHAPTER 1

JENNIFER AWOKE with a start - as if an electric current had passed through her body, and her brain scrambled to orientate itself.

She'd had that dream again; the one of her and her sister Sarah racing downstairs together on Christmas morning in anticipation of what lay at the bottom of the family Christmas tree.

She placed her hand on her chest as if to slow her heart rate. Even though the memory was old, the excitement she'd felt during that recurring dream was so real it had caused her pulse to physically race. As if she was right back there with her sister and folks in their old house in San Diego.

But this wasn't the family home, and The Snow Pine Lodge very *definitely* wasn't in San Diego.

Not in Kansas anymore, Toto.

Glancing at her watch, she was amazed she'd dozed off for the best part of an hour and altogether relieved that none of the other lodge staff, or indeed her boss, had walked in to find her quite literally, sleeping on the job.

Jennifer sat up on the couch, squinting at the unnaturally

bright light coming through the window, and raised her hand to shield her eyes.

Last night's blanket of fresh snowfall was now fully illuminated by the afternoon sun, and the entire valley in front of the Snow Pine Lodge very much lived up to its name.

That picture postcard card view of pine trees and snow-covered mountaintops again brought her thoughts back to her sister. Growing up, they had always dreamed of a fairytale Christmas complete with twinkling lights, freshly fallen snow and hot chocolate to warm the hands and soul.

Southern Cali wasn't best suited for that, and while Jennifer felt she was finally living that dream here in the Colorado Rockies, it didn't seem complete without her sister to share it.

Their lives had taken very different paths; Jennifer now getting to grips with her new event co-ordinator role here at the lodge, while Sarah had followed a family tradition going back generations by enlisting in the US Navy - a career choice that meant the once-close siblings were now worlds apart.

'Really wish you could see this view, sis,' Jennifer whispered as she studied various groups of guests in colourful ski gear relaxing on the terrace overlooking the valley and snow-capped mountains beyond.

The ski lift visible in the distance reminded her of an old Christmas ornament they had - a snow globe with a couple of snowmen sitting in a chair lift while others skied downhill.

She opened the window a little to allow in some cold crisp air in an attempt to kickstart her brain.

One thing Jennifer hadn't been prepared for was the altitude. Born and raised at sea level, it had been a real shock to the system getting to grips with the diminished oxygen levels up here.

Although in truth, she'd been finding it a bit hard to breathe back home anyway, since yet another great romance hit the rocks.

Story of her life.

But just as she was getting to grips with the uncertainty of starting a new position right in the middle of the winter season, even more anxiety beckoned - in particular, an upcoming high-end corporate event for a demanding Silicon Valley CEO.

Which combined with the lack of oxygen was starting to make Jennifer feel overwhelmed. Was she really capable of pulling this off?

Getting to her feet, she picked her way through boxes overflowing with ancient Christmas decorations; stuff she'd been sorting through before her eyelids grew so heavy that a power nap was in order.

She took a deep breath and surveyed all; her sister's voice echoing in her head yet again.

'You've got this Jen - time to shine. Nobody does Christmas like the Whytes.'

CHAPTER 2

JENNIFER'S PHONE chirped as she headed towards her office in the main lodge building. She rolled her eyes upon seeing the sender's details and accompanying subject line.

Re: Reception Drinks and Canapés

This was the guy's *third* email today alone, none of which she'd had a chance to respond to as yet.

The excitement of overseeing her first official holiday event was very quickly turning to annoyance because of this particular CEO's demands.

Peter McCarthy from MotionTech wanted to oversee every teeny-tiny little detail, instead of just letting her do her job.

Honestly, if she were to sit in her office all day answering his already lengthy list of queries and messages, she would get nothing at all done.

Better to just send a brief note and let her get on with it - she was the event specialist after all.

This guy's OCD about everything from the glassware to Wi-Fi speed was exhausting.

Who cared about wifi when your guests were here to enjoy everything else the Snow Pine Lodge offered? An escape from it all, a chance to marvel at the wonders of nature, to ski or sit in front of the many open fires with a glass of wine or a hot chocolate. Or toast s'mores around the fire pit by night.

If Jennifer had her way, wifi would be banned altogether so that people could truly disconnect and escape.

Not these tech types though, she mused groaning as her phone lit up once more with another missive from Mr McCarthy - this time with the subject line: *'party favors'.*

Seriously?

She put the phone down and surveyed the stack of invoices, kitchen menus, regular mail and various other tasks to be attended to.

When taking this position, Jennifer had been enchanted by visions of herself wandering along snowy trails in the mountains, wrapped up snug and warm in her newly purchased winter wardrobe of cosy knits and soft down jackets - the ones she hadn't yet had a chance to purchase.

She took a deep breath and resolved to attack the pile of work, so she could de-stress by doing the one thing that always brought balance to her life, getting out in nature.

Jennifer dreamed again of sauntering through that winter wonderland behind the glass in the crisp mountain air, fresh snow crunching beneath her feet.

Heaven...

PETER CHECKED HIS INBOX - AGAIN. Still no reply from the Snow Pine Lodge.

He knew things moved at a different pace in the analogue world and likely more so in the mountains, but this was getting ridiculous.

One of the most crucial, career-defining moments in his life was potentially in the hands of some yokel who had no inkling of just how important this upcoming event was.

Even his less-than-subtle correspondence thus far, where he tried to use every opportunity to convey its importance hadn't been met with the required response from jen.events@thesnowpinelodge, or indeed for the most part, any response at all.

Everything Peter poured into his career over the years had led to this, his chance to take everything he'd learned in the technology world, and finally make his mark in the world of fitness wearables.

His newly patented activity watch, Solas, was about to shake up the industry and make the big boys sit up and take notice.

Problem was you only got one chance to make a first impression.

Unfortunately, Peter's first impression was in the hands of a frustratingly blasé event planner, and if that meant hourly emails, text messages and phone calls to ensure everything went like clockwork so be it.

He reached for his phone and dialled the Colorado phone number.

Time to wake up the mountain yokels once and for all...

CHAPTER 3

Jennifer and her assistant Suzi stood in the middle of the Jack-alope banqueting room surrounded by the boxes of spare decorations she'd found in storage earlier.

Unfortunately, most of the good stuff had already been utilised around the lodge interior.

'Three days to turn this place into a Christmas wonderland,' she muttered dubiously, surveying the room.

'Don't you mean two days?' Suzi pointed out. 'Isn't the MotionTech CEO coming in the day before to check that everything is to his......taste?'

Jennifer grimaced, realising she was right; this place had to be perfect before Digi-Guy arrived, or what little oxygen was in the air up here would be sucked right out of it.

'Plenty of time,' she grinned, trying to convey the message that everything was under control. 'Nick said he's ours for the rest of today, so once we get him on fairy light duty, we'll have this place well on the way in no time.'

She surveyed the huge room and automatically started to feel calmer.

This place oozed character; from the wooden beams on the

high vaulted ceiling at one end, to the grand fireplace at the far side. But it was the massive floor-to-ceiling picture windows that afforded an incredible view of the snowy surrounds, that really gave this room the wow factor.

Even the questionably ethical moose head above the fire looked like it belonged here. A throwback to another era of this former hunting lodge, and while Jennifer wondered about maybe having Moe the Moose take a sabbatical, she figured he could stay put for now at least.

Something about the tech CEO's voice on the phone earlier had the air of an alpha male who may well have frequented such lodges in a bygone era.

'It's all the details,' Peter McCarthy insisted, and even though he'd been annoyingly brusque when bombarding her with request after request, there was also something about his voice that made his demands less … well, demanding.

A familiarity to it that she'd put down to the California twang. Weird too that she'd once gone to high school with a guy called Peter McCarthy, so that could be it either.

Though the Mack she'd known was a world apart from this anal fussy-wuss.

In any case, when Jennifer promised the guy that everything was in hand, she'd meant every word.

This was going to be a night to remember, not just a corporate knees-up, but the perfect opportunity to showcase her expertise and prove to her bosses that her employment at the Snow Pine Lodge was merited.

The perfect line in the snow between her past and her future.

She and the others set to work sorting through boxes, hanging fairy lights and decorating almost every surface of the banqueting room with festive finery.

Handyman Nick painstakingly wrapped the ceiling beams with individual light strands, and by the time they'd finished, even Moe the Moose got a festive makeover with an old-style berry wreath around his neck.

'Not much life left in these,' Suzi commented, kicking one of the still half-full boxes with her foot. 'This stuff of Christmas Past should have found its way into the recycle pile a long time ago.'

Jennifer picked up a stray bauble. While everything here had indeed long since seen better days, there was something comfortingly retro about it all too - a reminder of childhood Christmases gone by.

While this stuff certainly wouldn't do for a high-end corporate event, she hadn't the heart to throw it away and would find a way to make use of it somewhere - even if just in her own office.

'You'd have to wonder why you need anything in here with all *that* out there,' Nick commented, nodding to the windows with a perfectly framed view of the picturesque valley, framed by freshly snow-dusted pine trees.

Jennifer followed his gaze as a small flurry of snowflakes gently drifted past the window.

It was indeed a tableau that rendered everything else insignificant. 'Unfortunately, it'll be dark when the party kicks off.'

'True.' He nodded. 'I'll check out the garage; might be some outdoor lights we can string along the railings out there?'

'And maybe cut some Toyon berry bush from the garden,' Suzi commented. 'We often put it in vases at this time of year,' she said to Jennifer. 'It's kind of a Christmas tradition in these parts.'

'Toyon berry?'

'Some people call them Christmas Berries, or California Holly. They grow in creek beds and on the lower slopes,' Nick told her.

'Gives off a gorgeous festive scent too,' Suzi enthused. 'With that and the mulled wine, those tech dudes will literally be inhaling Christmas spirit when they walk in the room.'

'Now we're talking,' Jennifer grinned, already feeling some of the pressure lift, as she could see a vision for the event starting to form. 'Nick if you could organise those lights and the berries that would be fantastic, and then I can take some photos of everything and send them to the client.'

During their time decorating, her phone had pinged several times and Jennifer knew even without checking that Peter McCarthy would be responsible for some, if not all of those.

She picked up her notebook from a nearby table and flicked to a section for the launch event, ticking off some of her to-do list, before adding several more ideas.

'Suzi, maybe get a list of room allocations for MotionTech guests to housekeeping in advance so we can make ensure everything's in order in time for their arrival. Also, is there any way to check the wifi speed in here? Unsurprisingly these tech types view wifi on par with running water or flushing toilets,' she added archly. 'You know, the essentials.'

'My phone usually works fine with it, though cell reception is patchy at best up here as I'm sure you know,' Nick said, shrugging.

'Is it possible to measure the actual speed though? This guy's questions have been very specific, as in the exact download and upload capability.'

'Dunno, all I know is you don't have to wait too long for Twitter to load.'

'Nothing says happy holidays like super-fast wifi,' Suzi chuckled.

'Something to do with a PowerPoint presentation. To be honest, this guy doesn't sound like someone who cares a whole bunch about the festive side, it's *way* down the list of importance anyway.' Jennifer grimaced. 'Honestly, if I hear "it's all in the details," one more time I think I'll explode. Seems to be this guy's favourite catchphrase.'

'Weird. Why host a Christmas party if you don't care about Christmas? OK, let me ask Jake who looks after the IT here to get some numbers for you.'

'Thanks.'

Next, Jennifer checked in with the kitchen to ensure that the catering element was under control.

But things were already shaping up better than she'd anticipated.

Maybe she might even be able to fit in a ramble out and amongst those picture postcard views she'd been viewing from behind glass since her arrival?

Something told her not to expend too much energy outdoors though; Jennifer suspected she'd need every ounce she could muster by the time this weekend was over.

FINALLY ... Peter exhaled in relief upon seeing the email subject line, or indeed any email at all from the SnowPine Lodge, which he'd already decided wouldn't be getting any more business from him due to their event organiser's laid-back approach.

While the woman sounded fine on the phone, she was so low on formality that her emails didn't even include her full name and job title.

He clicked into the body of the email from jen.events@snowpinelodge.com and his heart dropped afresh to see a disappointingly brief update and a reference to precariously low wifi speed. Followed by a reassurance (again short on detail) that everything was in hand.

However, when he clicked on the attached images of the beautifully festive and welcoming banqueting room, he exhaled a little.

The location truly did look stunning.

Reminding him why he had decided on this spot in the first place. Exactly the kind of surroundings in which his brand-new fitness device would be right at home.

Hiking, kayaking, climbing, trail running in summer, skiing and snowboarding in winter ... the Solas watch could take photos and post activity directly to social media platforms in real-time.

The Colorado Mountains were an outdoor enthusiast's dream at this time of year, and for many adventure seekers, there was only one thing better than being in the great outdoors - and that was sharing it with others.

His PowerPoint presentation was ready to go, and sample model gift packs already winging their way to the hotel.

This time tomorrow, Peter would have his feet on the ground in the Snow Pine Lodge to ensure that the party planner - and indeed everyone concerned with this make-or-break event - was as motivated as he was.

CHAPTER 5

JENNIFER FELT the crisp air tighten the skin on her cheeks, and watched her breath turning into a mini-snow cloud right in front of her face.

The air was calm and still as she tentatively picked her way along the trail; the partly melted and refrozen snow on the gravel underneath gave her a decent grip.

Her legs were freezing though, even with two pairs of running tights on. A trip to the local sports store was definitely on the cards once this weekend was out of the way.

Her pace was slow as she consciously breathed deeply while picking her footing, not wanting to fall and end up in the emergency room ahead of her first big event.

The trail meandered alongside a partially frozen river, surrounded by a huge snow-capped boulder that almost seemed to float in the distance.

She stopped to take a photo of the picturesque beauty, only to find her phone was dead. Then took off a glove to turn it back on, before realising it was likely the icy temperature that had caused it to power off.

Oh well, plenty of time for photography in the future, she

mused, setting off again in the direction of the little resort village in the valley about a mile from the lodge, where the ski lift was based.

As she approached the main drag, she noticed an elderly guy shaping a block of ice outside an artisan cabin.

'Morning!' she offered by way of greeting.

'Oh, hello there,' he replied, glancing up.

'Wow, that's amazing,' Looking closer, Jennifer stared at the intricately sculpted side of the block of ice he was working on. Though only half-finished, it was easily identifiable as a snowboarder in motion.

'Thank you. Are you enjoying your vacation?'

'Oh, I'm not on vacation. I just started a new job up at the Snow Pine.'

'Ah, I see,' the older man grinned, gently blowing some ice shavings away from his project. 'I saw the trainers and figured you weren't local.'

She looked down at her feet, puzzled.

'Those look like road shoes; you might want to invest in some trail boots or yak tracks if you're going to be hitting the trails around here, higher up especially.'

'Thanks for the tip, I'll look into it. I have to say your work truly is amazing.' Jennifer repeated awestruck, an idea starting to form in her head as she thought about tomorrow night's event, and the fact that the tech company had some kind of sports connection. 'The detail on this is just incredible.' She stooped lower to inspect a finished piece on a platform off to one side. 'Do you do commissions?'

The man chuckled 'Nah, this is just a hobby. When it's cold I sculpt and when it's warm, I paint.'

She had to smile at this rather idyllic lifestyle description.

'A couple of the local businesses buy them off me from time to time, pays the bills,' he added modestly.

'I'm an event organiser for the Lodge and these in particular would be awesome for something I'm working on right now. Do you have any others ready-made?'

'Just these so far, but I'm a fast worker.'

Quick as you like, Jennifer arranged a price for two finished sculptures and shook on it, arranging for Nick to have them transported, before heading onwards with a pep in her step.

Talk about the wow factor.

'Just make sure to have your guy call me about collection before the weather turns,' the guy who'd introduced himself as Don told her.

'Should be fine, the weather seems pretty settled,' she shrugged, having been diligently watching the forecast to establish if the snow was due for her first-ever white Christmas.

But there was nothing on the radar just yet.

Don chuckled. 'You'll find this place has a climate all of its own. I'd put money on another fresh dumping soon.'

Jennifer looked up at the brilliant blue skies above the tree line and was dubious.

But hey, more snow could only be a positive for the Snow Pine Lodge's Christmas visitors, couldn't it?

CHAPTER 6

THE FOLLOWING MORNING, Jennifer pulled back the curtains in her room to be greeted by a blizzard blowing across the valley.

Evidently, the Ice Man was indeed better than Siri at predicting the weather.

The MotionTech crew was due to arrive later that day and she prayed that everything would go off smoothly.

Her first major event in a new job was always going to be stressful, but the combination of a new role, unfamiliar location and demanding client had her feeling the pressure more than she had anticipated.

In her old job, Jennifer had been part of an extensive team, but here, the buck stopped with her alone.

Though her new crew had worked out well so far, especially Suzi and Nick.

Now it was all about dealing with the client and making sure everything ran like clockwork.

No time for leisurely rambles this morning she thought, almost relieved, since yesterday's outing had felt more like a half-marathon given the underfoot conditions and oxygen scarcity.

She ran through a mental list of things to do before the MotionTech CEO and his guests turned up.

She needed to pull out all the stops for Peter McCarthy's arrival; somewhat dispirited that the images of the newly-decorated banqueting hall she'd since forwarded hadn't exactly been met with gushing acclaim.

An on-the-ground walkthrough was what was needed to get a true sense of just how special and festive this place was.

Tech-guy would have a chance to see for himself how everything looked, and more to the point how magical it felt this evening, before the main event tomorrow night.

'MORNING,' Jennifer mumbled to Suzi in the lobby, some half-chewed bagel in her mouth as she ate breakfast on the go. 'The first of the corporate crew arrives at lunchtime. Can you ensure that housekeeping is on top of the changeover? And just double-check that Mr McCarthy has been assigned the Juniper Suite; that one's vacant since Wednesday so we should be able to get him in right away.'

'Already on it,' the younger girl smiled as she passed.

Inside her office, Jennifer picked up the flashing phone to a message from the front desk informing her that there was somebody to see her.

As she made her way back out to the lobby, she spied a stylish woman in her thirties standing off to the side of reception, taking in the picture postcard view down the valley.

'Hi there, good morning. I'm Jennifer the events co-ordinator, how can I help?'

'Hello,' the woman replied, looking a little spellbound by the gentle flurry outside. 'Laura from MotionTech to carry out some advance planning for the event tomorrow.'

'Oh, will Mr McCarthy not be joining us? Last I heard he was checking in today.'

'Yes, he's on his way. I'm just here early to set up for the presentation, ensure our technology runs smoothly and carry out any troubleshooting.'

'Of course, let me take you through to the Jackalope Room and help get you set up.'

Having gone off to call the catering supplier and check their schedule for tomorrow's food delivery, a little later Jennifer went back to check on the assistant.

Walking into the room, she noticed the curtains drawn and a snazzy high-tech projector displaying activity images featuring a chunky sports watch called Solas.

The assistant had since been joined by someone else and they were getting to grips with an iPad and flicking between images and info pages.

'How's everything going?' Jennifer enquired amiably.

'So far so good,' Laura replied, and as her colleague looked up and the projector lights illuminated his face, Jennifer felt her head spin.

But this time it wasn't due to lack of oxygen.

She felt the blood drain from her face and almost felt herself stumble as she grabbed the back of a chair for support.

Mack ...

CHAPTER 7

HE SEEMED to recognise her at the same time.

'Jen? It can't be...' His voice trailed off as he too wore a look of total astonishment.

Her cheeks reddened as she gripped a nearby banqueting chair to balance herself.

'You two know each other?' Laura asked, rather unnecessarily.

'Yeah......' He ran his fingers through his sandy blond locks, now considerably shorter than she remembered. 'We were in high school together......about a million years ago.' He moved awkwardly to greet her, while Jennifer's knuckles had turned as white as the freshly fallen snow.

'I can't believe it's you ...' She scrambled to reconnect the dropped connection between her overloaded brain and her mouth. 'I knew you sounded familiar on the phone, but with the name, I didn't put two and two together... thought it was just the San Diego accent I was picking up on.'

'I go by my proper name now.' He shrugged. 'Business stuff, you know. And you never mentioned yours.'

As she moved to embrace her old high school flame in what

now felt like an out-of-body experience, Jennifer struggled to process her feelings.

There was a strained silence until Mack quickly mumbled something about catching up properly once he and Laura had finished prepping the presentation, and she agreed, practically backing out of the room.

It was all so surreal...

Though the fact that he'd mentioned going over plans first and catching up second left Jennifer in no doubt Mack wasn't quite as thrown by the twist of fate as she.

'You OK?' Back out in the main reception, Suzi looked puzzled. 'You look like you've just seen a ghost.

'Something like that,' she mumbled.

Peter McCarthy was indeed Jennifer's very own Ghost of Christmas Past.

A little later, she sat across from the first guy she had ever kissed ... loved, even?

Her thoughts had been in a tailspin since her discovery that the man who had been the proverbial thorn in her side for the last couple of weeks was no stranger - hell he'd even featured in a dream she'd had just a few nights ago.

Jennifer now wondered if some part of her brain had recognised Mack's voice, though his San Diego accent had taken on more of a Northern Cali twang these days.

It's all in the details...

'So everything is just how you want it for tomorrow?' she asked, as they shared a hot chocolate by the fire pit on the terrace overlooking the valley.

She was trying to remain professional while subconsciously thinking how great he looked these days and how much he'd changed - for the better.

Despite the bulky Canada Goose jacket he was wearing just now, she had seen enough to confirm he was in great shape.

As one would expect from the CEO of a soon-to-be stellar fitness tech company.

'All looks great. Gotta say, if I'd known it was you over-seeing this, I'd have been far less worried; you always had great attention to detail. As it is, I still can't believe we were having a blind back and forth for weeks. You must have thought I was an almighty pain in the butt.'

'Of course not,' she lied, deciding to spare his feelings. 'But it might have helped if I'd thought to question your name or I'd provided mine. But now that I truly understand how much this means to your future, and that it's not just your run-of-the-mill Christmas party, I get how much of a big deal this is.'

Jennifer took a sip of her rapidly cooling hot chocolate as its warmth penetrated her gloves. 'But hey, just because we know each other and have a ... history, it won't get in the way of any professionalism. And on both counts, I'm here to help.'

'Thanks. To be honest I feel so much better to be here on the ground and see for myself how much everything is under control. But what a place to live, how do you get anything done with all this outside your door?'

Mack gazed down the valley as the clouds from earlier began to break and sunbeams illuminated the surrounding granite boulders, causing them to almost sparkle.

'It's all new to me too, I only started working here.'

Before he could begin to digest the new revelation that possibly the most defining day of his career to date was in the hands of not only an ex-high school sweetheart but a rookie too, Jennifer stood up.

'Come with me a sec, I want to show you something,' she urged, catching sight of Nick driving a flatbed truck slowly up the avenue toward the storage yard.

CHAPTER 8

'So that was ... fun - especially with such precious cargo,' her colleague said, wiping his brow as she and Mack approached.

Once she'd made introductions, Jennifer headed to the back of the truck.

'Did you take a look?' she asked surveying the canvas-covered cargo in question.

'Yep. And they are *way* cool if you excuse the pun.' Nick climbed up on the back and carefully peeled back the canvas to reveal the snowboarder sculptures she'd commissioned from the artisan.

'Wow...' Eyes widening, Mack moved closer to inspect the freshly carved hunks of ice.

'Fitting given the theme, eh?' she said proudly.

He looked at her. 'These are for our event?'

'Yep, specially commissioned for you guys, I even got your logo engraved on the base.'

He looked so pleased, she didn't admit to how it was more a happy coincidence than her event management skills that was responsible.

'Incredible, but will they last? I mean won't they melt

indoors?' he mused out loud, as he tentatively touched a frozen arm.

'We'll keep them outside till the last minute, but in these temps, they won't be thawing any time soon,' Nick informed him knowledgeably. 'And these are Don Bailey sculptures, tough as you'll get. He uses a special freezing process for his blocks so there are no bubbles or fault lines. You'd need a hammer to crack these bad boys.'

He replaced the tarp and eased gently back down off the truck, before driving off again, leaving Mack and Jennifer to walk back towards the main lodge.

'So, everything really is under control. What about refreshments?'

He unzipped his jacket as they re-entered the warmth of the main reception area.

'Chef's got a fresh delivery of food coming in before noon tomorrow, and the kitchen is raring to go on the menu - so no worries on in that front either,' Jennifer reassured him. 'Why don't you go and get settled in your room? Check out the valley or do a little skiing or whatever. Time to relax a bit before your big night. Honestly, we've got it all covered.'

Mack took a deep breath and his face paled. 'Easier said than done. These presentations ... making speeches, this stuff's not ... my forte.'

She looked at him, surprised at how worried he sounded, and began to understand a little better why he'd been so demanding and insistent.

He really was stressed about all this.

'Try not to worry, Mack. Truly, everything is under control. If it helps, I'll go through a checklist with everyone again now, and ensure that we're all singing from the same hymn sheet, OK? No stone left unturned.'

'Thanks, I appreciate that. So... maybe I'll catch you later?' he called after her as she went to walk away.

'Sure, I'll be around. Anything you need just ask.'

'What about dinner? To um... show my appreciation for all your hard work,' he muttered, yet again sounding endearingly unsure of himself.

'Maybe, but I've got a lot to get through. There's this demanding tech CEO who's been breathing down my neck and I can't seem to shake him.' Jennifer winked, biting back a smile as she walked away with a fresh spring in her step.

And the kind of butterflies in her stomach she hadn't felt since high school.

CHAPTER 9

LATER THAT EVENING, Jennifer and Suzi packed away storage boxes and put the finishing touches to the festive decor, before switching on the lighting.

The banqueting room ceiling lit up like a brilliant night sky, and outside other newly-erected string lights reflected off the snow, casting an almost magical glow.

The light also illuminated the latest snowfall; the huge picture windows effectively turning it all into one giant snow globe.

Jennifer couldn't wait to see the ice sculptures in place; bringing them inside too soon was too risky given the temperature difference.

Plus it would surely be sensory overload for some of the newly arrived corporate guests, who by the noise emanating from the bar, were already full of festive cheer.

'Looks incredible,' Suzi gushed, snapping some photos with her phone.

Jennifer nodded. 'You know, I've done holiday events before but here it's almost effortless because it screams Christmas everywhere you look. Back home, we had to use twice as many decorations and bales of cotton to recreate that twinkling winter wonderland vibe. But this place....' she trailed off, marvelling at the decor and finally feeling the pressure of her first big gig subside, 'it doesn't have to try at all.'

Earlier the hotel's general manager (and Jennifer's boss) had popped in to inspect the room and seemed impressed by all the preparations, even if he still was a little hard to read just yet.

'There you are ...' At the sound of a voice she turned to see Mack approach. 'Wow, this truly is something...' he said, spinning around and slowly taking it all in.

'Better take these back to the office,' Suzi sang and winked as she picked up a couple of empty boxes and headed for the door. 'See you tomorrow.'

'So finished for the night then?' he asked, once he and Jennifer were once again alone.

'Yep, sounds like your guests are already enjoying themselves...'

'I know, apres-ski - isn't that what it's called up here?'

'Something like that - though I think you actually have to hit the slopes first,' Jennifer chuckled as she collected her phone and clipboard from a table beside the huge open fire.

'A few of them did, but the majority just hit the bar. There are a few pretty influential people to impress. For others, it's just a free jolly.'

'You truly are putting a lot into this.'

'Everything, I've literally put everything into it, Jen. Sometimes it feels like I should've just gone to Vegas and put it all on black.'

She could tell he was really feeling the pressure with every passing moment and her heart softened afresh.

'Well, for what it's worth I'd definitely buy a Solas device. Plenty of trails around here I intend to explore, and downloadable maps and GPS are perfect for someone like me who's always getting lost.'

'I'll get that taken care of - as a thanks for all this.'

'Emm no, I'll pay for it, thank you very much. And it's my job don't forget.'

'Glad to see you haven't changed much. Independent as ever.' He smiled fondly. Then took a couple of steps toward the window. 'The snow's starting to come down out there now.'

'Beautiful isn't it?' She followed his gaze as they stood together in silence, hypnotised.

'So, I need to get back out there and impress some Fitspo influencers enough to talk up my watch. Can I buy you a drink at least, since we didn't get a chance to do dinner?'

Jennifer's stomach growled as she remembered how hungry she was. Tempted as she was to accept his offer, it also played on her mind that socialising with clients under the watchful eye of her boss, may not be the wisest of moves.

'Go do your thing. I've still a lot to catch up on. But tomorrow night we can certainly grab that drink and celebrate a wildly successful launch.'

CHAPTER 10

THE FOLLOWING MORNING, Jennifer opened her eyes, when outside she heard the wind whistle and the sound of something buffeting the window.

She heaved herself upright, noting that she must be fully acclimatised to the elevation at last, given her head no longer felt like it had lead blocks inside.

Then moving to the window she opened back the curtain to see ... nothing, just pure blinding whiteness.

It must have snowed *all* night, and the accompanying high winds had created scarily blizzard conditions out there. So much so that even attempting to go outside looked impossible

She swallowed hard - today was going to be a long one if all Snow Pine guests ended up being confined to the lodge because of ski lift closures. Still, she thought brightening a little, it didn't get any more Christmassy than this, did it?

The phone on her bedside locker chimed and reading the message from Suzi, she quickly snapped back to reality.

'*Call me, we have a problem.*'

'Hey, just got your message what is it?'

'The catering company just called; the delivery truck is

stuck just off Route 9. The roads have been ploughed but the blizzard's made the main route into the valley impassable.'

'Oh no.' Jennifer sank back down on the edge of the bed. 'They'll be clearing it though, right?'

'They need the wind to ease off first, there are some pretty big drifts out there.'

Jennifer's heart lurched. 'Tell me this isn't happening. How does a goddamn snow resort get shut down because of ... snow?'

The weather forecast had said moderate snow.... what the hell was moderate about this?

'Doesn't happen that often,' Suzi said, resignedly. 'But the timing's not great ... considering.'

Jennifer tried to think fast.

OK, so the morning had started on a bad footing, she mused, trying to calm her heart rate.

She just needed to make sure that the day didn't end up like a snowboarder in the valley - going downhill fast.

A LITTLE LATER DOWN IN the lobby, Jennifer was met with a rabble of multi-coloured, skiwear-clad guests.

Some hovered around the front desk looking for updates on their ill-fated ski/snowboarding excursions. Others waited bleary-eyed for tables to become available in the packed restaurant since the combination of stranded would-be departures and incoming new arrivals caused a logjam of too many guests with nowhere to go.

Suddenly, the walls of the atrium seemed to shake as the entryway doors slammed open with a loud bang.

Then everyone turned towards the sound of an almighty crash, as the doorman struggled to secure the now-shattered main entrance glass door - while the wind swirled through reception, taking out the nearby 20-foot Christmas tree and setting many of the hanging lights into a frenzy.

Powder-like snow snaked in trails across the floor, melting as it met warmer air from the log fire.

'Talk about going from bad to worse ...' Jennifer mourned wide-eyed, reaching Suzi. 'Any word on the food?

'It's not looking good - the main drag is still totally impassable and the weather doesn't look like breaking until later this evening. Seems it'll be morning at the earliest before the ploughs can go back out.'

Oh. My. God.

Her heart pounding with anxiety as her brain struggled to figure out a backup plan, Jennifer spotted Mack chatting to his assistant and some others outside the restaurant.

He looked calm and relaxed, apparently blissfully unaware that the storm raging outside was about to be mirrored by an equally severe one inside.

'My office, quick - we need to figure this out.' Jennifer walked head down so as not to draw his attention, knowing he'd read the concern in her face and she'd have no answers to his inevitable questions.

'OK, let's see - the drinks are covered at least. This lot's already proven that free-flowing wine will buy us some grace. Let's check in with the kitchen; see if they can maybe work with what they've already got, and come up with some menu alternatives?'

She needed to rescue this - fast.

CHAPTER 11

SHE AND SUZI duly worked with the Snow Pine head chef to come up with a workable solution to their food shortage, and afterwards, Jennifer felt brave enough to seek out Mack, who was still holed up in the lobby sweet-talking influencers.

'Thanks, you saved my life,' he said, once she politely interrupted. 'Two point five million followers on Insta and TikTok combined. Can you believe these guys? A free weekend away, some merchandise and a gratis $600 sports watch and I'll get one post. One post that could well make or break the product launch.'

But he was smiling, and she noticed that he seemed way more relaxed about all of this than before - to the point that she felt guilty about having to stir up his worries once again.

'I need to talk to you.'

Immediately picking up on her more sombre mood, his eyes grew wide with bewilderment as she tried to lead him to a quieter spot in the rear of the lobby, but there was nowhere to be found.

Eventually, they stepped back into the Jackalope Room and Jennifer closed the door on the din.

'Kinda manic out there - shame about the weather, though I do think there is a fair chunk happy enough to not have to go up the mountain. Where did that come from?' Mack chattered, glancing outside at the drifting snow.

'I know, it's crazy.' She rolled her eyes as the huge window panes bowed and bellied with the strong gusts. Then she took a deep breath. 'Just wanted to reassure you that everything is under control - we had a moment when it came to the catering, but we've got it covered.'

There was nothing to be gained by worrying him. She was going to make this work regardless.

He nodded as the noise of the wind in the chimney above Moe the Moose howled afresh, and the roof lurched.

'Great,' he said a trace of concern crossing his face now. Though she could tell he appreciated being told about a problem already solved, rather than being presented with one that needed a solution.

'So dark in here. It's not sundown for about three hours. Good thing we got so many lights eh?'

Not five seconds later those lights flickered before going dark - to ironic cheers from the lobby.

Jennifer and Mack looked at one another in horror in the half-light flickering shadows of the fire.

On another occasion, it could have been romantic. But now a whirlwind of anxiety was going through both their minds.

Mack's on the digital presentation he'd spent months preparing.

Jennifer's with other, just as pressing matters - like a functioning kitchen and a freezing cold hotel.

'How long does it take for the generator to kick in? You do have a backup? Jen? he demanded, a little more urgently, given her hesitation.

'I'm not ... sure like I said, I've only been here a few weeks. Let me call Nick and ask.'

They took out their phones and began to swipe screens, the blue light of the screens illuminating the worried expressions they both wore.

'No signal,' Jennifer cursed

'No WIFI either.' Mack ran his fingers through his hair and his brow moistened with sweat.

'I'm sure all will be sorted quickly,' she reassured, trying to inject some belief into her statement, as he went through his phone settings, looking to connect with alternative network providers - without success.

Jennifer watched the winter storm raging outside and the freshly erected, though now lifeless fairy-light strings being tossed and battered in the driving wind.

'Let, me go check with my boss and get an update on when we can expect the power back at least.'

Mack nodded as he looked at the expensive device on his arm - his pride and joy Solas watch.

'We have a couple of hours tops until the presentation. If this goes belly up Jen, I'm done. It has to happen tonight. If I can't get secure enough orders from retail buyers by Christmas, the bank won't extend the finance....'

He trailed off, his mind racing with the ramifications of a disastrous launch, and an empty MotionTech order book that would effectively end his life's dream.

CHAPTER 12

JENNIFER STRODE THROUGH THE LOBBY, where background festive music was now absent, but the din of chat and laughter remained as guests seemed to enjoy the novelty of the situation, without yet realising the wider-reaching connotations.

Namely being marooned in a freezing and full-capacity hotel in the middle of a major snowstorm with no electricity and dwindling supplies.

Trying to quell from her mind the image of a frozen Jack Nicholson in *The Shining,* she went in search of Nick or the general manager to ascertain why no backup generator had kicked in as yet.

There had to be a backup, surely? They were halfway up a mountain in a ski resort; surely there had to be precedent for this.

Having soon discovered that there was indeed a backup generator, but it was awaiting a long overdue maintenance service call, thus dysfunctional, Jennifer spent the next hour frantically praying the lights would just magically come back on.

Even though the supply company was estimating eight

hours for service restoration, a nearby substation was buried beneath heavy snowfall.

Meaning the kitchen was quite literally powerless to work on the catering.

This was a disaster of epic proportions - for more reasons than one.

Mack truly needed this event to work and Jennifer had no clue how to help him.

Tomorrow the storm might clear as would the roads, but by then people would need to be on their way. Rescheduling wasn't an option.

This had to work now or never.

Jennifer took a deep breath.

She didn't know a whole lot about technology or fitness wearables, but she did know how to throw a party.

Come hell or high water, or more to the point, deep snow, she'd just have to rely on every ounce of her ability to pull this off.

CHAPTER 13

Back in the kitchen, Suzi was deep in conversation with the head chef, Julian. The rest of the staff stood around casually chatting, their spirits heightened by this unscheduled, extended break from what would typically be a frantic day.

'What's the latest?' Jennifer asked.

'Working to see if we can come up with an emergency menu using just the gas stove, but options are limited,' the chef said. 'The ovens are down, obviously. While we could consider using the wood-fired pizza oven on the terrace, with these winds that's just not an option. So while I can probably still feed the crowd, we're talking basic sustenance here as opposed to a lavish banquet.'

'Well, that's something at least.'

Jennifer rubbed her temple as if trying to coax out a brainwave.

'Suzi, can you give me a hand in the banqueting room? We need to go through those old decorations again and see what we can find that doesn't need to be plugged in. Perhaps we can make it all work with a more retro vibe?'

'Gotcha.'

The two duly fetched the boxes with the decades-old decorations that Jennifer was now glad she hadn't had the heart to throw out. 'Some of the tinsel is OK - these strings of golden bells too.'

Suzi lifted a faded ancient mistletoe garland, looking dubious. 'Are we sure there's no way the power will be back in time? It sounds like the wind has dropped off.'

They looked out the window where lighter snowflakes now seemed to be falling straight down as opposed to sideways.

Jennifer moved to the doorway; the sky had indeed lightened as darker clouds parted to reveal patches of blue and golden clouds as dusk approached.

She opened the door, pushing back some snow that had blown under the canopy above the patio.

The air felt calm and crisp. Thank goodness.

'This is either the eye of a storm or it's over,' she called back over her shoulder as she took a further step out.

To one side she could see the wood fire oven the chef had mentioned earlier. 'I wonder ...' she mused, nodding at it.

Suzi's eyes widened. 'You think these guys would honestly be OK with pizza?'

'Not really, but at least it'll expand the capabilities of the kitchen. The chef mentioned that dish that needs no cooking; Ensalada de Manzana. Perhaps a few warmer accompaniments could be done out here?'

'Good idea; I'm sure Nick can have that up and going in no time - if nothing else it will give a little more atmosphere too.'

'Exactly.' Jennifer's mind was racing now. 'Actually, I have another idea in mind for it too - something to distract this tech-dependent lot from their precious cell coverage.'

When she explained, Suzi raised an eyebrow.

CHAPTER 14

MINUTES LATER, Jennifer was joined by a still-ashen-faced Mack. 'Hey, what's the update? It seems to have blown itself out - have you heard anything about the power reconnection?'

She shook her head. 'No change I'm afraid. If it were a downed line or something they said it would be a simple fix, but the dud transponder means a longer outage. I'm afraid it'll be tomorrow before it's back.'

There was no denying the crestfallen look on his face.

'Hey, we can still make this work,' she reassured him. 'Use it to our advantage even, and make this product launch one to remember - like I promised. We've put up some more decorations, we'll have candlelight, some food ... plenty of wine, and you can distribute your launch packs and make your presentation the old-fashioned way.'

'It's not as simple as that, Jen. These people are used to bullet points and snazzy audiovisuals. Me standing there like a fool pleading for orders won't cut the mustard.'

'Hey, I know this isn't ideal. But trust me ... you can do this. *We* can do this,' Jennifer touched his arm reassuringly. 'Let's take a look at your launch material, and see what we can do. At the end of the day, a good presentation is about passion, not paraphernalia. I know you'll make a presentation that will blow them all away.'

A WHILE LATER, she looked around the room; her new stripped-back, low-tech vision already beginning to take shape.

Nick got the fire going in the pizza oven. Suzi was busy putting the finishing touches to the decorating, while the wait and kitchen staff prepared the drinks and food.

When Mack returned with his launch packs and a selection of Solas devices he'd planned to use as influencer giveaways, he gave Jennifer a brief rundown on their functionality.

As he did so, his own watch started to chime and the blue screen flashed on and off.

'What's that?'

'My one-hour warning to remind me to get changed.'

Jennifer studied him, as a brand new idea entered her head.

'Go. I'll make the announcement to guests that the launch is starting on schedule.'

Once Mack left, she went to have a word with Nick to fill him in on her plan.

'OK, see all these watches? Take them out of those boxes; I've thought of a better spot for them.'

Suzi and Nick duly went to work on the devices to help Jennifer carry out her piece de resistance.

She then announced to all guests that drinks were served and the reception would begin on time.

Jennifer figured the promise of food, which could be smelt from outdoors where their now ski-gear-clad chef was busy cooking up a storm, would quite literally light a fire under everyone.

Heartened, she walked through the now-calm candlelit lobby, as the majority of people had returned to their rooms (albeit with battery-operated candles instead of flaming ones) to freshen up.

She took a deep breath, and for the first time all day felt calm.

This was going to work.

She was pretty sure some of her ideas would raise eyebrows with the powers that be, but hey, that was event management.

Or more often than not; crisis management.

If anything, the next few hours would prove to Mack, her bosses and indeed herself, that unlike snow, Jennifer Whyte didn't melt when the heat was on.

CHAPTER 15

THE JACKALOPE ROOM buzzed with energy as people stood with drinks and ate plates of cobbled-together, but admittedly mouthwatering food, as Jennifer stood outside the door with a now-formal clad MotionTech CEO.

'You all set?'

Mack blew out hard, trying to shake his nerves.

She had seen his persona change when the storm had thrown its curveball. For so many weeks his emails had been full of questions about Wi-Fi speed and screens for presentations. Now all that scaffolding had been stripped away, and he had no choice but to present his product with nothing but his wits.

'Remember, that crowd in there has seen spreadsheets and PowerPoints a million times over. Just go in there and explain your passion to them like you did to me. Only then can they truly understand what it is they are being asked to back. It's not just the device - it's you.'

He looked at her, a lump in his throat. 'Thank you.'

'I also have a little trick up my sleeve to help make sure your product steals the show. So just relax, OK?'

Mack looked at her, confused but unable to ask her to elaborate since she'd already opened the door to the banqueting room.

Those closest to the entrance, including his staff, started to whistle and applaud, leaving him no option but to put his game face on.

'See you in there. Go get 'em, Tiger,' Jennifer whispered as she ushered him inside.

MACK GRINNED at her subtle joke about their high school football team, his nerves abating somewhat as he came into the room.

The place looked ... incredible.

The expectant atmosphere for him and the product seemed almost heightened by the absence of the bright lights and PowerPoint backdrops he'd been so concerned about, and he remembered Jennifer's wise words.

It's about passion, not paraphernalia...

As he made his way through the applauding crowds, he noticed the ice sculptures had since been brought in from outside. They looked even more impressive standing upright and installed so they acted almost sentinel to his arrival.

Mack's eyes widened further when he realised those icy snow-boarders were in fact, 'wearing' his devices - all fifty or so of the watch samples he'd kept hidden in their boxes.

And as he reached the top of the room to stand beneath the icy tableau, the display screen of every single Solas flashed to life all at once, their emitting blue light dramatically illuminating, not only the sculptures themselves but the entire room.

From everywhere Mack could hear breathless gasps, and even a few cheers, and amid the applause and palpable sense of amazement, his nerves disappeared.

He didn't need to worry about anything.

Thanks to Jennifer, this audience was already blown away.

CHAPTER 16

FOLLOWING some truly impassioned words from Mack about the Solas device and her own personal journey to its origins; evidently having taken her advice about showing everyone his passion for the product, Jennifer knew he had his audience eating out of his hand.

Her ice sculpture display brainwave thankfully also seemed to have had the desired dual effect of both wowing the attendees and distracting him from his stage fright.

Mack suffering from such debilitating performance anxiety - who knew?

Though Jennifer could of course now better understand his desire to ensure that everything about this launch went like clockwork, given how much he had riding on it. And while clocks might be predictable, they weren't all that interesting.

Later, Mack pulled her aside with a spring in his step.

Formalities over and MotionTech's order book bulging, the hotel wait staff were now involving attendees with decorating snowboarder-shaped cookies fresh from the pizza oven - as per Jennifer's instructions - while others gathered happily around the fireplace drinking mulled wine and making s'mores.

'All this is incredible,' he cried, eyes sparkling as he shook his head in bewilderment. 'Solas is getting the kind of interest I could never have even dreamed of. I still can't believe you pulled this off.'

'*We* did.' She winked and passed him a well-earned glass of mulled wine. 'And yeah, I think it's going pretty well. Getting back to basics is good sometimes.'

He chuckled, still unable to believe it had all gone so well. 'Honestly, they'll be talking about this in the valley for years - the night everything went analogue.'

'*And* the night Peter McCarthy sold out his entire inventory and then some.'

The chatter and buzz carried on well into the evening, and everyone seemed to be having a whale of a time, until all of a sudden the main lights flickered on.

This pretty much had the effect of throwing a bucket of water onto a blazing fire, and the disappointment amongst the crowd was palpable.

Jennifer moved to the light switch and promptly turned everything back off, to rapturous cheers from the guests.

Mack went to join her, suddenly clocking the ancient wreath draped around Moe the Moose's head immediately above them.

'Mistletoe? You really do know how to throw a retro Christmas event, don't you?' He grinned, encircling her in his arms

And Jennifer smiled as he leaned down to kiss her. 'All in the details.'

CHRISTMAS IN VENICE

A HOLIDAY NOVELLA

CHAPTER 1

"She is beautiful, no?"

"What?" Max shook himself out of his daze. He was huddled uncomfortably at the back of a Venetian water taxi, trying to ignore the swaying of the little boat and the lapping water of the canal only inches away.

"The city, Venice. She is beautiful?" The driver beckoned with both hands to the scenery around them, seemingly unperturbed about steering the vessel.

"Oh. Yes—of course."

The Italian man beamed and went back to zooming along the canal. Max tightened his grip on the wooden seat and tried not to show his extreme discomfort at being forced to ride in this treacherous little bucket. Instead, he focused his attention on his wife Naomi, who was gazing around at the city in pure delight.

If this makes her happy, then it will be worth it. Max tried to keep that thought in the forefront of his mind. It would be worth the long flight, the chilly December air, and yes even the endless network of canals, if only his wife enjoyed their trip.

It was a much-needed getaway for both of them. They

hadn't had a moment to themselves, let alone a whole weekend, since the birth of their daughter eight months prior. Max loved baby Julia and adored being a father—he wouldn't trade it for anything in the world—but in truth, the craziness of having a newborn in the house was taking its toll on their marriage.

Julia had only just begun to sleep through the night, and Naomi's constant fussing over the baby was hard to take. She was reluctant to leave her alone with a babysitter for more than a few hours; the fact that he'd convinced her to leave her with her parents for a whole weekend was a minor miracle.

But she'd agreed—reluctantly, but even so—and Max had put together a romantic weekend getaway as an early Christmas present for her. He knew she'd dreamed of visiting Venice all her life.

As for himself, he had no love of the water, no taste for Italian food, and no knowledge whatsoever of the language or history of this odd little place. But if the break could help them reconnect as a couple—no demanding infant in the background, no baby paraphernalia to cart around everywhere—then it would be well worth the discomfort.

He snuck another glance at his wife. *So far, so good.*

She'd nearly had a change of heart at the last minute, fretting over how Julia would do on a full weekend without her. Luckily, Naomi's mother had all but shoved her out the door of their home. "You need a break." she'd said firmly. "You have a husband, remember? Spend some time with him. Try and remember what your relationship was like before the baby came along."

"But what if she misses me?" Naomi protested feebly, and her mother waved a hand in dismissal.

"There's such a thing as being too attached, darling. She'll be fine. She has to learn to spend a little time away from you sooner or later. What will you do when she goes to preschool? When she has friends and wants to go to a sleepover? Do you want her to be so attached to you that she can't function on her own?"

Naomi hadn't liked that very much, Max could tell, but she didn't really have a reply. And so, taking wheeled suitcases packed with warm clothing and rain gear—Max had read that Venice could be rainy this time of year—they took a taxi to Gatwick and set off for Italy, Naomi fretting about what she was leaving behind, and Max thinking warily about everything that lay ahead.

THEIR HOTEL WAS on the water—*right* on the water, as was everything in Venice, with guests stepping out of water taxis onto a dock with an awning and large double doors welcoming them into the lobby.

The concierge checked Max and Naomi in quickly and summoned another employee to help them carry their luggage up the stairs; apparently there was no lift in the building.

Their room was small but cosy, and there was a little kitchenette with a coffee maker and a microwave. The wooden headboard and dresser were ornately carved and there was a vase of perky fresh flowers on the nightstand.

Max stowed their suitcases and checked his watch; they'd arrived in the late afternoon, and there was still some weak winter sunshine outside as the sunset. "Well. We're here. Dominic we head out for a bite of dinner?" Travel always made him hungry.

But Naomi was already on the phone. "I'm just going to call Mum and Dad quickly and check in on Julia," she explained, covering the mouthpiece with one hand. "It'll only take a minute."

Max nodded and stifled a sigh. *She's going to be calling multiple times a day*, he thought gloomily. *I'm going to have to work hard to keep her distracted.*

Naomi was making cooing noises into the phone, talking to their daughter.

He could tell when her mother came back on the line because the cooing stopped and his wife said reluctantly: "Well, I know it's still early but I just wanted to—oh, the flight was fine. Did she sleep through her afternoon nap? Oh, that's good." Max thought his wife almost sounded a little disappointed to hear that Julia seemed to be doing fine without her.

When Naomi finally put down the phone he suggested brightly that they find a place to eat lunch but she still seemed worried and distracted.

"Mum says she slept this afternoon but I can't help worrying—I mean, we'll be gone for three nights, and what if she doesn't sleep through the night for any of them? Maybe a full weekend was too much too soon, Max. Maybe we should have stuck to just a night in London in case something goes wrong and she needs us…"

He stifled a groan and wrapped his wife in a hug. "Look, you're an amazing mother, and it's brilliant that you love our daughter so much. I do too. But your mum will take great care of her! I'm sure she's thrilled to get some grandma-granddaughter time in. In the meantime, let me spoil you, okay? A night in London is nothing out of the ordinary. You've always wanted to visit Venice and I want us to really make the most of this weekend."

"Well, okay." Naomi melted a little in his arms, returning his hug. She smelled like vanilla and pears—the perfume she'd worn since they first started dating over six years ago.

Max breathed deeply of her scent and promised himself that he would make sure she enjoyed herself with the most perfect, romantic vacation possible. *Even if we do have to go everywhere in a bloody boat.*

He couldn't actually understand why he feared the water so much. When people asked, he usually told them that as a toddler he fell off a dock into a deep lake while at a family reunion. Unable to swim, he would have drowned if an older cousin hadn't quickly pulled him out.

In truth, though, the story was a lie. Max had never fallen off a dock and never even come close to drowning; in fact, he'd taken swimming lessons and learned to swim perfectly well.

He just didn't like water, or boats or being piloted every-where in one of these low-riding gondola things that Venetian tourists seemed to view as so romantic. All the same, there was no way to get from their hotel to the restaurant he'd selected from the guidebook unless they went via water, so again they climbed into a water taxi and set off.

The driver chatted to them in a mix of English and Italian. Max truly only grasped every other word the guy was saying, so he tried to smile and pretend he was too wrapped up in the city sights to talk.

Naomi leaned forward to talk to the driver, asking him about sights as they glided down the Grand Canal and asking him how to say basic words and phrases in Italian.

Finally, they reached the area of the restaurant and disem-barked from the water taxi.

There were only a few other diners—apparently a Thursday evening in December was not the busiest time in Venice for tourists—and Max and Naomi were given a quiet table with a nice view of the canal.

Nice if you enjoyed looking at the water, Max thought bleakly and turned his attention to the menu.

Once again his lack of Italian was flustering him. He read through the dishes suspiciously. Culinary exploration was not one of his strong points; in fact, when he and Naomi had first started going out, it had been a bit of an inside joke between them.

After a while, though, it turned into a slight sore spot. Naomi loved ethnic foods, trying new recipes, and sampling new cuisine at new restaurants. For Max, the definition of "trying a new food" meant using a different brand of ketchup on his burger. He preferred good old English cooking—burgers, meat-and-potatoes dishes, that sort of thing—and tried new stuff only with the greatest of reluctance.

As far as Italian food, spaghetti and meatballs were about as familiar as he got with the cuisine. *Antipasto?* That sounded like something that would require an antacid later on. *Secondi?* He didn't know what it was, but it sounded like a side effect of a bad illness. *Brioches?* Were they made of shoe leather? There were plenty of other items on the menu that he couldn't even pronounce.

When the waiter finally appeared to take their order, Max explained haltingly his trouble with the choices. The waiter smiled and explained several of the dishes.

Finally, Max settled on polenta with grilled meat and vegetables. The way the waiter explained it, the polenta sounded like a kind of cornmeal porridge, which seemed like a weird choice for a dinner item, but he supposed it was better than pumpkin ravioli or calf liver and onions, both of which the waiter explained were Venetian specialities and seemed to think were very fine dishes.

Max ordered a bottle of red wine for the table while Naomi picked out her own meal—some type of fried sardine and onion dish, risotto, and vegetables. It didn't sound in the least bit appetising to Max, but he wasn't about to admit that.

The food arrived quickly and they dug in. Max decided the polenta wasn't half bad; at least there was a generous helping of meat to be had, though he couldn't help wishing for a bottle of ketchup to smother it in. He poked through the vegetables and wondered idly if Italian supermarkets sold anything like Heinz; he could buy a bottle and carry it around with him.

Dessert was at least a touch more familiar; Naomi ordered tiramisu, that strange, spongy creation which looked like cake but was soaked in espresso and a dark cocoa powder that made his nose feel itchy.

For himself, he managed to order, of all things, a small plate of fried doughnuts and a cup of coffee. The doughnuts were suspiciously filled with raisins and bits of orange, and the coffee was extremely strong, but at least it somewhat resembled something he might find back at home in England.

He was pleased at least to see that Naomi was enjoying the meal though. She'd *ooh*ed and *aah*ed at every dish the waiter presented and blissfully downed two glasses of wine.

They'd lingered over their meal for over two hours; now she seemed quite ready to return to the hotel for an early bedtime.

"Great food," Max exclaimed, more enthusiastically than he felt, as he paid the bill and then hailed yet another water taxi. *How many more of these meals will I have to eat? Not to mention get water taxis.... Let's see, tomorrow is Friday and our flight leaves Monday morning...*

The driver helped them into the boat and they sat down at the back, Max somewhat awkwardly, Naomi leaning her head on his shoulder.

"This was a good idea," she surprised him by saying. He put one arm around her shoulders and squeezed gently, forgetting momentarily the uncomfortable rocking of the boat.

The sun had set, leaving Venice dark and quiet for the night. City lights reflected on the canal and lent the scene a sort of peace that even Max could appreciate. Bright lights twinkled here and there; the city was getting ready for the Christmas season.

Back at the hotel they hung up their coats, scarves and gloves and turned down the bed. After the earlier flight and the heavy dinner, Max was ready for an early bedtime.

Naomi's hand wavered momentarily over the phone, and Max hesitated, holding a spare blanket. Then she let out a massive yawn, covering her mouth in surprise. "Oh my goodness! I don't know where that came from."

"I do," he said smiling. "You're just worn out from the journey and all the excitement of finally being here."

"I suppose that is it," she agreed.

Max duly spread the extra blanket over the bed for added warmth and watched with relief as Naomi switched off the lamp and curled up in bed, phone call forgotten.

He switched off his own bedside lamp and curled up next to her, breathing in her vanilla-pear perfume and stroking her hair as she snored softly.

Maybe Venice can work its magic on us yet, he thought sleepily, before he too drifted off to sleep.

CHAPTER 2

Lucy stared forlornly out the window of the plane. They were descending into Venice and in the late afternoon sunshine, she could see the city laid out below her, full of promise.

But she didn't have eyes for the snow on the cobbled rooftops, or the maze of canals in the place of city streets. She was too wrapped up in her thoughts to notice any of those picturesque details.

She exited the plane with the other passengers and collected her luggage mechanically, moving through the airport terminal with a heavy heart. She flagged down a cab that would take her as far as the outskirts of the city, and from there she needed to get a water taxi to take her to the hotel for the night. After the flight from Dublin, she needed a hot bath, a simple meal and a long, deep sleep in a plush bed.

At the Piazzale Roma - the main transport hub of the city — her water taxi driver helped her load up her luggage and steered the little boat quietly along the canals of San Marco, sensing she wasn't in the mood for small talk.

Reaching the stop-off point to the hotel which was located

a couple of blocks away from the Grand Canal, Lucy got out near Rialto bridge and dragged her single suitcase along the cobbled streets to the hotel.

She checked in and accepted her room key with a smile and a nod, trudging quietly up the stairs to her room and dropping the suitcase on the floor.

One year.

It seemed so much longer. Only one year had passed since she and Dominic had enjoyed the weekend of their dreams here in Venice.

Gliding along the canals, drinking too much wine in trattorias, taking in the theatres and the opera of the festive season— it had been a magical time, full of romance.

Then towards the end, they had capped it all by stealing away to a quiet corner of the city — a tiny bridge off a side street, away from the hustle and bustle of central San Marco.

There, on the picturesque wrought-iron bridge and above the inky black canal waters, they had marked their initials on a metal padlock and hung it from the rail of the bridge, sealing in a promise of their love in this most romantic of cities.

What a difference a year makes, Lucy thought forlornly. Maybe the trip had been *too* romantic, too perfect, because not long after they returned to Dublin everything seemed to start going downhill.

For starters, they'd got into a fight at a friend's party on New Year's Eve over a simple understanding made much worse by the copious amounts of drunken champagne. Then Lucy suffered from a cold on and off for the rest of the winter, and feeling rundown only made her more irritable, which led to more fighting.

Spring was supposed to be a breath of fresh air, but a promotion at work meant more hours away from home, which Dominic resented. Once summer came she thought they might get away for a mini-break to make up for all the stress, but then he was busy with family issues. By the time autumn arrived, there was barely a shred left of the relationship they had once had, and one day Dominic announced out of the blue that it was over.

He was moving on, and so should she.

In retrospect Lucy supposed she shouldn't be surprised. But she was still hurt. How could someone just walk away so easily, without putting up a fight? Surely everyone had a bad year now and then, and it was worth sorting through it all to save your relationship.

In any case, Dominic was gone, and Lucy was back in Venice alone.

She shrugged off her coat and scarf, hanging them over the back of a chair, and slipped her tired feet out of her boots. When she and Dominic had come here last year, she'd packed two suitcases full of clothes—gorgeous dresses, cashmere scarfs, plenty of jewellery, and of course silky negligees to wear underneath. Now she had a single suitcase with a few sweaters and pyjamas in it. What was the point in dressing up, when there was no one special to see it?

Lucy slowly got ready for bed, changing into cosy flannel pyjamas and brushing out the knots in her hair. *Once this weekend is over, I'll feel better,* she promised herself.

Eating Ben and Jerry's in front of the TV and crying on the phone with her friends wasn't helping her feel better about her break-up, so she was trying a more radical plan.

She would unlock the padlock from the bridge, thereby unsealing their promise of last year. Maybe then she could finally move on with her life and accept that Dominic was gone for good.

CHAPTER 3

IN THE MORNING Lucy located a café and sat down for a lonely breakfast. The skies were full of the promise of snow, much as they had been here this time last year.

She ordered a cappuccino and biscuits and gazed out the window of the café. San Marco was twinkling with holiday lights; festive greenery hung from balconies and decorated windows and shop fronts. All along the canals, glowing decorations were reflected in the water. Venice was well and truly ready for Christmas.

Other tourists were enjoying the morning, gliding down the canals in gondolas or hoofing it on one of the narrow cobblestone side streets. Some were shopping, enjoying an early morning cup of coffee, and others had their heads down, chatting on cell phones and planning out their day. Lucy watched idly as they passed her by. People were walking alone, but there were many couples or families out and about, too. It gave her a small pang to see so many carefree people happily striding by when she herself felt so down in the dumps.

She sipped her cappuccino and considered what she should

do over the next two days. She truly adored Venice and would love nothing more than to spend more time exploring it, so she hadn't booked her return ticket until Monday morning.

That gave her plenty of time to hit the major sites—St. Mark's Square, perhaps a concert at the Basilica—and maybe just float around the city a bit on a gondola, looking at all of the lights and enjoying the gentle chatter of other tourists. It would be a nice, relaxing, and well-deserved weekend break.

Since the sun was peeking weakly through the clouds and the temperature seemed fairly moderate, Lucy decided to make her first stop at the Piazza San Marco—St. Mark's Square—for a refreshing stroll and some more people-watching. She didn't fancy lingering outdoors in the cold but as she was bundled up in a wool coat and cuddly scarf, she thought a little walking about wouldn't hurt. Besides, she wanted to get a closer look at the architecture of St. Mark's Basilica. She and Dominic had briefly visited it last year, but one visit was not enough.

Her memories of that visit with Dominic stabbed a bit. They had strolled through the square, surrounded by the cooing of pigeons and the lightly falling snow, admiring the cathedral but mostly admiring each other. *Well, this time I'll be alone, so maybe I'll get a better look at the details,* Lucy thought ruefully.

And the Basilica was magnificent, even if she had no one to share the view with. The murals on the outside and the gleaming domes were beautiful. She stood for a moment on the stones of the piazza, contemplating the work that must have gone into planning and building such a magnificent structure.

Other tourists nearby were talking about the cathedral and snapping pictures, and she amused herself by watching them, too.

One couple in particular caught her eye. Something about them reminded Lucy of Dominic and herself on their prior trip; something about their cosy posture that said clearly "We're head over heels in love".

The girl had red hair tumbling down under a knitted hat and was wearing a bright red pea coat that complimented rather than competed with her hair. The young man was clearly enamoured of her, though he also seemed a bit distracted. Lucy looked closer. Not distracted...nervous? Suddenly he slipped down to one knee in the crowd, and Lucy realised what he was about to do.

A proposal! The romance of it touched her as much as it hurt, and she turned away quickly, partly to give the young couple their privacy, and also to spare her own feelings. She wouldn't deny that when she and Dominic had visited the city, she'd secretly hoped it might lead to a proposal. Clearly, it wasn't meant to be.

Lucy decided to warm up a little by touring the inside of the Basilica. The interior was just as impressive; gleaming gold and bronze mosaics on the ceiling gave the cathedral a warm, shimmering appearance. Between the mosaics and the enormous paintings everywhere the eye could travel, Lucy had the feeling of being inside a Faberge egg. It was incredibly beautiful and a little overwhelming. She found a pew away from other groups of tourists and sat down to admire the interior of the cathedral.

She was still musing about Dominic when she had the oddest feeling of being watched. Turning, she glanced around the back of the pews, but it was so large and there were so many other groups of people that it was hard to tell if anyone in particular had been looking at her.

Nonsense, she thought sadly. *You're so lonely that now you're imagining you might bump into a friend, at least for the duration of your trip. Snap out of it!*

She looked back up to the religious paintings on the ceiling and resolved to put the feeling behind her. If someone could put so much effort into a project of this scale, I think I can manage the very tiny project of rebuilding my love life, she thought resolutely.

And with that notion, she decided to put Dominic out of her mind for the rest of her trip.

She would enjoy herself, unlock that padlock, and fly home again ready to start over fresh and enjoy her newly single life.

CHAPTER 4

OUTSIDE THE CATHEDRAL Lucy had to make a decision about what tourist site to visit next. The Basilica tour guide had recommended the Doge's Palace, across the Square, but she wasn't altogether interested in another tour of rooms and historical artefacts.

Instead she decided to take a boat tour.

She'd heard that the slow-moving vaporetto on the Grand Canal offered a great water tour of the San Marco, and somehow she and Dominic had never gotten around to taking one last year. It would be nice to see the city during the daytime when she could really peer at the sights.

She bought a ticket and a hot chocolate and took her seat, with her guidebook at the ready. The views were pretty decent: she could see the bridges on the main canal and the side streets, including Rialto Bridge, which was decorated with festive lights for the season. Gradually she stopped thinking about everything she saw in the context of whether she and Dominic had seen it the year before; she was simply enjoying the colourful buildings and festive displays as they slid by, simply because they were beautiful—not because they evoked any particular memories.

The water bus ran around the city for about an hour. Finally, Lucy collected her guidebook and empty cup and stepped off to plan the next part of her day. She fancied going out to Murano Island to visit a glass-blowing studio, and since the next water bus wasn't leaving for nearly an hour, she decided to grab a quick bite of lunch first.

There were plenty of cafes and small restaurants offering both traditional Italian lunches and more standardised tourist offerings, like miniature pizzas. Lucy chose a hot sandwich and another frothy cappuccino and watched the tourists around her while she ate. She'd always enjoyed people-watching, and it helped to distract her from the fact that she was alone.

Finally, it was time to board the water bus and head out to Murano. Lucy was happy to see that there weren't quite as many tourists out here; the island was much quieter by comparison to San Marco, though there were still some tourists here and there exploring on foot. She wandered the streets until she found a quiet glass-blowing shop that appeared to be open, and ducked inside.

The man in the workshop was skillfully blowing and moulding glass before the delighted eyes of a few other tourists. Lucy watched with wonder as the man shaped the molten glass into a vase. The tourists broke into applause, and the man smiled. Lucy lingered on for a while to listen to him explain his craft, the history of glass-blowing in the city, and the time that went into crafting each piece.

In display cabinets there were glass vases, abstract sculptures and glassware for the kitchen; Lucy marvelled at the work that went into each piece. Ultimately she left without purchasing anything; she certainly didn't need anything for herself and she was terrified of something breaking in transit back to Dublin. *Maybe another time,* she thought wistfully, giving the colourful, fragile pieces one last look before exiting into the street.

Almost before she knew it the sun was setting over the island and it was time to take the water bus back to San Marco. By the time Lucy reached her hotel, she was famished, and she was happy to pop into a small trattoria down the street for her evening meal. *I don't think I'll ever tire of the food here,* she thought as she dug into a fragrant bowl of pasta and washed it down with a glass of wine.

By the time Lucy returned to her room and crawled into bed, it was fully dark in Venice, and the city was slowly quieting down as people returned to their homes or hotels for the night. Somewhere in the distance, Lucy thought she could hear Christmas carols playing in Italian.

"Goodnight, Venice," she mumbled sleepily, burrowing deeper into her blankets. For the first time in weeks, she was looking forward to the coming weekend.

CHAPTER 5

SCOTT CHECKED the pocket of his coat for what seemed like the hundredth time.

Still there.

He patted his pocket and zipped up his coat, stepping out of the hotel lobby into the brisk December air.

Rachel was waiting for him outside. Her red hair was gleaming under a knit cap and she was wearing a red woollen pea coat that made her look as though she belonged on a Christmas postcard.

Scott stood back for a moment, silently admiring his girlfriend as she chatted to an older woman in fluent Italian. Rachel was obsessed with Italy—the language, the art, the food, everything—so of course when everyone else chose to study Spanish or French in high school, she picked Italian.

She'd even spent a college semester abroad in Italy as an exchange student. Her efforts were paying off now; she'd been eagerly chatting to everyone she met since they'd touched down from New York on Thursday night. She seemed to be having the time of her life.

Everything is going according to plan, Scott thought with

relief. After all, when your girlfriend is obsessed with all things Italian, what better place to whisk her away for a romantic vacation…and a Christmas proposal?

He'd spent nearly six months planning everything out. Step one: find the perfect ring, a combo of diamonds and emeralds that would appeal to Rachel's non-traditional tastes. Step two: book the perfect hotel in Venice, a five-star affair with a gorgeous view of the Grand Canal. He wanted their long weekend in the city to be one of utmost luxury; nothing less would do.

Step three: choose a romantic site for his proposal. Venice had such a reputation as a romantic city, he was sure he'd have no shortage of memorable spots to choose from, so he planned to take Rachel on an extended tour of the city and just wait until the mood felt right. They had plans to visit the Basilica, have a romantic dinner or two, and perhaps tour the canals, so he was confident the perfect magical setting for a proposal would present itself in no time.

But first, they needed to get breakfast. A small café near their hotel offered piping hot cappuccinos, pastries and more for a tasty Italian breakfast. They sat at a small table by the window, looking out at the festively decorated streets, sipping their coffee and chatting about their plans for the day.

"Where do you want to go first?" Scott asked, still absent-mindedly fingering the ring box in his pocket.

"Oh, I don't know." Rachel nibbled at a pastry, her eyes alight with happiness. "There's so much to see! Did you have a preference?"

"I was thinking St. Mark's Square," he said casually. "It's pretty mild today, so it's a good day to be outside. And after that, we could tour the Basilica, since you did say you wanted to go there."

"Oh, I'd love that." Rachel gestured expressively with her hands when she was excited; just like an Italian, Scott thought.

"We should go to the sung Mass there on Sunday. I hear it's amazing."

"We will," he promised. They finished breakfast and went outside to navigate their way to St Mark's Square. Scott hoped he was keeping his excitement under wraps; he didn't want Rachel to have a hint of the surprise that was waiting for her.

CHAPTER 6

T HEY WERE able to zigzag their way to the Square on foot, crossing small canals via ancient stone bridges and finally emerging into the crowded piazza.

It was full of tourists and pigeons, exactly as it had looked in hundreds of postcard-worthy pictures that Scott had seen online.

Weak winter sunshine peeked through the clouds to illuminate the masses taking pictures of the Basilica or each other.

The Basilica was an impressive sight even to Scott, who knew little enough about the history of the place. The sheer size of the structure and the murals on the front of the building were enough to make anyone pause for a second look. Rachel was fairly glowing with excitement, rattling off a steady stream of facts about the architecture and construction of the cathedral. Scott looped an arm through hers as they walked, meandering slowly through the crowd. He loved her intelligence and enthusiasm for the world and was happy to listen to her talk.

Rachel trailed off and leaned her head on his shoulder, smiling. Scott gave her a quick kiss on the forehead. "What are you thinking about?"

She snuggled closer to him. "How nice it is to be here with you."

"Yeah?" He gave her an affectionate squeeze, and she grinned up at him.

"Yeah. I love it here. This is the best Christmas present ever." She stood up on tiptoe and kissed him.

He kissed her back, not caring about the crowds of tourists around them. For a moment it was as if everyone and everything else faded away, and it was only the two of them, arm in arm in this romantic city. Rachel's eyes sparkled as she turned away with a contented smile, gazing at the spires of the Basilica.

The perfect moment...

"Actually, there was something else..." Scott started to say, kneeling on the cobblestones and feeling for the ring box in his pocket.

Splat! Suddenly he felt something wet land on his head.

Horrified, he quickly stood up as Rachel turned back to him. He touched one hand to his hair and stared at the white smear on his fingers in disgust.

"Ew!" Rachel exclaimed, quickly pulling tissues out of her coat pocket. "Is that..."

"Stupid pigeons." Scott wiped at his head and looked around the square for the offending pigeon in question, but they were all busily cooing at tourists trying to get scraps of food.

"Come on," Rachel said, already tugging him toward a café on the edge of the piazza, "you can duck in the bathroom and get cleaned up, and I'll get us something hot to drink. It's kind of cold out here anyway."

"Okay," Scott said reluctantly, fingering the box in his pocket. He let her lead him across the crowded stones through even more flocks of pigeons. In the cafe, he popped upstairs to the tiny bathroom and quickly cleaned up, mortified and irritated in equal measure.

So much for that...

CHAPTER 7

WHEN HE EMERGED Rachel had ordered two hot coffees to go. They headed back out into the piazza, and Scott hopefully slipped an arm around her shoulders, but the earlier magic was lost.

It was late morning now, and St Mark's Square was filling up with winter tourists taking pictures and talking loudly in a mixture of languages. It was difficult to have an intimate conversation with all the noise and bustle, and Scott soon gave up trying.

When they had finished their coffees they entered the Basilica, and for a moment left the hustle and bustle of the outside masses behind. Stepping into the cathedral was an experience that Scott could only classify as otherworldly; the paintings stretched up the walls and all over the ceilings of the domes above, combined with swirling mosaics and inlays that made the entire interior seem to spring to life.

Rachel pointed out several of the paintings. "St. Mark's Basilica was constructed in the eleventh century," she whispered. "The paintings and mosaics were constructed and touched up over the centuries. Very little of the original mosaic tiling on the ceiling is left—probably only a third—due to restorations over the centuries. If you look up to the roof you can see scenes depicting the life of Christ and the lives of the patron saints of Venice."

Scott admired the scenes overhead. Every available nook and cranny of the walls and the ceiling was covered in some Biblical scene or another—some that he recognised, and some that he didn't. The press of tourists meant that they had to move fairly quickly through the church interior, and soon they were back out in the Square.

Rachel hooked her arm through Scott's and laced their fingers together. "So, where to next?"

"You're the tour guide," he said, and she grinned a little. "True. How about a tour of the clock tower? One should be starting soon. We can get a good view of San Marco from up there."

"Sounds good to me," Scott said, wondering if the clock tower would provide him with a good spot for a proposal. Surely a quiet spot overlooking all of the city would be romantic enough for that?

Unfortunately, the stairs were steep and crowded with tourists, and their tour guide kept up a brisk pace as he told them about the history of the construction of the piazza, the Basilica, Doge's Palace, and the clock tower itself.

"The clock tower, Torre dell'Orologio, was designed by Maurizio Codussi and took ten years to complete, beginning in 1496 and ending in 1506. The wings were added later on, perhaps by Pietro Lombardo. You can see the original workings of the clock, which was wound manually until 1998; now it runs off of electricity."

The tour ended on the roof, with a magnificent view of St Mark's Square. Scott didn't regret the tour for a second, but with all of the people, there was no way he could propose.

Rachel was enjoying herself though, even if she was distracted by all of the chatter around her. She conversed for a moment in Italian with their tour guide and turned back to him. "He says that if we love the view here, we should go to the Campanile. It's the tallest building in the city."

"Off we go, then." Scott let Rachel lead the way as they completed the tour and bounded away to the Campanile, where they climbed yet more steep stairs to reach the top. The view, however, was reward enough: at 325 feet tall, the bell tower offered them an amazing view of the city, even more so than what they had seen from the other one. All of Venice was visible from here, and even Rachel stopped talking long enough to be enchanted by the sight.

Snow dusted the rooftops of Venice like powdered sugar. Holiday decorations could be seen strung in streets and along canals; here and there a brightly lit Christmas tree was visible. From up so high the people of Venice looked like brightly coloured ants, rushing here and there in the streets. Scott's stomach rumbled, and he realised it must be dinner time; many of those people below were likely rushing off to eat.

With this in mind, he and Rachel descended the steep flights of stairs back to street level and set off in search of a restaurant.

It wasn't hard to find one, and once they were settled in and dining on appetisers of fried meatballs and calamari, waiting for their *Secondi* to appear, Scott started to relax. This day certainly hadn't lent itself to the perfect romantic moment, but it was only Friday afternoon; he had two more days to make it happen. He'd already sought out a charming restaurant and a gondola ride, both of which he imagined would be perfect settings for a proposal that would surprise and delight Rachel.

The waiter arrived with part of their order, and she chatted to him in Italian. Scott sipped contentedly at his wine. Rachel was having a blast, and he had to admit that he was having fun, too.

He just needed to be patient and wait for the right moment.

In a city so famed for romance, surely it couldn't be far away?

CHAPTER 8

Naomi woke slowly, stretching languorously. The winter sunshine was barely peeking around the curtains of their hotel room, and she snuggled deeper under the fluffy duvet. Max was still sleeping, blissfully unaware of the world, and she smiled to herself.

Poor, dear Max.

She knew he was probably dreaming of being back at home in England, where he didn't have to travel by boat and where Frosted Flakes and bacon sandwiches were easy to come by.

The fact that he would go to such lengths to treat her to a dream holiday in Italy when he was so clearly out of his element spoke volumes about how he felt about her.

She stole a glance at the clock and bit her lip, feeling momentarily guilty for having not called before she went to bed for the night.

What if Julia fussed, or had trouble sleeping, or wasn't feeling well? What sort of mother didn't check up on these things?

Almost as if he could sense her consternation, Max woke

beside her, stretching and groaning. Naomi smiled as she rolled over to face him. He always looked so rumpled when he woke up—hair sticking up in multiple directions, pillow creases on his face—and somehow she found it charming. He looked so relaxed and unassuming, much like he had in college when they had first started dating. She leaned over now and planted a quick kiss on his forehead. "Good morning, sleepyhead."

"Morning." He rubbed the sleep out of his eyes and looked around. "Mmm. What time is it?"

"Eight o'clock, aka time to rise and shine and get some breakfast." Naomi threw back the covers and raced to the bathroom for a hot shower. Max protested weakly from the bed, laughing. "Not fair. You had a head start."

Naomi laughed and pulled a fluffy towel down from the rack. Her guilt over not calling home was fading a little. Julia was in the most capable of hands, she reminded herself, and after all, she had to admit spending time alone with Max was a luxury she'd sorely missed.

She'd gotten so used to building her daily routine around the baby that she'd forgotten what it was like to spend a romantic evening with her husband and wake up slowly, on her own timetable, the next morning.

It was rather a lovely feeling.

Once they had both dressed for the day, in warm sweaters and coats, they set out to find breakfast. Naomi was thrilled to get a chance to experience a real Italian menu, though she could sense Max's trepidation.

To say he wasn't big on trying new foods would be putting it nicely, but luckily a traditional Continental breakfast didn't veer too far from what he was used to eating back home. At the café near their hotel, they ordered frothy cappuccinos and plates of flaky pastries filled with sweet cream or chocolate.

There was fruit, yoghurt and muesli on the side and hot choco-late. Max seemed pleasantly surprised, and Naomi found herself relishing her breakfast without having to worry about feeding the baby.

CHAPTER 9

AFTER BREAKFAST they set out to see the sights.

Naomi had read plenty of guidebooks on Venice before they had left, taking meticulous notes in a small notebook to carry in her purse, but nothing could have prepared her for the reality of the city.

The narrow stone side streets felt almost like hidden passageways, beckoning to visitors with the promise that they might lead to some secret location. Even with the winter chill, the canals were a sight to see, with gondolas gliding past and colourfully attired gondoliers calling out to each other as they went. Everywhere there were strings of Christmas lights and oversized decorations for the upcoming festivities.

Wandering through the streets and over the stone bridges that crisscrossed the canals, Naomi felt like she was melting away into another time and place entirely. Shop windows with signs in Italian and English advertised blown glass, Venetian masks, and leather goods. They stopped to browse in a few shops and when Naomi admired a hand-blown glass Christmas ornament, Max promptly bought it for their tree back home. She eagerly pressed her face to the windows of other shops, admiring the handiwork within even though she couldn't decipher most of the signs.

There were plenty of other tourists about, but as she strolled hand in hand with her husband, Naomi was starting to feel like it was just the two of them. Max seemed happy to find plenty of streets that could be walked rather than toured by boat, and he was starting to relax.

Italian music drifted from shops and trattorias as tourists entered or exited, holding the doors open just long enough for the sounds and smells within to escape onto the street. There was an intoxicating blend of spices, perfumes, leather, food, and wine in the air, and it fueled Naomi's excitement at seeing the city.

According to her guidebooks, one of the must-see attractions in the city was the Piazza san Marco, or St. Mark's Square, which was bordered by several attractions: St. Mark's Basilica, the Doge's Palace, a historic clock tower, and a bell tower of impressive height, the tallest building in the city. Naomi had planned ahead and booked a multi-attraction ticket and tours, so they could take in all of the sights in one day.

She had no intention of missing out on anything so magnificent; after all, who knew when they might be able to take a trip like this again?

CHAPTER 10

As it turned out, the tours were every bit as amazing as promised online.

The Square was packed with tourists and flocks of pigeons; Max snapped a few shots of Naomi trying to coax one onto her outstretched hand, laughing as it flew away, disgruntled, because it realised she didn't have a snack for it. They lined up with other tourists for the trip through the Basilica and were rewarded with hearty neck cramps from gawking at the mosaics and paintings inside.

"When we get back to the hotel, I'm wrapping a hot towel around my neck," Naomi said with a laugh. Max wrapped an arm around her as they moved leisurely across the Square to the clock tower, where their next tour awaited. "Maybe the front desk could recommend a spa or something? You know, one of those places that do couples' massages?"

"You'd be up for that?" Naomi looked at him in surprise. Normally any mention of a new activity would have him wrinkling his nose in suspicion. But he nodded. "You'd enjoy it. And I would…try to enjoy it!"

Naomi nestled closer to him as they joined the line for the

Doge's Palace. She couldn't even remember the last time they'd been able to do something like this—well over a year ago, she supposed, before the late stages of pregnancy and then the baby left her essentially housebound. She was startled to realise she was truly enjoying herself, not worrying about Julia. She snuck a glance at Max, who only smiled. She smiled back a little. Was he thinking the same thing—that they were long overdue for this kind of date? As if to answer her question, he pulled her close and gave her a quick kiss.

Their guide was enthusiastic about her subject and gave them a richly detailed rundown of the history of the Palazzo Ducale. Even Max looked interested as she explained that the Palace was the hub of political power in Venice from the ninth century onwards, and its proximity to the Basilica was no accident, but rather a result of the intertwining of church and state in Italy at that time. Gothic arches and an impressive array of sculptures, paintings and frescoes covered the inside of the palace. The tour wound through multiple floors, through staterooms, criminal courts, cells, cramped administrative offices, and finally outside to the Bridge of Sighs.

"Why is it called that?" asked one of the tourists, and the guide explained that the bridge connected the interrogation rooms of the Palace to the outside world. Built-in 1600, the bridge earned its name from Lord Byron centuries later based on the somewhat romantic notion that it offered convicts their last view of Venice before entering their cells; prompted by the beauty of the city, they would sigh over their city.

"Of course," she added, tapping on the stone bars on one of the bridge's tiny windows, "there wasn't a lot to back up that notion. By the time the bridge was built, there wasn't a lot of criminal traffic going in and out of the palace. And with the small windows and the roof, there wasn't much you could see of the outside city. But it makes for a very poetic name, in any case."

Following the tour of the palace Max and Naomi joined the line leading into the Torre dell'Orologio clock tower. The stairs inside the clock tower were steep, and Naomi marvelled at the idea that for years someone had actually climbed the tower regularly to wind it up. Thank goodness for the modern marvel of electricity.

If she thought that tower was steep, however, the Campanile bell tower was even more staggering. The guide explained the story of the tower's 1902 collapse and rebuilding and pointed out the view of the Dolomite mountains in the distance. Naomi sighed with delight as she leaned on the railing, surveying Venice below. It looked to her like one of those miniature Christmas towns that people assembled on their mantels in December, complete with tiny people, glowing shop windows, and snow-powdered rooftops. She could almost picture the spot where a tiny horse and carriage would travel, laden with packages to be delivered to homes in the city. Her mother loved to create such miniature cityscapes in her home every Christmas; she was probably setting one up now, or shopping for new pieces with baby Julia in tow.

The thought of her daughter made her start suddenly. She looked quickly at her phone. Time to call and check in!

She slipped the phone back into her bag and joined the crowd of tourists edging their way slowly down the steep stairs.

CHAPTER 11

Night was falling in Venice, and while another city might have quieted down with the dying light, San Marco seemed even more beautiful now as the Christmas lights blazed to life.

The Basilica was gloriously illuminated, and everywhere Naomi looked festive displays were being lit up in the darkness. The city looked like a romantic postcard at night.

Unfortunately, the dying daylight also meant the temperature was dropping, and Naomi and Max hastily moved on from the Square to find a restaurant. Naomi hadn't realised her stomach was growling; now she realised they had skipped lunch in the excitement of the tours. It didn't take long to find a little trattoria that wasn't too crowded and sit down to order their dinner.

Max let Naomi take the reins in ordering, and she found it hard to pick just a few dishes. There was calamari, a favourite of hers already; pumpkin risotto and seafood risotto; seafood dishes she'd never even heard of, including squid ink and cuttlefish; and of course plenty of tempting noodle and vegetable dishes, often with seafood in the mix. Max visibly paled at the mention of the squid ink but bravely ordered a tamer seafood dish with crab meat and vegetables. Naomi finally settled on her order and also asked for a bottle of wine for the table; the waiter produced one with a flourish, along with two very generously sized wine glasses.

The concept of lingering over a meal at a restaurant had always seemed a little odd back home since Julia, but somehow here in this ancient and magical city, it seemed that hurrying through the meal would be an affront to Venice itself.

Max and Naomi ate slowly, talking about everything they had seen during their tours. By the time dessert had been served, they drank the last of the wine, paid the bill and got ready to leave, they had been at the restaurant for nearly three hours.

It was only once they had returned to their hotel room that Naomi realised she hadn't called her parents to check in on Julia. While Max brushed his teeth in the bathroom, she guiltily dialled her mother's cell phone.

She answered after several rings. "Naomi! How is Venice?"

"Beautiful," she answered truthfully. "Amazing. We're seeing so much. And the food is incredible."

Her mother chuckled. "And how is Max coping?"

Naomi laughed a little, remembering her husband's face as they perused the menu at the restaurant. "Well, he's a little alarmed by some of it, and he doesn't like the boats. But he's having fun. How is Julia doing?"

"Oh, she's as perky as ever! We're out shopping for Christmas decorations now."

"You remembered to bundle her up?" Naomi immediately thought of a dozen other things to ask: *Did you pack her favourite stuffed animal? Do you have an extra soother in case she loses hers? What about a bottle? What about...did you...what if...*

But her mother seemed to anticipate the questions. "She's wearing her favourite teddy bear coat, I packed Mr. Hippo in her diaper bag, she has an extra soother and a bottle of formula, and she ate and got a clean nappy on before we left the house. And we'll be home in plenty of time for a little pre-dinner nap. Don't worry, Naomi, she's doing fine! Concentrate on enjoying yourself. Your weekend will be over far too soon."

"I suppose you're right," Naomi said, giving her 'I love you's' and hanging up. Max emerged from the bathroom and collapsed onto the bed. "Oof. I'm worn out from all that walking. How's Julia?"

"She's doing great," Naomi said, fiddling with her phone. She felt torn—on the one hand, she was glad to hear that her daughter was doing well, but on the other, she still felt bad for being so far away. And yet, she'd truly enjoyed her day and knew this entire trip would have been impossible with a baby in tow. "You're still up for more sightseeing tomorrow?"

"Of course," he said quickly, trying to look alert and failing utterly. She leaned down and kissed him. "Get some rest. There will be plenty of time to make plans in the morning."

Max fell asleep almost immediately, and Naomi slipped under the blankets.

For a moment she debated leaving the phone on in case her mother tried to call, but then she resolutely turned the ringer to the "silent" mode. *Mum's right,* she thought sleepily, pulling the blankets up to her chin. *This weekend will be over in a heartbeat. I'm going to enjoy it while I can.* With thoughts of decadent desserts and twinkling lights still filling her head, she drifted off to sleep.

CHAPTER 12

Lucy woke on Saturday morning feeling strangely refreshed.

She wasn't sure what had changed overnight, but somehow as she stretched and stood in front of her window, gazing down at the canal below, she somehow felt lighter, brighter, and full of excitement for the rest of the weekend.

She chalked it up in part to the delightfully fluffy mound of blankets and pillows on her bed—a good night's rest always made her feel so much better about things—and partly to her visits to the Basilica and Murano the day before. She couldn't exactly explain why, but seeing something so magnificent made her feel a little better about her own small problems. Even if her relationship had crashed and burned, there was still so much beauty to enjoy in the world, so why should she mope? She felt ready to get out and enjoy herself.

She hummed a little to herself as she dressed, pulling on warm black pants and a black turtleneck sweater with her boots and coat. She slightly regretted not bringing anything more colourful with her; she'd been in a bit of a funk when she packed. She pulled her blonde hair up into a French twist and added her everyday diamond stud earrings. On impulse, she popped down to the front desk and asked for the nearest chemist.

Twenty minutes later, she stood in front of the glass window of the shop, surveying her reflection as she applied red lipstick from a freshly purchased tube. She looked over her appearance with a small amount of satisfaction. The lipstick seemed to make all the difference in the world. She no longer saw a sad post-breakup woman in the mirror; now she saw a sassy single gal out to have a fun holiday weekend in a foreign city. Just this thought excited her.

She had a new sway in her step as she popped into a small coffee shop for a frothy hot coffee and biscotti. The only Italian she knew was *'grazie'* but she grinned nonetheless as she thanked the girl at the counter for her food. Sipping the coffee and munching on the crunchy-sweet biscotti, she set off down the street to the nearest dock to catch a vaporetto.

Lucy made it a point to visit museums and art galleries in any city she visited, and her main destination today was the Gallerie dell'Accademia—an amazing collection of artwork that spanned back over centuries, and included work by the sixteenth-century Venetian painter Titian—followed closely by a trip to the Peggy Guggenheim collection, which boasted a dazzling array of more modern art by American and European artists alike, including Picasso and Jackson Pollack. She was certain the museums would hold her for most of the day. After that, she could spend her Sunday doing a bit of leisurely souvenir shopping—what better Christmas gifts to bring home than genuine Italian stuff from Venice? Then, she thought sadly, she would return to the bridge and do what she came here to do.

The Gallerie proved every bit as involved as her guidebook had promised, and the hours flew by as she toured the various rooms. The tour was guided, but the group that day was fairly small, so she was able to linger and enjoy the various pieces of art. At one point she thought she saw a man who reminded her of Dominic in one of the adjoining rooms, and for a moment she wished he could be there to share the tour with her, but she quickly pushed that thought aside. *Today is for me to enjoy the present, not linger on the past.*

In one of the rooms, surveying Giorgione's *Tempest*, Lucy found herself near an English couple. She commented casually on the artwork and hearing her Irish accent, they immediately introduced themselves, and the trio quickly fell into small chat about all they'd seen in the city.

"We're here as an early Christmas present to ourselves," the man who was called Max explained, beaming at his wife. "It's our first outing since our daughter was born."

"Oh! You have a daughter?" Lucy had always loved the idea of having a little girl. "How old?"

"Eight months." His wife, Naomi was clearly a proud mum, pulling up pictures on her smartphone to show off. Lucy made appropriate compliments on the little girl's cute looks and wide smile. "Is it hard to be away from her?"

Naomi hesitated for a moment. "A little," she confessed. Max looked like he wanted to say something but wisely didn't, and Lucy guessed that it was harder than the mother wanted to admit. She tactfully changed the subject. "What's been your favourite sight in Venice so far?"

"I think the bell tower at St. Mark's Square," Naomi said dreamily. "The view makes you feel like you're looking at a postcard. It's such a romantic city."

Yes, it is, Lucy thought with a pang. She couldn't help envying the couple a bit for their romantic trip. It was clear they were relishing the time spent together, without the demands of parenthood interrupting their time together. She supposed that *was* one perk to the single life—no worries about other people imposing on your routine, especially "people" of the nappy-and-bottle variety.

Naomi was asking Lucy about her own trip to the city, and she struggled for a moment to explain what she was doing there. She finally settled on the generic half-truth "It's a gift to myself" rather than explaining that she was there to forget about love lost. It seemed like too sad a tale to share with strangers, especially those celebrating their own happy romance.

SHE HAD a bit of time in between tours to grab lunch and found herself munching on a hot panini and coffee at a tiny cafe.

Afterwards, she joined the tour through the Guggenheim collection and quickly lost herself in room after room of art. The variety presented made it impossible to get bored, and the tour almost seemed to end too quickly.

Outside the weak afternoon light signalled the close of day. Tourists were moving in groups to find dinner, attend an evening mass at one of the city's cathedrals, or rent a gondola for a private cruise up and down the canals to view the holiday lights.

Not quite yet ready to move on to dinner so early, Lucy opted to hire a gondolier and relax on the canals.

She was glad she'd bundled up warmly because the air off the water was freezing. However, the view of San Marco at night by boat was worth the chill. One of Lucy's favourite childhood memories was that of piling into the family car with her parents and siblings and driving around their hometown to look at the Christmas light displays on homes and businesses. Lucy and her sisters had given imaginary ratings to the displays as they passed and debated seriously about the merits of each display, awarding scores to the decorations based on imagination, colourfulness, and sheer size of the displays.

Some of their favourite houses went all out, with all of the trees in the front gardens ablaze in ropes of lights and lighted figures across the driveway and even on the roof. As a child Lucy had found it delightful; now she thought about how much work those displays must have entailed.

The displays in Venice evoked a similar feeling of awe.

Large lighted stars hung above her, seemingly suspended in thin air. Strings of lights outlined windows and doorways or encircled trees on balconies. Here and there a business had a brightly lit nativity or other display in their shop windows. Most of the bridges, too, were brightly lit for night, and the cathedrals all featured lighting of their own. Christmas music floated down the canals from nearby businesses; though most of it was in Italian, Lucy recognised the tunes and hummed along.

Her good-natured gondolier hummed too and occasionally sang along to the tunes.

By the end of her forty-minute boat ride, Lucy had pretty well lost the feeling in her nose and fingertips, but her heart and soul felt warmer. She asked the gondolier for a nearby restaurant recommendation and thanked him warmly, rubbing her hands together as she walked down the street. The joyful Christmas spirit combined with the obvious magic of the city was improving her mood more and more with every passing hour.

She ducked into a trattoria playing an Italian rotation of sacred festive music; Lucy recognised the tunes of "Silent Night" and several other hymns that had played on heavy rotation during her childhood. She smiled at the thought of how she had squirmed through Mass services at church while thinking ahead to opening presents!

The waiter brought appetisers and wine and soon returned to the table with a hearty order of seafood risotto, crusty bread and marinated anchovies. Lucy ate her fill and lingered at the table afterwards, enjoying a strong cup of espresso despite the late hour. She nibbled her tiramisu and asked the waiter to add an extra bottle of wine to her order; she could take that back to one of her sisters in Dublin as a Christmas gift.

Satisfied and laden down with a bag containing her wine, Lucy strolled down the street, lost in thought. She felt almost giddy from the fun of the day and of course, the delicious food. She was so lost in thought (and more than a little tipsy) that for a moment, she imagined Dominic standing at the corner of the narrow streets, waiting for her.

She sighed to herself and continued walking.

My imagination is just not going to let me be, she thought ruefully. *Now I know what unrequited love means.*

Even a full day of great fun and good food can't get a person out of your head. You still see them everywhere you go.

CHAPTER 14

Back at the hotel Lucy tucked the wine safely in her suitcase, and drew a hot bath scented with plenty of lavender and chamomile.

Soaking blissfully in the bubbles, she considered what to do the following day.

First, a lazy breakfast. Second, shopping; she was already compiling a mental list of things to look for in the little shops: a leather-bound journal for Dad, some blown-glass trinket for Mum (maybe a Venetian mask or a paperweight)?, perhaps a knitted scarf for her younger sister.

And of course, if I find some little things for myself, too, that wouldn't be half bad.

Her eyes fell on her smartphone, sitting on the bathroom counter. It was tempting—oh so tempting—to call Dominic's number, just to see what he was doing. They hadn't spoken since the breakup, but that didn't mean she couldn't call just to say hi. She might get his voicemail, and then that would solve a lot of the awkwardness of having an actual conversation. And wouldn't he be surprised when he heard she was calling from Venice?

She composed a message in her head:

Hi, Dominic, I'm in Venice and I was just thinking of you—remembering all the fun we had here last year. God, no—that was far too needy. Maybe: *Hey Dominic, was just thinking of you and wanted to wish you a Merry Christmas.*

Too casual? What about: *Hi Dominic, hope you're doing well. Maybe we could grab a coffee sometime and catch up?*

She half reached out for the phone before she pulled her arm back. *Nope. Don't do it.*

This trip was about getting over heartbreak, not inviting it back in. Besides, she wasn't sure what might be worse—having to talk to Dominic and dealing with a stilted conversation, or leaving a message that he might not return.

After all, it was possible he didn't want to speak to her at all, and calling him might just confirm that for good—something she'd rather not deal with, in all honesty.

Or, he might return her call with some news about a new girlfriend—something she *definitely* didn't want to hear about. At least if she didn't call, she didn't have to face the complications of a conversation. Dominic could stay safely tucked away in her memories and one day he would be just that—a memory.

Lucy finally drained the bathtub and wrapped herself up in a fluffy robe before settling down in bed with a magazine. She was drowsy from the wine and the warm water, and it was easy to put Dominic out of mind and curl up for bed.

She dreamed that night of standing on the bridge last winter with Dominic in the snow, hand in hand as they locked the padlock.

But in the morning she didn't remember her dreams, and she whistled cheerily to herself as she got ready for another day.

CHAPTER 15

SATURDAY MORNING DAWNED colder than the previous day, but Scott wasn't daunted in the least.

He'd already bounced back from the disappointment of his failed proposal at St. Mark's Square, and he'd moved on to an even better idea: a romantic candlelit dinner near Rialto Bridge, followed by a stroll along some of the quieter streets nearby.

There, under a starry sky, away from all the hustle and bustle of the tourist crowds, he would get down on one knee and propose to the love of his life. He could already picture the scene in his head; he'd replayed it a dozen times since he got out of bed that morning.

But first, the day ahead promised plenty more sightseeing in the historic city. Rachel, enamoured of Italian art, was eager to tour the Gallerie dell'Accademia, which boasted centuries' worth of Italian paintings, frescoes, sculptures and more. For his part Scott didn't know the difference between the various periods and styles of painting, nor did he understand the polit-ical significance of some of the pieces, but Rachel was having fun and for her sake, he made an effort to have fun, too. It was hard to concentrate on the tour, though, when he kept thinking forward to the table he'd booked for the evening.

Even as they sat at lunch, he was only half-listening to Rachel as she chattered on eagerly about the art they'd seen. Inside he was playing out the proposal as he intended it to happen:

First, they would go to the restaurant. Scott had found one near the impressive Rialto bridge; if you sat near windows you had an excellent view of the bridge, and for the festive season the bridge was lit up much like the rest of the Grand Canal.

They would enjoy a lovely dinner, then take a walk across the bridge and enjoy the sight of the holiday lights across the Grand Canal. Perhaps, if the mood struck them, they would take a gondola down the canal and marvel at the lights from the water.

Then, they would take a quiet walk through the less-populated city streets. Then, on a quiet bridge, away from the crowds, Scott would get down on one knee, pull out the ring, and…

"Earth to Scott." He snapped out of his reverie to see that Rachel was staring at him, looking slightly bemused. He realised she must have asked a question, and he felt his ears reddening a little. "Sorry, babe, I was lost in thought. What were you saying?"

She smiled and said, "I was suggesting we do a little shopping today. Instead of hitting another museum. I could tell you were a bit bored with the last one."

Scott winced a little. "Was it that obvious?"

She laughed out loud. "It's okay. I know I'm the one who's crazy about Italy; I know you're not as big of a fan."

"We can do whatever you want today," he promised, and meant it. He wanted her to enjoy herself, and more importantly, he wanted her to be in good spirits for their dinner date.

He patted his coat pocket once more and followed her out of the cafe and through the city streets.

Shopping proved to be a bit of an interesting experience. Rachel was enjoying chatting with the shopkeepers in Italian, and she found several small items that she wanted to purchase: a leather bag, a cashmere scarf with a gossamer texture and a price tag to match, and some beautiful tiny glass birds, which were wrapped carefully and placed in a sturdy box for safe-keeping.

CHAPTER 16

By THE TIME they had finished touring the shops and returned Rachel's purchases to the hotel, it was time to get ready for dinner. As usual, Scott was astounded by how a few simple changes could turn Rachel from a daytime tourist into an evening beauty.

She emerged from the bathroom with her hair swept back up from her face, showing off a pair of diamond earrings he had bought her for her birthday. She'd added a little makeup but not much—she didn't need it—and swapped out her sweater for a silky, low-cut black top. She'd kept the warm black pants and boots, though, and bundled up in a thick scarf, gloves and coat.

"It's freezing out here!" she exclaimed, as their water taxi took them to the restaurant. "I'm so glad we're not going on a gondola tour tonight."

"Yeah, me too," Scott echoed, privately disappointed. *Well, there's always tomorrow...*

As promised, the Rialto Bridge was aglow with lights that changed colour as festive tunes played over the water. Scott and Rachel *ooh*ed appreciatively at the sight and hurried into the restaurant to their table.

The waiter frowned when Scott mentioned his reservation. "We seem to have had some issues with our booking, sir," he said, and Scott's heart sank. "Somehow there are mixups with the seating. That table is not available this evening."

His expression made it clear he wasn't going to offer any further explanations or help, so Scott tried politely, "Could you find us another table then? I promised my girlfriend a romantic dinner tonight."

The man looked irritated at this request, as though the endless romantic trials of visiting tourists were of no concern to him. However, he consulted his book and grouchily conceded that he did have an available table.

"This way," he said, marching off briskly without a backward glance, and Scott and Rachel glanced at each other in concern. Nonetheless, Scott was determined to make the most of the night, and they hurried after the man to the table he indicated.

Scott thought that it was almost as if the guy had deliberately selected the worst table in the restaurant. Tucked into a dark corner, it offered no view of the bridge whatsoever, but a very good earful of the clamour from the kitchen.

He reached under the table and squeezed Rachel's hand in apology. "I'm so sorry, I didn't know this would happen. Do you want to go somewhere else?"

"No, this is fine." She busied herself studying the menu. Scott also buried himself in the menu, and when a waiter appeared to take their order, they decided to start with a round of appetisers. This waiter also seemed a little on the surly side, but Scott decided it could just be the busy evening—the restaurant was packed—and tried to brush it off.

Wine appeared on the table in short order, and Scott and Rachel tried to strike up a conversation. It was difficult to chat quietly with the din of their fellow diners and the noise from the kitchen, and after a while, they fell silent. Some time passed before it occurred to Scott that their appetisers had yet to appear. He finally caught the attention of their waiter and inquired about their order, only to be met with a terse, "I'll check" before the man disappeared without a second look.

Scott glanced at Rachel, but she was carefully studying the other diners, trying not to let on that she was disappointed. After what seemed like forever, the waiter finally returned with a plate of bread and olive oil and fried meatballs—all rather lukewarm, now, after what Scott suspected was a long period sitting on a side counter waiting to be served. They picked halfheartedly at the food and waited for their Secondi to be served.

The second round of the meal came out with decidedly more speed, but when the waiter set Rachel's dish down in front of her, she said something haltingly in Italian. The waiter did a double-take and apologised curtly, whisking the dish away. Scott didn't need a translation to know that whatever the man had brought was definitely *not* the risotto dish she'd ordered.

Next, the waiter brought out another dish, but after a couple of bites, she had to signal him back. "Sorry," she said, "it's just that this has cuttlefish in it, and I asked for the chicken."

This time the waiter was duly embarrassed, and muttered several apologies as he took away her plate. In the meantime another order had arrived—polenta with porcini and sausage—and Rachel nibbled a bit at it while they waited. She urged Scott to go ahead and eat his, but he felt bad eating when she was having so many issues with her own order.

Finally, the waiter brought out fresh risotto with chicken, and Rachel dug in. By now Scott's food was growing cold, but he ate as much of it as he could anyway. When Rachel finished eating he leaned across the table and whispered, "Do you want to order dessert?"

"No thanks!" She shook her head and glanced at the kitchen, as though expecting to see the waiter again. "No, this was terrible. Let's just go."

They paid and left, Rachel shivering in the cold. Scott quickly abandoned the idea of either a gondola ride or a walk; he guessed she wouldn't enjoy either, and after their disastrous meal, he felt terrible that he hadn't planned out better entertainment for the night.

BACK AT THE HOTEL, he scrolled through Internet listings of local late-night happenings while Rachel warmed up with a hot shower. When she emerged, wrapped up in a cosy robe, he queried, "Would you want to go out again? We could catch a late-night movie, maybe, or go to one of the local bars for a drink?"

Rachel made a face as she crawled into bed. "Ugh, I don't think so. I'm so worn out, and it's so cold. Let's just stay in for the rest of the night, okay?"

"Okay." Scott closed his laptop and decided to take a quick shower to warm up, too; Rachel was right about the temperature outside. By the time he emerged ten minutes later, however, soft snores could be heard coming from Rachel's side of the bed. Stifling a sigh of disappointment, he switched off her bedside lamp and crawled in beside her.

The ring box was still waiting in his coat pocket. Scott thought sadly of his ruined evening and wondered if the following day would provide any better chances for the proposal he wanted to make.

Come on, Venice, he thought desperately, *show me a little romantic magic before we go home.*

CHAPTER 17

SATURDAY MORNING, Max and Naomi got off to a sluggish start.

He noticed happily that she was relaxing more with each passing day; today she slept much later than usual, and seemed happy to cuddle in bed rather than rushing to get up and out the door. He took it as a good sign that the beauty of the city was working its magic.

He didn't want to say it out loud and spoil the mood, but he missed mornings like this—just the two of them, cuddled up in bed, then perhaps picking out an activity for the day. No baby needing to be fed, clothed, changed and coddled; no schedule that included mandatory feedings and naps. Just he and Naomi, the way it used to be.

Part of him felt so guilty for even thinking that though. Of course, he loved Julia—until she was born, he hadn't quite understood how people fell head over heels in love with infants, but one look into her serious green eyes and he was a goner.

He adored his daughter, loved playing with her, napping with her on his chest, dancing around in the living room holding her and listening to her laugh. He looked forward to many years of firsts—first day of school, first pet, first date, first car—and to many father-daughter chats. He was thrilled with his daughter and thrilled with what a wonderful mother Naomi was to their baby.

He just missed having his wife around, too.

He sat in bed and watched her put on makeup in the bathroom mirror. It seemed like so much of her energy these days went into the baby, not into herself. It wasn't just their relationship that had been put on the back burner; he realised that now, a bit belatedly.

Little things like putting on mascara in the mornings, or picking up a novel she wanted to read—they had gone out the window in favour of feedings, changings and caring for Julia. Max realised a bit guiltily that his wife didn't have a lot of time for her own interests anymore and he wondered if maybe he should be chipping in a lot more than he was. Either way, he wanted to do something to help make it up to her.

So, while she was busy getting ready for the day, he popped down to the hotel reception desk and asked the manager on duty to help him find a good couple's massage therapist in the city. "I don't speak Italian, so perhaps you could set something up for us? Preferably with someone who speaks a little English?"

The manager seemed only too happy to help and promised to have something lined up for the afternoon, after they came back from their museum tour but before dinner. That treat all taken care of, Max went back upstairs to collect his wife and whisk her off to tour the art galleries.

The first one was full of classical Italian art from the past several centuries, and Max looked around with amazement at the extensive collection. He didn't necessarily know anything about the artists featured—none of the names jumped out at him—but even so, it was hard not to be impressed with the huge collection. Their tour guide was fairly chatty but also let them have plenty of time to study the pictures on their own.

In one of the rooms, he and Naomi struck up a conversation with an Irish girl visiting the city—from Dublin, as it turned out. "Oh, we're from Newcastle," Naomi explained. "So we're used to this cold!"

The woman laughed. "At least the city isn't flooded," she said. "It happens from time to time. I've been lucky though; both times I've visited it's been dry."

They chatted for a while about everything they'd seen so far, and Naomi asked if Lucy was travelling solo or with a partner. For a moment the woman looked sad, but she laughed. "No romantic trip for me, I'm afraid. I'm just taking a little break as a Christmas gift to myself."

After the galleries, Max and Naomi found a nearby café where they ordered miniature pizzas and drinks for lunch.

Naomi checked her phone, scrolling across the screen to check the time. Max could see that she was calculating the time difference and whether it was too early yet to call home, and he said quickly, "I have a surprise for you."

"Oh?" Naomi was distracted enough to put the phone back in her bag. He nodded, encouraged. "Remember I mentioned that massage yesterday? Well, I asked the hotel manager to book us one. I've got the paper in my coat pocket with the address; we can have a water taxi take us straight there. Our appointment is at two o'clock."

"Really?" He'd expected her to be excited, but he hadn't realised she would light up so much at the idea. She quickly checked the time. "Oh, we should leave now! We don't want to be late."

At her insistence, Max hurried through the rest of his pizza. *That wasn't even half-bad,* he thought reluctantly. *Maybe Italian food is growing on me.*

CHAPTER 18

THE DIRECTIONS WERE clear enough to follow, and the water-taxi easily deposited them outside a luxurious looking day spa.

To Max's relief, the masseuses who were handling their appointment both spoke fluent English, so at least he didn't have to feel awkward about *that* part of things.

If Max tolerated the treatments—he thought they were a little frilly, to be honest—he could tell Naomi was beside herself. They started with a foot bath and moved through a series of massages and body treatments, rubbing in fragrant oils that Max supposed were relaxing or calming. Naomi certainly looked relaxed, and he settled down onto his treatment table, feeling a touch better himself.

By the time their hour session was up, Naomi was practically radiant, and Max could definitely feel that the kinks in his neck were long gone.

She was beaming as they glided back down a canal to another restaurant for dinner. "Have you ever felt so relaxed before?" she said dreamily, and he couldn't help but grin. He supposed he hadn't, but better than that was seeing how relaxed she was. It was like her old self was coming back—the one who wasn't constantly stressed and fussing over the baby.

Dinner was the usual mix of terrifying choices, but somehow Max didn't care so much. He discovered that he could order pasta with a tomato and meat sauce, and did so without caring if it looked too English. He didn't even know the names of the dishes Naomi ordered, though he could smell seafood in at least one of them. When dessert came around he even tried a bite of her tiramisu, even though he still thought the espresso and chocolate were too strong.

They finally left the restaurant late and went to hail a boat to take them back to their hotel. Max noticed all the gondoliers lining up outside nearby and on impulse said, "Shall we take a detour?"

Naomi was snuggled up tightly against him. She followed his gaze, looking delighted. "Are you sure? I know you don't like being so close to the water…"

"I can put up with it." *I think.*

Max asked the gondolier to take them on a short tour of the canals, and off they went, poling out into the Grand Canal and taking in the sights of San Marco by night.

Naomi sighed contentedly. The lights strung up along buildings and over bridges reflected on the lapping waters of the canals, leaving the whole city aglow. It was hard to not feel festive gliding under lit snowflakes and stars and listening to classic Christmas hymns sung in Italian playing through loud-speakers on Rialto Bridge and in shops closing up for the night.

Max tried carefully to avoid looking down at the water as they glided along. He found that if he just kept his eyes on the level, looking at the colourful paint of the buildings or the lights overhead, he could almost forget they were in a glorified canoe.

Naomi seemed perfectly content. Out of the blue, the gondolier gently sang something Italian in a baritone voice, and although Max couldn't understand a word, he thought he could sense some of the joy in the man's voice.

Their gondolier ended their tour right at the dock of their hotel, and Max released a breath as he climbed out of the shallow boat. A dock wasn't solid ground, but it sure beat a gondola for stability.

Upstairs he shrugged out of his heavy clothes into pyjamas and listened as Naomi drew a bath and changed into night-clothes. To his surprise and delight, she emerged from the bathroom smelling like her perfume and wearing a silky black slip that was not intended for sleeping in. Apparently, she'd forgotten all about calling home promptly each evening, and once she'd climbed into bed he forgot all about it too.

Later that night he woke up for no reason, startled out of a dream, or maybe hearing some noise outside the hotel. He got up quietly and went to the bathroom to get a drink of water, and when he came back he lay propped up on one elbow, studying his wife.

For the first time in over a year, she seemed totally at peace, breathing softly, her hair spread out over the pillow.

It was a good idea to come here, he thought, satisfied, as he curled up next to his wife. They hadn't had so much quality time together since the baby came, and he thought it was worth every moment spent in those darn boats.

A feeling of extreme contentment spread through him as he listened to Naomi's soft breathing, and he eased himself care-fully back under the blankets to cuddle up next to her, drifting away to sleep.

CHAPTER 19

When Sunday morning dawned cold and overcast, with a chance of snow, Scott knew at once that his chances of getting Rachel to take a scenic gondola ride were probably low.

After the crowds, the disastrous dinner, and now with the cold, it was obvious her excitement at visiting Venice was waning. She was already talking about what they might do the next weekend at home, discussing the possibility of a movie and drinks with friends, and his heart sank.

Was he never going to get a chance to propose here?

But when he asked if she was game for a gondola tour on the Grand Canal, to his surprise, she agreed. "It'll be cold," he added, almost as an afterthought, expecting her to change her mind. But she just shrugged and said that she would wear an extra layer of clothing.

They attended the late morning Mass at St. Mark's Basilica, as he'd promised they would, and they were not disappointed. The sacred chorale was sung in Italian, and echoing off the gilded domes of the cathedral it sounded otherworldly.

Scott didn't know much about Catholicism or how Mass

progressed, but he was able to appreciate the obvious meaning behind the service. They emerged onto the steps of the Basilica to light snow, oversized fluffy flakes drifting down to the stones like tiny down feathers.

He was more than happy to spend a quiet afternoon at the hotel, and when they left for their evening gondola ride, he made sure Rachel had bundled up in extra thermals and a warm sweater. He didn't want anything to ruin the night; this was his last big chance to propose before the weekend was over, and nothing would mess it up if he could help it.

But the line for gondola rides was long, and the gondoliers themselves seemed jaded and in a less-than-cheerful mood. Scott tried to put a positive face on things; Rachel remained silent. The minutes in the queue dragged by, and soon it became apparent that they were going nowhere fast if they intended to go in a gondola.

After nearly an hour, they finally secured a free gondola, and Scott sat down next to Rachel with relief. At last, they were underway!

Rachel tried chatting a bit with the gondolier, switching from English to Italian, but he seemed dismissive and uninterested in making tourist small talk. Finally, she gave up, sitting back and snuggling up against Scott to take in the sights.

The view of the Grand Canal was even more impressive from this vantage point, with views of the buildings and also the side canals and bridges that led off to smaller businesses and homes.

However, after just a few minutes floating along, their boat came to a halt. The large number of vessels out on the canal for the night had led to a water-locked traffic jam, and now boat traffic was nearly at a standstill as gondoliers and water taxi drivers shouted and argued with each other.

Beside him, Rachel was shivering. Scott hugged her a little

tighter. *This was a terrible idea,* he realised, listening to their gondolier mutter to himself in his native language. English or Italian, the tone was the same with a complaint, and it was clear to Scott that the man was not having a good night.

The ride was supposed to last about forty minutes, though Scott knew he could pay for a longer period if he wanted.

However, by the time the forty minutes were up, it felt as though they'd been in the boat for hours. As soon as the gondolier pulled up at a dock, Rachel nearly bolted out of the boat, and Scott hastily paid the man and followed her.

From the set of her shoulders and the way she walked, Scott could tell his girlfriend was dejected. He could also tell she was freezing, and when she ducked into a small café and ordered hot chocolate he asked the waiter to make it two and followed her to a quiet corner table.

They sat in silence for a moment, warming their hands on the cups and sipping their drinks without speaking. Scott finally reached out to touch Rachel's hand. "Babe, I'm so sorry for how this weekend's been going. It seems to have just got worse and worse as it went on."

"It's not your fault," she said gently, wrapping her hands more tightly around the cup to steal its warmth. "I guess I thought Venice would be so much more … magical I guess."

"We've just had some bad luck, that's all." Timidly he asked, "Do you want to try and find something else to do for the evening…maybe sit by that cafe orchestra in Piazza San Marco?"

Rachel shook her head firmly and she looked sad. "No. The city was fun at first, but like I said I'm a little …disenchanted by now," she admitted. "It's cold, people are in a bad mood, and there are so many tourists. It just isn't the romantic getaway I thought it would be."

"Yeah, I guess I'm bummed too," he admitted. *For more reasons than one.*

Rachel drained the last of her hot chocolate. "So while it's been fun, I think I'm ready to go home."

"Me too," he agreed halfheartedly, even though he didn't feel the same way. He quickly finished his hot chocolate and they returned to their hotel by the quickest route possible, avoiding the packed Grand Canal.

CHAPTER 20

IN THE LOBBY, Christmas music was playing softly, and Scott took a moment to admire the nativity scene by the front desk. He hadn't paid it much mind before, but now he thought wistfully of the romantic Christmas break he'd planned and how things had run downhill so fast. There didn't seem to be much for it but to admit defeat and head back home.

Maybe I can arrange a more romantic proposal back home, he conceded. *It won't be as good as Venice, but it will be better than nothing.*

Scott climbed into bed as quietly as possible, thinking Rachel was already asleep, but to his surprise, she rolled over to face him and said quietly, "Remember our first date?"

Scott was surprised by the question. "How could I forget?" he said, snuggling up to her. He had planned the day for nearly two weeks, down to the restaurant reservation, tickets to a movie starring her favourite actor, and dessert at a local hotspot he knew she'd been dying to try.

It had taken no small shortage of planning and a considerable chunk of his wallet, but he'd managed to pull off the best first date he could imagine, and Rachel had been delighted.

Now she rested her head on his arm, closing her eyes. "And remember when you put together that surprise birthday party for me at that new nightclub, and I had no idea you'd invited my best friends because they were all sworn to secrecy?"

"It wouldn't be a surprise otherwise," he protested, and she smiled.

"You always go to such lengths to make things perfect," she said sleepily. "But I'm happy just spending time with you. Isn't that enough?"

"I guess," he said reluctantly, nuzzling her cheek.

She opened her eyes and gave him a wry look. "It's not, though."

"It's not that," Scott sputtered, trying to put his feelings into words. "It's just that…well, I feel like you deserve the best of everything. And I know how much you love Italy, and Venice is supposed to be such a romantic city…and I wanted you to have the time of your life on this trip. That's all."

"I did have a lot of fun," Rachel said, rolling over to tuck her back against him. He curled around her, enjoying the softness of her skin. "But I've had fun because I was here with you. It wouldn't have mattered if it was a five-star trip if I was alone. Everything—the dinners, the bell tower, touring the Basilica—it was all amazing because I was sharing it with you."

Scott buried a sigh in her hair. "I've had an amazing time with you, too. I just wish I could have created more perfect romantic surprises for you. That was part of the whole point of coming here."

"Well," Rachel said, sounding suspiciously less sleepy, "I have a little romantic surprise of my own …"

"What's that?" Scott ran a hand down her side, lingering on her hip, and was surprised when she suddenly pulled his hand around to rest on her stomach.

"I was going to wait to tell you until we got home. I was

surprised you didn't say something about me skipping the wine and the seafood."

For a moment Scott could only stare down at her in shock, and she rolled onto her back, peering up at him in concern. "Babe? Say something. You're worrying me."

Scott racked his brain, thinking of the perfect most romantic thing to say. Instead, all he could blurt out was, "I can't believe you climbed all those stairs in the tower yesterday!" and Rachel started laughing and pulled him down for a kiss.

ON SUNDAY MORNING Max and Naomi decided to attend the late morning Mass at St. Mark's.

Max had attended a few Masses as a child and Naomi had attended more than her share throughout her childhood and teens, but there was something different about standing in a cathedral, listening to a carol sung in a foreign language. It gave a person chills, and yet at the same time it was beautiful. The voices of the choir echoed off the domed roofs and filtered back over the assembled worshippers in the pews.

After the Mass, they walked slowly through St. Mark's Square, under a cloud of softly falling snow. There were fewer tourists out today, and fewer pigeons due to the weather. Max noticed a young couple of tourists also walking through the Square and pointed them out to Naomi. "Don't they kind of remind you of us, before we got married and had Julia?"

Naomi looked at the pair and smiled. The girl was bundled up against the cold and clearly not enjoying it; she pulled her hood up over her red hair in a bid to stay warm. The boyfriend kept one arm protectively around her. "We were always glued at the hip," she mused. "Whatever happened to us?"

"We got busy," Max conceded. They stopped at a café for coffee and took a quiet table where they could watch the falling snow and talk. Naomi wrapped her hands around her coffee mug and studied the scene outside without speaking.

"Sometimes I think you don't worry about Julia like I do," she said suddenly, and almost immediately her cheeks reddened, as though she hadn't meant to speak out loud and was embarrassed that she'd done so.

Max was a little startled, but he thought guiltily of how often he wished they could have more time apart from the baby. "It's not that," he began. "It's just that I miss you—I miss *us* before we got so wrapped up in real life—and now you're so wrapped up in being a mum, it feels like we don't get much time together. And I don't like that. I miss my wife."

To his utter bewilderment, Naomi suddenly started to cry. Alarmed, Max patted her arm and fished in her bag for tissues, unsure of how to react.

She dabbed at her eyes, trying to wipe away the tears without disturbing her makeup. "I just get so worried about her! I'm afraid to be a bad mother. I'm constantly thinking, what if something happens, and I'm not there? What if she needs me, and I'm busy doing something else? It feels so—so selfish to have fun!"

Max blinked, still unsure of how to respond to this sudden outburst. "But I am having fun, and now I feel terrible for it!" she continued, sniffling. "I'm enjoying spending time together, just the two of us. I enjoy going out for dinner and sleeping without listening for a baby monitor. I like getting dressed up and going out, instead of packing a nappy bag. This whole weekend, it's been—"She flailed her arms a bit as she tried to find the words. "It's been brilliant, and I don't want it to end. But I feel like a bad mum because I'm not checking in on my daughter every few hours."

"I don't think that makes you a bad mum," Max said

cautiously. He still wasn't sure if this was his cue to say something, or if he should let her keep talking. She didn't respond though, only sniffled, so he kept going. "I think you're an amazing mum to Julia. And I love you for it. I wouldn't want you any other way. But you need to take care of yourself, too. And I don't want us to be so wrapped up in being parents that we forget about each other. That was the whole point of this trip—for us to reconnect." He grabbed her hands in his own and gave her a pleading look. "Please don't feel bad for that. I don't want you to feel bad, I want you to be happy."

Naomi sniffled and nodded. "I am happy," she admitted. "This whole trip has been so lovely. I just...I'm torn. I feel guilty for not missing Julia more, and I feel guilty for being away from her, and I feel guilty for ignoring you..."

"You can be all those things. It's normal, I promise. I feel them too."

"Really?" Naomi looked doubtful, but Max nodded. "I miss her, and then I feel bad for not missing her enough. And I feel bad because I don't think about how you're feeling sometimes."

Naomi wiped her eyes and drained her mug of cappuccino nearly in one swallow. She set her mug down with a sigh. "Today I woke up glad that I'll see my daughter tomorrow, and then I felt sad that it's our last day in Venice."

"Then we should enjoy it," Max said firmly. "Tuck the phone away in your bag. You know your mum is perfectly capable of handling anything that comes up."

"I know but..."

"So let's get going. We can tour the city, eat as much Italian food as we can, and go home tomorrow happy and contented. How does that sound for a plan? C'mon. We might only get this one chance to explore the city. Let's make the most of it."

Naomi seemed to finally make up her mind. "OK," she said, tucking the phone in her bag. She gave Max an apologetic look.

"Just don't get upset if I check it now and then throughout the day."

"Promise," he said, grabbing her hand. "C'mon. I know you have a notebook full of destinations and notes tucked away in your bag; tell me where we're going today."

THEY STARTED with a map of the city and no real destination. It was cold out, but they were dressed warmly and there were plenty of cafes dotting the streets where they could buy hot coffee, hot chocolate or a snack to eat while they warmed up.

The snow was falling only lightly, drifting past them without a whisper. They started out from their hotel and began wandering across the map, exploring tiny side streets and playing a sort of treasure hunt game. Could they find the narrowest lane in the city, Calle Varisco? Could they find the house labelled "1"? They also looked for street addresses that reflected their birth years and anniversary years. All of this was marked down with a pen on the map.

When they had crisscrossed the city, they ended up near Rialto Bridge. Naomi's notebook listed the Rialto food market as an interesting place to linger, and while Max had no interest in the actual food on offer (lots and lots of seafood), he did find it interesting to see the cultural side of the markets. He hadn't put a lot of thought into the lack of farmland available or how most Venetians got their food, and a look at the market gave him a greater appreciation of the many types of seafood up for grabs at local restaurants. *I still want English fish and chips when I get home,* he thought with amusement as a vendor showed off fresh squid.

After that, tired of walking, they decided to hop a water bus and cruise the Grand Canal for a daylight look at the city. The snow had stopped by now, and they had a nice view of the hotels and other businesses lining the water, along with glimpses of some of the side streets and canals. It was nearly dusk now, and the Rialto Bridge was well lit up for the night. Further down they spotted the Bridge of Sighs—somehow less impressive now that they had heard the story of its name—as well as a myriad smaller bridges, quiet and deserted in the gathering dusk.

Rising above all they spotted the bell tower and clock tower in St. Mark's Square, and the spires on the cathedral. Max checked his watch. "If we're ready, we can get through a quick meal and make the late Mass. You up for it?"

"Definitely." Naomi's eyes were sparkling.

They grabbed food at a small takeaway cafe nearby—more pizza for Max and a panini for Naomi—and then headed into the Basilica with the other tourists and worshippers who were joining the Mass.

They were in for a treat. They'd been expecting a regular service, but tonight there was a visiting choir who would be singing the Mass. The voices that rose up to the gilded domes filled the cathedral with the same spine-tingling sound they'd heard that morning, yet somehow it seemed even more impressive at night.

Outside, the Basilica was flooded with light for the night-time hours, and Max and Naomi took a moment to admire it as they stood in the piazza. Finally, the cold got the better of them, and they all but ran back to the hotel, laughing at their attempts to hurry without slipping on the fresh snow.

Back at the hotel, Naomi made a quick check of her phone. "No calls," she said happily, and stayed it away again.

Max plumped up a pillow and handed it to her. "Aren't you going to call and check in?"

She thought about that for a moment. "I don't think so — not today," she said at last. "It's our last day and I'll let my mom do what I asked her to do—watch Julia. And I'll enjoy us for one more night before we go home."

"Speaking of the night— look at this." Max turned off the lamps and opened the curtains, gesturing out the window. Naomi joined him and gasped a little. They could just see down the canal to Rialto Bridge, and it was still lit up with an ever-changing rainbow of Christmas lights, even at this late hour. Very faintly, they could hear the stream of a jazzy-sounding Christmas carol drifting down the water.

"It's magical," said Naomi. "Like something you see in a movie. And we were lucky enough to see it in person."

They stood in the window for a while longer, holding each other and not speaking. Sometimes, they both realised, you didn't need words to express a feeling.

Just being in the moment and sharing it was enough.

CHAPTER 23

ON HER LAST full day in Venice, Lucy slept late.

She indulged a little, ordering room service so she could linger in bed a while longer, watching a local English-language morning news program and nibbling on a croissant. Finally, she took a hot shower and dressed for the day.

She made sure to pick out the nicest outfit she had and tied a scarf around her neck. She wanted to see the morning Mass at the Basilica, and afterwards, she would do a bit more sightseeing in the city, and go to dinner.

Then return to the bridge, do what she came here to do and go home.

After the late Mass she found a café where she could get a quick snack—more coffee and croissants sounded just about right—and then set off to do her shopping. She wandered through the Rialto food market and was fascinated by the variety of items available for purchase, but declined the vendors' inquiring nods regretfully. Unfortunately, she had no way to take home fresh squid or crab meat in her suitcase, however delicious they might be. She would have to settle for one more evening of stuffing herself with local delicacies before heading home.

After the food market, she spent some time admiring Rialto Bridge from the windows of a local café, where she snacked on deep-fried meatballs, olives and bread drizzled with plenty of olive oil and herbs.

The waiter who dished up her antipasti had plenty of suggestions for where to shop on her last day, along with a warning that if something seemed cheap, it probably was: "Many shops import goods from China," he explained, "so stay away from the cheap stuff. Real Italian quality, it will cost you. But it's worth it!"

Lucy kept his warning in mind when she caught a water bus out to the island of Burano. She wanted to take a peek into the Church of San Martino, which looked positively rustic after the decadence of the Basilica, and the Oblique Bell Tower.

She also hoped to see the school of lace-making, where she was told a few dedicated Venetians hung onto the craft of making fine lace by hand. She was impressed by the number of hours that went into the craft; for herself, she'd never had the patience for fine handicrafts, so she couldn't imagine spending hours and hours on one tiny piece.

Besides the church and the lace-making museum and school, Burano boasted rows of colourful houses along the main canals that looked even prettier with a dusting of snow on the roofs. They reminded Lucy of colourful cupcakes with icing on top. Too soon it was time to board the bus back to San Marco, and she looked one more time at the colourful waterfront as they sailed away.

Back in the city, it didn't take long to find all manner of shops with tempting goods that she knew her family and friends would love. Leather goods, Venetian masks, handmade chocolate and more—it was hard to pick out just a few things.

Finally, she settled on a tooled leather journal for her dad, one which she knew he would enjoy writing in and would look lovely sitting out on his desk. He prided himself on keeping a neat study and this journal would fit right in. There were lovely cashmere scarves and tiny blown-glass paperweights for her mother and sisters.

She picked up an extra blown-glass necklace charm for herself—a souvenir of her trip—and finally returned to her hotel as dusk fell and the shops began to close up for the day. In the distance, she could hear the bell tower chiming out the hour, and she knew it was time to find something to eat—her stomach was rumbling even louder than the chatter of passing tourists.

CHAPTER 24

SHE TUCKED her bags safely away in her room and went down the street to a cosy restaurant that was just gearing up for the dinner rush. There were lots of other tourists out and about at this hour too, but Lucy had no trouble getting a small corner table and her dinner arrived quickly.

She had a little trouble choosing what to order—there were so many delicious things to choose from, and this would be her last dinner in Venice—but finally, she picked out fried crab and pasta with an anchovy and onion sauce. Fried doughnuts and strong coffee for dessert prepared her for the walk ahead of her, to find that cursed bridge.

Unfortunately, there was one small detail Lucy had overlooked in her planning: she couldn't remember where, exactly, the bridge was located.

She had a map of Venice and she thought she knew the name of the area, but now she realised that she was somewhat off on the name. It hadn't seemed important at the time—why would it be? She wasn't planning on going back there—but now she belatedly realised that she had a bit of a search ahead of her.

It took the better part of an hour, but eventually, she had circled several possible bridges on the map and was methodically setting out to each one.

The first bridge was a bust; not only did it not bear any locks at all, it was made of solid stone whereas the one she wanted was wrought iron. Another had some padlocks on it, but it was so close to the busier tourist districts that Lucy was almost certain it couldn't be the right one. Nonetheless, she checked each of the padlocks, wanting to be certain.

It was getting late now, and it was getting cold too. Lucy was discouraged, and she muttered under her breath as she marched to her last location. *Stupid romantic ideas, stupid lock, stupid bridge in the middle of this stupid city...*She thought she might start crying if she got mad enough, and she took a deep breath to calm down. It was just a symbolic thing, after all. Nothing to get all worked up about.

When she turned onto another street, suddenly she knew she was in the right spot. She walked to the middle of the bridge and gazed out over the quiet water. If she closed her eyes, she could picture it all: she and Dominic standing her under a snowy sky, their breath coming out in puffs, writing their initials on a lock and then locking it around one of the metal rails on the bridge. What a silly, romantic, yet lovely thing to do.

She opened her eyes and knelt in the fresh snow, feeling for the lock. There were a few on the bridge, and her fingers were getting cold when she found theirs. Feeling in her pocket for the key, she was about to unlock it when she heard footsteps crunching in the snow.

Lucy dropped the lock and stood up. A man was standing at the foot of the bridge, hesitating.

"Hello?" she called out cautiously.

"Lucy?"

Lucy froze to the spot. *It can't be! There's no way...*

But even while her brain was denying it, her eyes confirmed that Dominic was, indeed, standing in front of her now. He walked hesitantly onto the bridge, shoulders hunched up in his coat against the cold.

CHAPTER 25

THEY STOOD LOOKING at each other for a long moment, neither sure of what they should say next.

Then they both started speaking at once. "What are you doing here?" she blurted out, even as he started to say, "I was hoping I'd catch you..."

Embarrassed, they both stopped. "You go first."

"No, you go ahead," she said quickly, and he shuffled his feet in the snow.

"Maybe we could go somewhere warmer to talk? There are a few places around the piazza open late."

"What are you doing here Dominic?" she demanded, remembering her original question.

In answer, he took a key out of his pocket. "I was hoping to persuade you to not use this."

She stared at his key for a moment, then took her hand out of her own coat pocket and opened it to reveal a matching key. They stood silently, looking at each other and at the tiny keys that had once meant so much.

Lucy closed her hand and thrust the key back into her

pocket. "Why are you here?" she repeated defiantly. "You broke up with me, remember?"

"I do. But I made a mistake."

"And now what? You fly halfway around the world to stop me from unlocking our old padlock?"

"That sort of thing usually works in the movies," Dominic said, looking desperate. She snorted, and he burst out suddenly, "Look, the real reason I flew here was that I was too stubborn to call you and admit I made a mistake. I thought you'd laugh or hang up on me, and I hoped eventually you'd be the one to call, and then I wouldn't have to hurt my stupid pride by begging you to take me back. But obviously, that didn't work, and when I found out you were coming here— well, I knew what you were planning, or thought I did, and I hoped I would catch you in time to stop you. And to tell you that I still love you, and I want to give us a second chance."

She stared at him for a moment. "I almost called you," she said finally. "I've missed you. I thought unlocking the padlock was the best way to let go of our past together and move on."

"I don't want to let go of our past," Dominic said, moving closer to her.

There was just enough moonlight peeking out of the clouds to show the blue of his eyes and the gleam of his hair. He took Lucy's hands in his own and drew her close. "I made the biggest mistake of my life when I let you go. But I want you back if you'll have me. I think we can give that promise a second chance."

Her heart soaring, Lucy looked down at the padlock on the bridge, and then up at Dominic. Around them, the snow had started again, softly.

"I think so too," she whispered, leaning into him. His lips brushed hers, and for a moment she forgot all about the cold.

Only for a moment, though.

"I think you're right," she said, leaning back from him. "We should definitely go somewhere warmer to talk about this. Preferably somewhere serving hot chocolate."

"I know just the place." Dominic tucked his arm through hers and pulled her closer as they walked slowly over the bridge, their bridge.

She leaned in to him and as the snow fell, touched the key in her pocket once more.

I think I'll hang on to this, she thought, *but not to unlock the padlock.*

I'm going to tuck it away somewhere to remind me that even when it seems impossible, miracles can still happen.

CHAPTER 26

DOMINIC AND LUCY spent the next hour sitting in a small café, drinking hot chocolate and mostly ignoring the plate of fried doughnuts that they'd ordered.

What started as awkward small talk quickly turned into rapid-fire chatter about everything that had been going on in their lives since the split.

And more pertinently, how Dominic had come to find her in Venice.

Lucy had been on his mind ever since that disastrous night when he said he wanted to break up. Okay, so he *had* wanted to at the time—they'd had a terrible stretch of months, and it seemed like they fought more than they enjoyed each other's company. There was the nasty blow-up at Mick and Jenny's party and then a general period of friction that he honestly couldn't put down to any single thing. It was as if they had just stopped "clicking".

Oh, and that ridiculous summer barbecue at his parent's house. Even now Dominic cringed. He shouldn't have badgered her to go. He still wished she would make more of an effort to get along with his parents, and he did *not* think his mother was overbearing—well maybe a little bit, but not enough to warrant a fight—but he had to admit that if he hadn't pushed Lucy to go when she would rather stay home...

Weeks of rehashing all their arguments from the past year only seemed to bring him back to the same conclusion, time and time again: they didn't have any major problems, they just happened to make very big mountains out of totally manageable molehills. They were both strong-willed—something Dominic loved in Lucy, as much as it often irritated him—and neither was willing to back down when they thought they were in the right. They'd had too many complications thrown at them too quickly, and they just weren't good at working through them. But breaking up? That had been a stupid move, too impulsive and too unthinking. And afterwards, he couldn't figure out how to talk to her without admitting he felt like an idiot.

So he said nothing. His friends assured him she would reach out first: "Women can't help it," his best mate Tom said reassuringly, while they were out drinking and playing pool one night in a bid to help Dominic get over his misery. "She'll want you back, but she'll try to play it casual. She'll call and act like she just wants to say hello, or she'll make up an excuse to come to your place—she'll say she left a jumper there or something. And here's your chance to charm her and show her that you want her back. Seriously, everything will come together."

But how wrong his friend had been. Lucy didn't call, and she didn't turn up unannounced at his apartment. Dominic had spent a night hopefully going through drawers and wardrobes, thinking maybe he could find a wayward jumper or a lipstick and use it as an excuse to call her, but none surfaced. For a moment he was even tempted to head to the shops and buy something just so he could pretend it was hers, but he knew instantly that she would see through him, and then he would look like an idiot *and* a fool. That combo was too much for his pride.

But as the weeks went by and Dominic got more desperate, he finally decided to casually mention her to some other mutual friends—just to see how she was doing, he told himself.

Instead, he got the shock of his life.

"Lucy? She's great. Going to Italy next week, I heard," Mick said when they met up to watch the football last Saturday. Dominic felt his mouth go dry. He didn't need to ask what part of Italy; he knew Lucy well enough to know exactly where she was going: Venice, where this time last year they had pledged to love each other forever.

If he knew Lucy's mind—and he thought he did quite well—she wouldn't be content to just move on from a breakup. She would need to get rid of any romantic symbols that lingered on as a reminder of their relationship. It seemed extreme, but somehow he wasn't surprised by the realisation that she intended to unlock the padlock in Venice and throw it into a canal to sink into oblivion. It was just the sort of strong-willed thing she would do.

It took only a little prying to get more details on the dates she intended to be gone—Mick and Jenny typically kept an eye on her flat whenever she was away, watering the plants and feeding her fish—and within mere hours Dominic had in his possession a ticket to Venice.

En route, his nerves were jangling. He supposed he could have just *called* her, but what if she didn't want to talk to him? No, if ever there was a time to pull out all the stops with a big romantic gesture, this was it. And if flying to a foreign city to declare your love for someone didn't count as a big romantic gesture, then Dominic honestly didn't know what did.

It was a gamble of course, that he wouldn't catch up to her in the city, but he was pretty sure he knew how she would plot out her trip. According to Jenny she was flying in on Thursday night and leaving again on Monday morning.

Dominic guessed she would spend Friday sightseeing, probably catching up on the major attractions. She'd been particularly impressed by St. Mark's Basilica last time, he remembered, so it was almost certain she'd go there. She also loved art and he remembered regretfully that they hadn't made time to visit the museums during their trip, so she would likely spend Saturday touring the art galleries and culture hotspots.

He had a hunch she would wait to retrieve the padlock until the last day. It would be her farewell to the city and to that chapter in her life. In Lucy's mind, it would be the final touch to her trip, so it made sense that she would save it for the very end.

Dominic wasn't senseless enough to try to catch Lucy anywhere on Thursday night; he knew she was flying in too late to hit any tourist destinations. Instead, he set out on Friday morning, trying to put himself in her shoes and guess where she'd go first.

It was impossible to find her among the tourists in St. Mark's Square. He thought he caught a glimpse of her inside the Basilica and quickly shrank back behind a pillar. He wasn't ready to talk to her just yet, and by the time he got up his courage and looked for her again in the crowd, she was gone.

The next day he bought tickets to a couple of art gallery tours in the city. Browsing through one long collection of classical art, he again thought he caught a glimpse of Lucy, chatting with a couple. Was it possible she came with friends? He wondered. Then she parted ways with the couple, and he decided she must be alone.

Dominic almost decided to approach her outside of the museum, but he lost his nerve. For a moment his impulsive trip began to look like a bad idea. What, exactly, was he supposed to say to her when he materialised out of thin air? *Hi, I've been* *semi-stalking you around Venice in hopes of persuading you to get back together with me...*Probably not the best opening line.

And so he had decided that the best possible place would be their bridge.

Thank goodness, he thought now, sipping his coffee and staring at his beloved, it had worked.

LUCY WAS TELLING him that she had stepped down from her newly awarded position at work. "I thought I liked it," she confessed, "but the hours were terrible and the extra stress wasn't worth the pay. I wasn't seeing my family and friends as much as I wanted to. So I kicked myself back down a level."

"I'm sorry," Dominic said and meant it. He knew how much the promotion had meant to her when she got it.

But Lucy shrugged. "You know, I was annoyed for a while. And then I started thinking about it, and I realised I didn't care that much about the job itself. I just wanted the extra cash, and I realised I valued my free time more than the money. Lesson learned, I guess."

Dominic told her about his endless struggle to find a way to get in touch with her and reconnect, and Tom's terrible advice. Lucy laughed and told him about the night she'd nearly phoned him from her bathtub. "To think I was going to tell you I was in Venice just to see what you would do," she said, giggling, "and you were here, too!"

Eventually, the café owner made it clear he was ready to close up shop, and Dominic and Lucy left, strolling hand in hand through the quiet streets of San Marco. Even the gondoliers had mostly disappeared, leaving any late-night wanderers to find their own way around on foot.

They weren't really walking in any particular direction, but soon Dominic and Lucy wound up in a deserted St. Mark's Square. If the piazza was picturesque in the daylight, it was beautiful at night. Deserted save for one or two other hardy souls braving the cold—and devoid of the flocks of pigeons that called it home during the day—the Square now had a romantic ambience, like a piece of the city carved out of ancient times and deposited into modern Venice. It was well-lit, even at night, along with St. Mark's Basilica and the towers at the edge.

"When we were here last year," Dominic said, "remember the café orchestras that played here in the evenings?" Though the cafes in question, situated right on the edge of the square were long closed by now. "We danced in the piazza. Remember?"

Lucy nodded. They were surrounded by tourists, but it felt like they were the only two people there.

Dominic took her hand and gently led her out into the square, and they began slowly waltzing in place to an imaginary orchestra. "I think we should have a tradition," he whispered in her ear. "We should come back here every winter, or as many winters as we can manage. And we should visit our padlock on the bridge, and dance here in the square, and eat fried doughnuts until we burst."

"That sounds good to me," Lucy said dreamily, snuggling into his coat. She suppressed a yawn, and Dominic hugged her. "Aw, you're tired. I'll take you back to your hotel."

"I'm not that tired," Lucy started to protest, but a jaw-cracking yawn cut her off, and she admitted sheepishly that she was ready to drop.

Back at the hotel, Dominic sat gingerly on the foot of her bed. "How soon are you flying home?"

"I'm supposed to go tomorrow," she said, shucking her boots and coat.

"Do you think you could change the flight?"

"I'd imagine so. Why?"

He got to his feet, a slow grin spreading across his face.

"Because I have a few days off, and we're here in the most romantic city in the world, and I think we should make the most of it."

"I like the sound of that." Lucy looked at him speculatively. "Are you going to stay? Here, tonight, I mean?"

"Are you inviting me?"

In response, she smiled and scooped up her pyjamas from her open suitcase.

"Tell me if I need these," she asked coquettishly.

Without another word, Dominic took them from her hands and dropped them back into the suitcase, pulling her down on the bed next to him.

"I guess that would be a no then," Lucy said, smiling as she kissed him, and reached to flick off the lamp.

CHAPTER 27

When morning dawned Lucy went online and rescheduled her return flight.

Dominic left to gather his things and check out of his hotel and returned an hour later, scrubbed up and ready for the day.

He still wouldn't tell Lucy what he had in mind for the day, though he insisted she check out at the front desk and bring her suitcase.

Then they boarded a water bus out to an island close by.

To Lucy's surprise and delight, Dominic had taken the liberty of calling ahead to the island's lone but massively exclusive hotel, the Cipriani and making a reservation for the two of them.

At this time of the year, the luxurious hotel was well decorated for Christmas but luckily was not brimming with guests, with most people opting to stay in the busier and less expensive hotels in San Marco.

As the older woman at the front desk explained, most of the island was now a dedicated nature reserve, with some hiking available to tourists. Obviously in this weather walking all over the island wasn't high on most visitors' priorities but from the wink Dominic gave her, Lucy guessed he didn't intend for them to spend a lot of time out and about anyway.

The windswept little island seemed almost bleak in the December light, yet there was a sort of peacefulness to it. She could easily imagine returning here for a future getaway, though perhaps in a warmer month.

"Do you really think we'll spend every winter in Venice?" Lucy asked, snuggling closer to him.

Dominic shrugged. "I hope so. But I don't think superstitions should change our fate, though. I think it's up to us to decide our future." He stopped and looked down at her, tracing her chin with his thumb. "And I for one, am very serious about our future. I want to make sure our love stays locked in place forever."

"I want that too," Lucy whispered. He tipped her chin up for a kiss, and she melted into him, forgetting all about the cold.

THE FLIGHT from Venice back to England had to be rerouted due to weather, and when Max and Naomi finally arrived home late that night they were exhausted.

Max was thrilled to be home, but he would be most thrilled once he was tucked into his bed.

Naomi's parents were up waiting for them, but baby Julia was tucked safely in bed, sleeping. Naomi beamed down at her daughter despite her fatigue. "She's such a good sleeper," she whispered proudly to Max, who smiled and rubbed her back.

Naomi's mother poked her head into the bedroom. "You know," she said, a hint of a smile on her lips, "she's done so well this weekend. Why don't you leave her here one more night? That way you can get some solid sleep after your flight, and unpack at your leisure tomorrow."

One more night without the baby in tow sounded heavenly,

but Max could see Naomi wavering. He held back, waiting to see what she would say.

To his surprise, she tiptoed out of the bedroom with a reticent—but exhausted—smile on her face. "You're sure you don't mind?"

"Absolutely not," her mother said, looking as surprised as Max felt.

Naomi gave her a quick hug. "Thank you! We'll come over tomorrow afternoon to pick her up."

They collected their coats and went back out to the cab, waiting for them at the curb. *Did I really just hear "tomorrow afternoon" from my wife?* Max wondered.

As if reading his thoughts, Naomi grinned sleepily at him. "I hope Mum is up for a lot of babysitting. I'm getting kind of used to these baby-free nights."

"I'm assuming that is the jet lag talking," Max said in amazement, and she laughed and leaned against him, snoring almost before the cab pulled out of the driveway.

MONDAY MORNING, Scott was reluctant to drag himself out of bed. He was still beaming with the news of Rachel's pregnancy, and now he noticed that she had an extra glow to her as well.

He rubbed her stomach affectionately as she lay in bed. "Good morning to you too," he whispered, and she laughed as his breath tickled her skin. "Are you a he or a she? Either way, I hope you get your mom's brains because your dad doesn't have a lot going for you in that category."

They dressed and ate breakfast in their hotel room, with Scott springing down to a café for a large bag that included everything from pastries to muesli.

"You're eating for two now," he reminded Rachel, and finally she laughingly told him to stop hovering over her while she ate.

"Finish packing. I can feed myself just fine," she said, planting a kiss on his cheek. He quickly turned his head to plant a deeper one on her lips. "Are you sure you're fine? You don't need anything else? Is the baby moving yet?"

"Goodness no, I'm only eight weeks along." Rachel tucked herself up into a comfortable cross-legged position on the sofa.

"Eat, and pack. We want plenty of time to get to the airport. I imagine it will be busy today."

Soon enough they were packed and checked out of the hotel.

Scott bundled Rachel gently into a water taxi, fussing about the weather until they were safely on dry land and bundled into a cab. She leaned into him in the back seat with a contented sigh. "Venice was lovely. But I think home sounds even lovelier."

"Actually, I agree with you." He wouldn't have thought it twenty-four hours ago, but now Scott couldn't think of anywhere in the world more appealing than their cosy apartment back in New York. He was already thinking ahead to everything they would have to do to get ready for the baby. He supposed this meant cleaning out the spare bedroom so Rachel could turn it into a nursery.

Maybe that can wait until after Christmas.

There wasn't too much traffic on the roads, and soon enough they were unloading their suitcases at the airport. Scott checked everything in and they moved through the security lines to board their flight.

Scott kept one hand tucked firmly in Rachel's, and the other he jammed absentmindedly into his coat pocket.

His fingers touched the ring box and he froze. In all the excitement of Rachel's announcement, he'd completely forgotten about the original reason for their trip. Now they were mere minutes away from going through the metal detectors, and the box was still sitting unopened in his pocket.

A bored-looking official was checking passports at the top of the line.

He took Scott's passport and studied it with a glazed expression. "Anything liquids/metals or anything to declare?"

Scott stood stock-still for a moment, the man staring

blankly at him. "Yes," he said, his voice sounding foreign to his own ears. "Yes, I do have something to declare."

He turned around to face Rachel. Other passengers in the line were staring, some curious, some irritated at the holdup, but he ignored them all.

Rachel was staring at him, puzzled, as he took her hands. "Rachel, you are the best thing that has ever happened to me. You're beautiful, intelligent, funny, and have a gentle soul. You're everything I could want in a partner, and now I'm blessed enough to learn that you'll be all that and more as the mother of my child.

I brought you to Venice because I thought there was no more romantic place in the world to ask you to marry me. Obviously, that didn't work out the way I'd planned, but I'm not about to leave before at least giving it my best shot. So with that in mind..." Scott heard audible gasps as he dropped to one knee and pulled the ring box from his coat pocket. "Rachel, will you marry me?"

A woman in line let out an excited squeal, and Rachel burst into tears.

He quickly stood up and caught her as she grabbed him in a hug, nodding and trying to wipe her tears away with her coat sleeve. He pulled a wad of tissues from her coat pocket and handed them to her, to the happy clapping and cheers of the passengers in line behind him.

CHAPTER 29

RACHEL SLEPT through most of the flight home, and when they landed at JFK, Scott quickly collected their luggage and hailed a cab, settling her in the backseat where she dozed off again.

When they got home he made sure she was settled on the couch with a hot cup of cider and dumped the suitcases in a corner. They could unpack tomorrow or the next day. He didn't see any reason to rush.

Their Christmas tree was all set up in the corner of the living room, and he plugged in the lights, bathing the living room in a soft glow. Scott sat down next to Rachel, and she snuggled into him. She was still admiring the way the stones in her ring sparkled, and he laced his fingers through hers, admiring the stones too. "Do you like it?"

"It's perfect," she whispered, leaning back into him. They sat still for a moment, admiring the tree.

Finally, Rachel broke the silence. "Are you hoping for a girl or a boy?"

"I don't care," Scott said after a moment's thought. "You?"

She shook her head. "I'm happy with either one," she said. Then after another moment, she said, "Promise me something."

"Anything."

"When we're getting ready for the baby—fixing the nursery, whatever…"

"Yeah?"

"Don't try to make it perfect, okay?" She rubbed her stomach, smiling a little. "Let's just enjoy these moments together and not worry about how they happen."

"You got it." Scott kissed her. "Merry Christmas, my perfect wife-to-be, who wishes for imperfect but totally real and romantic moments."

Rachel smiled. "Merry Christmas, my perfect husband-to-be who will never stop trying."

After a few moments, Scott could tell by her breathing that she'd fallen asleep. Gently he pried the cider mug out of her hands and placed it on the coffee table, then picked her up and carried her into the bedroom, tucking her gently under the blankets. She twitched and sighed in her sleep, smiling a little to herself.

"Merry Christmas," he said softly, pulling the blankets up over her shoulders. "Here's to years of imperfectly wonderful Christmases ahead."

And here's to the romance of Venice, he thought as he went back to the living room to unplug the tree lights. He smiled a little to himself as he tiptoed back into the bedroom. *I guess the best romantic moments happen when you stop looking for them.*

With Christmas hymns in Italian still echoing in his head, Scott snuggled up to his fiancée and drifted off to sleep.

ABOUT THE AUTHOR

International #1 and USA Today bestselling author Melissa Hill lives in County Wicklow, Ireland.

Her page-turning emotional stories of family, friendship and romance have been translated into 25 different languages and are regular chart-toppers internationally.

A Reese Witherspoon x Hello Sunshine adaptation of her bestseller SOMETHING FROM TIFFANY'S hit screens worldwide in Dec '22 and is airing now on Prime Video.

THE CHARM BRACELET was adapted in 2020 as a holiday movie *A Little Christmas Charm*. A GIFT TO REMEMBER (and a sequel) was also adapted for screen by Hallmark Channel. Multiple other titles by Melissa are currently in development for film and TV.

Visit her website at
www.melissahill.info
Or get in touch via the social media links below.

Printed in Great Britain
by Amazon